continued . . .

Also by S. L. Wright

Confessions of a Demon

DEMON UNDERGROUND

S. L. Wright

A ROC BOOK

ROC
Published by New American Library, a division of
Penguin Group (USA) Inc., 375 Hudson Street,
New York, New York 10014, USA

Penguin Group (Canada), 90 Eglinton Avenue East, Suite 700, Toronto,
Ontario M4P 2Y3, Canada (a division of Pearson Penguin Canada Inc.)
Penguin Books Ltd., 80 Strand, London WC2R 0RL, England
Penguin Ireland, 25 St. Stephen's Green, Dublin 2,
Ireland (a division of Penguin Books Ltd.)
Penguin Group (Australia), 250 Camberwell Road, Camberwell, Victoria 3124,
Australia (a division of Pearson Australia Group Pty. Ltd.)
Penguin Books India Pvt. Ltd., 11 Community Centre, Panchsheel Park,
New Delhi - 110 017, India
Penguin Group (NZ), 67 Apollo Drive, Rosedale, North Shore 0632,
New Zealand (a division of Pearson New Zealand Ltd.)
Penguin Books (South Africa) (Pty.) Ltd., 24 Sturdee Avenue,
Rosebank, Johannesburg 2196, South Africa

Penguin Books Ltd., Registered Offices:
80 Strand, London WC2R 0RL, England

First published by Roc, an imprint of New American Library,
a division of Penguin Group (USA) Inc.

First Printing, December 2010
10 9 8 7 6 5 4 3 2 1

Copyright © Susan Wright, 2010
All rights reserved

ROC REGISTERED TRADEMARK — MARCA REGISTRADA

Printed in the United States of America

PUBLISHER'S NOTE
This is a work of fiction. Names, characters, places, and incidents either are the
product of the author's imagination or are used fictitiously, and any resemblance
to actual persons, living or dead, business establishments, events, or locales is
entirely coincidental.

The publisher does not have any control over and does not assume any responsibility for author or third-party Web sites or their content.

This novel is dedicated to my loving husband, Kelly.

ACKNOWLEDGMENTS

I would like to thank Jessica Wade, my editor at Roc, and my agent, Lucienne Diver, for their dedication in making this novel the best it could be.

1

I was wiping down the top of the old mahogany bar, tenderly rubbing the scars and worn patches where the varnish had disappeared, when I got all choked up and sentimental again. *My bar...*

I wanted to smack myself, it was so dumb. But I'd just found out that the bar belonged to me. For too many years, I'd felt guilty about my business manager, Michael, and his languishing investment of a bar, knowing full well how infinitesimal my profit margin was.

Now—who cared? I suddenly felt like a wildly successful entrepreneur. I had everything I needed right here; I could make a living and provide myself with what I wanted the most: *relief. The sweet elixir of life.*

At least it was for me. I made people feel better so I could sip their contentment. I could feed on any emotions, of course, but my bar provided me with a lovely stream of people who needed release from their pain—my captive herd. I lived on them like the parasite that I was. I no longer needed to sleep or eat, and I could change my appearance any way I wanted.

I was Allay. A demon.

Bliss came around the corner. "The ice maker isn't working."

Startled, I looked up into the Hollywood eyes of my offspring. Though she'd literally been born only yesterday, with her platinum blond curls and perfect cheekbones, she could have stepped off the red carpet. This in spite of the fact that she was wearing a pair of my old jeans and a threadbare Affliction T-shirt as she helped me prep the bar. I had offered to open up the Den to entice her into staying around. Call it some kind of misplaced maternal instinct.

"There's a trick to it." I dried off my hands on my tiny black apron, heading to the back room.

"I know." Bliss tapped her head. "Memories. Remember?"

All demons were born with trace memories from their progenitor. But this stopped me in my tracks. "You know about the *ice maker*?"

Bliss rolled her eyes. "Every morning for the past ten years, you've checked the ice maker. Believe me, something that repetitive is bound to stick."

I felt exposed. How could someone know my thoughts and feelings, yet not be me? From the little I'd seen so far, Bliss was very different from me, much more knowing and brusque.

I tried to turn the conversation away from me. "We'll have to go buy bags of ice, then."

As if I hadn't spoken, Bliss added, "I wish you hadn't blocked the memories of Plea. I'd like to know what it's like for a real demon. Instead of a possessed human."

"Sorry to disappoint you."

It wasn't my fault that I hadn't been able to handle the haunting flashes of Plea's life when, as a teenager, I had accidentally absorbed her essence as she lay dying. I had built a wall that remained to this day around my progenitor's life. I had tried to be exactly who I was before I was turned: a California free spirit, spiced with a bit of New York City. I'd even kept my appearance the same: slender yet strong, with short dark hair and muddy green eyes. I blended into the mix of artsy bohemians and working-class Latinos my bar drew, keeping a low profile and inviting no questions.

But there was no denying that my strongest desire now was to feed off the emotions of other people. It changed everything. Like other demons, I manipulated people so I could touch them, so I could live off them.

With my offspring, it was completely different. I didn't want to touch Bliss. Having her this close was bad enough. She stared at me curiously, clearly knowing so much yet understanding so little about me.

Shock kicked open the door of the bathroom, wrestling the mop and bucket on wheels onto the chipped tile floor. She took one look at me and Bliss standing barely an arm's length apart behind the bar and went on high alert.

"Back off!" she snapped at Bliss. Shock's persona was petite with buzzed white hair, but she radiated fierceness like an angry terrier. You knew it could bite.

But I trusted Shock with my life. She was my only demon friend. She had saved my sanity for the past ten years; she was the only one who really knew me. The only one I had. That was why I had risked everything to save her. Nothing less would have driven me to seek help from Vex and Dread, the two-headed monster that had once ruled my demon line. Vex had thought he owned me, but in the end I had killed him.

Actually Ram had killed Vex, sucking the life force from his body and absorbing it into his own. But I had stood there and watched the battle between the ancient demons, mesmerized by Ram, as I always seemed to be. I had no self-control with him. Even at the height of my distress at having to kill another demon in order to survive, I let him make love to me in the park. My energy overload had almost instantly resulted in Bliss, my offspring, who would now spend her life craving to feed off others' ecstasy because that was what she had been born from.

I raised my hands to get Shock to slow down as she approached Bliss at the bar. I didn't like it that my best friend was defensive around my offspring. "Bliss isn't doing anything, Shock."

"Then why are you so freaked-out?" Shock gestured with her chin at my aura, the visual radiance that clearly mapped out my uneasiness.

"This progenitor stuff is a little weird. It'll take some time getting used to having an offspring."

"*Don't* get used to it. You're not supposed to. Your instincts are telling you to *get away* from her. She knows you, Allay. Your strengths and weaknesses. She has your muscle memories of aikido, too. She could really hurt you."

I turned to Bliss. "Do you want to hurt me?"

"Nope." She crossed her arms and smirked. "I don't plan on hurting you, either, Shock. The only interesting memories Allay has—other than the past few days—are about you."

Shock refused to look at her. "New demons can't be trusted. They're unstable, unpredictable. You know that, Allay."

"I can't push her into the street," I argued. "Vex brought in all kinds of demons to attack Glory. It's not safe for a newbie—"

"I can take care of myself," Bliss told me.

I could hear myself in her voice. How much of her assurance came from her own abilities and how much came from my memories? "When I was first transformed, I had help from Vex," I reminded her. "A lot of help—he even gave me the Den. That's what we have to do for each other from now on. You don't want to be going to Dread for help someday."

"Dread isn't going to protect us," Shock said. "He tried

to kill you, Allay. That makes us fair game for any demon, including Goad and his horde of offspring. You know Vex was the only one who could keep Goad in line."

The memory of Goad pressing his finger into my face, drawing out my energy as he practically licked his chops, was enough to make me shiver. He had kidnapped me from the street on Vex's orders, wrapped me in a strait-jacket, and handed me over to Dread. I still hadn't managed to process that horrible, helpless feeling.

"We'll feel Goad coming from at least a block away," I said. "We'll have plenty of time to barricade ourselves upstairs if any demon tries to get close."

Shock crossed her arms. "If you open up the bar, Ram is going to come skulking back here disguised as a patron. We would never know."

I remembered his expression as he left; it was the face of Theo Ram, the persona he'd been wearing when I first met him, a cabbie and womanizer with a thing for damsels in distress. Handsome in a rugged way, with a strong-boned face, dark curling hair, and gray eyes that spoke to me across the room.

I couldn't think about Ram. It made me feel flushed and no amount of effort to control my own physiological responses could stop my reaction. I didn't want to expose myself any more than I already had.

"If you hadn't been messing around with *him*," Shock added, "you wouldn't have *her* as a problem."

"Bliss was coming anyway," I mumbled. "I just needed a . . . cleaner energy than what Pique had given me."

In the silence, Bliss said, "I wish Ram had told you how he hides his signature. I'd have a lot of fun sneaking up on other demons, if I knew how."

Shock kept ignoring her. "How are you going to explain Blondie here? The police will be back here asking questions. If another gunman doesn't get here first and shoot up the bar again."

I looked at Bliss carefully. "She can be a friend visiting from California. Someone I knew in high school."

Bliss shrugged as if she didn't care one way or the other. "As long as I don't have to pretend I'm a loser." Thankfully she didn't add, *like you*.

"Why don't you lift up the shutter, Bliss?" I suggested. "If I'm going to get shot at again, it better happen now while three indestructible demons are in here instead of a bar full of customers."

But I doubted there would be another drive-by shooting since I had told Dennis Mackleby, commissioner of New York City Planning, that if I was attacked again I would expose the evidence I had of him taking bribes from the Fellowship of Truth. The Fellowship, a so-called church, had been run by Vex and Dread like an organized-crime family, paying off politicians and city employees to get what they wanted—and they had used my bar as the drop-off for those payments. Over the past fifty years, the Fellowship's message of self-empowerment and philosophy of "There's No Such Thing as a Free Lunch" had garnered nearly a million faithful followers. But I knew it was just the latest in a series of churches the two demons had controlled, going all the way back to Constantinople.

Bliss went straight to the peg under the bar where I hid the padlock key, and then outside to open the metal shutter that pulled down over the front windows and door. It was a little eerie to see her practiced motions. Before yesterday, she didn't exist. Now she moved around listening to my voice in her head. Why didn't it make her crazy, like it drove me out of my mind to think my progenitor's thoughts?

She pushed the shutter partway up and left it so the sun came in the lower half of the front windows. Just like I did when I was opening up.

Shock was frowning. "Ram's going to come back. I

saw how he was looking at you, like he wanted to eat you up. Like you belong to him."

"I know he tried to kill you, Shock—"

"Twice," she reminded me. "After he seduced you to get inside your apartment, where I was lying in a stupor, unable to defend myself."

"You think I haven't been telling myself that? I know what Ram did, better than anyone. He lied to me over and over. But he also saved my life—twice, if you count helping me steal Pique's essence. . . ."

I couldn't go on. I still wasn't sure about that gaping, yawning hole in my celebrated return from the near dead. The price of my life had been bought with Pique's death. Though I had been born a human, after murdering Pique, I could no longer lay claim to my humanity. I was a killer, a cannibal, a monster with a guilty conscience.

"Ram is a demon assassin, Allay. He's been killing his own offspring's offspring for thousands of years. You can't possibly trust him. For one thing, he's a master emotional manipulator. Look how he got you to change your mind about killing another demon. You were adamant, remember—*I'm not going to kill anyone!* But he comes along and you do exactly what he says."

"That's true," Bliss agreed. "He convinced you it was okay."

I knew they were right. "He told me that's the only way demons die, that everyone has to die, so another demon will eventually kill each one of us because we're mortal. We're not gods. It seems . . . it *seemed* reasonable, at the time."

"He's got you under his spell," Shock insisted. "You have to tell him to get lost, and mean it, Allay. Stop acting like a lovesick teenager and get hold of yourself!"

That stung. "I know."

"Then don't open the bar," Shock demanded.

"I'm doing it for Bliss. She wants the company. And I need to feed."

Shock crossed her arms again. "Tell me you're not secretly hoping Ram will come back."

I opened my mouth, but I couldn't deny it. I had been thinking about him; would he come back and watch over me? Did he really care about me? It seemed impossible that I had caught his eye. Perhaps his rakish Theo Ram persona was not far from his true self, with a girl in every country, and I was just the latest diversion from his weary millennia-old battle with his wayward offspring.

I couldn't admit my fascination, so I tried to divert her. "If I touched him, I think I would know it was Ram. Even through his shields, he had a driving, aggressive energy that came through his persona."

Shock's eyes widened. "Really? That could be very useful." She shot a look at Bliss. "Don't tell anyone. It could mean life or death for us, and we don't want him to know we've found a chink in his armor."

Bliss nodded blandly. "Sure, that will really help when we ambush him after lunch."

I could tell she didn't like Shock's doubts about her. But Shock was too busy considering the implications of Ram's existence to care about Bliss's feelings. Shock must have been frightened out of her wits when she woke to find she was being killed by a strange demon whose signature she couldn't sense. She had holed up in Revel's apartment for days while I negotiated with Vex and Dread to try to find her attacker. Shock was not one to willingly put up with the circus at Revel's place for long, but she had been paralyzed by fear.

Until Ram had told me that he wouldn't kill demons anymore just because they were fertile, demons like Shock. He had pledged to kill only demons who hurt humans, either by taking too much of their emotional energy or harming them by other means.

The question is, Can I trust him?

I needed to know more about him. I had thought I understood Theo Ram, the cabbie, so well. But Ram the vengeful demon was a complete mystery to me. He admitted his first great love was Hope, who was also a possessed human. Like me.

Ram said he had killed Hope. That was the last thing I could tell Shock. Just last week, I would have denied it was possible—I talked over everything with Shock. Now I had only myself to question: What would make Ram kill his lover? What kind of betrayal would make his love turn to hate?

And what exactly did he want from me? I had learned my lesson about taking favors from ancient demons after Vex's beneficence turned out to be one big con job. All along he had intended to cut off my head so everyone could watch it rematerialize, turning me into a messiah for his church. I wasn't going to let anyone think I was their pawn, never again.

"You can't trust him, Allay," Shock said, more heated this time. "You have to be strong and guard against him."

"I also have to go get some ice, or we're never going to open up."

"Allay . . ." she warned.

"I hear what you're saying, Shock. I agree I can't trust him. The man I knew was just a persona. But there's nothing I can do about it now." I brought up the real problem that was staring me in the face. "I'm more worried about the new ERI machines that can tell demon energy from humans. They'll be hitting the airports soon, and then we'll all be in trouble."

Dread had showed me the infomercial for the Electromagnetic Resonance Imaging machine that revealed the difference between human and demon auras. Vex had intended to use the invention to prove that his messiah (me) was different from humans. The problem was that they were being mass-produced by the FAA and were going to be rolled out as the latest weapons detectors in security technology. No demons would be able to fly or enter government buildings after that or they would be discovered.

Shock waved her hand. "They said the same thing about X-rays and DNA genotyping, but nothing came of that panic. People see what they want to see, and our bodies are near-exact replicas of humans. Even when doctors see us heal, they don't believe their eyes. We'll get by as we always have."

I wasn't so sure. Even if Shock wasn't concerned, I was going to find out more. I couldn't imagine having demons exposed. It would wreak havoc on the world.

I was crouched down behind the ice maker when the bar phone rang. I extracted myself with a new appreciation for Pepe's devotion to cleanliness. The damage to my shirt wasn't too bad.

I knew who it was the second I heard his voice. "Is this Allay?"

"Dread," I said, to alert Shock. Her eyes narrowed in concern. "What do you want?"

I bit my lip, keeping myself from asking how he was doing. The last time I had seen him, he had looked like a dying lizard, curled up and defenseless. But I didn't want to remind him of that. Dread was not the kind of guy who revealed weakness to anyone. He had been Vex's right-hand man for too many centuries and had learned how to be invisible in order to stay out of the line of fire.

"We have to meet," he said flatly.

"Considering that you tried to kill me, I'd be pretty stupid to agree to that."

"I've solved my problem, Allay. Like you, I took a demon last night. So I have no need to consume your core."

"How reassuring." I wondered who the poor sod was. Not that I could feel self-righteous about it, having killed my own victim last night to replenish my life force for another two centuries. It made me nauseated to think I was just like Dread. He was even worse than his name indicated; he sought to instill fear in people, that special burning doubt that fed Dread's soul.

"We need to settle some things," Dread said impatiently. "Unless you intend to declare war against me?"

He wanted to see my aura to judge my emotions, and maybe even touch me so he could tell if I was deceiving him or not. That would be dangerous because demons killed other demons by touching them, sucking away all of their energy.

But I didn't want to fight Dread, not openly, anyway. He had too many resources at his command—including the entire might and wealth of the Fellowship of Truth as its prophet. I also couldn't forget that he had imprisoned me in his iron cage and tortured me so I would birth him a demon to consume. He put innocent people, and even his own demon-wife, Lash, in that cage and tormented them to produce the energy he craved. I knew what he was now, and so did everyone else because I had spilled the beans about how he got his kicks. Without his progenitor, Vex, to keep him in line, there was no telling which way Dread would jump.

That was why I needed to see Dread in person. I had to gauge that for myself.

"Okay, let's meet." I waved to hush Shock's indignant protest. "But I'm not going to Brooklyn."

"I wouldn't expect you to." His chilly tone indicated he didn't want to discuss what he had done to me on the top floor of the Prophet's Center. "I'm fairly certain that you're not going to try to kill me—"

"Because I could have before I left the Center," I put in. Now that I knew we were going to negotiate, I wanted to unnerve him.

I could hear him swallow, but he didn't respond to my taunt. "I can be at your bar in fifteen minutes."

"No way. You're not bringing Goad here." I shuddered at the thought of that slimy bastard in my bar. Vex had kept his henchman away from me for more than a decade—unfortunately now I knew why.

"I don't intend to bring Goad. Only Zeal."

That meant we'd be three against two, giving us the advantage. I glanced at Bliss. *If* she was willing to help us. Would she, if it came down to a fight with a sixteen-hundred-year-old demon and his trusty wingman?

"Okay, I'll see you here in fifteen."

I barely hung up before Shock exclaimed, "*Here?* You can't let Dread come here."

I shrugged. "It's better than meeting him out there." I gestured vaguely. "I know this place. At least this way if things get gnarly, we can bolt upstairs."

"You mean the survivors can escape."

"Shock, I just went to hell and back to make sure you wouldn't be killed. I'm not about to endanger you needlessly. We need to know where we stand with Dread now that Vex is gone. We need to make a deal with him, so he thinks we're more valuable alive than dead."

Bliss was sitting on a barstool swinging her foot. "Sounds like a good idea to me."

"Naturally you'd say that," Shock snapped. "You're practically a carbon copy of Allay right now."

"I don't think so," Bliss and I replied at the same time. We looked at each other. I was the first to turn away, uncomfortable.

*   *   *

I put in a quick call to the hospital to find out how Pepe, my janitor, was doing since he had been shot in the drive-by shooting of my bar. His wife was at his side, and she assured me that he was feeling much better since the anesthesia from the surgery had worn off. He spoke to me for a few minutes, thanking me over and over again for taking care of the bills for the doctors and hospitals. Michael had even sent over a Fresh Direct delivery for the family and signed it from me. I felt ashamed knowing that it was my own fault Pepe had been shot. I had been the real target.

I hung up with Pepe sooner than I wanted when my senses began tingling at the approach of demons. The signatures were strong, breaking through even Shock's buzzing signature, which rose in intensity until it broke off and started all over again. Now I suddenly began to feel as if the floor were tilting underneath my feet. That was Dread, coming from the south. With him was Zeal, a squeezing sensation. The cumulative effect felt as if I were being pushed down a steep incline. It was much more unpleasant than Dread and Vex together. Vex's halting sensation had tended to counteract Dread's slippery one.

In all that ambient "noise," Bliss was nonexistent.

She winked at me when I looked over. "Let's get the party started."

I shook my head. "You better not say a word while he's here."

Bliss shrugged as if she couldn't care less. At Shock's insistence, we had lowered and locked the metal shutter from the inside. With the wrought-iron bars over the windows and steel doors, the old bar was as demon-proof as it could be.

"You stay here, inside the bar." Shock opened the door and gestured curtly for Bliss to follow her into the tiny foyer at the base of the stairs. This door wasn't as strong as the outside one upstairs on my apartment. "Take your bat and brace it against the handle."

"Shock . . . if Dread wants us dead, he could do it a lot easier without getting his hands dirty."

"I'd rather not be stupid." Her expression was blank.

I didn't want to fight her, so I stayed in the bar. But I didn't get the bat. I would have preferred to open up and present myself to Dread as if I had nothing to fear. That would make him think he had something to fear from me. I was surprised that Shock didn't know that.

Things were feeling very different between us. We had both nearly died this week, each in our own way. While it made me want to bust out of my shell to proactively take care of myself, she seemed intent on retrenching her defenses.

"Okay, Allay. You can open up," Shock called through the door.

I let the door swing open. Dread was in a male persona, but not that of Prophet Thomas Anderson. His usual guise was an urbane, Ivy-league man in his late fifties with silvery short hair and the lightly bronzed skin of an outdoorsman. I had never fallen for his obvious warmth and glad-handing, because I knew Dread for the demon he was.

His current persona was much closer to what I would consider his "true" appearance, if physical attributes could indicate character. His eyes were narrow and black, and his features spare and sharp. He wasn't a big man, and there wasn't an ounce of extra flesh on his body, as if he ran hot, powered by pure cunning, in the service of his boss, his father, Vex. Now where would he turn?

He nodded to us all in greeting, saying merely, "Allay."

I knew my fear would intoxicate him like nothing else. But I felt as if I were back in his iron cage, as his hips pressed against me, his rigid erection rubbing painfully into me, as he choked the life out of me.

I retreated from him, since there was no use hiding the lurid orange flush of my fear in my aura, and watched his reaction carefully. Before he had locked me up and tried to kill me, I could have sworn he was crushing on me. He certainly opened up to me about Lash's abandonment, maybe more than he had to anyone else. I remembered how his voice had broken in long-suppressed rage as he talked about her betrayal after being inseparable for hundreds of years, how she had left him so publicly for Crave, a young incubus posing as a hip jewelry designer.

Dread remembered, too. He remembered it even as he had nearly raped and killed me, and it had added to his pleasure. If he couldn't control me, I knew he would enjoy stamping out the one person who had seen him vulnerable.

He couldn't hide his reaction, though I think he tried. The green flush of desire stained his varicolored aura. He wanted me to fear him. Though I hadn't meant to, I'd triggered his sexual cues.

Shock shot me a startled, reproving look that was all the more embarrassing because I couldn't explain that I hadn't meant to arouse Dread.

So I ignored the unsettling feeling of the floor falling out from under me and turned to Zeal. "Hello, Zeal. Finally we get to meet."

"I've wanted to," Zeal said shortly, "but Vex wouldn't let me."

"I guess things will be different now that he's gone." I wanted to keep reminding them that when Vex had crossed me, he had ended up dead.

Zeal frowned slightly. She was also not in her usual persona—the coordinator of ministries for the Fellowship of Truth, the drill sergeant who whipped the masses into a frenzy during their circles and inspirational seminars. As Missy van Dam, she was a doughy middle-aged, rather unattractive woman. But I'd seen her do interviews on television, and she paired her completely unremarkable appearance with such smart, witty observations about life, based on a solid folksy foundation accented by an idiosyncratic mix of clothing and metaphors. Her self-help patter, like much of the church's message of personal salvation through self-responsibility and enlightenment, was both appealing and unremittingly cheery.

But right now Zeal was in the guise of a dour, round-faced woman of indeterminate age. There was nothing distinguishable about her—light brown hair, bland eyes, striped tunic shirt, and khaki slacks. I forgot what she looked like the second I looked away. Clearly Zeal's job here today was to not distract anyone from Dread.

"Have a seat," I offered, gesturing at a two-top in the middle of the bar. I had the counter and the long mirror to my right, looking at the barred windows in the back, the most vulnerable part of the building. Shock took up a stance next to the locked door to the foyer, while Bliss sat behind the bar near the phone with instructions to dial 911 if anything "bad" happened. Zeal took a seat behind Dread, keeping her eyes downcast in a nonthreatening way.

Dread motioned to himself. "As you can see, I wasn't seriously depleted by Ram."

That was a lie. I had seen him a breath away from death on the floor of his cage. Curled up like a fetus. He had been drained more than Shock, and it had taken days for her to fully recover. Dread was sixteen hundred years old and a very powerful demon; I could honestly attest to that. But even he couldn't hide the telltale blush of his humiliation.

He doesn't want me to tell anyone that Ram almost killed him.

"So that's why you're here. It's about Ram." I refused

to commit to his version of the story. Not yet. I needed to know why he didn't want me telling tales. Was it pride or did it have strategic importance? How much could I get from him without pushing him too far?

"Yes, you know him better than anyone." Dread's eyes slid to Bliss. "My men tell me you were in the park with Ram last night. He walked out carrying you, with your new offspring by his side, all the way to this bar."

I was glad he skipped over the part about the wild sex I'd had with Ram in the park. Bliss's name was proof enough of what we'd done. No need for everyone to be talking about it. Though apparently they were.

"Yes?" I said encouragingly, committing to nothing.

"So, is he here now?"

My brows lifted in surprise. "You know Ram isn't here, or you wouldn't have come."

"In fact," Dread said, "I got a report of his signature on the Upper West Side not ten minutes ago. Unless he can fly, he won't be able to get here for another twenty minutes even if you called him the moment we set up this meeting."

He was so smug—and so stupid! He didn't know about Mystify, who could mimic other demons with his signature. Mystify had been born from Ram after Vex's death; I had watched as the influx of energy had split Ram in two. I would bet my last dollar that Mystify was having brunch on Columbus Avenue while Ram was lurking outside somewhere, probably dying over the fact that I'd let Dread into my bar.

"Ram left," I agreed. "And I didn't call him back. I want to hear what you have to say."

Dread swallowed, as if belatedly realizing he should have started with the sugar. "I'm sorry I hurt you, Allay. It was Vex's orders to put you in the cage, you know that. And it was his orders that Ram should be tortured to break you. I couldn't help it that I liked it. And I couldn't help it that my need to replenish my life force overwhelmed my good sense and I tried to kill you."

"Is this supposed to be an apology?"

"It's the truth. That's better than an apology." His back was ramrod straight. "I don't want to see you dead. In fact, I'd like to work with you. Now that Vex is gone and we all know it's been Ram killing off demons, that changes everything."

"You want to use me to get to Ram."

"Not to hurt him, Allay. He could have killed me, but he didn't. And he did me a favor, getting rid of Vex so handily. I owe him my thanks for that."

I almost wanted to laugh at the way he had turned this around. "Ram swore to kill any demon who harms humans. That includes torturing them in big iron cages."

He lifted a hand like that was a minor consideration. "Naturally my cage will be dismantled immediately. Now that I know the rules, I'll follow them. I always have. Vex would be the first to tell you that. I know plenty of consensual ways of getting what I need."

I wasn't sure if Ram would believe that. The desire for our favorite emotion was very powerful, almost like an addiction. Surely Dread would do whatever it took to make people afraid of him. But I said, "Ram will be glad to hear that."

"Will you tell him?"

"Sure, the next time I see him," I agreed. "For your part, can you keep the Vex demons off my back?"

"For that, you have to agree not to make baseless accusations about the church. Those were some very nasty calls you made, Allay. Why did you threaten to reveal Mackleby's bribes?"

"I wanted to make you let Ram go, remember? Now I know what a mistake that was. Having my window shot out was warning enough."

Dread shook his head. "Mackleby didn't shoot up

your bar, Allay. Believe me, I would know. He hires his muscle through us. Even if he wanted to go freelance, there wasn't enough time for him to find someone to pull that job. The surveillance camera on the corner of Second and Avenue C was disabled, so we know it was a pro. But as to who hired the gunman, I can't say for certain."

"Really?" If Dread was right, that changed everything. "Then who shot up my bar?"

"You must have an enemy. Perhaps a demon with a grudge?"

"A demon wouldn't use a gun."

Dread tilted his head. "Not unless the demon was sending a message, and wanted you frightened and confused. Not dead. Because he had other uses for you...."

"You think Vex sent the gunman." I felt that sinking feeling of the world reorienting itself. Vex had wanted me confused and scared enough to run to him, to agree to star in his religious resurrection.

"I'm glad you haven't said anything to the police about Mackleby," Dread went on smoothly. "Or our work together."

My shameful past as his bagman, handing off sums of money large and small to a bunch of crooks, was not something I really wanted to admit to. And he didn't want me to blow the whistle on the church's nefarious doings: bribes here, payouts there, with a little extortion thrown in for good measure. "I'm sure the police are already looking into it. They must think I'm crazy. But they'll find out that Vex bought this bar and put it into trust for me."

"Actually, it was purchased in the prophet's name." That was Dread's persona. "Rather than go into the details, I think it's best to say you grew up as part of the church and your parents were staunch members until their death. I took over care for you, even after you grew disgruntled with our philosophy."

"So you bought me a *bar*." I gave a short laugh.

Shock rolled her eyes, her first reaction to our discussion. "You've got to be kidding. The tabloids will say you two were sleeping together and you gave Allay this place as hush money."

I pounced on it. "That's right. So we might as well be up front about it. We'll tell the cops that I'm your discarded mistress."

That wasn't what Shock expected. Her mouth snapped shut.

Dread didn't like it, either. "I'd rather keep that as speculation. It would be less likely to be publicized."

"Well, I'd rather be explicit. I have to be able to work with the police in this neighborhood—I need to convince them that I'm finally being honest with them. Besides, with all the publicity you've had lately, isn't it time for you to be the one who's sweeping girls off their feet?"

It was a barb that lay close to home, seeing as his prophet persona was the unfortunate guy whose society wife had just run off with a playboy twenty years her junior. If the police did leak this to the media, I wouldn't shed any tears over Lash. If the prophet was publicly linked to a young goth bartender in Alphabet City, she'd probably get off on the humiliation.

Not that I wanted that kind of publicity. But I needed a hold over Dread. Having him admit to the police that there had been an affair between us gave me leverage on his prophet persona. I wanted more than his word that we were striking a truce.

And he knew it. But he needed me because of Ram. Ram could sneak up on him at any moment and kill him. My goodwill was a potential defense.

"Agreed," Dread said stiffly. "I'll tell the police we were lovers when you first came to the city. The bar was placed into trust for you nearly a year after you started working here. So that's how long we were together. I'm expecting, naturally, that you won't go to the press with this story."

I nodded. "Who wants that?" Almost casually, I asked, "Are you still planning on a resurrection? I know you wanted to be the star of that show, and now that Vex is gone, there's nothing stopping you."

Dread gave an all-too-real flinch. "No, no. I am not meant for the figurehead role." He was thinking about the degradation of his wife's abandonment splashed across the daily papers. "I couldn't take on the mantle of messiah."

"I thought you were raring to get rid of Vex and branch out on your own."

"Know thyself, I've always said. After all these years of acting as prophet, I've decided I'm much more effective as the power behind the throne, so to speak."

"What throne? You can't mean Goad."

His look was pure disdain. "Of course not. I work for no one. I intend to keep . . . behind-the-scenes would be a better term."

I wasn't sure how Dread was going to function alone. "Well, you're going to have your hands full dealing with Goad. He's head of his own line. More than a third of the Vex demons are his offspring, while you have none. How can you control him?"

Dread raised his head confidently. "I can handle him. And Glory, too." Glory was the only other powerhouse in the demon world, undisputed head of her own extensive line and snug in her Harlem territory surrounded by her most trustworthy offspring. Dread added, "I hear you made an agreement with her, as well."

"Considering that was yesterday, you're well-informed." It had to be Savor. I had trusted her, after she had told me that she was a double agent for Glory. But she must have gone straight back to Dread with what I told her.

I knew I couldn't trust Savor.

"I'll make the same bargain with you that I made with Glory," I offered. "I won't hurt you and yours, and you won't hurt me and mine." I gestured to Bliss and Shock. "And *nobody* pulls a demon resurrection."

"Agreed," Dread said, as if his word was his bond. "I wouldn't mind making the same pact with Glory. That raid on Harlem was Vex's idea, with Goad executing it."

"I told Glory that."

"I know." Dread smiled for the first time, pleased with all of the things he knew about me. He checked his watch, judging how long it would take Ram to return from the Upper West Side. "Our time is up. Come, Zeal."

He didn't know as much as he thought he did. It was a good lesson in not being too sure of yourself.

2

As Dread's slippery signature gradually disappeared, swallowed by Shock's repetitive buzzing, she carefully locked the door behind them.

"We can't live boarded up," I pointed out. "We'll have to take Dread at his word at some point."

Shock looked long and hard at me. "You really intend to open up the bar?"

I had to smile. "It's the beginning of a new era, Shock. Don't you want to celebrate?"

She frowned, but was interrupted by a loud banging on the front door. We all tensed.

"It could be the trap," Shock warned. "Both of you stay in here."

The bolt clicked into place as she closed the door to the foyer behind her.

I didn't want to be afraid, but I was. Bliss, Shock, and I were flotsam in a dangerous sea. Except for one thing: *Ram*. Everyone knew that Ram had exposed himself to save my life. I was going to be popular now for a very different reason than my alluring human-demon energy, which offered the best of both worlds, so to speak. Now because of Ram, I would have another spotlight focused on me.

"There's a cop car outside," Bliss said quietly, looking through the crack along the side of the shutter.

From the other side of the door, I heard voices; Shock

demanded that they identify themselves. Though her persona was petite, she had all the authority of a New York City EMT who was used to dealing with the most hardened criminals as well as panicked, hurt, and dying people. She fed until she overproduced, and when she had given birth to her latest offspring, Petrify, in my apartment, I had let him go rather than kill him and take his life force.

Would things have been different if I had killed Petrify? He would be dead now instead of Pique.

I doubted it would have mattered in the end. I would have still confronted Pique outside my bar, which would have led to Ram saving my life and me inviting him in for a midnight "snack." Which in turn drove me right into Vex's waiting arms.

"Allay?" Shock called through the door. "The police are here to speak to you."

I opened the door to let in two cops, a man and a woman. Lieutenant Markman, my nemesis in blue, wasn't with them, thank the gods. He'd probably show up soon. "I know you wanted to see me. I'm sorry I didn't get back to you sooner," I said to the officers. "I've been trying to get the bar open again, and I lost track of time."

They stood in the center of the bar, staring around intently as if it were the scene of a crime. Which technically it was, only not today. Right now, the smell of Pine-Sol was stronger than anything else.

Officer Suarez was as short as Shock, but much stockier with dark hair pulled tight back into a bun. The gear on her belt made her waist disappear. She looked like a small, efficient tank. Officer Rizzo was a bear of a man with buzzed blond hair and a good-natured expression. Only now he was frowning with his hands ready to go for his belt.

Either one of them could be Ram, and I wouldn't

know it. I could tell by the way Shock drew back, she was thinking the same thing.

"We're responding to a 911 call," Suarez said briskly. "There are reports of a disturbance taking place in the bar."

I shot Bliss a look. She had been sitting by the phone the whole time I spoke to Dread. "Nobody here called 911. There hasn't been any disturbance. Other than the ice machine not working. . . ."

Neither of them smiled back at me. Suarez flipped open her book to read, "Perps are male, Caucasian, black hair, five foot eight inches. Female, Caucasian, brown hair, five foot six inches."

My mouth opened slightly. This was Ram's doing. He must have called the cops when he realized Dread and Zeal were here. That meant he was nearby. "Uh, that sounds like the . . . insurance adjusters. They were just here checking on the repairs that have been done."

"Do you mind if we look around?" Suarez demanded.

"Not at all. Go ahead," I agreed.

They split up, one checking the bathroom while the other went into the stockroom and checked the cooler.

When they reconvened back out in the bar, Suarez asked, "We'd like to check upstairs, miss."

Shock made a slight motion with her hand, warding me off. I didn't need her advice. I didn't want anyone poking around in my place. Even if there weren't any bulky envelops of cash waiting for me to hand off to the Fellowship's stooges.

"I don't think so," I said flatly. "I don't know who called 911 to send you here, but I have to be very careful. My windows were shot out this past weekend, and I can't take any chances."

"We know that, Ms. Meyers." Her head turned at the sound of brakes squealing outside. "That would be

Lieutenant Markman. He radioed that he's on his way
to speak to you."

"Oh." Then I added hastily, "Good."

Shock went to let the lieutenant inside, along with another man. Lieutenant Markman was the oldest in the
bunch, rounding in the face and belly, with his silvering
hair cut very short. He knew I had been lying the last
time we spoke—I'd been sitting right here, soaked in
Pepe's blood and surrounded by shattered glass, claiming I had no idea who had shot out the windows of my
bar and nearly killed my janitor.

Did it make a difference that I'd been wrong? Maybe
it hadn't been Mackleby; maybe one of Vex's henchmen
had done it.

"You didn't come by the station this morning, Ms.
Meyers." Markman came close to intimidate me and get
control of the interview. "Why is that?"

"I'm sorry," I repeated sincerely. People liked it when
you apologized. "There's been a lot to do to open up the
bar, and the insurance adjusters just came by to sign off
on everything."

"We've got a few leads on who might be behind the
shooting, Ms. Meyers. And I'd like to hear more from
you about your relationship with the Fellowship of
Truth."

"You think they have something to do with this?"
I asked, in hopefully genuine surprise. "I don't think
so."

"Three days ago you were ready to file a police report
accusing Prophet Anderson of kidnapping your friend
Mr. Theo Ram, who subsequently turned out to be nonexistent. What was that about?"

I gestured to the same chair Dread had used during
our discussion. "Let's sit down and talk about this. But
I'd rather it be more private, if you don't mind."

Lieutenant Markman dismissed Suarez and Rizzo,

who both looked disappointed to be cut out of the loop. "This is Detective Paulo. He's in charge of your case."

The detective sat down to Markman's right, the better to watch me as I was questioned. Paulo had unattractive stubble and bleary, narrow eyes, shifting them between the three of us, trying to catch every nuance of our reactions.

It put me immediately on guard, when what I wanted to do was make Lieutenant Markman trust me. "You probably already know," I explained. "Thomas Anderson bought this bar and put it into trust for me. But I was misinformed last week that it wasn't really in trust for me, that the church still owned it and the prophet could throw me out whenever he wanted to." This part was a bit vague. "I went over there demanding to know the truth, and . . . he was angry and pretended that it was true. Just to provoke me. See, we were lovers a long time ago, and he promised he would always take care of me. I was hurt when I thought he went back on that promise, and he was hurt when he thought I was questioning his honor. But now we've sorted it all out. I own the bar, like he always told me."

I took a deep breath and waited to see his reaction.

Markman nodded. "Yes, we found out about the trust. Why didn't you tell me the truth?"

"Are you kidding me? If the media gets hold of this, I'm toast. There'll be photographers all over me. The *Post* has Mr. and Mrs. Prophet on their front page at least once a week, as it is. Instead of Mark Cravet, it would be my photo splashed everywhere." I shook my head. "I made a mistake ten years ago, but I left all that behind me."

Markman looked around the bar. "You're still reaping the rewards."

"Yeah, if you call working sixteen-hour days a reward."

He raised a brow and consulted his notes. "What about 'Theo Ram'? Did he even exist? Or was that trumped up as a handy accusation against Mr. Anderson?"

"Yes, there was a guy who called himself Theo Ram. Like I told you, he lied to me. But I really don't think he's the kind who would shoot up my bar. He seems more interested in . . . conning women into intimacy."

Shock looked pleased at that accusation. Since "Theo Ram" would likely never appear again, I didn't see any harm in pointing the finger at Ram's old persona. The one he had used to lure me into his web.

"Have you seen him since that time?"

Suddenly I remembered all the surveillance cameras that now dotted the city streets. "He helped me home last night after I had too much sake to drink. Bl-"—I stumbled over her name—"Belissa was with us."

This was veering off my plan, and from Shock's expression she didn't like it. But it turned out my instincts were correct when Markman consulted his pad. "At eleven forty-one last night, two officers reported seeing a man carrying a woman out of the park accompanied by her sister."

"Belissa is my friend from high school, back in L.A. She just arrived for a visit. We went out to celebrate at a Japanese restaurant, but I had a bit too much sake."

"Why did you go to dinner with a man who lied to you about Mr. Anderson?"

"We didn't. We ran into Theo afterwards, while we were walking home through the park. I was feeling bad, and he helped me get home."

"You just ran into him?" Markman asked skeptically.

"He probably followed us," I conceded. "He said he wanted to apologize for lying about who he was. His name is really Rick." For some reason, *Casablanca* was in my head. Maybe it was the interrogation scene. . . .

"Last name," Markman demanded.

"I don't know," I said. "I don't plan on seeing him again, so I didn't ask. He's caused me enough trouble. But he paid some of that back by helping me out last night."

"If you see him again, get his contact information for us," Markman ordered.

"Uh, sure," I agreed. "But I don't think he had anything to do with the shooting."

Bliss suddenly spoke up. "I think he kind of likes Allay. But she's not so sure about him."

I shot her a "shut the hell up" look that both men caught. "I don't want anything to do with him," I said doggedly.

But Markman finally seemed pleased to see a real reaction from me. "Where did you have dinner?"

I gave him the name of a sushi place off Delancey. It was usually so busy they wouldn't notice even someone as markedly gorgeous as Bliss. In fact, it looked like her breasts were growing rounder by the minute, drawing Detective Paulo's eye as I told my story. It made sense from a demon perspective. Bliss instinctively pleased people so she could feed off their delight.

But now she had caught Markman's attention. "Miss?" the lieutenant said pointedly to Bliss. "Can I see your ID?"

My throat closed. It was too bad our brief cover preparations hadn't extended that far.

But Bliss gave them both a brilliant smile. "I'm Belissa Madrigal. You can call me Belissa, Officers."

Madrigal, that was the name of a family who had lived down the street from my house when I was growing up. Bliss knew that because she had my memories. But I couldn't get distracted now by the thought of her wrinkling her nose at my boring childhood in the endless bedroom communities of Orange County.

Paulo looked slightly stunned as Bliss came out from

behind the bar and walked over to them. I could almost hear the boom-chick-a-wow-wow music going. The way she moved, she could have been in a porn shoot. All I could see were breasts and hips and wet lips.

Shock rolled her eyes, but I was glad Bliss was taking some initiative. I couldn't carry this by myself. Shock was a city EMT; surely she could be talking to the cops to put them at ease. But she was standing there with her arms crossed, acting as suspicious as they were.

"I'll have to get it from my purse," Bliss told them. "It's upstairs."

They both watched her leave; then Paulo had to shake himself awake as the door closed behind her.

Markman retreated to his notebook, while the detective sat there looking dazed. I did my level best not to laugh. After a few moments, Markman said, "We checked on your janitor. He's still in the hospital, but should be released tomorrow, they tell me. He claims he doesn't have any enemies. He's clean, paid up on taxes, has children on the honor roll. So why do you think someone shot your bar, Ms. Meyers?"

"I don't know why anyone would want to hurt me," I said plaintively. "Maybe it was all a huge mistake. Maybe it was a random drive-by shooting."

"At the same time some mystery man is telling you that your bar belongs to someone else? That's some coincidence."

"What about that man who attacked me on Saturday?" Sure, blame Pique, the guy I killed. Might as well slander him now that I had offed him. "Do you think it could be him, or some other patron who has a grudge against me? People get set off by the stupidest things."

"Yes, there was something else. . . ." Markman flipped through his book. "The surveillance camera recorded an altercation between you and a guy on Sunday evening. Late forties, leather jacket, shoulder-length dirty blond hair. You were trying to open the gate to your car, but he stopped you. You do remember that, don't you, Ms. Meyers?"

Whoa, these cops were well-informed. I would have to blame Revel's surveillance cameras for this one. "Yes, that was Phil. Phil Anchor. He's just a patron."

Actually, he was one of the men I passed off payments to from the Fellowship of Truth—their pet journalist who dug out the dirt on their enemies.

"Why were you arguing?"

I sighed. "Phil's troubled. A cocaine addict, in fact. He's been coming to the bar forever. He wanted a drink that day, but I refused to open for him. He comes around after hours all the time, and I have to turn him away."

Phil had come by the bar to complain that I hadn't made his drop to the prophet. And I had gotten so exasperated with him that I had threatened to expose his petty crimes. It's what gave me the idea to threaten Mackleby in order to get Vex to let Ram go.

"Hmm. . . ." Markman was good—his suspicions were raised, but on the face of it there appeared to be nothing of concern. "I think this Rick, aka Theo Ram, is our prime suspect. Are you sure he didn't say anything about where he lived?"

Slowly I shook my head, as if thinking back. "Last night's a wash. Sorry. I barely would have remembered it if Belissa hadn't told me this morning. And everything else he told me turned out to be a lie—"

Bliss suddenly returned in a pounding rush down the stairs, bursting open the door into the bar. Her long blond hair was ruffled up and her eyes huge with fear. "M-my purse! I can't find it. Oh, Allay, what if I left it in the park last night? It had *everything* in it! My money, my credit cards . . ."

Bliss turned to Lieutenant Markman with a beseeching expression. Where sex appeal had no affect on him, her innocent helpless act melted him instantly. It was perfect—not in the least bit overdone—trembling as her eyes glistened, she radiated sweet despair.

How did she know that would get to him? Did she sense it somehow?

I hadn't been able to make a dent in the hardened cop. Now he fell all over himself to be reassuring. Markman ordered one of the officers outside to go retrace our route through the park. Bliss turned to me when asked where we walked, so I sketched it out, feigning hung-over vagueness about the entire thing.

Bliss insisted on going out to the park to search for her lost purse. I knew she was just angling to get out of the bar, and who could blame her? It had been a lousy birthday for her so far. So I agreed we needed to go search, hoping to end the interview, while mentally reminding myself we needed to get Bliss a fake ID ASAP.

As Markman got into the car, he cautioned us both to be careful. "If this guy Rick contacts you again, Ms. Meyers, let us know right away."

"I will," I agreed fervently. "And I'd appreciate it if you would be discreet about my previous relationship with Prophet Anderson. You understand why I don't want it to become public knowledge."

"Of course," Markman agreed, smiling good-bye to Bliss.

She touched his arm, sucking off his pleasure. "Thank you very much for helping me, Lieutenant Markman. I can't tell you how much I appreciate it."

They let us go with more goodwill than I would have dared to imagine a half hour ago. It looked like we had pulled it off, Bliss and I. She had completely distracted them from grilling me.

If only all of my problems could be solved so easily. "Okay, Bliss. Let's go for a walk in the park. Are you coming, Shock?"

She snorted. "As if I'm letting you two out alone. Let's do this thing."

"That was quick thinking," I murmured to Bliss. "Good job."

She just smiled, much more smugly than I would have. She seemed to delight in showing me that she was already a better demon than me.

That was all right by me.

3

We walked through the Wild Houses Projects, on the sidewalk that curved between the squat brick apartment towers. Then across the turquoise pedestrian walkway over the FDR Drive to reach the park, making a pretence of looking for Bliss's lost purse. It was a nice day; the trees swayed lushly in the breeze off the river, and there were lots of people out eating their lunch or taking a midday jog.

"If any cops *are* watching us, they're going to wonder what you're so happy about," Shock muttered.

I realized I had a big, sloppy grin plastered across my face. "I can't help it. I was supposed to be dead today."

"I told you it wouldn't change you, Allay. The only thing different is that you've gained two centuries."

Bliss added, "And there's one less asshole in the world."

My smile faded. It always came back to Pique. I couldn't be happy about killing him. It was wrong—premeditated murder, for my own gain. The worst thing anyone could do. It was as if Pique would always be with me now that I had consumed him, as if he were an alien head sprouting from my back. Always watching me. Waiting for me to remember. I could forget him for a while, but he was right here, leering at my demon nature that I tried so hard to deny.

But I had fought hard to survive this past week, and

I had come out far ahead of where I had started. I had a real chance to live now, on my own terms. The threat of Vex forcing me to die and live again for his church was gone forever.

Then there was Ram. With all the confusion I felt about him, there were a lot of possibilities that made me start smiling again. How could I not think about him here, in this park, where we had joined together to create Bliss? I stared out at the water, lost in the swoony feeling of his arms around me, holding me as if he couldn't let go. . . .

Bliss straightened up from where she had been looking under a bench. "Wow! Check this out."

She held up the front page of the *New York Post*. The banner screamed THE PROPHET STRIKES BACK? The question mark was the barest nod to journalist ethics while the article examined in lurid detail the connections between the prophet of the Fellowship of Truth and the man who had been wounded in Crave's backyard—"in the garden of their love nest," as described by the tabloid. The man had once been Dread's driver, and performed jobs for the church in various capacities. For the *Post*, that was evidence enough of the prophet's complicity in the midnight attack against Crave and Lash. Apparently the wounded hit man wasn't talking.

"That's about as bad as I expected," I conceded. Vex's raid on Harlem had been ill-conceived from the start. But it was unusually sloppy for him to send a man who had obvious connections to the church to back up the demon horde sent to kill Glory's demons.

"The only thing worse would be if you were mixed up in it," Bliss agreed. "Good thing you hid in the closet when the police came."

Shock grimaced. "I don't see why you had to go warn Glory, Allay. Stay out of other demons' wars, I always say." She tucked the paper under her arm. "Come on, let's keep moving in case the police are watching."

I sighed. "If the cops don't have anything better to do than follow me, then the city is doing pretty good, I'd say."

Shock's phone buzzed. She stared at the keypad for a few seconds. "It's a text from Glory," she said grimly.

My phone had been stolen by Goad. I didn't want to know what he was doing with it. "What does she want?"

"To meet with you, Allay. On the Upper East Side."

"Now?" I asked.

"Yeah, now. Ninety-eighth Street."

Bliss had flung herself down on a bench, giving up the effort of looking for her purse. "That could be very interesting. Maybe Lash and Crave will be there."

I knew she was thinking about the scene I had watched, unbeknownst to them, as Crave fed Lash's masochism. I was no better than a cheap Peeping Tom, and Bliss knew it. I didn't like it that she had a window into my head, but she had been very useful with the cops.

"You want to come with me?" I asked her, then turned to include Shock.

"You bet," Bliss said eagerly.

Shock didn't even try to argue about it. It made sense for us to stick together. Safety in numbers. At least until everything settled down. "There's a walkway across at Delancey," she said. "We can take that to get to the subway."

It was only a few blocks from the station to the address Glory had texted: Ninety-eighth Street and Madison Avenue. It was an old brownstone town house sitting on the corner, with bow windows along the side and stained glass ovals in the stairwells. The shrubbery in front was as manicured as a toy poodle, and even the sidewalks were scrubbed clean. There was a jewelry store on the ground floor, but Glory had instructed us to go upstairs.

It was only as we entered the side door that Bliss whispered, "I bet this is Crave's shop."

I realized she was right. Several demon signatures were waiting for us at the top of the stairs—Glory's lifting, swirling sensation was enhanced by Crave's whirlpool-like effect, as if I were being sucked into a tornado. I also felt the stinging of Lash's signature, but it was so much like Shock's that they melded together.

Piano music was playing, soulful in a minor key. In one of the round alcoves formed by the bay window, Glory sat at a desk looking down onto the street. She was clicking away on the keyboard, firmly in her Selma Brown persona—voluptuous, bold, and boundlessly confident. Her dress and head scarf were patterned in white, yellow, and red flowers bigger than my hand, setting off the darkness of her skin.

Glory had made the right choice when she bought dozens of homes in Harlem for her entourage in the mid- to late nineties. She had cashed in at the right time on the gentrification she had helped instigate with her renovation projects. She was a well-known figure in the community, a regular on the stage at the Apollo Theater singing backup for a lot of big names.

Crave was at the grand piano that mostly filled the parlor space, playing like a seduction. His Mark Cravet persona wore all black, from his dark hair to his ebony boots. His skin was dusky and his eyes big and soulful, as if he had aristocratic Spanish ancestors. He was compelling, and never seemed to try very hard to get women to fall for him.

"Hello, Allay," he said with a special smile, reminding me that he had fed me yesterday.

I knew he was doing it to piss off Lash, who was sitting next to him on the piano bench, staking her claim on him from the moment we walked into the room. Her impeccable silhouette-hugging Marc Jacobs dress was made of creamy satin, matching her perfect blond hair and Grace Kelly features. She didn't bother with her guise of the aging prophet's wife among other demons, and was giving Bliss a run for her money. But I thought Bliss's young hipster beauty was preferable to Lash's patrician elegance.

Lash flicked a glance at me. "I knew it. She did consort with Ram last night."

Glory turned away from the keyboard with a final click, and fastened her dark eyes on me. "Is it true, Allay? Is that how you got Bliss?"

"Surely that's old news by now." I didn't look at Bliss, but I knew she was smiling and looking around curiously.

"I was wondering if you would deny it," Glory said.

"Why should I?" I held out both hands innocently. "I've told you everything that I know about Ram. As long as you don't hurt people, he won't hunt you. The demons who do will continue to disappear. Whether we can trust his word is another story."

"What about Dread?" Glory pressed. "Does he have an alliance with Ram?"

I sat down on the upholstered chair closest to her. She hadn't bothered to invite me to sit, but I wasn't going to stand in front of her like a child being scolded. "I don't know what Ram intends to do about Dread," I said honestly.

"Someone has to kill him before he kills us all." Lash was defiant, too loud in the small room.

"Who? Dread or Ram?" I asked.

"Both!"

Glory was pointedly not looking at Lash. Crave quietly played a tinkling melody in the background. Neither seemed interested in placating Lash right now.

"I tell you what I'm worried about," I said. "The new ERI machine. Dread said it's supposed to hit the market in a couple of months. It can show the difference between humans and demons. Dread said the FAA already has it in production to replace their old metal detectors. What are we going to do?"

"I've got a lab working on it," Glory said dismissively. "They think we can disrupt the electrical field with low-frequency waves. We've always gotten around technological advances before, and this one won't be any different."

"But they'll be in place next month."

"If we have to stay off planes for a while, that's all the better. Dread has to send back all of the Vex demons who flew in for Goad's raid. That's nonnegotiable. It would help stabilize things if everyone stayed in their own territory."

I didn't think she understood the seriousness of the situation. It was almost intoxicating to think about—what if we were all exposed and I didn't have to lie about who I was anymore? "But the ERIs will be in government buildings. Shock, you'd be seen for sure. You have to go everywhere with your job."

But Shock was shaking her head at me in a mirror image of Glory. "I think it was a trick Dread and Vex played on you, Allay. There is no ERI. They just wanted to scare you into cooperating with them."

Now, there was a possibility I hadn't considered. I wished she had said something about it when we were alone. We'd have to talk about it later, not in front of Glory.

Glory pounced on my moment of weakness. "What's happening with you and Dread, Allay?"

So that was why she ordered me up here.

"We made a truce—he leaves me and mine alone"—I gestured to Shock and Bliss—"I won't go after him. He said he would offer the same truce to you. Since he claims to have half the demon population more or less under his control, I thought it was a good bargain."

"He's not in control of Goad." Glory glanced at the screen. "Goad and his horde took down Amaze last night."

I vaguely knew Amaze. She was harmless; she worked at the Carousel in Central Park, soaking up the kids' delight. She had been Glory's last offspring, born a hundred and fifty years ago, around the same time as Shock.

No wonder Crave was still tinkering softly away at the mournful music. No wonder Lash was glaring at me so indignantly. Vex was dead, but their people were still being killed.

"Is that who Dread consumed?" I asked.

Glory narrowed her eyes. "No, he took Petrify, Shock's recent offspring. Goad tracked him down in Jersey City, on the piers. He was hiding in a sea of cars, probably hoping to be shipped overseas."

Petrify had tried to escape New York—like I'd told him. I gave Shock a stricken look, but she was disgusted. "You should have done it," she told me.

"He was an infant, unable to defend himself." I glanced at Lash, wondering if she knew I had killed her offspring Pique, instead. I wondered if she cared. Pique had been a sick, twisted product of her sick, twisted love for Crave. All of the newbies were dying like flies. "So Dread got Petrify in the end. What happened to Amaze?"

"Stun killed her, I'm told. He didn't even need to replenish his core."

We fell silent, thinking of the implications of that. The only person Stun ever listened to was Vex, but now with him gone . . . and to make matters worse, he was Shock's first offspring. Not that she had anything to do with him. Except for making him the horror he was.

Bliss suddenly gave a long, sensual shiver. "Umm . . .

Petrify had the most frightening signature. I think he would have had a hard time making friends."

That was my fault, because I had fed Shock my panic when she came to my place to give birth. Who was I to judge her for her offspring?

Lash nudged Crave, who was watching Bliss so intently that his fingers faltered on the keys. Bliss was doing it again, changing subtly, throwing out cues, trying to please the only man in the room.

This time it was the *wrong* thing to do.

"Stop it, Bliss," I ordered under my breath.

"Feeling jealous?" Crave asked Lash. Slowly Lash eased back into place. He made eye contact with Bliss again, letting Lash see. She touched his thigh, soaking up his desire to hurt her.

Bliss was watching them, a smile shadowing her lips.

Low enough that I almost couldn't hear her, Lash said, "You know I can never get enough of you."

He kept playing. "So I've discovered."

"I'll do anything for you," she said louder, willing to abase herself in front of everyone if that would make him pay attention to her. "Anything you want, just tell me, and I'll get it for you."

"I don't keep you because you're rich," Crave drawled.

"No, you depend on me for that," Glory snapped.

I watched it all go down. Crave was sick of playing the role of devoted lover, especially when it suited no purpose except to stroke Lash's pride. But Glory was determined to indulge Lash because she wanted her to be happy in Harlem. Lash was her only hold over Dread. She had probably told Crave to treat Lash better because this was no time to be harboring a viper in their bosom.

"Dread is sure rich." Bliss sighed. "All those clothes you left behind, Lash . . . You should see Allay's closet.

It's embarrassing. How much black can one person wear?"

"Bliss!" I exclaimed. Shock rolled her eyes as if she expected nothing better from Bliss.

"What?" Bliss asked innocently. "I would have pegged Lash for the sugar-daddy kind, not the benevolent cougar."

All eyes turned to Lash, who glared at Bliss. "Shut up!"

Bliss laughed, a startlingly clear sound. "You think I don't know Dread's thing? When he was wooing Allay, he couldn't even bend over, he had such a long stick up his ass."

Crave snorted, then hid his mouth behind his hand. Glory didn't look happy about it, so I kept my expression blank. Once again, Bliss had perfect recall.

Lash stood up and started fanning herself. "It's crowded in here. Maybe some of you who have no reason to be here should step outside." She looked pointedly at Bliss.

Bliss laughed again. "That's okay, Lash. Don't get into a twist. I'll wait downstairs on the corner."

Shock suddenly spoke for the first time. "Then one of them has to leave, too. I won't sit here outnumbered."

It was annoying, but I didn't want to openly contradict Shock. They had just revealed a lot about the inner tensions inside the Glory camp. I didn't want to give them the same insight into ours.

Glory gestured to Lash, her voice kind. "Why don't you go upstairs, honey? I'll call you when we're through here."

Lash hesitated, glancing suspiciously at me. With Bliss out of the room, I had reverted to being the primary target of her jealousy. But she was dependent on Glory, as she had been dependent on Dread to sustain her. I could smell it on her, something anachronistic, as though she had never left the era she had been born in, when women were property to be cared for and tended. I couldn't imagine spending sixteen hundred years living that way.

Lash waited until Bliss headed downstairs; then she swished out of the room, as if compelling us to watch her retreat upstairs.

Crave continued to play softly, but the melody was markedly lighter. Shock folded her arms as if she could wait all day.

"Dread would do anything for you if you get Lash to meet with him," I told Glory.

"Yes," Glory agreed thoughtfully. "I expect he wants to possess her again rather than kill her. In spite of all the secrets she knows about him."

"That's a powerful bargaining chip. And he's in a bargaining mood right now."

Glory gave me a bland smile. "Ah, the impatience of youth. I prefer to wait to see which way the wind blows. I'm not going to get caught out in a mass raid again. And it's not just Dread I'm concerned about. I'm certain Goad won't bend his knee to anyone now that Vex is dead."

A soft bell rang. Glory gestured to Crave, dismissing him like a servant. He went quickly through the back archway, presumably going down to his jewelry shop. Shock smiled slightly, relaxing even more now that it was just the three of us.

As Glory questioned me about my conversation with Dread, I kept thinking about Bliss down on the street, alone. I didn't like it. What if she wandered off? Or got into trouble. I didn't have any responsibility for her, but for some reason I felt I had to do my best to help her. Other demons didn't feel that way about their offspring. But in a real sense, she was the only kind of child I would ever have.

So I rushed through my answers and finally told

Glory, "I've got to go get Bliss. She doesn't make the best choices sometimes. As you noticed."

Glory wasn't satisfied, but that was only to be expected while things were in a state of flux. Shock and I got out of there with more promises of cooperation and goodwill.

When we got down to the corner, Bliss was nowhere to be seen.

I raised my hands. "Crap! I knew it! She's run off."

"Good riddance," Shock said with feeling. "I thought she'd never leave."

"Don't say that." I felt awful. I tried to think like a demon—Bliss was nothing more than too much energy I had absorbed, overloading my system until I'd fissioned in two. But with her memories of my life, it felt much more intimate than that. I'd always considered Shock to be my sister because her progenitor, Revel, was also the progenitor of Plea, the demon I'd absorbed when I became possessed. I knew Bliss wasn't my child, but I couldn't convince my heart of that.

I tried to sense her signature, but with all the demons at the jewelry shop, including Shock right next to me, Bliss was gone.

"You look that way." I ran across the street and down Madison Avenue. Surely Bliss would be drawn downtown while looking at all the boutiques. But even after several blocks, with Shock falling behind, I still didn't sense her signature.

I headed back uptown. If Bliss was smart, she would go deeper into Harlem instead of exposing herself to Goad's horde.

But she wasn't farther up Madison, either. As I paused on the corner, indecisive, a black limousine car with dark windows whipped past, and I glanced at Shock as we both felt Glory's strong and distinctive signature. Glory was going home.

"Come on, Allay," Shock insisted. "This is useless. Let's go back to the bar. Bliss is bound to show up there. Unfortunately."

Shock hailed a cab, but I couldn't make myself get inside. "I can't." It was the strangest feeling. As if I were walking away from a baby, leaving it helpless on the sidewalk. "I'm so stupid! I never should have let her come down to the street alone."

"Allay, you're being irrational. Bliss can take care of herself, believe me. I've been watching her from the moment she was born. That girl can get whatever she wants."

My feet stubbornly returned to Crave's jewelry shop. The leafy green of Central Park over on Fifth Avenue was enticing. Maybe she went that direction. Or she could have gone east toward the river.

As I was turning, something caught my eye through the window of the jewelry shop. A flash of brightness—blond hair. It was Bliss.

Now that I saw her, I could feel her floaty signature, as if my sight enhanced my sixth sense. I should have known.

I pushed against the glass door, but it was locked shut. Shading my eyes, I could see Bliss and Crave reflected in one of the case mirrors. Bliss was kissing Crave, wrapped around him as if they were molded together. Their auras sparked green and gold where they touched, unmistakable signs of their raging lust. His fingers tightened on her shirt, ready to rip it off her, and damn the consequences.

She's a succubus! I should have figured it out when she seduced the cops.

I banged my fist against the window, rattling the door in its frame. Startled, they looked over at me. At the same time, on the inside, Lash appeared at the top of the staircase calling for Crave.

When she saw him holding Bliss, Lash shrieked. Even through the glass, the sound was shattering.

"What is going on here?" Lash demanded in a shrill voice. "What are you doing with her!"

Caught, Crave kept grinding himself against Bliss even as they both stared over in surprise at Lash.

"Let go of her!" Lash screamed.

Lash growled as she approached Bliss, her fingers extended like talons, like she was going to suck the life out of Bliss.

"Let me in!" I cried, banging harder on the door. "Bliss, come open the door!"

Bliss managed to untangle herself from Crave, who stopped Lash from getting to her. There was no way for Bliss to straighten her hair or clothes enough to remove the image of them going at it. Bliss was breathing hard, trying to hide her face.

"Are they laughing?" I asked Shock, trying to see through the glass. "They are! Stop it, you idiots!" Glory wanted Crave to keep Lash happy. But Crave was grinning as he valiantly took the brunt of Lash's fists.

"You slut!" Lash screamed. People turned on the sidewalk, and I abruptly stopped banging on the door. Now we were drawing a lot of attention. Good thing there weren't any paparazzi in sight, but that was bound to change any second.

Thankfully Bliss came over and opened the door. "Okay, let's go," she said breezily.

Lash grabbed on to Crave. "So now you're going after dim-witted bimbo demons!" She raked Bliss with a scathing look. "*Must* you seduce every female who crosses your path?"

Crave didn't seem bothered. "Only the ones who irritate you the most, my dear."

Their gazes held, Lash proud, jealous, and defiant,

while Crave refused to back down. It went on for a long time, too long, as they silently battled it out. Neither shifted or glanced away. The tension was so thick that I held my breath.

Then slowly Lash began to crumple in on herself, her indignation disappearing as her eyes began to plead. "How could you, Crave? I gave up everything for you."

"I didn't ask you to."

She reached out for him, her eyes closing in ecstasy as she soaked up the full force of his disdain. It was her favorite emotion, the torment of her life. She had to be adored and pushed away at the same time. Dread had been the perfect symbiotic relationship for her. Crave was only going through the motions, an experienced incubus who was compelled to give women what they wanted so they in turn desired him.

And Bliss was cut from the same cloth—born with a desire to please and a need for ecstasy.

"Have you had enough?" Crave jerked his arm impatiently, as ruddy light flashed between them.

Her heavy-lidded glance went to Bliss, who was watching fascinated. I was, too, in spite of myself. "Don't make me do this, Crave. Not in front of her."

"You're the one who made a spectacle of yourself, Lash."

She was feeding off him in deep luxurious gulps. "Please, Crave."

She was practically pulsing with desire for him, which he was soaking up. Her expression was glazed, and the dark green swirls in her aura grew more pronounced. The green tendrils began to cycle between them, going faster.

Shock pulled me away, and Bliss followed. The last thing I saw was Crave staring after us, ignoring the groveling Lash in front of him.

*   *   *

I waited until we got in a cab. "What do you think you're doing, Bliss?"

"Crave was using me to play a game with Lash. He's very good at what he does, isn't he?"

I wasn't expecting that. "You don't care that he was using you?"

Bliss laughed. "He can use me anytime. He kisses really good."

"Please keep away from him. You hear me, Bliss? I need to stay on Glory's good side, and she needs Crave to keep Lash in line. That's her only hold on Dread. I don't want you getting mixed up in that." Bliss didn't reply. "Please, Bliss."

After a moment, she agreed, "All right, since it's important to you, Allay. But after this all settles down, I'm going to give him a whirl. He looks like a lot of fun."

I held my tongue on my warning. It was probably inevitable. They would either repel each other like magnets or go down in a glorious burst of passion. There wasn't anything I could do to stop it, and acting like the mom of a teenager would be the quickest way to drive Bliss away.

Shock was looking at me curiously. I knew she was thinking the same thing—somehow keeping Bliss happy had become very important to me.

4

Back at the bar, Shock took me aside and urged me to tell Bliss to leave. "She's doing something to you, something I've never seen before."

"I've never given birth before."

Shock shook her head, clearly not understanding. For demons, fissioning was a physiological function of absorbing too much energy, something akin to throwing up. Sometimes the new demons killed their progenitor while they were weakened and fallen into a stupor from the ordeal. Shock had come to my place to birth Petrify, in part because she feared he would consume her. Also, she wanted to give him to me so I could replenish my life force with his core.

Instead I had sent him out like a lamb to slaughter, bleating and unable to defend himself. And Dread had killed him. If I had killed Dread first, Petrify would still be alive.

Not that Shock cared about that.

"I feel responsible for her," I tried to explain.

Her piercing blue eyes searched mine. "Are you falling in love with her, Allay?"

"No!" I couldn't have been more appalled. "*Ick* ... how could you think that?"

"It happens." She shrugged. "Newbie demons retain a lot of their progenitor's personality traits as their memories battle with their own true nature. Their core desire wins out in the end, but when I met Mar in Singapore, she was in love with Stymie, her offspring. They were together for months before he finally left her, and it turned out bad. A whole neighborhood burned to the ground. They don't talk now."

"That's so narcissistic. It's sick, Shock. I can't believe you think that about me." But what was my fascinated need to keep Bliss close? It was more than duty. That was for sure. I had panicked when I thought we'd lost her on Madison Avenue.

Maybe I should rethink listening to my gut. I was a demon, after all. My own choices were suspect.

Shock saw my uncertainty. "It's time to cut the cord, Allay. Bliss isn't a human, and she isn't your baby."

I sighed. "I'm not kicking her out now, Shock. Not while everything is in turmoil. I feel guilty enough about Petrify."

"What do you mean?"

"I wish I'd helped him more. I didn't even give him shoes!"

"He tried to kill you, Allay. Where's your head? These are demons we're talking about."

I turned away. "We're demons, too."

I couldn't fix the ice machine. We needed to go several blocks to the supermarket to get the big bags, and it would take at least two of us to get enough in the hand-carts. I wanted all of us to go, but Shock insisted I stay in the bar, where it was safe. "Goad's horde could be waiting just out of range for you to wander into their hands."

I couldn't stand having another argument with Shock, so I let them go alone. I was busy prepping the bar when I realized I also needed limes and lemons. The fruit stand was on the corner, so I could get back inside the bar quickly if I felt anyone approaching.

I ran out and bought the fruit, fidgeting as I explained

to Raoul that I was opening the bar again. He was so happy that I didn't want to be rude and rush away, but Shock and recent events had made me too paranoid to have a nice chat with my neighbor on a nice spring afternoon.

I was crossing the street at the corner when I saw Ram. I felt an instant rush of anticipation, an almost itchy need to touch him. I'm ashamed to say I wanted to feel his ancient energy again, to feel the depths of time in him. I wasn't sure if it was the demon in me that wanted him more or the horny human who hadn't been laid in years before he came along.

Then I met his eyes, and nothing else mattered. Where there had been two of us, there was now one being united in common purpose—to protect and care for each other.

How could his eyes say so much?

It was only then I realized he was in his Theo Ram guise again. It seemed kind of dangerous since the cops were looking for that persona. I wondered if he did it to make me more comfortable, because I had learned to trust him in that guise. But I had also learned he had lied about who he was, riding on my coattails to infiltrate the Prophet's Center.

He was on Third Street behind the Spanish restaurant, in the short driveway in the back where they kept their Dumpster. He gestured for me to join him, then drew me in deeper, so we couldn't be seen behind the Dumpster.

"What are you doing here?" I asked. He must know Shock and Bliss had left. "Why didn't you come to the bar?"

"The surveillance cameras are aimed at the front. There's nothing on this side." He glanced away. "Revel's PI is at the other end of the block. There's a waitress in the Chinese joint he likes."

I narrowed my eyes at the reminder that Papa Revel's eyes were trained on me. Revel had been my first demon lover, the one who had taught me how manipulative demons could be. He had spent the past decade trying to win back my trust, while also protecting me for Vex. But I couldn't get over his first betrayal—I really thought he loved me, when all he wanted was to control me.

"Have you been watching me, too?"

He smiled slightly. "Every second."

I didn't like it, but in a strange way it was also flattering. Why did I hate it when Revel did it, but it made me go all girlish when Ram did?

I wanted to reach out to touch him, but resisted with everything I had. The fact that we had chemistry didn't mean anything, not really. Ram was the most dangerous creature I'd ever come close to, and I knew plenty of monsters by name.

"Every second?" I forced myself to ask coolly. "So you did call 911."

He hesitated, fighting a lifetime of concealment. "Yes, when Dread and Zeal were in the bar. I was worried."

I shifted back from him. "I've got everything under control, Ram. I wouldn't have invited them inside if I thought there would be trouble. But now Dread's agreed to order the Vex demons to keep away from me."

He ran his hand through his hair, tugging at the curling strands. It made me want to do the same, to feel how silky it was. He had lain with his head in my lap as I stroked his hair, doing everything I could to make him feel better after Dread's torture, while he was lying to me with every pained breath. I thought he was a human, but he wasn't. He had such deep reserves of energy that he could have healed himself instantly. I tried not to take that personally—it would have exposed him and prevented our escape. But I couldn't help thinking about it.

"What are you giving Dread in return?" he asked.

"He wants me to tell you that he won't hurt people anymore. He's dismantling his cage and getting out of the Abu Ghraib business. He wants to cut a deal with you."

Ram gave me a look. "I hope you don't believe him."

I shrugged. "He lives for fear, and he's used to a regular diet of it. I seriously doubt he's going to change now."

"He's going to want more from you, always more. You can't trust Dread, Allay. He's trying to form an alliance with Goad, and has promised him something huge. Everything's on the verge of exploding. The humans went through the enlightenment and the industrial revolution, but the way demons operated has remained the same for nearly two thousand years with Vex and Glory calling the shots. None of the modern demons has seen such a major paradigm shift within our culture. They don't realize that the old days have ended." He shook his head. "What does Glory want from you?"

"Information about Dread. And you." I took a deep breath. It was time for me to be fully honest with him. How could we develop any sort of trust if we lied to each other? "While I was at the Prophet's Center, Dread told me about a new machine that's been developed—the ERI. It uses a high-frequency, high-voltage, low-amperage electrical field to show the difference between humans and demons. They're going to be used as weapons detectors, but Vex found out they also reveal our unique energy pattern. Shock thinks he was just making it up to scare me into cooperating with them."

Again he hesitated, raising all sorts of flags in my mind. "I've been waiting for this. It's called a Kirlian field. It was invented by Professor Semyan Kirlian of

Russia in 1939. He discovered a way to use high frequencies to photograph the aura, the energy field of living matter. I met with him after the war. I'll never forget how he tore off a piece of a leaf and when he photographed it, a ghostly image of the missing part was left."

"Like us, when a limb is cut off," I said, remembering how Dread's arm had rematerialized after he cut it off with the cross of the Fellowship of Truth. "So it's really true? The ERI really exists."

"Yes. It's already in mass production."

"But that's ... earth-shattering." I could hardly imagine it. "Demons will be outed."

Ram nodded. "I've been waiting for this moment for a very long time. Perhaps in this scientific age, we'll finally be known for who we are. I hope we can leave behind the hysteria and xenophobia that always comes when we're discovered. If reason doesn't triumph, we're in for another witch hunt of epic proportions."

"We have to tell the others."

"It won't do any good to try to raise a panic about it, Allay. None of them will believe you."

"They didn't before, but they will if I tell them you agree with me."

"Even if you convince them it's true, there's nothing they can do about it. It might even provoke them into stupid acts, like Vex with his religious resurrection. Demons will always try to use what's at hand to their advantage."

"Does that include you?"

His slow smile melted me inside. "I always win. That's why I'm watching over you, to make sure you get through this transition period unharmed. These are chaotic times, and there's no telling who will turn on whom, who will become enemies or friends."

I suddenly got the oddest flash of a giant demon standing head and shoulders above the surrounding men. He was broad in the shoulders, a massive man with a huge helm on his head that made him seem even taller. His followers were in rags and brandishing sabers as he shouted commands, his flaming red beard streaming from his chin. "I know it's happened before. All those vampire and werewolf stories. Not to mention the Bible. And Redbeard . . ."

Behind the huge redheaded demon, I could see a castle high on a craggy coastline, the water bluer than I've ever seen before, like the purest turquoise. His people swarmed over to me, surrounding me. The ocean was booming not far in the distance as I passed slowly through the crowd. They reached out to touch me, begging for my blessing, for a miracle, forcing their desperate desire into me as I glutted myself. Pain blossomed in my hands as blood began to flow, shiny dark red against my pale flesh, dripping down my arms as I raised them high for everyone to see. A roar went up as they tried to get to me, squashing me among them as I writhed in ecstasy.

I blindly held out my hands, palms up. "I'm bleeding!"

"No, you're not." Ram took hold of my arm to steady me. "Allay, what's wrong?"

"Memories," I realized. "Plea's memories."

I could feel the stigmata in my palms, the searing lie. I had . . . Plea had conned those people into thinking she was a saint, just like Vex had wanted me to pose as a messiah. I wondered if he thought that Plea's memories would be an inducement to agree to his plan. Maybe he hoped I would want to relive the glory days. He couldn't have known that I remembered nothing about my progenitor. But from this taste, it would have made me even more reluctant to stage my own resurrection.

"Are you okay?" he asked.

"Yes." I swallowed back a burning in my throat. "I haven't had a flashback in a long time."

It was a little ominous that my self-control was slipping now. But that one memory made clearer than anything the true frenzy of the mob, the sheer weight of humanity that could crush anything in its path.

I should have known better than other demons; I had lived my human life. I knew how schoolkids stuck to those who were like them, shunning the ones who were different. I knew what that revulsion for the other felt like, and sympathized with it, even though I was now "the other."

It was what kept me in hiding, in shame, holed up in my bar instead of living my life for the past decade.

Now through Ram's touch, I could feel his driving aggression, everything rushing full speed ahead—his desire for me, his need to pull me closer, and his iron control so as to not frighten me. It washed over me, surrounding me with his energy, as he sighed, no longer hiding his need for me. His aura flushed verdant, staining my own aura with my response where he touched me.

"Thank you for helping me," I told Ram. "And thank you for Bliss."

His smile was wistful. "You like her. I'm glad."

It surprised me after Shock's dire warnings. "You don't think it's dangerous?"

"Between your memories and influence, and her own core desire for pleasure, I doubt she's capable of harming anyone."

It was nice to have my judgment confirmed for a change. Very nice to touch him and feel that warmth I craved—my own skin was cool, as was all demons'. But Ram was different, far more ancient than any of us.

He was completely immoral. How could he not be, when he was able to do exactly as he wanted and controlled everything in his reach?

He was looking at me, his eyes locked on mine for far longer than I was used to. I kept glancing away, but he was still watching me when I looked back. It made me confused, almost heady with delight. How could such a simple thing, his eyes on mine, be so powerful?

I leaned forward as he bent closer. I wasn't sure if I kissed him or he kissed me, but our gentle, sweet brush of the lips lingered on as I pressed against him. Touching him was even better than being devoured by his eyes. I was lost in his arms around me, holding me close as his mouth caressed mine.

Then I realized Ram was feeding me, pouring his potent energy into me. I almost stopped him, but it tasted so good, and was so freely given, that I couldn't refuse. I hated stealing from my patrons to survive. He was like a river of wealth flowing into me.

He turned, pushing me against the chain-link fence, which gave comfortably against my back. He was already hard, so hard and hot that he pressed into my belly, and I arched against him, buoyed by the fence.

He grasped my hips through my skirt and rubbed against me with one long, hard thrust. His intent was unmistakable. "Allay," he breathed. "I must have you."

"Here?" I said, a little too loudly, shaken out of my fog of lust. True, we were hidden behind the rusted green Dumpster, but the sidewalk was just on the other side and I could suddenly hear the sound of cars and people talking as they passed by.

"Your place," he urged. "I'll go around the block and come in through the roof."

Shock was coming back any minute. The thought of her expression when she found me having sex with Ram was like a cold dash of water. "No!"

He eased back, letting me rest against the fence, our auras sparking with brilliant green where his hands held my waist. To his credit, he was still feeding me his energy despite my rebuff. "You don't want me?"

"Yes! I do. Only . . ."

"You don't trust me," he said flatly.

My mouth moved to protest, but that was what it came down to. Did I trust him? How could I?

Then again, how could I not? He had saved my life twice. My best chance of survival was with him at my back. Shock's and Bliss's best chance of survival, as well. If I was a cynical, conniving demon, I would fuck him senseless just to keep him on my side.

But I wasn't that kind of girl.

Ram traced a light finger down my cheek to my wet lips. "Of course you don't trust me. There's no reason you should. But I have an eternity to prove myself to you."

I really wanted to ask him to lower his shields, so I could feel his powerful signature throbbing through me. So I could feel how old he was, like history itself, wrapping the thread of human existence around the spool of one man.

I clasped his hand, and reached up to cup his palm that lay against my cheek. "I do want you, Ram."

I pulled him closer to kiss him, making him lean into the fence, pressing against my entire body. All of a sudden, my fear was gone. All I cared about was him in that moment.

I wrapped my leg around his to lock him in close. He arched his back, stroking himself against me, raising up my skirt with one hand so he could feel my cool thigh. His fingers dug into me urgently. "Don't deny me, Allay."

I murmured against his lips, "I want to feel you inside me."

"Now?"

"Now."

I pulled up my skirt all the way. He moaned at the feel of my skin against him. With a quick twist, he ripped my panties as if they were tissue paper, making me gasp at his power. As if I were close to a volcano about to erupt, bathing in the heat.

He pulled my knee high around his hip, holding me up as I wrapped my arms around his neck. We fit together, balancing each other as my back braced against the chain-link fence. All I could see was his face.

I was open to him, and he pushed himself inside me slowly, sliding ever deeper like I was drawing him in. He let out a sighing breath almost as if he was climaxing, trembling throughout his body at the intensity of burying himself inside me.

"I belong inside you," he murmured.

I kissed him as he thrust into me, soaking up the adoration, the desire that raged inside him, the need to take me and keep me safe. He couldn't hide any of it. It was overwhelming as it poured into me, filling me up.

As I cried out in pleasure, somewhere in the back of my mind I still questioned—how could he feel so much for me, so soon? Could Ram really be in love with me? Maybe it was just because I was like Hope....

Then everything vanished as I climaxed, giving myself over to pure sensation. Nothing else mattered. There was only perfect joy, the essence of Bliss, in every touch, in every sweet kiss.

As I came back to myself, a light sheen of sweat covered my skin, raising goose bumps in the breeze. He had fed me so much, my skin felt warm.

Then I remembered where I was. I was as shameless as Bliss. No wonder, poor girl! I'd made her that way.

Ram felt my sudden blush of embarrassment, staining my aura blue. I disentangled myself from him, and as I straightened my skirt, I felt the need to say, "I don't usually go around having sex in public places, if that's what you're thinking."

"Not at all." He sounded as if he was trying not to laugh.

I shot him a silent warning not to. And he didn't. But he was amused at my modern sensibilities. I could see why; after all, he was born in a time when everyone, including children, slept in a pile and had sex in front of everyone else. Orgies must look awfully self-conscious to him.

"Come around to the bar and see me next time," I blurted out. "I don't like hiding from Shock."

His brow rose as he realized that was why I didn't want to go back to my place. "I don't mind your friends knowing about us, but I don't want Dread and Glory's spies finding out. Revel is working for Dread now, you know."

"You want me to lie to everyone about seeing you?"

"I don't want them to get the idea to use you against me. If they know how important you are to me, they could kidnap you and try to trap me."

It sounded reasonable enough. But I didn't like to lie. I lied too much as it was, living among humans. I wanted to be honest about my feelings for Ram. I would have to start with Shock and Bliss, and damn the consequences. Because it was the truth. Despite my doubts, I couldn't turn my back on these feelings—his or my own.

Ram lifted his head. "Shock's coming. I've got something to do tonight, but I'll try to be back before you close. *You* . . . be careful while I'm away."

He gave me a lingering kiss, and then he was gone before they came into my range. As I emerged from behind the Dumpster and made my way back to the bar with the crumpled bag holding the fruit, I couldn't stop smiling. I'm sure my customers would never recognize the wanton sex kitten that I had become with Ram.

I made it back to the bar just before Shock and Bliss. They took one look at my highly charged aura, glowing green and still edged with blue from the realization of how uninhibited I had been, taking him right there on the street. . . .

"Allay!" Shock breathed in dismay. She seemed to be at a loss for words over the fact that I had made love to Ram.

"Yes," I told her and Bliss. "You might as well get used to it. I finally found someone I can be honest with. A guy I'm mad about. I'm not giving it up, not for anything."

"Not even your life? Or mine." She shot Bliss a look. "Or hers?"

Bliss tilted her head. "You told me to stay away from Crave until things settle down."

"Yeah, Allay," Shock agreed. "The least you could do is the same. Ram is dangerous, and getting too close to him puts *another* target on you."

"No, that's not what I meant," Bliss denied. "I meant I should be able to do Crave now. Otherwise it's a double standard."

I shook my head. "You know why I asked you to stay away from Crave. Glory is our ally now, but if you start messing with Lash, her only hold on Dread, she's going to turn against you. And me, because I'm going to defend you. Could you wait just a few days, even, before pursuing this?"

"Can you?" Shock asked me, her arms folded.

"Do you want me to piss off Ram by rejecting him? Now, when we could use all the help we can get?"

"Don't tell me you're using him. You're in this up to your eyeballs. I can tell. But he's using you. That's what demons do."

That was exactly what Ram had said. I had survived a long time by listening to Shock. But I couldn't force myself to agree.

I clapped my hands together once, ready to be done

with this. "Can we talk about all this later?" I pointed to the bar. "It's time to open up."

She held my gaze a moment longer, then gave a hard shrug as she turned away. It was awful. She had been my friend since I became a demon, my sister in word and deed. She used to come by the bar, regular as clockwork, to pretend to have a drink and tell me some of the gossip in the demon world. She was on the streets with her job, so she came across demons all the time and picked up bits and pieces of things. But she also refused to participate in the various intrigues. In that way we were a lot alike. I had stayed away from the others and hid out in my bar because too many demons had turned on me and tried to steal my hybrid energy. And my soul.

I couldn't live that way anymore, so no wonder I was at odds with Shock. I had to be strong and defend myself. I had been stuck in a cocoon spun by Vex, safe and warm and utterly dead to the world. Shock had her work and I had my bar, but there was a lot more to life than that.

I let Shock know I was taking her seriously by calling Revel when she was nearby and could listen in. Shock had already filled him in on what had happened since we left his apartment yesterday, but I had to endure another round of his offers to help up to and including buying me my own fortress in the sky like his penthouse on Park Avenue.

Revel had always gotten off on giving me things. And I had resisted him with all my might for the past ten years, ever since I had found out that he had seduced me into loving him on Vex's orders. He'd been my first love. And it had been wonderful—empowering, exciting, with everything at my fingertips bound up in one amazing man. It was too bad it was all a lie. You might say I'd never gotten over it. Not until this week, when

Revel had turned out to be one of my staunchest allies in a time of absolute need.

That said something. I didn't have many friends, but I could now say that Revel was one of them.

"You can't possibly keep working in that dive," Revel drawled through the phone. "It's a death trap."

I rolled my eyes, but Shock could hear his insistence and pointedly agreed, "I'm all for shutting the place down for good!"

"You can come live here for a while, until things calm down," Revel said. "You can't trust Dread or Glory, Allay. They'll smash you flat if it suits them."

"Has Dread contacted you?" I asked.

"Yes, he made me the same offer he made you—I cooperate with him and he'll make sure Goad's line leaves me alone."

"Why isn't Goad ousting Dread altogether? He's the head of his own line—there must be over thirty goons who would do what he says, with or without Dread."

"I'm not sure, but I think it has something to do with the church. Dread has a lot of real-world power with the Fellowship. The bigger his church grows, the more influence he has."

"Dread says he likes being the power behind the throne. Who else other than Goad could be the figurehead?"

Revel paused, considering it. "Goad is even older than me, but he's never impressed me much. If anything, I could see Goad handing over ultimate control of his line to Dread because he doesn't know what to do with it. He had impulse control issues—he likes immediate pleasure, and that's about it."

"He's creepy, a cockroach." I scrubbed at the place on my cheek where Goad had pushed his finger into me. "I doubt he could pull off anything big."

"There are too many things we don't know," Revel

said. "Everything's changed now, not the least of which is Ram. Why has he decided to come out now? Why did he unbalance the power structure by killing Vex?"

"That's why I called you, to find out. Are you having any luck on your research?" I had asked Revel to find out what he could about Ram in his historical documents.

"I've filled out the backstories in the myths and legends that I believe reference him. I can send it over to you now."

"Anything on Hope?" I tried to ask casually.

"One of my contacts says he has a line on a fifth-century Persian scroll. It's very rare—the Greeks were the victors and their version of history survived. But this scroll contains a nearly complete tale about a woman who became a goddess living 'half in the light and half in darkness.' It predates the Persephone myth."

"What does it say?"

"I'm trying to buy the scroll so I can find out. I'll probably have to go to Uzbekistan to get it. I'm the only one who can verify its authenticity before I pay that much money."

Revel was over a thousand years old and was undoubtedly the world's foremost expert on old manuscripts. "When are you going?"

"Maybe as soon as this evening. From what my contact says, this text may hold the key to Ram. While I'm gone, you and Shock should come stay here. And Bliss, if you want."

I shot Shock a look. She must have told Revel everything. A few days ago, that would have felt like a betrayal.

"Thanks, but I'm staying here," I told him. "But if Shock wants to . . ." Shock turned away, clearly irritated. So I told Revel, "Let me know when you get back."

We opened up the bar, speaking to each other only when necessary.

The regulars appeared like magic and were overly grateful that I had reopened the bar. I dabbled in their relief, not absorbing much of anything because I was already wallowing in the energy that Ram had given me. It felt great to be all charged up and able to protect my people, my bar, my territory, without having to sap them of their energy.

Bliss sat down with every one of them, introducing herself as my friend from Orange County. Using my memories, she deftly inserted herself into my childhood, even telling a few funny stories about my past. More than I had ever told my patrons before. She fed off them while she did it, but I kept a careful eye on her to make sure she didn't take too much from any one person.

Shock plunked herself down on the back corner barstool and gloomily stared at the liquor bottles along the back wall. Even when happy hour picked up and a flood of people were dropping by to ask why we had been closed for two days, she ignored everything. I left her alone, thinking it would be best. Besides, we were too busy and I didn't have time to draw her out of her funk.

Then my mouth started watering, and I swallowed a few times. *Savor.* Her signature was a very subtle warning, just before she appeared as Sebastian, her favorite male guise. He was an elf of a man, slender and young with black hair spiked up carefully. He was also knowing, sarcastic, and smug, with a drawl that could cut steel.

Savor strutted over to the bar as if he were on a catwalk. His cheeky grin said he expected to be welcomed. But Dread had found out about my agreement with Glory somehow. I was betting the informant was Savor.

"Hi, Allay. I heard the bar was open and I just *had*

to come in." Savor glanced toward the open door to the back room at the end of the bar. "Where's Lolita?"

"I haven't called the employees back yet." I lowered my voice. "I'm not sure if it's safe." I didn't actually believe that, but I wanted to see Savor's reaction.

"You think you're going to be attacked?"

"The police haven't found out who shot up my bar. It could happen again."

Savor pooh-poohed me, flapping his hand at me. "It was Vex. Everyone knows that. He was trying to frighten you back into the fold. You ran to him the first time because *someone* got into the bar and nearly killed Shock."

"Did Dread tell you that?" Savor was Dread's messenger, with a finger in every pie.

"Mmm-hmm. . . ."

Dread was really making sure I heard the message that Vex had shot my bar. But it was having the opposite effect—and I was left wondering who had really done the deed. Was it someone Dread was protecting?

But I had other things to talk to Savor about. "Did you tell Dread about my agreement with Glory?"

"Girl, I didn't have to. Stun sensed you inside Crave's house, and he told everyone that *you* warned the Glory demons. They were saying you had an agreement with her long before *I* know you made one."

Now I didn't know what to believe. I had distrusted Savor for so long that it was hard to believe him now. He was shifty by nature, first a man, then a woman, then another man. He tried on personas like changing jackets. Clearly his loyalties were also ever-shifting. Wasn't that the definition of a double agent?

But Savor dropped the exaggerated speech, looking me square in the eye. "I gave you something on me, Allay. I thought that would help you trust me. I see I was wrong."

"I trust people who stand by me in a crisis."

"Like Revel? Your trusty progenitor?" Savor leaned closer. "I could tell you a thing or two about Revel."

I wasn't sure I believed anything he said, but I had to bite. "Like what?"

"Vex ordered Revel to make a possessed human—*you*. Revel betrayed Plea, his own offspring. He lured her to the beach that night and sucked her almost dry. Then he left her like bait for some poor teenager to find. It was Vex's plan, but Revel is the one who did it."

I looked over sharply at Shock. "Shock never told me that."

"I don't think she knows. But I was there that day to make sure Revel carried out his orders."

A memory surfaced in spite of myself, Plea greeting Revel with a happy, trusting smile. There was the crash of the waves in the background, as Revel took my/Plea's hand. Then he started drawing on my/Plea's energy. I knew it the moment he started—*betrayed . . .*

I was betrayed.

It staggered me. I had just started believing in Revel again. I was tempted to call him to demand the truth, but he had sent a text earlier saying he was at JFK Airport leaving for Uzbekistan, but his boy Ki would let me into the penthouse any time I wanted.

I couldn't let Savor know how badly he had upset me. "That just proves I can't trust any of you. I mean, would *you* trust yourself, Savor?"

His smooth Sebastian guise slipped back into place. "Honey, I don't trust *anyone*."

"Then why are you here?"

His smug smile said it all. "My employers told me to drop around and see who shows up. I'm supposed to check out the new girl."

"Dread or Glory?"

"Does it matter?" He sniffed at Bliss, who was behind the bar, working hard to keep up with the ten-o'clock bump. "Looks like the spitting image of her dear mammy. But with better hair."

"Seriously, Savor. Stop spying on me."

"I only report what you ain't got to hide." Savor gave a high-pitched laugh. "A girl's got to earn a living."

Somehow I doubted that money was the only reason Savor played his dangerous games. But Bliss was definitely in need of a hand, so I couldn't talk anymore. Savor hung out for a while, watching everything and talking to my patrons. He touched a few of them, feeding right in front of me. I gritted my teeth and didn't say anything. I didn't have anything concrete against him, and I could use all the allies I could get.

Savor tried to speak to Shock, but she brushed him off. I hadn't told her that Savor was also working for Glory—that wasn't my secret to tell. So she treated him as I always had: a bottom-feeder who ran Dread's most unsavory errands.

Eventually Savor left, giving me a jaunty wave. Not long after that, I felt Goad's signature at the fringes of my senses. It stung like needles against my skin, then eased off as he pulled back. Then it happened again. And again. Like he was testing to see where my boundaries lay. He must have a longer reach than I, seeing as he was one of the oldest demons around.

Shock went and stood near the door. Even Bliss went on alert, the most serious I had ever seen her. She, too, remembered the way Goad had touched my cheek.

Then he was gone. But we were all on edge now. I was glad to have work to distract me. I had been ready to call Lolita to ask her to come back to work tomorrow, and bring my cats home, but I felt less inclined now. I wanted to let things settle a bit.

Over the next hour, Goad returned again and again from all different directions, never coming very close, sometimes alone and sometimes with Stun. I finally went over to Shock. "What do you think it means?"

"He's trying to drive you out."

"But I always go barricade myself upstairs when a demon comes after me."

"What about the other night, with Pique?" Her frown was speculative.

"Okay, except for that one time."

"Don't give me that, Allay. You ran around this neighborhood like you were superdemon, saving all of your customers."

"Only some of them." I liked her image of myself much better than the one in my own mind—huddled upstairs hiding from demons, exposing everyone close to me, making them vulnerable by my presence. It was why I kept away from my family and didn't even go home for visits.

"Do you think I should close up?" I asked her.

Shock sighed. "They're less likely to try anything in front of a crowd."

I could feel Goad's stinging signature racing across my body, even with Shock standing so close. "I'm not going to sit here and take this!"

I marched around the bar to the back wall. Bliss was sitting sideways on the cooler to get closer to a young engineer who lived up the avenue. She was stroking his arm, looking into his eyes, breaking off only to pour another beer or shot of vodka at the patrons' requests.

I picked up the phone and dialed Dread. His secretary, June, answered promptly of course, even at eleven p.m., her perky friendliness intact. "Ms. Meyers, how nice to speak to you again. The prophet said you're to be put through to him at any time. Please hold while I page him."

I could just imagine her smile, designed to show off

her pink braces. I wondered how much she knew about what had happened to me and Ram in the Prophet's Center. She was human, but wore a guise as surely as any demon, hiding herself behind a petite, perky facade. There had to be more to her or Dread wouldn't keep her so close to himself. Unless she was as clueless as she appeared to be, so he could more easily hide his double life.

"What is it, Allay?" Dread said in greeting.

Equally as brusque, I retorted, "Why is Goad circling my bar?"

He let out a sigh of frustration. "I'll call him off. But you have to stick to your end of the bargain, Allay."

I knew Dread was a busy man, but he was being much more dismissive than earlier. "I did! I told the cops about us, like we agreed."

"I know, I had an interview with your Lieutenant Markman. I'm talking about Phil Anchor and the threats you made to expose him."

That got my attention. "Phil? You can't be serious. You aren't listening to that loony."

"Why not? You threatened Mackleby and then you threatened Anchor. You're getting very comfortable throwing around words like 'blackmail' and 'bribes,' Allay."

I couldn't believe that Phil Anchor, of all people, was causing me problems. Twenty years ago he might have been a famous journalist, but he had been the church's hand puppet ever since I started working for Vex and passing him his payola.

I faced the wall of shelves holding the liquor so nobody could hear me. "Dread, it was nothing. Phil came at me the other day, poking his finger in my face, claiming I'd stolen his drop. He was acting insane and I just wanted him off me. I didn't mean it. I told *him* I didn't mean it. But he was bingeing on coke and out of his mind."

"I can't have you threatening my people, Allay. All agreements are off if it happens again. Understand?"

"Well, then you better keep Goad off my back."

Dread hesitated. "Goad is . . . problematic at the moment."

"You don't have control over him? You said you did."

"He's considering his options. I'm in no position to deny him that."

I rolled my eyes. "So you can't keep the Vex demons away from me? That means you can't hold up your side of the bargain, Dread."

"He knows I won't abide him touching you." I remembered Dread's spike of lust when he saw me, and hoped that was true. "But he may not stay away from your friends. I wish I could do more, Allay. That's the honest truth. I intend to regain control of Goad and his line very soon, in a few days at the most."

I wished we were in the same room together so I could better judge his feelings. "That's not what we agreed," I said, hanging up abruptly. He had manufactured his little outrage over Phil Anchor in order to distract me from the fact that he had lied about being able to control Goad's horde.

Quietly, Shock came up behind me. "You can't make deals with Dread, Allay. You just broke free of them. Don't get sucked back in. You'll hate yourself if you do."

"I know." They had destroyed Phil Anchor, turning him into an aging caricature of the dashing man he had once been. "Goad's gone rogue. We have to be careful."

"That's what I've been saying."

"You were under Dread's protection, too," I reminded her.

"Only because I decided to stay and keep an eye on you. And Vex didn't know that I would do that anyway, no matter what he promised me."

I smiled at Shock. "I know. That was why I went to Vex, to find a way to protect you."

"Too bad it was your boyfriend who wanted me dead."

My smile froze, then faded. "Shock . . . Ram admitted it was a mistake to attack you. He's not going to do it again. You should try to get to know him before you judge him."

She gestured. "Show me which one is Ram, and I'll have a nice chat with him."

Startled, I looked around. "He's not here. At least, I haven't sensed him."

"But if you didn't touch him, you wouldn't know, right?"

I remembered how little I had felt from him earlier—not until I touched him could I sense his distinctive energy. "Probably not. But why would he hide from me?"

"Because he can."

With that, she turned on her heel and retreated to her solitary seat, pretending to drink a rum and Coke. She wouldn't meet my eye, but she continued to sweep a suspicious gaze over my patrons.

I sighed and made another round wiping down the tables, picking up empty glasses, and piling them on my tray. I wished I could tell Shock the truth—that I was disappointed Ram hadn't returned yet. I almost wished he was here keeping a low profile instead of staying away. What did that say about my judgment?

5

Not long after I spoke to Dread, Goad's signature pulled away again. I went back to my patrons as part of me kept expecting the stinging to reappear in its game of cat and mouse. But Goad didn't return.

Maybe Dread had more control over Goad than he had been letting on. Or maybe Goad had found someone else to harass.

Closing time on Wednesday was one a.m. I didn't have to tell any of my patrons to go; they all knew when it was time to leave as I started the closing routine.

Ram still hadn't returned when Bliss rolled down the metal shutter and locked us inside. I had invited him to come by the bar. Why didn't he?

Shock checked her beeper. "Richards called in sick. I can take a night shift and be back in time to help you open up tomorrow."

I was surprised, even though I knew that Shock was a workaholic. "You can't go out. What about Goad?"

"I'll have my partner with me at all times, and an open line to dispatch and police on call. Nobody's ever tried to get me while I'm working. They'd be stupid to try."

I was really hurt. I'd been waiting until everyone left so I could talk to her about Revel. I wanted to know what she knew about his involvement in making me.

Savor's revelation had shaken me to my core. Maybe everything I knew about Revel was wrong.

"I don't understand why you have to go," I said.

Her eyes blazed brighter blue. "I need to feed, Allay."

I gestured to the bar. "You could have fed all night, but you sat over there and sulked instead."

She wouldn't meet my eyes. "You know what I like."

She lived for other people's pain and suffering, sloughing it off in fat sheets as she patched their bodies back together enough so they could make it to a hospital. It blunted their agony when she took their pain, but she didn't do it for them. Let's be real. She wouldn't ever cause harm to anyone, but she had no qualms about feeding off tragedy whenever she could find it.

"What about you?" she asked. "Are you going to stay here where it's safe? Or are you going to let Ram lure you out?"

"I don't have anywhere to go."

"Call me if you do go out," Shock insisted. "Promise me, Allay."

I nodded, wishing she would agree to what I wanted so easily.

"What about me?" Bliss asked plaintively. "Do you want me to stay inside, too?"

"I don't care what you do," Shock shot back.

"Shock!" I had no patience for her hostility. "Why are you so hard on Bliss? She's been nothing but helpful."

"Yeah, seducing Crave was real helpful."

"Well, I like having her around."

"Thank you," Bliss said.

Shock lifted her hands, an angry scarlet swirling through her aura. "Do whatever you want. Both of you."

The door slammed behind her.

I'd never seen Shock so upset. It unnerved me to the point that I could hardly talk to Bliss. With the two of us working, we quickly closed down the bar and went upstairs. I jumped into a hot shower, wanting to rinse everything away in a long hot steam.

Shock was being such a bitch that I hadn't even had the chance to talk to her about the ERI machine that was going to expose all of us. She didn't know that Ram believed demons would be exposed. We had to figure out what to do about it. But Shock had shut me out.

And Ram never showed. Not all night. I had hoped we could sit down and talk about the ERI with everyone together. It would help if Shock saw him as an ally, but she was having a hard enough time accepting Bliss, who hadn't said an angry word to her.

"Bliss," I said as I came out of the bathroom, wrapping the terry cloth robe around myself. "I wanted to tell you what Ram said today about the ERI . . . Bliss?"

A quick look proved she wasn't in the front or the back room. That was when I realized her signature was gone. It was very light like mine, a floating sensation like fallen leaves being lifted on the breeze. I hated to admit that with Shock's numbing signature finally gone, it was a relief. Bliss's was similar enough to my own buoyant signature that I hadn't even noticed it. I also hadn't noticed it was gone.

I was alone for the first time since I had come back to the bar. I couldn't feel any other demons within range. I was snug in my bubble once again, my home and things around me exactly the same as always.

But everything had changed. I couldn't ignore what was going on out there anymore. It was as if my world had turned inside out.

It bothered me that Bliss had sneaked away. I was being too clingy. But I worried about her even though she seemed very capable of taking care of herself. I wondered where she went. To an after-hours club? She had been flipping through the *Village Voice* earlier, and talk-

ing to the patrons about places in Chelsea where there
was dancing until dawn.

Wherever she is, I bet she's having fun.

I threw on an old black hoodie that didn't quite reach
my slung-low sweatpants, and curled up on the sofa,
staring into the shadows, too keyed up to read. The place
was too quiet without the bar cats coming through the
duct and spatting with each other over the catnip.

Then from far away came the sound of the phone
ringing down in the bar. If I had been listening to my
iPod or watching TV, I wouldn't have heard it.

I was afraid I wouldn't make it in time, so I snatched
up my keys as I ran. While I raced down the stairs in the
dark, the phone kept ringing.

"Den on C," I answered breathlessly.

I was expecting it to be Shock checking in. Or hopefully Bliss.

Instead it was Glory's unmistakable deep-throated
drawl. "Allay, is that you?"

"Glory? What's wrong?"

"Do you know where your girl is at?" Glory demanded.

"Shock? She's at work." Then I realized who she was
talking about. "Oh, I don't know where Bliss is."

"I do. She's gone to Crave's shop. He lit out to meet
her. Lash is having fits. I tell you, Allay, I can't have
this."

I let out an aggravated sound. "I'm sorry, Glory. I told
her to stay away from Crave."

"You go tell her again!"

"She doesn't listen to me. Can't you order Crave to
stay away from Bliss? He's the one taking advantage of
her. She's so new she's practically mindless."

"Hardly that, I'm sure." Her voice grew grim. "I've
given Crave his orders. He knows the consequences of
defying me. If it was any other demon, I'd kill her before

I let her ruin my plans. But I can't kill her without alien- ating you. So that makes it your problem."

"Are you so worried Lash will turn on you?"

"Not at all. The issue is the timing. Tell your girl to keep her pants on. Surely she won't explode in frustra- tion."

That was exactly what I'd asked of Bliss, and she had agreed; then she'd gone up to see Crave anyway. But I didn't want to tell Glory that. Glory might just give that death order. "Okay, but I'm telling them that you sent me there to warn them both."

"Get going! I want him back with Lash tonight." Glory hung up.

I stood there with the phone in my hand. I could call Shock and tell her I was going out, but she would be hateful because it was about Bliss. I didn't have enough time to wait for her to get here to go with me, so there was no use in calling her just to upset her all over again.

I wished I had my car, but it was parked in a Chi- natown garage waiting for my aborted getaway, which Goad had interrupted by kidnapping me. It would take too much time to go back down there to get it, so I de- cided to take a cab up to Crave's place. That would be safer and quicker than the subway this time of night.

I grabbed some twenties from the cash drawer and headed out.

In my neighborhood there weren't many people walking around in the dead of night in the middle of the week. But up on Madison Avenue, it was a ghost town. I felt Crave and Bliss as the cab approached, but I doubted they would be able to sense me over each other.

A much more fancy version of my metal shutter, complete with decorative grillwork, was pulled down over the front of the shop. So I went to the side door and rang the buzzer.

I felt like a jealous lover running down her errant boyfriend. I didn't like it.

As soon as the door opened, Bliss said, "Obsessive much, Allay? It's like you can't stay away from me."

"It's not my idea, believe me." I thanked Crave as he let me inside.

Through the arch was his jewelry shop. He flicked on a switch and the crystal chandeliers filled the room with sparkling light. It was a surprise after the darkness outside. There were four long glass cases set in a square, allowing access from all sides. The bare walls appeared to be rustic stone in warm peach colors, with real ivy climbing up several trellises. It made the glass cases in the center feel like an altar.

Several groupings of plush chairs and a long, low sofa were arranged at the back end of the room, along with vanity tables with large tilting mirrors. You hardly noticed the ivory carpeting and the fabric, but the subtle design evoked the ultimate in luxury.

"Nice place, Crave," I said admiringly. "I'm sorry to show up like this, but Glory ordered me to break up your little party. She said you two have to stay apart or she's sending a goon to kill you, Bliss."

"She wouldn't kill Bliss," Crave denied.

"You think not?" When he couldn't answer, I added, "Don't make the mistake of relying on Glory's goodwill towards me to keep Bliss alive. She's already half turned on me."

"Screw her!" Crave lifted both his hands in frustration, glaring around at nothing. He was ruddy with enraged testosterone, the image of a bullfighter ready to slaughter large animals in front of a roaring crowd. I wondered how deeply he and Bliss had gotten into it before I had interrupted them. Bliss was wearing a long T-shirt as a dress along with my motorcycle boots; I knew from my time with Ram behind the Dumpster that an outfit like that made for easy access . . .

I didn't want to aggravate the situation, but it had to be said. "Maybe you should deal with your mess with Lash and Glory yourself, Crave. Leave Bliss and me out of it."

"I will settle it with Glory," Crave said, his black eyes snapping. "Believe me."

Bliss didn't seem at all concerned. She wandered over to the first case, lined with black and white velvet to show off the colors of the necklaces. The gems were grouped together in patterns and shapes, and were suspended by nearly invisible chains. The lights were set to reflect for maximum brilliance, dazzling the eyes.

"They're so beautiful." she sighed, bending forward to see them better. Crave was instantly beside her, watching every move as she pointed to a tiny landscape scene of pave gems that formed a belt buckle. She exclaimed at a dancing line of flames that turned out to be a choker.

Crave's anger melted away under her admiration. He must be used to it, but from his avid interest in her reactions, this was his passion. I'd never seen him so relaxed and smiling as he explained the inspiration for some of his pieces.

He bided his time until we came around the corner to the ring case and Bliss admired a perfect rose ring. It was rather large for a ring, a play on costume jewelry, but created in precious gems. Her admiration took on a note of delight.

"Here," he offered, opening up the case and removing the heavy ring. "Try it on."

His fingers brushed against hers as she took it. I could see the spark of desire flare between them. She held up her hand tilting it back and forth, admiring the sculptural effect of the petals and the shading of varying hues of pink diamonds and darker sapphires.

I sneaked a peek at the price tag—fifteen thousand dollars! It was a miniature masterpiece. But still . . .

Crave saw my expression, but his eyes just crinkled a bit. He seemed expectant, but Bliss slid off the ring and handed it back as if it was nothing.

That threw him. He kept looking at her, waiting for a covetous glance or reluctant sigh as she let it go. Those unmistakable signs when a girl really wants something. I realized that Crave was used to playing off a woman's desire for his jewels. He probably tempted them with his gifts, holding them out of reach like a sugar daddy dangling a toy for them to yearn after.

As we finished the circuit, Crave seemed a bit at a loss while Bliss was exactly the same as always. She walked over to the unobtrusive door in the back corner. "Where does this go?"

"My workshop." He followed her. "Want to see it?"

I had to grin at his seduction technique. "We should be going now."

Crave took Bliss's hand, looking down at her instead of me. "I never let anyone into my workshop. But I want to show you."

It wasn't true; he probably used that line with every girl he seduced in his shop. But I still trailed after them, feeling like an unwelcome chaperone. I would give them fifteen minutes; then we were out of here.

It was much brighter inside, with seamless white walls. "This room is a vault, with steel all around us in the floor and ceiling. That keeps thieves from breaking in upstairs and cutting through."

Crave's aura was boiling with emotion—lusty, eager, yet also vulnerable. While Bliss was as cool as could be, glowing with simple pleasure. They held hands and touched a lot as he walked her by each machine that was bolted to its own table. He explained how each gem required its own faceting depending on the alignment of the crystals and the flaws, as she peered through the eyepiece at gems held in the clamps.

When we reached the rough-cut saw, he pulled out the large raw ruby from the clamps and let us hold it. The ruby was dusty with tiny rocks embedded in the surface. When he clamped it back under the microscope, he pointed out the flaws deep inside the stone that he would have to cut around to form each gem. He keyed the computer next to the machine, and a projection of the interior of the ruby rotated on the flat-screen.

Crave paused the image to point out the large inclusion near the heart of the stone, frowning a bit. "I've been looking at this one for a while, trying to see the best solution. I'm afraid I'll only get two medium gems from this one, and a lot left over for smaller gems."

I squinted my eyes at it. "It seems a waste with a stone that large to not get a huge gem from it."

Bliss leaned in, watching as he highlighted the areas that he intended to cut in the diagram. He set it turning again so she could see it from all sides. "There's definitely no getting around that flaw," she agreed.

"Sometimes it happens that way," Crave said.

Bliss tilted her head. "Wait! Go back."

Crave dialed the rotating image back until she said, "I see something . . . those three lobes. You can get three gems as big as the two you've outlined, but there's no waste."

"Where?" he asked. Both of us leaned in closer, too.

She sketched out the gems, with the final one making two upper curves. "It's a heart, see? You said you can cut shapes."

"Yes! I see what you mean. Two ovals and one heart gem. Let's see if they have enough base for refraction." He sat down and quickly erased his earlier projection.

With a few clicks and swoops of the mouse, he traced out three new gems. "It works! How did you see that?"

Bliss seemed pleased. "It's the bloodred color. I kept thinking of a heart. And then I saw it inside the stone."

He couldn't take his eyes off her. "That's how it happens to me—I see the shapes inside the stone. I don't know why I couldn't with this one."

"I'm glad I could help," she said with a laugh.

He reached out to draw her into a hug. I felt like an complete intruder. Anyone else would have turned and left them to their privacy. Obviously there was something powerful going on between these two.

But before I could move, Bliss gently pulled back, pushing her hands against his chest. "No, Crave. We have to wait. Remember?"

He noticed me standing there awkwardly. "Right."

"Sorry," I said lamely.

Crave looked as if a bucket of cold water had been thrown on him. He couldn't hide his frustration and spikes of lust swirling through his aura, but he firmly took her hand and led us both from his workshop. From his seriousness, he did believe that Glory would kill Bliss, and he wasn't willing to risk her. "I'll help you catch a cab."

Bliss still smiled, though there was an edge of sadness to it.

The sidewalk was dark and deserted. There weren't any cars passing on the street. "What time is it?" Bliss asked.

"Nearly four," I said.

We stood for a few minutes on Madison waiting for a cab. A few cars finally passed, but the one cab was already full. "It's not easy getting one this late," Crave admitted. "Let's go down to Ninety-sixth. There'll be cabs going across town there."

The two of them sauntered down the block, drawing

out their last few minutes together, still holding hands. I followed them at a discreet distance so they could talk. I used to follow my big sister and her eighth-grade boyfriend like this. Maybe it was good that they were forced to take it slow. I'd have to ask Shock what happened when you crossed an incubus with a succubus. It could be interesting.

Suddenly Crave tilted his head. "What's that? I feel something."

I reached out, but there was nothing. "I don't feel anything."

"I do," Bliss agreed, concentrating.

Crave nodded. "A demon's coming. Could be Stun."

"Maybe we should go back to the shop," Bliss suggested.

His eyes lit up at the idea, but I was looking ahead to the cross street. "There's a cab! Come on."

I dashed off at top speed, with Bliss obediently behind me. Crave fell back, looking behind us, urging, "Go faster!"

I almost caught the cab, but the light changed too quickly. It was pulling across the intersection by the time I caught up.

Irritated by the near catch, I turned to flag another cab. But there were no other cabs. I realized that my ears were ringing. "Stun!"

Bliss also mouthed the name of the demon as she felt the signature. "It's getting stronger," she added, looking uptown. The blocks were short, so he was nearly two streets away, but there was no mistaking the tall, dark figure approaching us: Stun.

6

"He's cutting us off from my shop," Crave said, grabbing hold of Bliss's hand. "This way."

We turned the corner and ran down the block toward Park Avenue. This was a much longer block. I felt Stun turn the corner behind us as we passed the middle.

Suddenly Crave slid to a stop, dragging Bliss with him. "No! Goad's ahead, coming down Park. He must have been staked out east of my place."

We darted across Ninety-sixth Street, avoiding the lone car that refused to stop despite Crave's waving arms. I ran as fast as I could to reach Park Avenue before Goad made it to the corner. The angry stinging heralded his arrival like a plague of bees rapidly descending on us.

Despite the two-way boulevard, there weren't any distinctive yellow cabs in sight.

"Cross over Park," Crave barked. He skidded to a halt to let a black sedan zip past, then tugged Bliss along. I followed them into the strip of greenery down the center, scraping my shins on the evergreen bushes.

Across the uptown lane, we continued south, pushed away from Harlem and the safety of Crave's shop. All we needed was a cab, and we could break free of this footrace.

But by the time we reached Ninety-fifth Street, I felt the burning of another signature. Raze, coming at us rapidly from the south.

"It's a trap," Crave said. We turned onto Ninety-fifth Street, heading farther east toward Lexington Avenue. Orange sparks refracted like lasers between Crave's and Bliss's hands. That made me realize how scared I was. I didn't want to be trussed up in another straitjacket and hauled off to be tortured. Or worse.

But as we neared Lex, I felt another signature. It felt like Stun again, but he couldn't have gotten in front of us. There were so many demons surrounding us now that their signatures merged together, making it hard to distinguish the individual notes.

"Yo, Allay!" A guy at the corner waved an arm at us. "Over here!"

With a sudden shift, my ears stopped ringing and it turned into Mystify's signature—a floating, frightening void. Then back again. There was only one demon who could change his signature like that.

"It's Mystify," I gasped. "He'll help us."

"Who?" Crave demanded, trying to stop me from running forward.

"Ram's offspring. Born after he killed Vex."

Crave grabbed my arm harder. "What? You didn't tell us that!"

"There's no time to argue!" Bliss exclaimed. "It's true."

Between the two of us, we dragged Crave over to Mystify. As we reached him, demon signatures were closing from every direction, but in the darkness of Ninety-fifth Street, none of them was in sight yet. Mystify lifted the grate in the sidewalk. "Get in fast!"

Bliss didn't hesitate. She jumped into the pitch-dark, not caring how long the fall was. She hit quicker than I expected with a metallic *bong*. I jumped down next to her, and the impact jarred my spine all the way up to my neck. We were crouching on the ledge that held the tray that caught the debris falling from the sidewalk.

Crave landed next to me, and then Mystify, who swung from his fingers for a few seconds as he padlocked the grate. When he landed, he grinned at me, his face checkered by the meager light shining through the grid. He was wearing a jacket that was too big for his wiry frame—since he could adjust his body to any size, the look had to be deliberate. His shaggy brown hair stood out in all directions, but with that angel's face, it didn't matter. He looked barely eighteen with a pug nose and large doe eyes. I wanted to eat him up and take care of him at the same time.

"This is stupid," Crave hissed. "They'll know we're down here."

"I can take care of that." Mystify held his breath for a moment, and his signature changed to Crave's. That same magnetism that Crave exuded, drawing you inward, was coming from Mystify. When I closed my eyes, I couldn't tell them apart.

Crave stared at him openmouthed. I had felt the same way the first time I had experienced Mystify's ability.

"Follow me," Mystify urged, sitting down and swinging his legs over the side of the tray. "The platform is narrow here, so be careful when you land."

I gave Bliss a nod as I leaped off after Mystify, feeling the demon signatures rapidly approaching overhead. Crave came next, and he caught Bliss around the waist as she landed, steadying her. Mystify was right, the subway platform was only two feet wide at this point, hugging the wall. A black trench yawned in front of me with the gleaming rails forming the brightest spot. The concrete was marked with red-striped lines where we stood—passengers weren't supposed to venture into this area at the end of the station.

Mystify climbed down the ladder and motioned for us to hurry. I had to step over the rail, then back to hug the wall. "We have to be careful of trains," he cautioned them. "There's not much clearance here. About twenty feet further on, there's a door that I've left cracked open. Once it's shut, it will be locked from the track-side. Go down the stairs. At the bottom are some service tunnels. Get back in there and wait for me to draw off the gang. I'll head north in the subway tunnel."

"What if they catch you?" I asked.

"I know all sorts of hidey-holes. They won't get me. But once I ditch them, they'll come back and search along this line. So don't stay down there long. And don't get on the subway—Goad's got someone posted at both stations."

"How do you know?" Crave demanded.

"Earlier I was running with their gang, posing as one of them. Head toward Central Park. Demons don't go there at night. There's nothing for them to eat. Goad will expect you to go up to Harlem or down to Alphabet City."

Mystify grabbed the ladder to get back up on the platform. I called out, "Wait—how do I get hold of you? Give me your cell number."

Mystify grinned, abruptly looking much older. "No phone, but you can leave a message for me under the edge of the obelisk behind the Met."

Without another word, he dashed down the platform. There were only a few passengers waiting this time of night, and they drew back to get out of his way. He looked demented, but harmless enough. He was radiating Crave's distinctive whirlpooling sensation.

Directly above, demon signatures converged, at least six of them.

"Are they going to catch him?" Bliss asked breathlessly.

"They have to enter the subway on Ninety-sixth Street. That will give him time to get away," Crave assured her.

"Let's go," I urged. "We have to get down underneath. Otherwise they'll realize there are two Craves here."

I started into the darkness, crunching quickly across the blackened gravel. Faint sheets of light pierced through the arches down the middle of the track. Adjusting my pupils to see better, I saw the ground moving as rats rustled away in waves. My fingers brushed the wall and came off covered in soot. Now I was glad I was wearing boots.

As Mystify promised, there was a metal door not far down, set in the wall a couple of feet above the tracks. Two metal rungs were underneath with a handlebar high on one side to use for climbing up. The door was cracked open with a piece of cardboard stuck over the hole for the tongue latch.

Crave went up first, then held open the door while Bliss pulled herself inside. I followed, taking hold of his hand to get up quickly. Crave checked the handle, then slammed the door shut behind us. The latch clicked, but when he tried the handle, it opened.

I felt the edge of the step with my foot, and I quickly adjusted my eyes to the total darkness. Everything was gray and black, just the outlines of shapes as if I had on night-vision goggles.

"I don't even have a lighter," Crave muttered. I felt him move as he took Bliss's hand. "How well can you see?"

"Shapes," I said. "Not much else."

"Me, too."

"I'll go first," he said. "Feel your way down after me."

Bliss followed him, and I clung to the pipe railing after her, taking it one step at a time. The staircase was spiral, fitting into a narrow slot. My feet clanked on the perforated metal steps.

"I can't sense them," I called softly. "Crave, can you?"

"Mystify's signature should be strong enough to drown mine out. Yours and Bliss's are so mild they won't notice us down here."

I bumped into Bliss at the bottom. Crave groped his way forward over the uneven surface, and Bliss stumbled after him, both hands hanging on to his waist.

"There's a tunnel over here," Crave said.

We shuffled across the rubble-strewn floor as far as we could, until another locked door stopped us. The air was dank and moldy-smelling. The squeaking of rats kept me on my toes, far away from the surrounding walls.

The darkness was awful. Like we had no defenses. No wonder early man's first major triumph was fire.

There was nothing we could do but hold our breath and wait. I didn't have to say what was on everyone's mind—we were stuck in a dead end if Goad's horde came down after us.

"What a terrible place to die," Bliss said artlessly.

Crave laughed shortly. "Let's hope it doesn't come to that."

"Nobody would ever know if it did," I pointed out. Our bolt-hole was starting to feel like a trap.

"Our fate lies in Mystify's hands," Crave said. "Are you sure you can trust him?"

I wasn't even close to sure. "I saved him from Pique. Hopefully that counts for something."

Above, we could feel the rumble of a subway train approaching, then a long pause, then a building rumbling as it left the station again. Another train passed through at high speed, making the metal staircase rattle like it was going to come down. Then the noise subsided and there was only the scuffle of animals in the darkness.

"Tell me about Mystify," Crave said.

Mostly Bliss filled him in, using my memories of his birth under the Williamsburg Bridge and how Mystify could imitate any demon's signature he encountered.

"Why didn't you tell us?" Crave asked. "You know Glory won't like it that you held out on her."

"It wasn't deliberate," I said. "There was so much else going on, it wasn't high on my radar."

"She's not going to believe that. And neither do I."

"You don't have to tell her," Bliss told him. "Or do you?"

He shook his head, but he didn't agree out loud.

"Crave belongs to Glory," I reminded Bliss.

Crave flared up. "You're trying to distract me from Mystify. You must have a reason for hiding him."

I hadn't even admitted it to myself. "Call it misplaced protective feelings. I worry about our offspring."

"Especially because he's Ram's," Bliss said.

I gave her a look that she probably couldn't see in the darkness. "I'm getting tired of you saying everything that pops into your mind, Bliss. Don't you have any filters?"

"Maybe not," she laughed. "I'll have to work on that."

"Do." I was getting antsy. "I can't stand it any longer. Let's go up."

Climbing up the staircase was easier because a faint light shone around the door at the top. Now that my eyes had opened as far as they could, I could see at least a dozen pipes running down the concrete wall next to the spiral staircase.

"I don't feel any demons," Crave said, cautiously opening the door.

I peeked around his shoulder. "We'll have to go up a block to get out of the subway."

He looked back at both of us. "Run for it."

He leaped down with me right behind him. With a

few handholds and tugs here and there, working together as a team, we ran down the tunnel and up onto
the platform. I kept my eye on Crave—he could sense
much farther than me. But there was no sign of alarm
when we reached the subway entrance. We flew through
the turnstiles and up the stairs to the street as if we were
fleeing a fire.

The air was a welcome relief after the stinking underground. The dark wilderness of the park lay three blocks
away. I had the terrible feeling that we would never
make it, that we were doomed prey. Last time Goad's
horde had come after me, it was like being run down by
a pack of wild dogs, unbeatable. They had set their trap
then with cold calculation, just as they had done again
now.

Why were they hunting me? Did Goad want me for
himself? Or was Dread behind it?

I could be killed. I had thought I was past all that, but
it was happening again. I was caught up in other people's power plays.

Crave was grim, trying to see every direction at once
as he urged us, "Run!" But Bliss didn't seem panicked
at all. She had a slight smile as she sprinted down the
blocks, as if she was glad to finally be freed from con-
finement. Crave kept glancing at her as if he was afraid
to let her out of his sight.

In the yawning darkness of Fifth Avenue, a city bus
roared past us and pulled up to the stop across the street.
I was tempted only for a second to catch it—a bus was
too predictable and slow to get away from demons.

The entrance to Central Park was right in front of us.
I glanced at Crave, and he shook his head. No sign of
demon signatures.

Crave took hold of Bliss's hand as we hurried inside
the park. We needed to get deep enough so that any de-

mon passing on the streets along the outer perimeter wouldn't sense our signatures. Until then, we weren't safe.

We were all breathing heavily after our dead sprint from the subway. But none of us lagged behind now. I could still almost feel Goad's angry buzzing signature. That was *not* the last thing I wanted to feel before I died.

We passed the band shell and crossed the treelined Mall. Bliss tried to veer onto the broad lane, but Crave stopped her. "This slants back towards Fifth Ave. We need to stay away from the East Side."

"Down," I decided. Side by side we ran down several flights of stone steps to Bethesda Fountain. At the bottom we paused to catch our breath, extending our senses to see if any demons were coming.

"We should keep heading west," Crave insisted, as we paused to catch our breath.

"The West Side has always been a Vex stronghold," I disagreed. "Raze has apartments there. We'll have to go either north to Harlem or south to the Den. But to do that we'll have to back out to Fifth Avenue to catch a cab."

"Too dangerous," Crave said.

"We're more likely to attract attention moving around," Bliss said reasonably. "Let's find a place in the middle of the park where we can wait out their rampage. They'll give up searching in a few hours and by then lots of cabs will be on the streets."

Crave took both her hands. "You're right." Their auras were tinged with orange, as was mine from adrenaline and flight reflex. But Bliss's radiant energy was still mostly yellow; she was enjoying this experience the way she reveled in everything. My aura and Crave's were both tinted the darker hues reflecting our somber mood. It showed me clearer than anything else that despite our memories in common, Bliss was nothing like me.

I nodded when they both looked at me expectantly. I wasn't eager to venture out again, anyway. "I wonder where Mystify is. I hope he got away from the horde."

"He definitely saved our asses," Bliss agreed.

Crave's eyes narrowed, as if he wasn't ready to go that far.

"I'm going to leave him a message at the obelisk," I decided.

Crave shook his head. "No, it's too close to Fifth Ave, right behind the Metropolitan Museum. Any demon passing by would be able to feel us."

"I'll go alone," I told them. "My signature is so light they won't notice it. They'll be looking for yours, Crave. I tell you what—let's go wait at Belvedere Castle. That's in the middle of the park. From there I can nip over to the obelisk and leave a message for Mystify telling him where we are."

I started up the steps, and they followed still holding hands. I slipped into the shadows and avoided the lit paths in the Rambles, a dell densely filled with bushes and small trees interlaced with narrow paths. Shadows startled me at first, until I realized that men were there cruising for other men. Like cats, they melted away until we went by. I could smell the musky scent of sex in the air. Bliss perked right up, but she still didn't linger. Apparently Bliss could resist pleasure if her survival was at stake.

At the transverse overpass, exposed to prying eyes and passing demons on the roadway below, I dashed across with both of them at my heels.

From there, Bliss and Crave split off to head deeper into the park where the castle overlooked the tiny lake. If Shock had been with me, she wouldn't have let me go alone. But Crave was focused on Bliss, and Bliss didn't have a cautious bone in her body. That was actually a relief.

I had almost reached the Met when I realized I didn't have a pen or paper to leave a message. It stopped me short as I dug into my pockets. Money was the only thing I had.

I fingered a twenty-dollar bill; it would do fine as a writing surface. But it would be useless to search the park looking for a lost pen. So I turned over the rocks in the gravel, finding one with a sharp point.

Taking it slow, I punctured small dashes into the bill, holding it up to the light shining from the lamppost to check my work. I incised one word, all I could manage on the bill, signed with my initial, and then folded it up.

I almost passed the obelisk, as it reared out of the shadows to my left. I had expected it to be right behind the museum, not on the other side of the path. I hoped it was the right one—there weren't two obelisks in Central Park, were there? You never could tell in this city. It seemed that I was a fair ways from Fifth Avenue, which made me relax a bit.

I was tucking the bill under the corner of Cleopatra's Needle when I felt Crave coming. But I was confused at first because he was coming from the north, not the south.

"Mystify," I realized.

When he emerged in the small plaza, it was even worse. Mystify was wearing a Theo Ram guise. It made me catch my breath.

As Mystify came closer, I realized there were differences. He looked like Theo's younger brother, less jaded and world-weary, more energetic and eager. His dark hair was longer and wilder, his cheeks slightly rounded instead of cut by a chisel, and his body not so lean and whip-hard as Ram's.

My mind knew it wasn't Ram, but my body leaned toward him. Crave's whirlpool signature, drawing me in, didn't help matters.

"Allay," he said, an echo of Ram.

I cleared my throat. "That's not your guise."

"It's what I was born in. It feels natural to me."

"I thought androgynous personas were more your style." I forced myself to look away from him.

"I remember our passion," he told me, coming in closer.

He had Ram's memories—he had been born on the heels of our love affair. He knew all sorts of intimate details about me. "That's not fair. Between you and Bliss, I'm an open book."

"Not many could hold up under such scrutiny. But you are divine. . . ."

His hand ran up the outside of my arm, making me shiver. He absorbed my confusion, trembling as it overwhelmed his senses. That was the emotion he craved above all others, and I was gushing it into him.

"Ahhh . . ." he breathed, shuddering in satisfaction.

I pulled away. He knew what to do to confuse me, because he had seen how Ram manipulated me. "I don't think Ram would like you wearing his guise."

Mystify grinned, making his persona look even younger. "Ram won't risk contact with me, not so soon after my birth. Even under the best of circumstances, he would be highly suspicious of anyone who knows so much about him. He especially won't let me get close during this upheaval."

"So you do know everything about him." I wanted to ask him what Ram felt about me, but didn't dare. I also wanted to ask about Hope. But that would be playing into his hands, and I was already vulnerable enough trapped in Central Park. My questions could wait until we were on a more equal footing.

"I know one thing from Ram," he said. "When things are in flux, that creates opportunities we can take advantage of."

"Like what?"

"Getting control over other demons. That's what Glory and Dread are doing. And Goad. There may be other players who haven't revealed themselves."

"What about Ram?"

He looked at me hard. "He's spoken to you. Why don't you tell me?"

"I don't know what's true about Ram. He lives by lies."

"You shook his world, cracked his nut, so to speak. And he can hardly believe it himself, but you've got him hooked, sister."

Delighted confusion roiled through me again, and this time I didn't mind it when Mystify rubbed my arm, stealing a chunk of it away for himself. His eyes closed in pleasure. He definitely made his feeding a sensual experience.

It made me uncomfortable, so I pulled away.

When he could speak again, Mystify said, "I know Ram would want you to get to safety instead of standing in range of Fifth Avenue."

"Bliss and Crave are waiting for me. I just left you a note."

Mystify swiped the twenty from under the obelisk. He checked it for writing, then held it up higher, seeing the pinpricks of light shining through from the lamp by the path. The letters spelled out C-A-S-T-L-E. In the corner was an *A*.

Mystify blew out his breath in a long, low whistle. "Nice of you to let me know."

He started to pocket the bill carefully, as if it meant something to him. Maybe it was the first note he had ever gotten. "Oh, you'll want this back."

He held it out to me. There was something so vulnerable about him, in spite of his steely Ram facade. He was only a day older than Bliss, but he hadn't had her advantages. He had been running since the first second.

Mystify was definitely a survivor. What else he was, I couldn't tell.

"Keep it." I wanted to offer to help him if he ever needed it. But Shock's voice warning me to be careful with newbie demons kept echoing through my head.

He joined me as I cut through the bottom of the great lawn, heading to Belvedere Castle. "Where do you live?" I asked.

"Here. Mostly."

I glanced around. "You're always on the move? That must be hard."

He didn't meet my eyes. "Yes."

There was a world of truth in that one word. He was alone, fighting for his life every minute. He had Ram's memories, a vast wealth of knowledge, but none of his strength. In a fight with any other demon, he and Bliss would lose simply because of the weakness of their newly minted state.

"You can always come to the bar if you need a safe place to stay." It was out of my mouth before I could stop myself. Shock would kill me for offering. Ram, too. Maybe I was an idiot, but I had to find people I could trust. I had already proven that isolation was the slow road to ruin. And Mystify had saved our lives tonight. That made it my move.

"You'd let me stay with you?" He shook his head. "Are you kidding?"

"I'm letting Bliss stay with me. Why not you, too?"

"For one, because Ram would kill me."

I had to laugh at that. "This isn't Ram's decision. Believe me. I mean it. You can stay at the bar if you're ever in need."

He hesitated. "Thanks. That means a lot to me."

"You better switch back to your own signature," I reminded him. "Crave's suspicious enough without coming face-to-face with his own signature."

Mystify obediently reverted to his disorienting emanations as we climbed the hill and the stairs that led up to the castle. It had a small terrace around it with walls looking down the sheer cliff to the lake below.

Bliss peeked around the open archway of the castle. "Mystify? Is that you? Did you see Allay—oh, there you are."

Crave appeared from the other end of the terrace. "I thought there was an echo at first." He glared at Mystify.

"I ran into him at the obelisk," I said.

"What happened with Goad?" Bliss asked eagerly.

"I drew them up to Glory's border. She's posted sentries to warn her in case there's another mass raid on her territory. They peeled away as soon as they came into range. I wasn't challenged because they assumed I was Crave. I circled around to the park and headed south."

"You make it sound easy," Bliss said admiringly.

Crave frowned and tucked his arm around her. I hid a smile. Classic! Soon they would be sparring with each other over her favor. Better Bliss than me.

"Come on up, Allay," Bliss urged. "You should see the view from the top."

I followed her up the steps spiraling around a stone column to the second floor and on to the top. The parapet was lined by traditional crenellation, with buttresses thickening the walls. The park spread out darkly on every side, but the perimeter was marked by the straight lines of apartment buildings, the windows glowing and the pediments lit up to show off the most distinctive features.

The cool breeze was bracing. Bliss's hair blew back as if she were in a shampoo commercial. But the sound of rushing cars rising from the traverse roadway was loud enough to destroy the peace.

"We're too close to the road," I said. "We can't stay here. What if a demon passes by?"

"I realized that after we got here," Crave agreed.

We headed down the steps, and Bliss was the last to come, tearing herself away. At the bottom, standing over the glinting lake, I said, "Should we head further north? We'd be exposed in the center of the lawn."

"And the reservoir is above that," Crave said. "I think we should head south. There are more options down at that end of the park."

I turned to Mystify. "What do you think? You know this territory. We need a place to hang for a few hours where Goad won't find us."

He considered it for a few moments; then he nodded as if making a decision. "I've got the perfect place."

He led us down the side of the hill and across the traverse bridge heading south. Crave grumbled that the bridle path was too close to Central Park West, but we were going the way he wanted. In less than five minutes, we reached Strawberry Fields.

Mystify went straight to the small plaza with the memorial plaque inlaid in the center for John Lennon that read IMAGINE. Stumps of candles with rivulets of wax and flowers in various states of decay littered the area.

It was absolutely quiet, with hardly any traffic noise coming from Central Park West. Mystify said, "I'm trusting you with my life."

"I promise I won't tell anyone," I said without hesitation. Bliss agreed, but Crave was much slower to follow. "You better mean it," I told Crave. "That includes keeping this from Glory. Can you do that?"

His eyes narrowed. "I can do that."

Mystify must have heard the smidge of doubt behind his confident assurance. I exchanged looks with him and shrugged. I couldn't guarantee Crave's word. I was pretty sure Glory was pulling all of his strings.

Mystify grimaced and then shrugged, as if he was willing to take a chance.

He looked around to be sure no one was in sight. Then he gestured us over to the center of one of the paths that radiated from the terrace.

He took a tool from his pocket and inserted it into the manhole cover that lay flush with the paving stones.

With a twist, he swirled the cover up. "They're really heavy. It usually takes two men to drag one open. But if I put exactly the right leverage on it, I can get it to move."

I peered fascinated into the darkness. "What's down there?"

"An old tunnel that runs along Seventy-second Street. Hurry, I don't want anyone to see us."

I lowered myself onto the rungs of the ladder that descended into the darkness. I moved a lot more quickly than I wanted to, as Bliss and Crave came down after me. I reached the bottom as Mystify stepped onto the ladder, smiling up at him as he deftly slid the cover back into place overhead, cutting off the light.

Bliss bumped into me. "We really need to buy a lighter."

When Mystify got to the bottom of the ladder, he pulled out a green glow stick, the kind that recharged in the sunlight. It cast an eerie illumination on the rough ground and fallen concrete from the upper part of the tunnel. The tunnel stretched into the darkness in both directions.

"Mi casa es su casa," he said quietly.

"Another filthy hole in the ground," Crave muttered.

"Excuse me for saving your life. If you don't like it, I can let you back out." Mystify lifted his foot onto the first rung of the ladder.

"Be grateful, Crave," I ordered. "Or I'm letting him toss you back outside."

Crave puffed up like he was ready for a fight, but Bliss let out a trilling laugh. "I think it's cool! Let's see where it goes."

Crave instantly deflated. Mystify looked like he wanted to continue the fight, and I was reminded achingly of Ram confronting Pique outside my bar. The first night he had saved me.

"Won't they be able to sense us here from Central Park West?" I asked. "We're awful close."

Mystify finally broke eye contact with Crave. "We have to go further down. This is too near the surface. And there are too many people here."

"People come down here?" I asked in surprise.

"Sure, there are dozens who sleep right here."

Bliss followed Mystify on his heels, exclaiming over everything. The glow stick cast enough light for us to see clearly with our demon sight. As Mystify said, we passed a few groups of people sleeping in rows. Some called out for us to get away. One of them shouted and threw a bottle at us. Crave shouted back, his voice ringing through the hollow space.

Mystify pulled me along faster. "Shut up!" he ordered Crave.

"Don't tell me what to do," Crave countered.

Thankfully nobody came after us. Debris was sliding around under my feet. Crave was holding Bliss's arm, helping her.

"How did you find this place?" I asked Mystify.

"I followed the homeless. When I got down here, I realized that if I could get deep enough, I could be right underneath a demon, and they can't sense me because of the layers of concrete, asphalt, and wiring in between."

I wondered why I had never thought of it before. The subway could blank out a demon's signature, and I had often used the train to escape demons. But I never thought of checking out the tunnels under the city.

Mystify veered over to one side. He knelt down where the bricks were knocked out of the side of the tunnel, about a foot off the ground. Beyond was a big open space filled with deeper blackness. "Down the rabbit hole," he prompted.

I swallowed. "We have to go in there?"

Crave took one look and crossed his arms. "You've got to be crazy."

7

"It's either that, or I'm dumping you back in the park," Mystify snapped.

They went face-to-face, both with their fists clenched. Mystify looked a lot tougher in the semblance of Ram's guise. The ethereal personas I'd seen him in before hid the steely backing of Ram's memories.

"I'd like to see you try," Crave said menacingly.

"He saved our lives," Bliss pointed out. "We would have been caught by Goad's horde if Mystify hadn't helped us."

The tension bound us motionless. Then I pointed to the hole. "I'm going down. It's got to be safer than the surface."

"Me, too," Bliss agreed. "I want to see what it's like."

Crave pressed his lips together. "I'm not letting you go alone. With him."

Mystify was blocking the hole. "Maybe I don't want you to come."

His slight sneer reminded me of Ram, the way he had stared down at Dread lying drained and helpless on the floor of his own cage. The ruthlessness of it made me shiver.

I shook myself out of it. "Can you both please stop with the chest-beating? We'll be caught while you stand here and figure out who's more of a man."

Bliss laughed again, breaking the tension. "I'll go first."

"No, let me show you." Mystify turned away like he didn't care about Crave. Crave had more trouble getting hold of his anger, but he managed to swallow it down. Clearly now was not the time. A demon could be driving by on Central Park West any second, and we would be exposed.

"You have to go in backward and feel your way down the rungs of the ladder. Hold on to this," Mystify told us, slipping his fingers around a bar that was wedged into the broken wall.

Mystify turned and put his foot down where he knew the rung would be. As he disappeared down, Bliss leaned out fearlessly to watch. His voice drifted up hollowly, "Okay, you can start down now, Bliss.

As she swung around, reaching down with one foot, I put my hand to my mouth. It looked really scary. But she disappeared into the hole as easily as Mystify.

Crave took the glow stick from me. "You next," he said shortly. He clearly didn't like being one-upped by the newbie.

I turned and put my foot through the hole. My stomach dropped as if it fell into the hole without me, until I felt the top rung on the other side. I had to be careful to lower myself as I backed into the hole, groping for the next rung with my foot. I was so focused on my feet and holding on that I bumped my head as I stepped down and inside.

The ladder was an old aluminum one that was folded shut and roped to the wall by subterranean Sherpas. It rested on a plank set across another ladder beneath it. The whole contraption swayed alarmingly with every movement I made. I descended faster than was comfortable. Some of the ropes looked frayed.

There was a push of air blowing past me, smelling

more damp than above. The deeper tunnel was much smaller—we could barely stand up inside. It was set at a ninety-degree angle to the one above, running roughly north and south. The walls were broken and seeping white crusty gunk along the cracks. The floor was uneven, filled with chunks of bricks and cement that had fallen from the inside. There was more sickening movement as mice, rats, and roaches scuttled away at the arrival of Crave and the green glow stick. A faint rumble of a subway train passing nearby made dust filter down from the curved ceiling. It felt like the tunnel was about to collapse.

"We're far enough underground that our signatures can't be felt on the surface," Mystify assured Bliss.

Crave had his arm over his nose. "This place is disgusting. Please don't tell me you live here."

"This is one of the underground highways. It's an old water main. See how the walls are made of brick? When the city installed new pipes in the fifties, they put the mains up higher, about eight feet deep, and smaller for better pressure. It's easier for them to maintain the cement pipes."

"How do you know that?"

"I talk to the people I meet down here. I'm alone, an obvious misfit, so sometimes they talk back. An old guy showed me this place. I found an ancient gas main yesterday—you have to crawl through that one, but it took me straight to the 1 subway tunnel on the west side. I keep finding new levels and natural underground caverns."

"How cool is that?" Bliss marveled.

Crave glowered but didn't say anything as Mystify turned south. I stopped him. "Does this go all the way to Harlem?"

"There's a collapse at the north end of the park. But Harlem is only a few blocks away."

I turned to Crave. "You have to go see Glory. She's expecting you."

Crave stiffened, looking the picture of offended pride. "I'm not at Glory's beck and call. Why don't you come back to my place? You'll be safe there until morning, and I can call a car to take you home."

Bliss's eyes lit up, but I asked, "Isn't Lash there?"

Crave hesitated. "Yes, but I can take care of her."

"That's the last thing Glory wants—you bringing Bliss home to Lash. You two are supposed to be lying low for a few days. You think it will help if you're walking around holding hands in front of her?"

Bliss shrugged. "Whatever."

"Why don't you go home, Crave?" I urged. "We'll be fine with Mystify."

"Not a chance. I'm not leaving you two alone with him." Crave's arms crossed as he shook his head. "This place is too dangerous. I'm going with you."

Damn male pride! He couldn't stand Bliss's interest in Mystify. "Could you at least call Glory to let her know about Goad's horde chasing us down?"

"Why don't you?" he shot back.

"Because Goad stole my phone when he kidnapped me for Vex."

Silently Crave handed me his phone. But when I opened it, there were no bars. We were cut off from the streets above. "No reception."

"I know a place where you can call out," Mystify offered.

I handed back Crave's phone. He was adamant about staying with us. So I sighed and followed Mystify south.

It was rough going, but I soon realized there was a path worn through the uneven floor by the trampling of many feet. If you stuck to that path, it was much easier.

Soon we came on another ladder angling down through a hole in the curved ceiling. The deep rumble of a subway train going by overhead was much louder. Several dark lumps were lying end to end near the wall, recognizable as human only by their glowing auras. They were bundled up in blankets cocooned around their heads. After a second, I realized it was to protect their skin from the rats.

"Passing by, passing by . . ." Mystify intoned in warning.

He tensed as if ready to react, and that made me more concerned than anything. But the sodden lumps curled up tighter as we stepped carefully along the edge to get by. Their bundles of goods were piled at either end.

When we got far enough away, Crave asked, "What are they doing down here?"

"Most of them go up on the street to beg during the day, and come down here at night to sleep in safety."

"Safety! Give me a nice park bench any day."

"The cops won't let you. They hustle people away if they try to sleep on the streets. There's not enough housing to go around and lots of the shelters are dangerous— their stuff gets stolen and people get raped. They aren't allowed to stay if they drink or do drugs. And mothers lose their children if they're seen on the street, so they come down here."

Now Crave was truly appalled. "There are children down here?"

Mystify glanced at me and Bliss. "You'll see."

We had been walking for some time when the racket of subway trains grew much louder. Eventually we came to another ladder that led back up to the tracks. "We're under Grand Central Station," Mystify said, raising his voice to be heard.

He quickly climbed the ladder up to the hole above, where light faintly gleamed. He blocked the hole for a moment as he climbed through.

"Come on!" Mystify called down.

As I climbed up, the rush of air and rumble was getting very loud. A train rushed by as I was emerging. It blew a bunch of nasty-smelling soot into my eyes.

Mystify pulled me choking from the hole. There were a few feet between us and the silver side of the car. Next to us was the end of the subway tunnel. Built into the wall was a giant train stopper, nothing more than a giant spring that was designed to stop runaway trains.

I crouched down next to the hole, suddenly seeing much better. Mystify had streaks of dirt on his cheeks, as did Bliss when she emerged. I copied them as they subtly shifted their features to flake off the soot and grime clinging to my skin. My clothes were another matter, but I would have to live with that until we got home. Crave came out of the hole looking practically as pristine as he had entered, the original metrosexual.

We walked toward the glow of the subway platform. A gaping hole in the brick underneath glowed with a faint light.

"Watch out," Mystify cautioned. "People are under the platform. Don't ever go inside one. It smells awful. Mostly it's drug addicts in the subway tunnels because those spaces are the easiest to get to. They sleep right where they shit."

A train rushed by on an adjacent track, buffeting us with the suction. I had to adjust my eyes again at the comparative rush of light.

To avoid notice of the security cameras, we waited until another train pulled in on our track and people were filing off before we climbed up onto the platform.

Mystify headed for the other end. "Hurry. If there are any demons around, they'll be able to sense us."

Crave grabbed on to Bliss's hand again, as if staking his claim on protecting her. We jogged down the platform to the arched entrance where the train entered the station. Down the other side were steps for the track workers. A short way farther was another door inlaid into the wall, this one at the same level as the track.

Mystify opened up the door leading to metal stairs jackknifing down into the darkness. He pulled out the glow stick again so we could see more easily. At each landing, there was another door. I counted down six levels before we reached the bottom. Mystify had to bump hard against the bottom door to open it.

We stepped into a very low tunnel. Crave had to hunch to walk through it. Trash was piled everywhere, with large cardboard boxes lying crushed to one side, spilling out dirty bedding. It reeked like a urinal.

Gagging from the stench, I put my nose deep in my elbow. Bliss was also covering her nose, but her eyes were laughing.

"It gets worse." Mystify's voice was muffled behind his cupped hands.

Crave did the same. "Of course it does."

We picked our way carefully through the abandoned tunnel. At the front end, the smell was even worse, as Mystify had promised.

A huge metal grate had been welded into place near the end, blocking off a short span of tunnel.

Mystify pulled out a key from his pocket. "You can buy passkeys for the MTA system at a few different places. All you have to do is tell them the location of one of these gates. The transit police used to come down here every few months and destroy the condos down below. Then they got the bright idea to cut off access with this gate. Now they just come to check the gate to be sure it isn't broken. The moles told me about a guy who lost his key a couple years ago, and instead of waiting for someone to come along and let him in, he broke the lock. The condo association brought a locksmith down here to fix it so the transit police wouldn't go down and bust up the place. They evicted the guy, but someone said the Second Ave tunnel let him into their community."

The hinges creaked as Mystify opened the gate and he carefully made sure it locked behind us. Inside, he lifted a piece of board that was leaning against the wall. A faint glow of light came up from the hole he exposed.

"This ladder is much longer," he warned, as he stepped through backward.

I was glad he warned us because I got a bit of vertigo as I started down, realizing I was suspended high on the side of a cliff inside a natural cavern. Down below were a few dots of campfires and the roofs of dozens of shacks lining the bottom of the crevice. The ladders were rigged to the wall with brightly colored mountaineering rope.

With the metal clanging and banging, I rapidly descended. Bliss came down nimbly after me, hardly making a sound. The ceiling arched just above the hole where the ladder entered, and the cavern was much longer than it was wide. Two rows of shacks lined the sides, and down the center were fires and open hearths where people were cooking.

"This deep, you'll find more established communities," said Mystify. "Some elect their mayor or spokesperson. They say some of the mole people won't let you go once you find them, but I haven't run across any of those."

A girl about ten years old passed by us. Her yellow hair gleamed in the dim light, pulled into a single pigtail. There were smudges on her cheeks and chin. "Hi, Mystify! Is this your girlfriend?"

She was looking at me. I smiled. "I'm his friend. Allay. Who are you?"

Without waiting to reply, the girl ran up the ladder like a spider, chanting, "Mystify and Allay sitting on a ledge, k-i-s-s-i-n-g!"

My eyes went wide. Mystify leaned in. "She's going

to use the bathroom upstairs. That keeps it clean down here. And it discourages other people from setting up a camp on their doorstep."

"Nice deterrent," Crave said dryly.

The sounds of early morning rising drifted out. Several other kids appeared, kicking a dusty ball. Their laughter was muted, as if they were mindful of echoes.

"What do they do all day down here?" I asked.

"They go to public school up above," Mystify explained. "They use a relative's address to get their report cards."

As we walked between the shacks, people wished us a good morning. Mystify pulled out small things from his deep pockets: a bottle of aspirin for an older woman and a packet of Halls cough drops for another. "They get their electricity from the extension cords dangling down from tracks above," he pointed out. "That keeps the rats from chewing on them. The water comes from a sprinkler pipe at the other end, and they carry it home in five-gallon buckets."

A filthy cat rubbed up against my leg. I couldn't tell what its original color was, but now it was gray all over. I tried to pet it, but it felt so nasty I didn't want to do much more than rub its cheek. "Poor cat," I murmured.

"The cats keep the rats away." Mystify swooped it up and gave it a cuddle despite its appearance. The cat purred, closing its eyes and radiating bliss. "They bathe them every once in a while, but the cats hate it. They wouldn't have a community without the cats. They'd be run over by vermin."

From the giant flies buzzing around the exposed bulbs, I would have said they still had a vermin problem. But I had to admit that everyone looked reasonably clean and healthy. The smells from the coffee and the eggs starting to sizzle over the fires smelled as good as any restaurant. It looked like several shacks shared a common fire in metal barrels that were cut in half to hold the grill.

Mystify stopped at a corrugated-metal hut near the middle of the row. It was as humble as the rest, but a huge man emerged from the cloth-draped door stretching and yawning. His skin was as dusty black as his clothes, and though his shoulders were broad and he topped the other men by several inches, his pants drooped on his hips and his hands seemed to hang huge on his bony wrists.

"Travis, I've brought some friends. They're passing through with me."

Travis was wary as he settled into an old bench seat that had been removed from the back of a car. "You're new to be bringing guests."

"I won't do it again," Mystify instantly promised. "We were being chased. I didn't want to leave them exposed."

"Never again," Travis warned, giving us all a hard look. "You can't speak of this place."

"No problem," Crave interjected.

I hurried to add, "We wouldn't want to bring harm to you. It's amazing what you've accomplished down here."

"We try," he said simply.

The condos certainly looked snug enough in the dim light. They didn't have to contend with rain or cold or heat since underground it stayed a constant, perfect temperature. We saw one guy reclining in a hammock strung between two shacks, and a woman was singing as she washed some dishes in a bucket. There wasn't the same frantic pace like up on the streets, as if they were untouched by outside events. It was relaxing, and I felt myself slowing down to match the more contemplative pace.

Mystify sat down on a cushion next to Travis, who was asking him questions about getting a new generator. I chose a stool nearby. Bliss was petting the dirty cat, wandering here and there after it. Crave kept one eye on her and the other on the local head honcho as he leaned against one of the poles that supported the shack.

"Do you have reception down here?" I asked Crave. The thought of Glory waiting to hear from him bothered me. I wanted her on my side, not against me.

Crave checked his phone as Mystify said, "You have to go up to the tank room. The back ladder is at the other end of the street." He gestured farther down the double row of shacks. "I'll take you there in a minute."

I could tell that he wanted to stay in good with Travis, having endangered his place by bringing us here. From his copious pockets, he pulled out a few MetroCards. "These still have fares left on them."

Travis nodded, pocketing the cards. His people would need them to get back in from the street. "What about Charlene?"

"I found a clinic that will see her for free as long as she brings her disability card. It's up in Harlem, but she can take the highway almost all the way there."

"She won't like going topside," Travis agreed.

"If she doesn't get a prescription for her blood pressure, then she'll die."

Travis nodded slowly. "I tell her that."

With that, he ambled back up the street to one of the corrugated lean-tos. "Charlene! We're coming to see you."

As I watched Mystify try to convince a sad old woman to go up into the light for the first time in five years, I realized that Crave and Bliss had disappeared. I could still feel Crave's signature, so I knew they hadn't gone far.

Walking a few steps away from the shack, I could see the ladder we had come down. There was nobody on it, or in the dusty end of the cavern beyond the condos where the kids were still playing.

I figured Crave had sneaked off with Bliss to try to

charm some more kisses out of her. I hated it that Glory had made it my business what they did with each other. Surely if she couldn't control her own incubus, then how could she expect me to?

Mystify came out from the shack, assuring Travis that he would make the appointment, before he rejoined me. "They've wandered off," I explained.

"Travis says they went up the back exit."

"Maybe they went to try to get cell reception." But I didn't hold out hope that speaking to Glory was on the top of Crave's mind.

Mystify smiled, looking a lot like Theo Ram. But I didn't get that same yearning to reach out and touch him, to stroke his hair and press my body into him. Mostly it just reminded me of Ram. What would he do in this situation?

I had no way of getting hold of him. Not even a message drop under a statue. Why hadn't he given me some way to get hold of him?

"Let's go find Bliss," I said.

We walked through the double strip of shacks to the back end. A pipe was rigged up to drop water into a spigot, with damp paving stones forming a small catch basin below. Not far from the pipe was another ladder slanting up the cliff at the end of the cavern. This ladder wasn't straight up and down like the other one, but as I started up, I realized that made it even harder to climb.

At the very top, I stood on the shelf of the cliff looking down at the condos. I waved down to Mystify, who was halfway up. I nodded, giving him the thumbs-up.

I looked around but didn't see any way off the narrow rocky shelf until Mystify arrived. He showed me a crack in the very end. Another ladder disappeared into the narrowest of openings.

"They don't use this as an entrance," he said. "It's too

awkward. But they need to have a way to get out if the transit authority comes down."

"Every bolt-hole needs a back door. Unlike that spiral staircase to nowhere you sent us down to get away from Goad."

He grinned. "No choice. It was the closest."

Mystify shimmied between the rocks of the crevice. It would be hard for anyone with any real padding on their bones to get through. But everyone I had seen in the condos had that spare leanness that came with hard living.

The end of another ladder stuck up into the downward-curved end of a discharge pipe. The hole was about two feet across.

I crawled up after him, then had to bend and contort to get around the ninety-degree turn into the horizontal part of the pipe. Mystify's rubber boots were right in front of my nose.

In a claustrophobic moment of panic, I thought I was trapped. I couldn't catch my breath, there was no air, and my throat closed. I grabbed on to Mystify's ankle, crushing the rubber.

"Ouch! Allay, what's wrong?" He tried to see me, but the pipe was too narrow.

I couldn't answer, lost in the midst of a memory. The walls closed in oppressively as I scrabbling at the stones trying to pry them apart. Voices on the other side grew more hysterical with each passing moment. I was stuck in the darkness, buried under rock, while people busily moved among the buildings above, oblivious of the horror under their feet. . . .

"Allay? Are you okay?" His feet pulled away. "I'm opening the grate so we can get out."

I forced myself to crawl after him, keeping one hand on his ankle as if it were a lifeline. My head swam from the lack of air, or was it too much? I heaved, barely able to see for the purple spots in front of my eyes.

I was in a panic.

It was Plea's memory. One of those disturbing pieces of my progenitor's life that I had sealed off from myself.

Mystify swung open the grate with a muffled clank, then a slight squeak. He held it open for me as I slithered out and onto the floor. There was barely an inch-high lip between the floor and the pipe.

I lay there gasping like a beached fish.

"What's wrong, Allay? Are you sick?"

Putting my hands to my head, I managed to say, "A flashback. Plea."

He frowned. "You mean memories?" When I nodded, he said, "Mine aren't that strong. It's more like remembering a movie I saw."

My heart wasn't racing as badly now that I was out of that pipe. I couldn't explain that I had forcibly kept Plea's memories at bay for a decade. Now they were breaking through with a vengeance. I was losing the fight to not see and feel things my progenitor experienced.

I took a deep breath and let go of the struggle. The images flooded over me. I was surrounded by walls built of small round stones, stacked nearly to the ceiling of the cavern just above my head. Then slowly I realized the stones were bones, human bones, neatly stacked higher than my head. Tibias and femurs were laced together by the thousands, interspersed with neat rows of skulls.

The smell alone should have told me—decay despite the lack of flesh. My instinctive reaction was to flee, to get away from death, but I was walled in by the bones of dead people. Frightened Parisians were rounding up everyone who was different, everyone they called a *vampyr*. Plea had been caught and dragged here in chains, left to slowly die entombed by the bones.

"No," I managed to say. "No, I didn't die."

"Allay!" Mystify was growing anxious.

Giving in to the memory did the trick. I was no longer

overcome by it. Rationally, I knew it was Plea, not me, who had been cemented into the catacombs. Those days trapped behind the bones had written itself deeply into Plea's mind. Never again. . . .

"It's okay," I told Mystify. "It's passing now."

Doubtfully, he helped me stand up. "Those are some powerful memories. Are you sure there isn't something wrong?"

"You've got that right," I admitted. I needed to sit down when I had a moment and start going through the memories. I couldn't risk another flashback like that at a critical moment.

He snorted. "I wish Ram's memories were that vivid, but he was usually so detached that it's like he wasn't even living his own life."

I wanted to find out more about Ram in the worst way, but the yearning with which Mystify was looking down at me made me uncomfortable. We were standing too close to each other, in a narrow curving corridor twenty feet tall. "Where are we?" I asked to break the moment.

The wall to our right was metal, and he tapped his hand against it, making a sullen boom. "We just came through the emergency drain that was installed in case this water tank busts. They don't want it flowing into the underground power station next door, so they sent any spillage down into the cavern." He bent over and closed the grate after him, pushing until it clicked. Then he pulled to make sure it was latched shut. "They don't want people coming in this way. Only out."

"But you've cut us off. We can't go back."

"There are other exits from here."

I could feel Crave's signature again, so I knew we were following them. But I couldn't hear anything.

We circled the water tank to a long ladder leading up. It was almost pitch-black, but I'd gotten to the point where I could adjust my eyes to see in the barest of light. There was an outline of a hatch far above. "Where exactly are we?"

"Right now we're five levels down, a little east of Lexington and Forty-third Street. The Chrysler Building is just south of us. This tank was part of the building's power station, providing steam heat and power for the offices. But most of the equipment was removed when it was shut down."

"You really know your way around after two days."

"This is the area I know best, between here and the park." We reached the bottom of the ladder. He put his hand on one rung and pointed halfway up to a shadowy rectangle about ten feet square. "See that dark hole in the wall to the right? That's my place. It's tricky to get to—you have to lean over really far and stretch, literally, to grab on to the rope I've rigged there. Travis told me the last guy who tried to use that spot slipped and broke his leg. They had to drag him all the way back to the tracks and up the stairs to get him out. Nobody's tried since. I think that's what made him trust me when he realized I was giving it a go."

I closed my eyes to sense them. "They aren't up there. Is that the way out?"

"No." He moved closer to me, his hands reaching out for my hips. "Come up with me. I have cushions there. It's comfortable and safe. . . ."

His face was getting closer to mine, and his hands pulled me in. "Come with me, Allay. Let me please you."

8

I pushed him away. "Mystify! What are you trying to do?"

"What do you think? I like you, Allay. You're the only sane demon around, and that includes my progenitor."

"I don't even know you."

"You didn't know Ram, either. You barely met him that night you took him upstairs."

My eyes widened. "That doesn't mean I sleep with every guy who crosses my path!"

"I'm no stranger. I know everything about you, Allay. What you like, what you don't like." His hand slid lower to rub my groin. "You can cash my check anytime."

My cheeks flushed red before I could stop my embarrassment from showing. "That's private!" I had taunted Ram into going down on me by saying that, to see if Dread had cameras trained on me in the Prophet's Center. "That's not for you."

"Allay, listen to me. Ram's no good for you. He'll take over your life. He has to be in complete control. Why do you think he's played the hidden and all-powerful Oz to the rest of us for two thousand years? He can't bear to be on an equal footing with anyone else."

"He's never been that way with me. In fact, he's done things my way even when he didn't want to. He didn't kill *you*."

"He did that to manipulate you. My life was a small price to pay to get you to trust him."

I shook my head. "Then why? Why does he want me?"

"The truth?" He took a deep breath. "You're like Hope."

For a second, I thought he meant "hope," not the woman's name, Hope. But Hope had been Ram's first love. My head whirled as if the floor were dropping out from under me.

"You're a lot like her," Mystify said. "He's never loved anyone since her. You feel like her." His hand rose to brush my aura. "Possessed humans are so juicy, especially when you're charged up like you are now."

I batted his hand away. "I think *you're* trying to manipulate me."

He shrugged. "I know Ram better than anyone. His heart leaped the first time he sensed your signature. It's a lot like Hope's was, that lifting sensation, like anything is possible. You don't know how important that is to Ram. He lives in despair. Even though he wants to think he's helping humanity, deep down he's afraid that it's all for nothing. That demons and mankind are destined to prey on each other unto oblivion."

It was my worst fear—Ram didn't really care about me. He was reenacting an old love affair gone terribly wrong.

Mystify reached out to pat my arm as if to comfort me, but he soaked up some of my distress. I forgot that he longed to feed on confusion. Maybe this was just his way of getting what he needed most.

I pulled away from him. I couldn't let him distract me with questions about Ram and Hope right now. I'd have to think about it later. "Let's find Bliss and Crave."

I tried to get hold of myself as we continued on around the tank. When we reached an archway in the wall, several pipes led out of the tank and through a narrow corridor. I had to go up several steps chiseled into the bedrock, and then slide alongside the pipes to get through the narrow gap.

It opened out into a large room several stories tall. There were currents in the air, leading my eye to the dark openings high in the walls and into the maze of pipes ahead. I touched the wall, rough stone, unfaced with brick. It was very dark, but I was starting to see fine gradations of color in the shades of gray—the gleam of a red plastic toggle switch, broad olive green streaks curving down the sides of the pipes, and the cool silvery blue of an old steel catwalk.

I gave in to the otherworldliness of the place, moving silently so I could hear the tiny rustles of the other occupants of the abandoned power station. The smell was dank and musty, but not as bad as the entrance to the condos. Or maybe I was getting used to it.

Mystify climbed up to the catwalk. It curved around a corner and behind a pipe that was at least six feet thick. Smaller pipes ran in parallel lines above it.

From up here, I couldn't see anything but blackness above and below through the metal mesh of the catwalk.

A scuffling sound drew my attention over to the far side. Two eyes shone in the darkness. Even when I enhanced my sight as much as I could, the only thing I could see was their shiny glow in the distance.

I almost called out, thinking it was Bliss or Crave. I could feel them very close. But Mystify put his hand on my arm, shaking his head. "A couple of guys live up in the electrical room. They're scared of us because we're walking without any light. Only real mole people can do that. The ones who don't ever go back up. They can see almost as well as us."

"That's . . . crazy." What kind of person would come underground and never leave?

"You do what you have to."

Mystify led me to the other end and through the arched doorway. He stopped short, putting his finger to his lips. Up ahead, I saw Bliss and Crave.

She was bent over the railing of the catwalk that crossed the small room. Her hips were braced against it, as she leaned out into the darkness, her hands holding on to the bar to keep from falling over it.

Crave had hooked one arm under her shoulder and the other was on her butt cheek, spreading her open so he could push his cock inside. He pulled her up as he buried himself deeper, so she leaned back into his chest, and they pressed against each other.

My entire body flushed. He pumped into her slowly, relentlessly, as she arched against him, moaning and writhing. Their auras merged, enveloping them both in a brilliant emerald glow, like the burning heart of a perfect gem. She turned to look over her shoulder and their lips met. The scent of musky sex filled the air, banishing the metallic tang of wet metal.

I started to turn away as he cried out deep inside her, his arms wrapped around her, his face buried in her neck. Now their energy truly merged, sending sparks flying back and forth as they fed off each other's fervor. His voice echoed against the walls. Bliss was almost as loud in her climax.

In the ringing silence afterward, there were a few muffled claps from unseen people down below.

Bliss laughed, collapsing back against Crave, letting him hold her up. "Looks like everyone enjoyed it." Then she saw me. "Including them."

"I can't let you go," he murmured, holding her close.

"You're going to have to," she told him, gesturing toward us.

Crave finally saw me and Mystify. I was trying to back down the catwalk, but Mystify was grinning openly at

Crave and wouldn't let me. What was it with men and their stupid games?

"Sorry," I told them both, turning away as they slowly pulled apart and started straightening their clothing. "I didn't realize we were interrupting. We'll wait back here."

"That's the way out," Mystify said with a laugh.

Bliss looked completely satiated, languid in her post-coital pleasure. Pain clenched at my heart, blurred the sight of her upturned face, so innocent and uninhibited.

"Give us a second, will you?" Crave was defensive, putting himself between Bliss and Mystify. I almost wanted to tell him to get over himself, that Mystify wanted me, not her.

But Mystify put up his hands. "Whoa, big guy. I can wait until you lose interest in her. That should be about two months, if you hold true to form."

"You don't know anything," Crave shot back.

"But he's right," Bliss said reasonably. "You'll never be satisfied by one woman."

"You're different," Crave told her.

"Spoken like a true Don Juan," Mystify murmured loud enough for him to hear.

"Don't listen to him, Bliss." Crave took her hands. "I've never felt this way about anyone before. They always want me. I make them want me, so they chase after me. But I want *you*. Like I've never wanted anyone. . . ."

She reached up to stroke his cheek. "That's very sweet. But I don't mind if this burns out like a meteor. I'm going to enjoy it while it lasts."

Mystify checked his watch. "This round will be over in another ten minutes. That's when we'll reach the street and Crave can check in with his boss."

Crave made a growling sound and started for Mystify. I was surprised when Mystify held his ground, but then again, he was Ram's offspring.

"That's enough!" I ordered, stepping between them. "It's getting late. I don't want to hit the morning rush hour getting home."

Reluctantly, Mystify broke eye contact, giving in. Bliss tugged on Crave, making him come with her. They went first, even though Mystify was the one who knew the way.

"Please leave him alone," I whispered to him. "Glory's going to be livid if she finds out about this. I have to convince him to play along for a while."

"I think it's already too late for that," Mystify told me. "But I'll do it your way."

He didn't have to say "just like Ram did." But I knew he was thinking it.

We climbed up a long spiral staircase that led to the platform of the train. I thought we were still too deep, but Crave checked his phone as we approached the escalator. "I can call out."

"Great." Things were looking up. "Let Glory know you're on your way home."

He silently dialed as we hopped onto the escalator. After a few rings, he said, "Hello, Glory? Allay wanted me to call you to give you an update."

He listened for a few moments. "I'm with Allay and Bliss right now."

"Tell her about Goad," I prompted urgently.

"Yes, we ran into them last night, too. They took Fervor? When?" He listened for a moment. "No, I can't get back right now."

I grimaced at his tone. Glory wasn't going to like being defied.

"No, I won't," Crave was saying into the phone. "You tell Lash to get out of my house, or I'll call her and give her the news myself. I never told her to leave Dread. She went nuts over some slight of his, and came crying to me. I never asked her to move in."

I nearly died. This wasn't at all what I had planned.

Crave listened for a minute, then retorted, "You can use it to your advantage, Glory. Tell Dread you'll split up the two of us, stop the news stories, if he gives back Fervor in exchange for Lash."

As we reached the top of the escalator, he held the phone away from his ear so we could hear Glory saying, "... disobeyed my orders. Your misfortune is that everyone knows what I expected of you."

"I'm not starting a mutiny, Glory. I'm breaking up with my girlfriend."

From the phone came the tinny threat, "If you do this, Crave, you *will* regret it. For the last time, are you coming home to make Lash happy, or do I have to cut you off for good?"

His anger was returning. "What do you mean by that, Glory? Don't you make empty threats to me—"

The dial tone made it clear that she had hung up on him.

I stared at him. "She's really mad at you."

Even Bliss was uncomfortable, which was a lot for her. "Maybe you should go home, Crave. I can see you in a couple of days. We can both deal with it then."

"I may be a gigolo, but she's not my pimp."

Mystify snorted with laughter. I didn't think it was funny.

"What are you going to do?" Bliss asked.

He shoved the phone back in his pocket like he didn't care. "First, I'll check into a hotel. I don't want to go home until I'm sure Lash is gone. I'll deal with Glory later, when she's cooled off."

He knew Glory better than I did, so I should have been reassured. But the tinge of orange that sparked through his aura spoke louder than words. Crave was trying to hide it, but he was afraid. Maybe knowing that Fervor, another Glory demon, had been snatched from the street last night made him realize how vulnerable we all were. He had hidden under Glory's skirts ever since he was born. Surely she knew what was best for him.

We surfaced in Grand Central, the towering old-fashioned train station complete with wrought-iron flourishes and a vaulted blue ceiling painted with the night stars. The row of tall, arched windows at the end let in the meager light of dawn. After the underground, it was a relief to let my eyes go back to normal and see color again. People were moving all around us, cutting across the vast space in a feeble imitation of the rush hour crowds that were soon to come.

Now we were exposed again. There were too many of us together for me to be able to tell if there were any demons in the area. "Can you sense anything?" I asked Crave.

"Nothing," he confirmed.

"Are you sure you'd feel them if they were nearby, with all of us grouped together like this?"

He nodded, distracted. "Yes, I'm known for my range."

I had to say it again. "Why don't you go home and deal with this mess, Crave? You don't want her putting a hit out on Bliss, do you?"

Crave shook himself out of it. "No, it's beyond that now. I've made it about me. It's better if Glory cools down first. She's forgiven me before, and she will again. I'm going to stay out of her way until she's ready."

I filed that away as useful information. I was tempted to call her to try to smooth things over, but inserting myself at this moment might be a bad idea.

"If you want a hotel, there's an escalator to the Hyatt over on Lexington," Mystify suggested.

That would keep us inside the Grand Central complex, where we could disappear underground if a demon popped up.

Crave ignored Mystify, as usual, but he took Bliss's hand possessively and headed for the concourse off the grand hall.

I smiled at Mystify and gave a slight shrug as we followed them. He didn't seem at all interested in leaving us. I was actually glad. It was likely Bliss would stay with Crave. Then I'd be on my own getting home.

We went straight up to the glass atrium of the Grand Hyatt. Despite the graceful trees and hanging garden in the lofty space, I didn't like the hard surfaces of the shiny marble floor and gold metallic railings. Even the escalator was sided in gold, as flashy and cheap as an imitation watch.

I hung back with Mystify as Bliss and Crave went to check in. Generic music played in the background, and we had nothing to do but watch the tourists dragging their bags up the escalator or crossing through the lobby with cameras slung over their necks. Mystify was watching them with the same bemused smile as me—they all seemed overwhelmed in some way or another. The city did that to you. I remembered when I first arrived, how amazed I was; even a walk to the bodega on the corner showed me things I'd never seen before.

Next to me Mystify murmured, "This city was made for me."

"More than enough confusion to go around," I agreed.

He gave me a look. "I like the intensity of it. Too much of everything makes life interesting."

In spite of his blunt come-on earlier, I liked Mystify.

"Would you like to come back to the bar?" I impulsively asked.

"I showed you mine, now you show me yours?" he laughed.

"I'm not asking you to go to bed with me, Mystify." I tried, but I couldn't be mad. He was so unabashed in his pursuit. "I'd like you to meet Shock. She should be getting off work soon."

"What about Ram?"

"What do you mean?"

"Is he going to be there?"

"I invited him to come to the bar yesterday, but he didn't."

"He'll be there. He won't be able to let you alone for long. I'm surprised he hasn't popped up already."

I did my best not to look around me to see if we were being watched. "You make it sound inevitable."

"I hate to see you swallowed up by him. He subsumes everyone he comes in contact with."

"But I thought he was isolated. He's stayed away from other demons for so long."

"He has relationships with humans. You don't think he's lived completely alone all these years? He'd be more insane than he already is." Mystify rolled his eyes. "Ram has a girlfriend who lives in Williamsburg, not far from the Prophet's Center, in fact. And there's another girl who he's been seeing even longer, Sasha. She calls him whenever she wants sex. She's really good at playing his game, but secretly she's hoping he'll fall in love with her. It's been going on for so long that she'll never look at another man."

"Oh." Why did that hurt so much? It's exactly what I thought of his Theo Ram persona: a philanderer who played with women but never settled down. I had gone into this with my eyes open, thinking it would be a one-night stand—a moment I could seize in the darkness. Then let go.

Now I didn't know what I wanted from Ram. Except I wanted to hear everything Mystify could tell me. "So he has an apartment? A life beyond all the demon-slaying?"

"He's got several apartments and he lives lots of different lives, depending on his needs at the moment. That's what you don't get, Allay. He's used to doing whatever he wants, taking whatever he wants. He has enough wealth that he could buy Wells Fargo tomorrow, if he wanted to. There's no stopping a guy with that kind of power. He'll tuck you into a corner of his life, like he does with everyone and everything he acquires, and what you want won't matter anymore."

Mystify reached out to rub my arm, taking some of the confusion that flooded me at his words. His lips parted and his eyes half closed in satisfaction.

I moved away. "How can I trust anything you say when you're trying to baffle me so you can feed?"

He licked his lips. "That's just a side benefit of telling you the truth. I can't help being drawn to how you're feeling. You don't want to believe that he's no good."

No, I didn't. Even though I knew it was true. What kind of a man—or demon—would spend two thousand years culling his own offspring's offspring? True, he was doing it to rid the world of bad demons. But still . . .

Crave and Bliss returned; his expression was thunderous. "My credit cards have been declined. And my phone no longer works."

"It's Glory," Bliss said artlessly. "She's cut him off."

"Glory pays your phone bill?" I asked in surprise.

Crave swore under his breath. "I let her people set up my corporation, my finances, everything. I never thought she would do something like this."

"That was pretty dumb," Mystify said.

I shushed him. "Don't tell me that everything is in her name."

"Everything. Including my house. And my business."

Mystify gave a derisive laugh. "Even dumber."

Crave rounded on him, grabbing his upraised arm. Sparks flew from their contact, and they staggered back into the railing over the mezzanine with a loud bang. People turned to look from all over the lobby.

I waded in between them, trying to fend them off from each other. Crave hit me before he could pull his punch, and his fist glanced off my shoulder. Mystify disengaged the instant he realized I was between them.

"Stop it, both of you." I rubbed my shoulder as it quickly healed.

Crave was breathing fast. "I have to go to my shop. I have to see how far she's taking this charade of hers."

"What are you waiting for?" Mystify retorted. "Nobody's stopping you."

Bliss went to Crave, molding her body against his, trying to silently comfort him. "We'll all go," I insisted. "It's safer if we stick together." To cut off Mystify's protest, I told him, "Come on, let's get a cab."

Madison Avenue was fairly quiet so early in the morning. But a locksmith's truck was parked at the curb and two men were neatly packing away their gear.

"Hey!" Crave shouted, jumping from the cab as it was still moving.

The cabbie cursed words I didn't understand, but the meaning was clear. I flung a bill over the front seat and we all ran after Crave.

The truck pulled away and made the light at Fifth Avenue. Crave couldn't catch up.

When he returned to his shop, we already knew what we would find. None of his keys worked.

His aura was a dense rainbow of conflicting emotions—pain, fear, humiliation, anger, with a healthy dose of bravado. He had to buck up in front of his girl. Not that she was the judgmental type. She stayed close to him.

"Has Glory ever done this to you before?" I asked.

He shot me a look. "No. I would have taken precautions if I ever thought it was possible."

I winced. "Not good."

Crave couldn't seem to tear himself away, lingering by the door. "My treasures are in there," he said quietly to her. "My best pieces, the finest jewelry I ever created."

There must be millions of dollars worth of gems and equipment in his shop. "You never set up a safe-deposit box? Siphoned off a few diamonds as a safety net?"

"No," he said through clenched teeth.

It boggled my mind. He had trusted Glory utterly. Yet she had cut him off completely, it seemed. Was Lash really worth so much to her?

"Not for nothing, but maybe you should call Glory and apologize," I suggested. "What's a few days with Lash compared to losing everything?"

"Yes," Bliss urged. "Just do it, Crave. It's not worth this."

For a mercy, Mystify didn't have a sarcastic word to say. I think we all were struck by the extent of Glory's retaliation. I was impressed by the fact that she was able to get a locksmith to the shop at this ungodly hour. It happened so fast. Crave had spoken to her barely half an hour ago. The efficiency was chilling.

Mutely, Crave shook his head. I'd never seen him so flattened. Even his usual magnetism, largely helped by his whirlpool signature, was dampened.

"You have to mend this with her, Crave," I insisted. "What else are you going to do? Live underground with the homeless?"

He shuddered, glancing down at his smeared and smelly clothing. We all looked like refugees from a war zone. "I'd rather risk the horde than go down there again."

"Hey, buddy, that's where I live," Mystify shot back, ready for another fight now that Crave's superior attitude was reasserting itself.

"You can come to the bar with us," Bliss told Crave.

No! I shouted internally. But I couldn't say it out loud. "Glory will be furious if I take you in." I glanced at Mystify, remembering what he had said about Ram. These ancient demons lived by manipulating others. "Then again, that could be exactly what she wants me to do."

Crave got it instantly, as did Mystify. Crave started looking more hopeful—if Glory was manipulating us all, then she hadn't truly cut him off. "Let's hope so."

Bliss didn't understand, and she didn't care. "You're coming home with us," she told him, putting her arm through his.

I was glad to hear her call the bar "home." Maybe I was finally striking the right balance with her. From now on, I was going to stay out of her love life. Even if I did think that she and Crave were destined to blow sky-high.

After all, who was I to judge? I had my own doomed relationship to deal with.

9

Ram appeared in his usual guise as I was letting everyone into the bar. He didn't say a word, and I couldn't tell how he was feeling from his aura. He looked like an ordinary human, with the pale swirl of color of people who were calm and comfortable. Ram could hide that he was a demon—hiding his feelings was a snap.

Crave was looking disoriented, as demons typically were when they encountered Ram. He felt and looked human, even though he was demon. I doubted Ram would drop his shields to reveal his driving signature—he didn't like to broadcast his whereabouts.

Inside the shadowed bar, familiar and safe with the metal shutter pulled down over the front windows, we spread out facing each other warily.

Ram went over to Mystify, who backed up slightly. "Get that look off your face," he said quietly.

Mystify instantly reverted to his angelic-faced boy persona, the one he'd been wearing when he saved us from Goad's horde last night.

I kept thinking about what Mystify had told me. Maybe Ram had been with his girlfriend last night, and that was why he hadn't come to the bar. He had said he was watching me "every second," but apparently he wasn't or he wouldn't have lost track of me last night. That was actually good. I didn't need a stalker for a boyfriend.

Ram was still very close to Mystify. In the same conversational tone, he said, "Now it's time for you to be going."

Mystify nodded shortly, keeping his eyes down. He headed to the door.

"Wait! Mystify, you don't have to go." I gave Ram a hard look. "I invited him here."

Ram waited, looking at Mystify, who gave me a slight shrug. "It's okay, Allay. I should leave."

Mystify passed close by me to get to the door. "I'll call you," he mouthed, with his back to Ram so he couldn't see it.

It made me mad. But I couldn't stop Mystify from leaving. "Why did you do that?" I demanded as the door closed behind him.

"He's wearing that guise to try to get to you, Allay. You can't trust him."

"Funny, he said the same thing about you."

Bliss gave Crave a "we're caught in the cross fire" look, and took his hand. "We're going upstairs."

I silently gave her the key, and Ram waited until they went through the door. He had seen the green tendrils weaving their hands together, and shook his head silently. "She moves fast."

I wanted to defend my slutty offspring by saying "Like mother, like daughter." But I was too unsure of him and what he wanted from me to joke about how much I lusted after him.

Yet there was no denying it. I was swept up in his spell just being near him. Maybe it was the power in his every movement, as if he was so sure of himself and his place in the world. Maybe it was the timbre of his voice, reaching deep inside me. Maybe it was his scent, subliminal yet overwhelming my senses, making me breathe faster as I longed to take him into myself.

I wanted to cry, "Yes, fit me into a corner of your life!

I don't care. I can be in a nonmonogamous relationship. I can try, anyway. Anything just so I can be near you...."

Pathetic! I clamped my mouth shut against my shameful desire. I had to get hold of myself. I didn't need Mystify to tell me how dangerous Ram was.

"Where were you?" he asked.

I looked down at myself. My skin was clean thanks to my shifting, but I would probably have to throw away my hoodie and sweatpants; the grime was ground into my knees and elbows from that awful pipe coming out of the condos.

"In the subway. Hiding from Goad's horde." I had promised Mystify I wouldn't tell anyone about the underground tunnels. "You could have been nicer to your offspring. He was there when I really needed him." I didn't add that Ram hadn't been there to help me, but he knew what I was saying. I refused to ask about his girlfriends, but that was all I could think about. "I thought you weren't the jealous type."

His brow rose. "He's manipulating you. I can only imagine what he's told you."

"Can you?" I asked. "Like what?"

"He told you about Sasha. And Meredith—even though they don't mean anything to me. I'm sure he held back on a few things so he can shock you later. He told you that I'm using you like I use everyone. That I put people into pretty boxes and take them out to play with them. That I'll do the same to you."

I blinked a few times. So much for confirmation. "Not quite that eloquently, but yes, that's the gist of it."

Ram stepped closer. "He could have told you that you're different. That I'm honest with you."

"Are you?" I asked, searching his face for the truth, even though I knew he could control every twitch. "Are you really?"

"Since I revealed myself, I haven't lied to you. I'll answer anything truthfully. I swear." He reached out to touch me.

I sighed, feeling his surging energy through his hand. No one else felt like him. No one had such deep reserves to call on.

"You're hungry," he murmured, feeding me his energy. It was so sweet that I couldn't protest anymore. "Let me . . ."

He pulled me close so we were hugging, our bodies pressing against each other. I soaked up his energy through every pore. It was like a rush of drugs to my head, as if I were blasting off into space. We seemed to spin together in silence, the universe stretching away from us as we pulsed in the very center.

He kissed my cheek, loving, cherishing kisses so as to not disturb my feeding. In his arms, I felt like nothing could reach me, nothing could hurt me. I could let go of the struggles of the past week and not worry that I was going to be consumed by a fellow demon. Not worry that I had become one of them through murder.

Guilt, shame, horror disappeared in the swelling rush of delight. We kissed, and I dived in, ready to be swallowed whole.

Before I knew it, he was unzipping my hoodie, pulling it off me with one jerk. My sweats followed, tugging at my flesh as he sundered the fabric. He was stronger than other demons.

When he had me naked, I was suddenly afraid.

I was still overwhelmed by him, wanting him with every part of my being. But I was playing with fire and would get burned. It was too intense, too impossible to continue. I would lie broken and hurt on the ground when he was through with me.

And what does a monster do with his toys when he's through with them?

I wrapped my arms around myself, shivering but not from chill air. The shadows hid more than I realized.

"Allay." He hugged me close again, as naked as I was. His breath blew against my ear as he tucked my face into his neck. "You're everything to me."

His arms encircled my back, holding me tightly as he enveloped me. I held on to his shoulders, fear and desire resonating against each other. It was horrible and wonderful at the same time, as exhilarating as walking along the ledge of a skyscraper. I knew one misstep and I could fall, dashing my brains out. But right now I felt as if I were flying, as if I were invincible. Only Ram could give that to me.

Oh, his lips! The feel of his body . . . the sound of his moan . . .

I couldn't think, couldn't remember who I was, only that this man consumed me. So shocking, too sudden, but true nonetheless. He couldn't be playing a role with me, not when we were stripped this bare, emotions echoing between us, feeling his fear at exposing himself utterly to me.

I want him.

He lifted me off my feet, easily carrying me. As he laid me down on the bench under the back windows, it felt as if I were floating in his arms.

I gave myself to him, beyond my own ability to control myself. As he penetrated me, it was as if I had never felt true desire before, only a pale imitation, a faint longing without fulfillment. I let him drink deep of me, kissing and biting my neck, squirming in his grasp as I cried out for more. He bit his way down the curve of my neck onto my shoulder, pressing his teeth in, as if feeling an unreasoning urge to mark me, to make me his own.

I was impaled on him, as we rocked together, surging ever higher. It felt like he belonged inside me. That with him, it was finally real.

"Yes!" I cried out in pain and ecstasy, twining together like my fear and passion. Where did one stop and the other begin . . . ?

We seemed to meld into one. Joined together at our most tender point, our cores pressed together, we became something new.

He came as deep inside me as he could get, his arms wrapped around me, lifting his face to the heavens as if surrendering himself.

It was perfect. At least I wanted to think it was.

I was snuggled into his arms on the narrow bench, savoring every moment. It was one of those rare times when everything stood still. I didn't want anything else but what I had right now.

Then Ram said, "I have something to tell you, Allay. But I don't want you to be afraid."

My fingers stopped stroking his chest. "What is it?"

He rested his chin on the top of my head so I couldn't see him. "Dread has made another possessed human. He had one of his Fellows absorb Fervor's essence."

"What?!" I wrenched myself out of his arms. "Are you serious?"

"I wish it wasn't true, but Dread intends to go through with his resurrection. He turned Cherie. You remember her from the Fellowship circle we attended?"

Cherie was the former supermodel, aging and emaciated from decades of stringent dieting. I had held her hand during the circle and fed off her fervid faith. "Why didn't you tell me?"

But I knew. I would never have had sex with him if he had blurted it out right away. Mystify was right—Ram manipulated me into doing what he wanted as naturally as he breathed.

I pulled farther away. "Why? Why is Dread doing this? Why would Cherie go along with it?"

"Cherie isn't known for her intelligence. I doubt Dread told her anything. Besides, Dread is no Vex. He's not interested in world domination. He's doing this to get control of Vex's line. By gaining more power and offering to share it with Goad, he gets to keep his enforcers and his power base among the demons."

I felt spun around, but it did make some kind of sense. That was where Ram had been, finding out what was going on inside the Prophet's Center. He could sneak in posing as any of the human employees, hiding his signature from Dread and Zeal. "Why didn't you tell me in the first place?" I demanded.

Ram tried to draw me back closer. "When you said Goad was chasing you, I lost my head. If he had caught you last night instead of Fervor, Dread would have used you to transform Cherie into a demon. I wasn't there to protect you."

I resisted, until he let go. "So Dread is going to pull a resurrection?"

"Yes, in a day or two, I'm sure. Hybrids usually burn out within a few weeks, and Cherie is not likely to take easily to the transition. She's nearly fifty and set in her ways. Once she commits suicide, Dread will be left with nothing to prove his assertion. But that should be enough to destabilize the situation and gain the Fellowship a sizeable following. Goad would be a fool to walk away from that."

"We have to stop him. We can't let Dread con millions of people by staging a religious miracle."

"It's too late, Allay. He's set up ERI machines at the entrances to the Prophet's Center. I can't get back inside without being detected."

I remembered our meeting in the bar. Dread had denied any interest in a resurrection. "Dread was stalling me when he came here. He lied to me. But I didn't see it in his aura. How did he do that?"

"Old demons can hide their emotions better than young ones. Much better," Ram admitted.

I stood up, suddenly not caring that I was naked. My body was another set of clothes to me, something I could change at will. "What else haven't you told me, Ram?"

He looked up at me steadily, reclining on one elbow on the bench. He could have been a sculpture of a Greek god lying on grape leaves. Maybe he had posed like that before.

"I already knew about the ERI machine because I bugged you in the Prophet's Center. I heard Dread's presentation in the media room, and your discussion with Vex. That's why I checked into it and found out that it's based on Kirlian's work. I don't see any way to fool a machine based on that technology. Glory hired a lab that I happen to own to find out how to do it. I told them to stall her for a few weeks, then let her know it's impossible."

My mouth opened. "Why didn't you tell me that *yesterday*?"

He ran his hand through his hair. "I should have, but I don't want you to be afraid of me. Every time I tell you something, you rear back like this and stop trusting me."

"That's because you keep lying to me. You let me tell you about the ERI even though you already knew." I patted my bare hips and thighs. "Do you have me bugged right now? Were you following along 'every second' while I was with Mystify?"

"No! I wouldn't eavesdrop on you now, Allay. That happened before I told you who I really was."

It was falling into place. "So you knew about the ERI all this time. You knew it would expose us. Is that why you revealed yourself to Dread? Is that why you killed Vex?"

He hesitated, and I felt my heart sink.

"I didn't know then whether the ERI used the Kirlian

field," he said. "I did know that I couldn't save you without revealing myself, and that I couldn't let you die. So I did it. But in truth, I suspected we'd soon be exposed one way or another—through Dread's resurrection or the ERI. Something. There's a rhythm to our coexistence with humans, and periodically we're exposed. Sometimes it's on a small scale, like tabloid reports of spontaneous combustion, and other times it becomes legend. During those times, demons are destroyed— buried alive usually. If it goes badly, I can hardly imagine what they'll do to us today with science at hand. We're past time for exposure, and the only question is, what will the repercussions be?"

I stared at him lying there, so cold and detached as if he could stand by and watch demons die by the bucket load. But I could hear Plea's screams echoing in my head, feel her raw throat from days of entombment in the catacombs.

I scrubbed my hand down my neck in sympathetic reflex. "You're going to let it happen."

"It's inevitable."

He had used the same ruthless logic to convince me to kill Pique so I could live. Then he had told me that the only way demons die is by the hand of other demons. But if I had listened to my memories, I would have known that demons also die at the hands of humans. If you isolate a demon so it can't absorb any human energy, it eventually disappeared in a puff of smoke.

I shuddered and crossed my arms around myself. "Genocide is never inevitable."

"There are too many demons. That's the plain fact. Pique would have been the one to expose us all if he had killed you on the sidewalk last week. It's going to happen and there's nothing I can do to stop it."

"You're glad about it. It saves you having to kill them all yourself." It was now or never. "Since you're being so honest, finally, answer me this, Ram. Do you want me because I remind you of Hope?"

He sat up quickly, his control slipping. He instantly took in my expression, looking for signs of what I knew, what Mystify had told me. I lifted my chin, refusing to turn away. I had the right to know.

As he stood up, his aura was stained with violet sadness. He couldn't hide his reaction to the mention of her name. "Your energy does feel a lot like hers . . . and your signature, as well. And there are similarities in your strength and clarity of purpose . . . but I never knew Hope as a young woman. She was at the height of her power at the time I was born. In many ways, she controlled everything between us, playing me for a fool."

"Playing me must be a nice way of remaking the past."

"I'm with you because of who you are, Allay. I love watching you blossom into your full potential. You're different from Hope, very different. You don't use people, for one thing. And I hope you never become jaded enough to start."

I wanted to believe it, but . . . "Tell me the truth. Do you think about Hope when you're with me?"

Slowly he admitted, "In the beginning, yes. I couldn't help it—you feel so similar. But now it's you, Allay. Only you."

Every instinctive alarm inside me went off. I knew it from the moment I'd found out about Hope, but I'd tried to ignore it. I was just a rerun, a faded echo of the original. I was an innocent toy he could use to work through his issues.

"Thank you for being so honest," I managed to get out.

His voice lowered. "I've upset you. I'm sorry, Allay. I don't want to lie to you. Ever."

I backed away from his outstretched hand. I wanted

to let him hold me so badly that it made me ache. But he was manipulating me, using me. My feelings were so conflicted that I couldn't stand it.

I turned away. "I think you should go, Ram."

"I understand."

That made me even more angry. "Sure, you understand! Stand there and be all understanding and superior, while I'm nothing but confused. Mystify should be here. He would love this."

"Mystify," Ram muttered savagely.

"Don't! Don't you dare do anything to him. He's my friend."

"Allay, you can't trust him—"

"Why? Because he's a template of you?"

"Mystify isn't me. If he feels anything for you, it's because he remembers *my* feelings."

I grabbed my clothes and marched over to the door, opening it. "You can let yourself out, Ram."

I didn't wait to hear what he said, running lightly up the stairs. Bliss had thoughtfully left the key in the door so I could get inside. I let the bolt snick shut behind me. Downstairs I could hear the bolt on the front door do the same as Ram let himself out.

I willed myself to let him go. I couldn't think when I was around him, and right now I needed to think.

It was my worst nightmare. Unless I did something fast, there was a resurrection coming.

10

Bliss and Crave were going at it in the back room, moaning and panting. They were probably on the very same chaise where I had seduced Ram that first night. Or rather, was manipulated into seducing him while feeling guilty for taking advantage of a poor human.

Ha! I was the poor sucker being taken advantage of.

I hopped into the shower and blasted the hot water. I was clean enough from shifting off the dirt and grime, but there was nothing like the psychological reassurance of water to make me feel better after our underground trek.

I thought better in the shower; maybe it was the steam, or the lack of things to look at. I was hoping for a brilliant idea on how to thwart Dread. But all I could think about was Ram. I didn't want to, but my body resonated with the memory of the way he touched me, his slight shiver when I stroked him, the way he looked at me with love in his eyes—

Bliss banged on the door at the same time I felt it. "Allay! Crave says Glory's coming."

"Now, why didn't I think of that?" I muttered. Maybe because Ram had turned my brains to mush.

"And Lash," Bliss added more doubtfully.

"I'm coming," I called back.

I threw on black leggings and a tank top, and slicked back my wet hair. By the time we got downstairs, Glory and Lash were at the front door waiting. Bliss opened up the bar and turned on the lights as I let them in.

Glory's guise was a short, middle-aged, possibly Dominican woman, with chaffed, capable hands and a retiring demeanor. *She's appearing to be harmless. Is that for my benefit?*

Or was someone else here the target? I glanced at Crave, who refused to look at either woman, while Lash drifted across the room closer to him as if she couldn't help herself.

Crave took a stool at the bar, half turned away as if he wasn't interested in speaking to them. Bliss unfortunately looked as if she was about to laugh. And for the first time I noticed she was wearing a pair of wildly colored boxer shorts rolled up at the bottom and an undershirt that barely reached her exposed belly button. Crave's shirt was untucked and unbuttoned, still smeared and stained from the underground.

Lash was hungrily staring at him, practically quivering in anticipation. She looked even more beautiful than Bliss—honey blond, with high cheekbones and luscious lips the same color as her red suit. The skirt was tight and split up the back, and the jacket was décolleté and snug-waisted. But her lack of confidence, her naked need for him, destroyed the effect of sexy glamour she was trying for.

"It's time to settle this," Glory said softly, pulling all of our eyes back to the least likely looking person in the room. "Crave, are you going to obey me?"

Crave slowly turned in his barstool, then got to his feet facing her. "I've been loyal to you for almost two hundred years, Glory, even over my own progenitor. Never once did you have to doubt me. Yet over this one personal choice, you've cast me out and stolen everything I worked for. I don't care what 'higher purposes' you intended for this. I'll never forgive you."

"No!" Lash blurted out. "Crave, you don't mean it—"

"I mean it." He turned to her. "We're over, Lash. I never should have let you move in. I did it only because Glory ordered me to."

"But . . . Crave, I know that isn't true." Lash hesitated, breathless. "I know what you feel for me."

"I gave you what you wanted, not what I wanted. Now I know what I want, and it isn't you." He reached out and took Bliss's hand, giving it a kiss. "I want joy in my life, not pain."

"Oh, please," I groaned. I wanted to smack him. "Spare us the theatrics, Crave."

Crave led Bliss over to the door as we all turned to watch them. "I'm sorry I couldn't give you what you wanted, Lash. Good-bye."

Lash took a few steps toward the door as it closed behind them. Her hands were out as if to draw him back to her. Then she clutched them to her chest. "I don't understand," she murmured to herself.

I had stood in that very same spot and said the same thing a few minutes ago. "I'm with you, sister."

Lash narrowed her eyes at me. "What do you know?"

I held up my hands. "Nothing. Nothing about this."

Glory smiled, showing a missing tooth on the upper side. "Did Ram tell you about the new hybrid in town, Allay?"

"Yes," I admitted. Should I have said that first? "He just left."

"Did he tell you anything else I need to know?" At the shake of my head, she added, "I was informed of the birth an hour ago. The new demon's name is Elude."

Elude—that meant to flee, withdraw, secret away. Poor Fervor. She must have wanted to disappear when faced with Dread, Zeal, and Cherie the supermodel. Even then she couldn't have known that Dread didn't intend to kill her himself as he drained her of nearly all of her energy, exposing her core for Cherie to take. To create a new possessed human.

"Dread's going to use Cherie to stage a resurrection for his church," I said. "Unless we can stop him."

Glory nodded to her offspring. "I think that's up to Lash. Don't you? Lash?" she called gently.

Lash had her back to us, staring out the windows into the narrow courtyard. Glory had to say her name again to get her attention. "Lash?"

"Yes?" Her eyes were dull.

"You have to go to Dread and convince him to stop this stupid power play."

"I can't do that." Lash blinked. "He'll kill me!"

"He won't kill you. He wants you too badly to see you dead."

"I couldn't, Glory. You don't understand . . . not after Crave . . ."

"You'll do it." Glory didn't seem to care that I was standing between them, awkwardly watching everything. "You're my eyes and ears, and I need you there. I can't have you stop now, not for wounded vanity or pride. You go back to your husband and you continue to age gracefully in the public eye while you support him. And you will convince him to cancel this scheme of his. Do you understand?"

Lash had both hands to her mouth. "Oh, Glory! No! I can't do it. I'll die before I go back to that . . . existence."

Glory's pleasant smile never faltered. "You'll exist on the street if you don't do as I say, Lash. Or you can join Crave in exile. If he'll have you."

Her head cocked at the ceiling. The muffled rhythmic thumping was unmistakable—Bliss and Crave were having sex again. Glory gave a slight shrug. "Maybe there's another room so you won't have to actually watch your lover fuck his new girl."

Lash was in such shock she didn't even consider

about how she looked with her mouth hanging open. "You can't mean it, Glory."

"This is your only chance at redemption," Glory said, still smiling. "Good-bye, Allay. It's been nice seeing you again."

"You're leaving?" I asked. "What about Lash?"

"Brooklyn's right over the bridge. I'm sure she can make it there." Glory didn't even glance at Lash, but she gave me a slight wave of her fingertips.

I couldn't believe she was leaving Lash here. Neither could Lash. But Glory swept out and jumped in the waiting town car. Anyone watching would wonder why the maid was leaving the lady behind in a dingy bar.

I'd been played again.

Lash and I looked at each other as the thumping overhead increasing in tempo. It was too cruel. How could they, knowing Lash was down here?

Lash put her hands to her ears. "I can't stand it!"

I didn't know what to say. I didn't exactly feel sorry for her, seeing as she had brought it on herself. And then refused to acknowledge reality.

Lash let out a growl that rose to a roar. She grabbed the table next to her and flung it away with all her might, then the next one, smashing it against the wall. I ducked the flying debris as she picked up a chair and threw it at the pool table.

I leaped forward to grab her before she destroyed my bar. "Stop it, Lash!"

She was screaming and crying Crave's name over and over again, raging at Glory for causing her ruin. I had to exert all my strength to keep hold of her, as she flung herself against the furniture, bloodying herself. Every time I thought she was subsiding, she would start up again.

I would have lost all of my tables if Shock hadn't arrived home from work. Once Lash was stretched between two demons, she soon stopped her hysterics and promised to behave. We left her curled up in a corner sobbing quietly.

"Why are they both here?" Shock asked, looking around at the mess Lash had made.

"Crave's upstairs with Bliss." I listened but there were no sounds of lovemaking. That was when I realized Lash had pitched a fit to draw Crave downstairs. They must have heard the noise, but they had stayed locked in my apartment.

"So much for Bliss backing you up," Shock said.

I was so relieved to see her familiar face that I didn't care how bitchy she was. "I'm glad you're home, Shock. It must have been a good shift."

She was glowing with energy. "The best. But I heard Fervor was taken by Goad's horde."

I quickly filled her in on Dread's renewed resurrection plans. She wasn't as shocked by Dread's deception as I was. "I figured that was all a show to try to get you on his good side," she said. "You can't trust Dread. Vex kept his word, but Dread lied whenever it suited Vex's purposes. That's who he is."

I glanced at the quiescent Lash, her forehead pressed against her knees, exhausted from her screaming rampage. "Glory wants Lash to stop him."

Shock rolled her eyes. "Do you have any other ideas?"

"We can't rely on Ram," I said.

"I'm glad you finally realize that," Shock said.

There was silence for a while, with Shock whistling tunelessly as she thought.

Finally Lash raised her head from where she crouched. Her voice was roughened from her screaming. "Just tell me one thing. Why her? Why Bliss? Why doesn't he love me?"

I glanced at Shock, but she didn't have a clue. Would the truth help? If someone could tell me the truth about

Ram, I would snatch at it, damn the consequences. "Bliss is different because she doesn't want anything from him, not like other women. He doesn't have to conform to her idea of the perfect lover. He craves *her*, instead of her craving him."

I braced myself for another outburst, as Lash took a deep breath. Then she sighed. "I'm screwed."

"What was that?" I asked, thinking I must not have heard right. Was the uptight, superior Lash really swearing?

"I have to do it." Lash banged her head for emphasis against the wall. "If I don't go back to Dread, I'll be out on the street with no money, no place to go. Just like Crave."

"What about Crave?" Shock asked sharply.

"He lives here now," Lash said tonelessly. "With Bliss."

Shock glared at me. "None of you lives here. Allay lives here. Not Bliss, not Crave, and definitely not *you*. You might as well go back to Dread, because once he hears Glory has cast you out, he'll send Goad to get you."

I didn't want Shock speaking for me, but I couldn't protest. I didn't want Lash around, especially not after she had busted up my place. I didn't want Crave here, either. I wasn't even sure it was a good idea for Bliss to live with me. It was turning out that Shock was right about a lot of things.

Shock held out her cell phone to Lash. "Call him."

She slowly pushed herself up. "No, I have to see him. He needs to feel my fear, sense my crawling skin."

I winced at the ugly image.

"I'll call a car to take you to the Prophet's Center." Shock started to dial.

Lash nodded, a new determination in her eyes. She pulled herself to her feet, brushing off her expensive suit. Both her shoes were off and her hair was messed up. But with a few quick adjustments, she was back to her usual pristine self.

I felt bad, like we were throwing her off the back of our troika to placate the wolves. If Lash was a nicer person, maybe I would have mustered up more of an effort to help her, despite the fact that she was our last, best hope to stop Dread.

Lash put on her stilettos and paced up and down the bar, deep in thought. She could be headed straight for Dread's iron cage, to be tortured at his whim. He might even kill her like he had threatened to.

"Are you sure you want to go back?" I finally asked.

Lash frowned as if I was interrupting her. "You know I have no choice. I won't throw everything away. I'm not like Crave." She sniffed delicately. "You can't expect me to live like you do."

Shock came over to me. "Don't bother. Her kind won't speak to the likes of us unless they want something."

"*My kind* are the ones who run things," Lash said.

"What if you can't get Dread to stop the resurrection?" I asked.

She was silent for a moment. "I suspect Glory would prefer that I kill him."

I shivered; she was so ruthless I could believe she would do it. "Are you sure?"

The look she gave me left no doubt she thought I was clueless.

A car honked from outside. "That's your car," Shock said.

I let Lash out. I wondered if it was the last time I would ever see her. Typical of Lash, she didn't bother to apologize or thank me or anything.

As she was getting into the sleek black town car, I heard my name called, "Allay!"

I was so wrapped up in demon-business that it took

a second for me to realize it was Phil Anchor. He was across the street waving at me. He was disheveled as always, though trying to look dashing and sexy and failing miserably.

Lash pulled away in the town car. I caught a glimpse of her profile, determined and unafraid. I hoped she could pull off a miracle.

Phil ran across the street and puffed up to me. "I've been looking for you, Allay. Why did you close the bar?" His hand clasped around my arm as he eyed Shock in the foyer. "We need to talk. Now."

I wrested my arm away from him. "Not now, Phil."

Phil was breathing alcohol fumes in my face. "You threatened me, Allay. I'm not going to let you ruin me."

I wanted to scream in frustration. "Stop being crazy, Phil! You do too many drugs and you take it out on me. Go talk to a therapist—you need help."

Phil wouldn't stop coming, so I had to use his leverage points to unbalance him. He rolled down onto the sidewalk. "Sorry, Phil. But you have to stay away from me."

I pulled back into the bar. Shock closed the door in Phil's face. "Nice clientele, Allay."

"Actually he's a friend of Dread's. One of the pettiest of petty criminals I used to hand off money to."

Shock snorted.

Instead of turning into the bar after Shock, I ran up the steps to the apartment. The door was unlocked. So much for my security.

Now Bliss and Crave were in the front room, curled up together on the couch, playing hand games as they talked quietly.

"Thanks for freaking out Lash," I said pointedly.

Crave waved one hand. "She gets off on it."

"I don't think so. You could have come down to help me."

"I thought it would be worse if we came down," Bliss said offhandedly. "I knew you could deal with it."

"Shock helped." I waited, but Bliss had no remorse for leaving me to deal with their mess. "Lash has gone back to Dread to try to stop the resurrection. She didn't want to, but Glory threatened to cut her off, too."

"So that's what Glory wanted." Crave sat up straighter as he realized it. "She took everything from me in order to convince Lash she would do the same thing to her unless she went back to Dread."

"Does that mean she'll give you your shop back now?" Bliss asked.

He tightened his arms around her. "I don't want it back. I'll open a new place. I'll do it on my own this time. Nobody's ever controlling me again."

"Amen!" I agreed wholeheartedly.

Bliss also agreed, though she and Crave were making googly eyes at each other again. I wanted to suggest they go out and get jobs so they could get their own apartment, but clearly they were too enthralled with each other to do anything else right now.

And to think I had been so worried about Bliss yesterday that I panicked when I lost her on the street. From toddler to teenager had been an awfully quick trip.

11

Bliss tried to cajole me into opening up the bar again, but Shock was so angry that I'd gone out the night before without telling her that I decided to placate her by staying closed. I couldn't tell her about the underground tunnels, because we had all promised, but I told her about Mystify and how he had helped us. It seemed to make her only more upset to know how close I'd come to being snatched by Goad's horde.

It was so distracting that I could hardly think of a way to stop Dread. I wanted to charge out and do something, anything, but nothing seemed feasible. Shock shot down every suggestion I came up with.

Would Lash succeed in stopping him? It hardly seemed possible. I was hopeful—that would be the fitting end to Dread to have his long-suffering wife deal the final blow. But Shock scoffed at the idea. "Maybe we shouldn't have let her go off alone. We could have used her to bargain with Dread."

"She's not a piece of meat," I said.

"Close enough."

Crave and Bliss were no help at all. Crave would take a sudden interest, giving me all sorts of inside information about Dread that he had pulled out of Lash, like the fact that he consumed a steady supply of girls bought on the international sex-slave market.

For the first time, I wished I had killed Dread when I'd had the chance.

I kept waiting for the phone to ring—surely Glory would hear from Lash and would let us know, but the minutes ticked by. Bliss and Crave went out together around dinnertime to feed. They had been living on a steady diet of each other since last night. I felt no worry as Bliss gave me a cheery wave good-bye. She was safe with Crave, probably safer than with me.

When they came back hours later, I saw Crave counting some cash. "Where did you get that?" I asked him.

"I've called in some favors." He gave me a bland smile. "I'll be out of your hair soon, I promise, Allay. Maybe as soon as tomorrow."

His feelings were too conflicted for that to be the whole truth. "Did you take it from some poor woman, Crave?"

His eyes narrowed. "Actually, Bliss took it from some rich old man."

I could just see it—she seduced some guy and got him to buy her something. Maybe he paid her for sex. "So now you're her pimp? You're going from living off Glory to living off Bliss."

"Don't you worry. I'll contribute my fair share. Cultivating women takes longer but pays off better in the long run."

"I can see that, since you're the one holding the cash."

Crave laughed and flung himself down on the chaise. I waited until Bliss came out of the bathroom, where she had been washing up. "Bliss, why is Crave holding on to the money that you made?"

"He helped. He introduced me to the guy and made all of the arrangements. I wouldn't have known what to say. All I had to do was go down on him, and he handed over a hundred bucks." She licked her lips in pure pleasure. "I was afraid it wouldn't be as good as with Crave, but that ultimate pleasure is . . . hmm . . . It's sublime. He was satisfied. I was satisfied. I can't wait to do it again."

Crave was frowning, staring straight past both of us. It was the first chink in their mutual-admiration club that I'd seen.

"Bliss, I don't care if you're a sex worker, as long as you're honest about it. But you can't give your money to Crave. Cut him in, if you want, but you have to take care of yourself. Look what happened to Crave—he depended on Glory and now he's paying the price for it."

"Money is everywhere. Easy to get." Her sunny smile couldn't be daunted. "I could go get more right now if I wanted to. Why not give it to Crave?"

"Because if you wanted to go somewhere right now, you'd have to get money from me or Crave."

Bliss giggled. "Oh, I don't think that would be a problem."

I sighed, shaking my head.

From the front room, Shock called, "Allay! Get in here now!"

The local evening news was on the television: " . . . and this just in. In Williamsburg, Brooklyn, a local preacher is reported to have decapitated a woman during a religious rite." The anchorwoman on NY1 was earnest, emphasizing every third word as if she couldn't believe it herself. "We have shots of the scene outside the Prophet's Arena."

A slightly tilted frame righted itself, looking down Kent Avenue. People were packed between the industrial warehouses, running in both directions in and around the cars that were stopped dead. The sound of incessant honking and sirens in the distance made the reporter on the scene press his earpiece to his ear and shout to be heard over the din.

"It's pandemonium here, Rebecca, as you can see behind me. Less than an hour ago, the Fellowship held a special circle here in the Prophet's Arena. Insiders claim that nearly three thousand people showed up for what they thought was a special healing service that would be performed by Prophet Anderson himself. Instead, they saw this. A special warning, this footage is very graphic. You might want to send the children away if they're watching."

"He did it," I finally managed to get out. "He really did it."

The screen went to a close-up of Cherie's peaceful face. Her remarkable beauty was back. No baggy, craggy skin and bulging veins. No knobby bones poking through paper-thin flesh, no rigid skeletal mask. Her skin was as bright and clear as the day she stepped onto her first New York catwalk at sixteen. Her proud, high-bridged nose was once again the epitome of elegance and sophistication. That exquisite jawline, and wide-open turquoise eyes ... even her hair was a luxurious mane of cinnamon red that only a true redhead could pull off.

The voice-over of the reporter narrated the shots. He sounded breathless, overexcited, like a junior reporter who knows he's in on the scoop of the century: "A limited number of the media were invited to the City Arena, more popularly known as the 'Prophet's Arena,' on barely an hour's notice. We were told that Cherie— one of the first supermodels who rose to prominence in the 1980s and more recently a celebrity spokesperson for the Fellowship of Truth—would be featured in a special church circle."

The camera angle pulled back to show at least a dozen people forming a circle on the stage in the middle of the arena. They were dressed all in white, and were surrounded by thousands of Followers who stood holding hands on the tiered arena seating around them.

Dread wore his white preacher's robes, holding up

the distinctive Fellowship cross with its flared arms. The glad-handing televangelist had replaced the beady-eyed persona that had sat here in my bar and promised to never, ever pull a demon resurrection. *Cross my heart.*

His profile was serene as he stepped forward to stand next to the altar where Cherie lay flat on her back, her hands clasped on her breast. Dread stroked Cherie's forehead, murmuring something to her.

Then he stepped back and raised the cross like an axe.

There was a gasp, but the circle didn't break. With a two-handed grip, Dread slashed the flared arm of the cross down across Cherie's neck.

Her head was severed off in one blow, as the axe clanked against the marble, taking out a big chip of the altar. Her hair flew into the air as her head bounced off the altar and fell onto the stage, rolling out a red river of blood. It was awful, more real than any movie. More blood was spurting from her neck stem as her body convulsed, flopping her arm down the side of the altar.

I gulped back my stomach. That could have been me. If Ram hadn't killed Vex . . .

Crave was leaning forward in interest. "The guy has balls. I'll give him that."

The roar inside the arena almost drowned out the commentary. Even the anchorwoman protested in horror. The camera kept shaking as the commentary continued. "As we warned you, this footage is graphic, but we have to show it without any cuts, Rebecca, so you can see for yourself that the film hasn't been doctored or changed in any way."

The circle on the stage was wavering and threatening to break with some of the fellows trying to get to the altar while others restrained them. A phalanx of black-garbed security ran out from all four arches and took up a stance to keep people from rushing the stage.

The prophet was kneeling next to the altar, his head

bowed over the cross, which he now held upside down. The dripping red blade stained the stage in a puddle around his knee.

"Behold the resurrection!" Dread announced, lifting his head dramatically.

The booming of his voice filled the arena. Everyone cringed and put their hands over their ears. Even through the television it was too loud. I wasn't sure if it was done mechanically or if Dread had altered his throat to achieve the effect.

"Cherie is not dead," Dread proclaimed. "Cherie has been touched by God! She has been transformed into spirit! She has gained everlasting immortality through the perfection of her being."

The camera came in close on Cherie's severed neck. The blood had splattered across her breast, making vivid red tracks on the white chiffon. The Fellowship's philosophy was that anyone could achieve immortality by completely accepting themselves; it was known as perfecting the self to dig deep into the psyche and embrace one's internal motivations.

"Behold, her resurrection!" Dread intoned.

Almost imperceptibly Cherie's neck lengthened. The bloody end blurred and stopped dripping. As the shadow of her jaw and chin appeared, shocked cries began echoing through the onlookers.

The camera angle included Dread beyond the altar, and Cherie's severed head lying at the base. Her head was wavering, growing insubstantial with every passing second. As it faded away, her head reappeared on her body. It looked ghostly at first, then settled into solid flesh as Dread watched her with a burning, reverent gaze.

Cherie opened her eyes. The screams hit an even higher pitch. Now people were fighting to get out, while others collapsed on floor, wailing for God to save them.

The circle had finally broken, and half the leadership was on their knees, while others were wrestling with the guards to get off the stage.

The noise level rose again almost as loud as when Dread had chopped off her head.

Cherie sat up, smiling in triumph. Dread held out his hand to help her stand up. She lifted her skirts to avoid the puddle of blood, stepping daintily to the rear of the altar.

Dread lifted her hand and gestured to her. She looked warily up at everyone watching, vulnerable in a way I had never seen before. "I give you Cherie! Immortal perfection through unwavering truth!"

His words boomed around the arena. The place looked as if it were boiling; everyone was moving at once. It was chaos. Only Dread and Cherie in the center were calm, smiling at the cameras, turning and posing for the frantic press. Some had crawled up on the stage and were aiming their cameras from nearly at their feet.

Dread had timed it perfectly to make the evening news.

"Well, that changes everything," I said flatly.

"Now people know about us," Bliss agreed.

"They think it was a religious thing," Crave said. "It has nothing to do with demons."

I wasn't sure about that. "Ram says we've been discovered periodically throughout history. But it's always distorted, never the real truth."

On the TV, the reporter was trying to maintain his professionalism, but he practically babbled as Cherie's smug, aristocratic face covered the screen. She seemed very satisfied with herself, preening as if she were at a modeling shoot showing off her angles.

"People won't believe it," Shock declared. "They'll think it's a hoax. Like sawing a girl in half or making an elephant disappear."

"Maybe," I said doubtfully.

The crawl at the bottom of the screen read MIRACLE IN BROOKLYN? More shots were shown panning the circle and the crowd right after Dread cut off Cherie's head. It paused on a close-up of Lash's face—Prophet Anderson's dignified, aging wife, returned to stand faithfully by his side in his finest hour.

Crave laughed out loud. "I wish I could see Glory now! I bet Lash turned on her the moment Dread crooked his little finger. He sure got one over on her this time."

"There are bigger things at stake here," I told him.

Shock shrugged. "Like I said, we should have tied her up and bargained with Dread directly. We would have stood a chance that way."

I was wringing my hands. "This is awful."

"What's the big deal?" Crave asked, putting his arm around Bliss's shoulders. "Cherie will burn out in a couple of weeks, and this will all blow over."

The anchorwoman deftly took back the broadcast. "Cherie is being taken to NYU Medical Center now for tests. We'll report to you live from that location." Then she segued into talking heads. They were scornful in their disbelief, talking down the Fellowship of Truth as a "religious self-help" movement with some political influence and a socially progressive agenda.

The worst had happened. "It's a terrible con on humanity, a monumental lie," I told them all. "No good can come from this."

It didn't take long for the disruption on the streets of Williamsburg to turn into a full-scale riot as even more crowds poured into Brooklyn. Helicopters hovered overhead taking shots of the Williamsburg Bridge jammed with people and cars as police on horseback tried to forge a path for emergency vehicles. There were reports of heart attacks inside the Prophet's Arena among those who had watched Cherie's resurrection, and more people were hurt in the crush outside.

The church was accepting a "small donation" to allow the faithful to pass by the stage to see the bloody altar for themselves. The news channels continued to show the streets around the Prophet's Arena, marked by flashing police lights, while traffic was at a standstill.

I started to hear shouts outside as cars backed up and snarled in my own neighborhood. The riot lapped up from Delancey Street, where the bridge was completely blocked, and started rippling through Manhattan.

I leaned out my front windows. There was a feeling of anything-goes in the air, as the street noise grew louder. People were running, everyone desperate to get somewhere else.

I called Glory, but all I got was a busy signal. The circuits were overloaded. I really wanted to hear what she had to say about all this.

Then Shock was called in to work during the emergency. As soon as she saw the number on her beeper, she got that eager, glazed expression. She wanted to feed off the misery this tragedy was causing. Ugly, but true.

She took only a few moments to insist that I stay locked up in my apartment. I had to promise not to open the bar. Then she was gone to feed her inner beast.

Crave and Bliss, with her hair flying wild, left soon afterward, diving into the seething humanity on the streets.

Neither of them bothered to ask if I would be all right alone. It didn't occur to them. Maybe they knew I wasn't demon enough to enjoy the thought of mixing it up in the middle of mayhem.

After they left, I wandered aimlessly around my apartment. I had to admit that some tension had eased. There was a certain relief in finally having the worst happen. I'd been fighting it from the moment I saw Zeal's slick infomercial. Now I no longer had to dread it.

The only thing I could do was deal with it. I had to see Cherie for myself.

Frantic honking filled the air. The "miracle in Brooklyn" had clashed with the evening rush hour, making for maximum disruption. People were dashing across the street, edging between the cars, with everyone in a hurry to get somewhere else. I took one look and knew that my only option was to go by foot. NYU Medical Center was thirty blocks north.

After a few blocks of being jostled and bumped by people racing past me, I wished I had a way to contact Mystify. There was probably a tunnel right underneath me that I could use, if I only knew how to find the entrance.

But it was lucky that I was on the street because I passed by a medical supply store, and was inspired to buy a set of scrubs for camouflage so I could sneak into the hospital to find Cherie. I pulled them on over my leggings and tank top right outside the store as I looked around for Ram.

Was he following me?

Thousands of people had the same idea as I did to see Cherie, and they were milling about, blocking the streets around NYU Medical Center, as cops tried to clear lanes for emergency vehicles. I looked longingly after a familiar white and red truck with the yellow strip down the middle, wondering if Shock was inside. She could have gotten me into the medical complex in a snap. But she would be angry to know that I had left the bar.

The cops saw me in my scrubs and made way for me, gesturing which way to go to enter the hospital. I was afraid I would be stopped at the door without any ID, but in the mass confusion my scrubs got me close to the building. I was routed toward the Ambulatory Care Pavilion along with people holding bloodied cloths to their heads or trying to soothe screaming children.

I slipped past the pavilion and entered the main lobby of Bellevue, a soaring pavilion of glass pasted onto the front of the old brick mausoleum that housed the hospital. The place was rocking from the influx of injuries, and with nearly two thousand physicians and interns on staff, nobody looked twice at me. I made sure to ride others' coattails, getting through ID-locked doors on their heels. There was so much rushing around that nobody noticed.

But I kept one eye trained behind me, always looking for who was following me. I half expected to see Ram on my heels any moment. I ignored the faces and concentrated on the clothes and shoes. I didn't see any repeat themselves, and I knew that I had lost him. If he had been following me in the first place.

It took some searching around, but I listened in on nurses and orderlies gossiping about Cherie. I followed up a dead lead that said Cherie was here in Bellevue's trauma center, but I couldn't find her. Surely wherever Cherie was, Dread would be. So I kept my senses open, casting around for Dread.

I finally sensed him in the NYU Cardiac and Vascular Institute in the building on the next block. Zeal's signature was with Dread. Closer to me, in a different part of the hospital, was Cherie. Her signature was a receding sensation as if I were being pulled backward, very disconcerting. *Elude,* to avoid . . .

I could only hope that my mild buoyant sensation would be lost in the push-pull competition between Zeal's and Cherie's.

I zeroed in on Cherie until I knew she was on the other side of the wall, but I was blocked from the lower entrance. Up a flight of stairs, I found the mezzanine of a training operating room with tiered seating where over a hundred people could observe. It was packed to capacity, with the hallways outside crowded with doctors and nurses, many on their cell phones despite the rules against their use.

I elbowed my way inside.

"What are they doing?" I asked the guy who I had squashed into the fellow next to him.

He rattled off a series of words that had no meaning to me, but I did catch "incisions." Standing on my toes, I could glimpse the masked, gloved surgeon down below making a series of deep cuts down Cherie's bare back. Blood was flowing, being soaked up by nurses with forceps stuffed with cotton. As they scrubbed Cherie's back clean, the flesh pulled together by itself, leaving a red and then pink line where her skin had healed. Then it faded and disappeared: from gaping wound to smooth skin in less than a minute.

I was more fascinated by the watchers. After all, I had seen this unbelievable sight on my own body, albeit using the coarser steak knife approach. Everywhere I looked there was openmouthed shock, disbelief, revulsion, and horror. Even worse were the ones who leaned forward instead of back, whose cold eyes were already assessing the possibilities. Those were the ones who wanted to strap Cherie to that table and experiment on her for the rest of their lives.

I shuddered. Didn't she know the danger she was in?

But she only spoke to the doctors working over her, and I realized that we were behind mirrored glass. She didn't know everyone was watching.

I staggered into the poor guy next to me, feeling off-balanced. It wasn't due to Cherie; it was Dread, coming closer with Zeal. Probably to claim Cherie as his prized property. Apparently if you were a religious prophet, you could get away with beheading a supermodel on TV.

There was a sudden hush as Cherie sat up, holding the sheet to her breast. The surgeon stood back, still masked and mute, shaking his head in amazement.

Her voice rang with conviction. "It's a miracle. You won't find a scientific explanation for this. Miracles defy belief. They defy conventional wisdom. By its very definition, a miracle can't be rationalized."

Some of the observers around me were actually nodding.

"I am one with God now," Cherie told the doctors. "I have perfected myself through absolute truth, making myself a pure vessel of immortality. God communes with me, through me, to enlighten everyone and bring about a new world order, one based on peace and harmony through self-knowledge . . ."

She continued to spout the Fellowship creed mixed in with memories she had acquired from Fervor, an intense young Glory demon who was drawn to religious extremists, much like Zeal. Having seen some of Plea's memories, I could only imagine what Cherie was remembering—snake handling and talking in tongues must be the least of the bizarre rituals Fervor had indulged in.

Those memories must dovetail perfectly with Cherie's fanaticism. As she stood up and slipped on her robe, thanking the surgeon for his work, she seemed remarkably composed. I had gone from babbling on the streets to landing in a psych ward right after I was turned.

Cherie is stable.

There were all sorts of reasons Cherie could and, by rights, should burn out, but I had a sinking feeling that she wouldn't. Either Dread had been extremely smart in his choice of Fervor, or her kidnapping was a fortunate accident for Cherie.

This con was going to stick. I could already see it in the faces around me. Too many people wanted to believe in something bigger than themselves. They had lost touch with their spiritual wonder, and here was Cherie handing it to them gift wrapped. All they had to do was accept themselves completely. As much as they were put off by her rant, they wanted to believe.

I had seen enough.

12

I had to get out before Dread arrived.

Unfortunately the examination broke up, and Cherie was whisked away. I was caught in a sea of medical professionals all speaking a language I didn't understand about what they'd observed. As I edged into the hallway and inched toward the stairs, I managed to gather that they had already sent for samples from Cherie's previous plastic surgeries to analyze along with the samples they had just taken, along with X-rays and various scans.

I was stuck in the stairwell, with everyone stopped around me, grumbling and calling out for those ahead of us to move, when I felt Dread pass by in the lobby below.

Holding my breath, I waited for him to veer and turn toward the stairs where I was trapped. But he continued on and converged with Cherie's signature in the glass lobby. Zeal was not far away.

My heart was racing. Apparently my signature disappeared in the midst of their powerful energy vibrations. I stayed at the top of the stairs, stuck between retreating to a dead end and trying to stay as far away as I could. There was no other way out of the mezzanine of the operating theater, except down to the lobby.

It was nerve-racking, but I didn't bolt. I eased down the stairs and saw Dread and Cherie marching through the lobby with a phalanx of lawyers and hospital administrators. They were leaving. I couldn't see Zeal, but I could tell she was just outside.

Emboldened, I slipped through the revolving door at the end, following them out of the medical center. Surely they wouldn't sense me in the midst of three clashing, and very strong, signatures. It had gotten dark outside while I had searched through the hospital, but the glare of artificial light made it seem like day. The sidewalk was a sea of faceless people being held back by blue police barriers and rows of NYPD officers. Media cameras and satellite antennas on white trucks nearby accounted for some of the glare.

A roar went up when Cherie emerged. Dread held up both hands in victory, smiling the prophet's patented smile. Projecting his voice to reach down the block, he announced, "Cherie is the first member of the Fellowship of Truth to achieve immortality by following the tenets of self-perfection set forth by our first prophet, Dale Williams. Perfection is the state of balance with one's self achieved by accepting ultimate responsibility for the reality of our lives. Come pray with us to be absolved of your conflicts, your inner doubts and miseries! Come join the Fellowship in savoring the unique individual that you are. As Cherie has done."

With a flourish, he presented Cherie to the crowd. She was more glorious than she had ever been in her youth, her natural beauty enhanced by her demon powers to remove every flaw. She looked like an angel come down to earth. She repeated almost word for word what she had said in the operating room, and this time I was struck by her trembling hands and shrinking back in the face of so many flashing lights and shouting people. She had practically been raised as celebrity; I expected her to be eating up all this attention. But something was wrong.

I looked for some sign whether Dread knew I was

nearby. Maybe he didn't care if I was. Zeal also didn't look in my direction. She was in the middle of the crowd, wearing the persona of a young, gangly guy who looked like an ordinary college student.

I was confused by it until Zeal raised her hand, pointing a sleek black gun at Cherie. Dread turned her slightly to make a broader target for Zeal. Nobody else noticed.

Zeal fired three rounds in rapid succession, striking Cherie's chest with every one.

The explosions split the air, echoing against the buildings around us. Cherie was thrown back, her chest a gaping blackened smear.

Screams rose as I was battered by everyone trying to flee. People were trampled and pushed as the temporary police barriers were turned over. I cried out as a guy stomped on my foot, shattering the bones. I rolled away into a ball and took the hits on my back and side, protecting my head.

Like a sea of calm in the center, Dread knelt next to Cherie. The news cameras recovered quicker than anyone else, jostled around them catching every second of her radical resurrection.

This time I had a ringside seat. The stampede receded, leaving behind hundreds of people, some of whom were on their knees praying amid the crying injured.

Cherie's chest healed rapidly, reforming into the luscious white flesh of her breasts. Her dress barely clung to her hips, threatening to expose her entire body.

As she sat up, there was an outcry that grew and swelled. Dread dragged her upright for the cameras. She was cringing as she covered herself with one arm. He spoke to her under his breath, forcing her to raise her arms along with him, lifting their palms high to the night sky.

Her body didn't have a mark on it. Her breasts were perfection, full and round with the pinkest of nipples. Washed in blood.

She twisted slightly but didn't break away from his grasp. I was directly to one side of her so I couldn't see her expression, but her movements said she was deeply uncomfortable. This from a woman who used to walk the runway practically naked, and whose red-carpet outfits left nothing to the imagination.

But from her body language and the flush of purple in her aura, it seemed as if Dread was forcing her to do this. Did Cherie understand what was really going on?

Zeal took Cherie's other arm, back in her usual earthy minister's guise. Apparently no one, not even me, had seen her transformation from assassin to trusted friend.

They were quickly surrounded by cops, who thrust them back inside the NYU Medical Center. It all happened so fast that I was pushed back down the sidewalk. The cops drove everyone away, and I stumbled off among the wounded.

People from all around were converging on the medical center. The towering white antennas at the entrance to the hospital meant that Dread's little assassination display had been carried live, as he intended. Young and old, they were flooding in to gawk and point and stare and not really believe, but wanting to believe that something out of the ordinary was happening and they were a part of it.

I took the streets that seemed to be the least clogged and was driven north and west. At Forty-second Street, I realized I was close to Grand Central, and that reminded me of Mystify. His casa was somewhere down below, but I didn't have a key to get in through the condos or from the subway tracks.

That left the message drop. It was another forty blocks north.

It was times like these that I wished I could just go home and curl up in bed and fall asleep. Worry about it tomorrow, when I was fresh and could think straight. But I didn't have that luxury. I had to keep on going, keep burning . . . forever.

I didn't want to think about the fact that I hadn't stopped Dread. In fact, I had let myself get distracted by everyone else while he put his plan into motion. In spite of all my efforts, I hadn't stopped the resurrection.

I felt responsible for it.

Ram could have stopped Dread, but he didn't care. He was probably glad it was Dread who was engineered our outing. He would stand back and watch the slaughter as humanity crushed his offspring for him.

He wasn't going to be any help.

Maybe Mystify would.

I started jogging, weaving between people and taking to the street when I could. Runners say that you get into a meditative state. I don't know about that; I'm usually running for my life if I'm running. But I tried it this time, tried to let everything go, clear my head.

The park was emptier than the streets, so I made good time heading uptown to the Metropolitan Museum. Once again I reached Cleopatra's Needle without anything to write on.

So I kept on running, taking a big look around the reservoir and back down and around. I wasn't sure if it was working, this meditation thing, but it was better than going back to the bar to wait alone for someone to show up. I loved the old place, but I was done with holing up there.

As I ran, I passed and was passed by other people. Some were joggers who couldn't forgo their usual late-night run. But others were clearly not prepared to be hustling along in their suits and stiff leather shoes, lugging briefcases as if it was hours after they had started the struggle home.

As I circled around for the third time—bless my demon lungs—I felt Mystify's signature appear quite suddenly, as if he emerged from underground. He was waiting by the obelisk as I finally ground to a halt, breathing much harder than I had expected.

"I knew you'd be here," he said. "It's like we're connected somehow."

He was back in his young Theo Ram guise, even though he knew Ram didn't like it. But I was glad to see a friendly face. "What do you think of this, Mystify? Dread's pulled off the resurrection without Vex."

"He learned at the knee of the master. We have to expect that he'll spread his wings now that he isn't under Vex's thumb. But he's moving fast, and that means he'll make mistakes."

"Dread seems to have everything under control. I was just at his last production at NYU Medical. Zeal pulled the trigger."

Mystify's brows went up. "I saw a clip of it. It reminded me of that awful infomercial Dread showed you."

I gave him a sharp look. "How do you know that?"

"Ram was watching through the bug he had on you." He reached out to touch me, expecting a big reaction from me.

I moved away so he couldn't. "Yeah, Ram told me."

He wasn't expecting that. Telling me Ram's secrets was one of his biggest holds on me. Now he was thrown. "I know you almost as well as he does."

"A lot has happened since you were born."

He smiled, looking a lot like Ram. "I don't think you've changed in essentials, Allay. Your desire to help people, to give them a second chance, even someone like Dread. It's because you want to spread comfort and relief. It's your nature to be forgiving, to shun killing because it's the antithesis of what you are."

That took me aback. "You're saying that came from my demon side, not my human side?"

"Yes, just like Ram will always be aggressive about getting what he wants. And Dread will always inspire fear and terror. And why Shock takes pleasure in tragedies. Those deepest desires form our personalities."

I was used to thinking my finer impulses were purely human. But maybe he had a point. Not that I was going to talk to him about that. "Ram wanted this to happen."

"He expected it would. There's no way to undo it now. But at least Cherie won't last long. Hybrids never do."

I gritted my teeth. "I wish everyone would stop saying that. Some of us do fine."

Mystify held up his hands, silently asking forgiveness.

"If only I could get to Cherie. She doesn't like what Dread's doing, I can tell." I gave him a considering look. I needed to share what I'd learned. "I want to talk to her. If I can get her to change her mind, she could stop this."

"You want to convince her to abandon her religion? Good luck."

"Why not? It's what demons are good at—talking people into things."

"Some demons are better at it than others."

"You're not like the others." I wasn't sure exactly what I meant by that, but his eyes lit up. "Can you help me find a way into the Prophet's Center from underground? We have to get past the ERIs that Dread installed."

"That place is ringed by demon guards. You can't get within blocks without being detected."

I smiled. "They won't even know I'm there. I was standing in the same lobby as Dread at the hospital and he didn't notice me. Zeal wasn't much further away, and she didn't, either."

Mystify frowned slightly, taking a moment to sense

my signature. "Hmmm ... Your signature does sort of fade into the background. Especially when there's another demon around."

"See?"

"Yeah, but getting inside the Prophet's Center isn't the hard part. What are you going to do when you find Cherie? What makes you think she'll talk to you instead of sounding the alarm?"

I gave a little dance at the base of the obelisk. "Because you, my friend Mystify, will be wearing Zeal's signature and guise when we go in. She'll think you're her good buddy Missy van Dam, and we're just going to have a nice chat. . . ."

13

I was ready to set off for Brooklyn right away, but Mystify insisted on doing some research first. So we took the underground tunnels back to his place deep under Grand Central. It wasn't as weird and frightening this time, though I couldn't get over the rustle of rats and cockroaches scurrying away from me—sometimes right over my shoes. But now I had learned to be especially careful in the wet areas where the multicolored nastiness would smear on my clothes and get in my eyes.

This time instead of going through the condos, Mystify took a "shortcut" that required us to walk sideways along a ledge inside an active subway tunnel. We were halfway there when I felt the suck of air. A train was coming.

"Get into the niche!" Mystify ordered, pulling me along faster. He shoved me into a depression in the wall, barely larger than the rest of the ledge. "Flatten yourself against the wall. Hang on tight with your fingers. There's going to be massive blowback."

His last words were shouted over the squealing racket bearing down on us as the white headlight bored into my skull. I wanted to run but that would put me right in its path.

Then it was on me, the screech of metal on metal and the suction of air lifting me from my feet. If I hadn't been a demon, I wouldn't have had the strength to hold on.

But the cars moved past much slower than I expected.

The faces blurring in the windows were crammed together, eyes rounded in fear, as if they were in cattle cars heading for the gas chamber. The city had been turned inside out by Dread's stunt.

The train rumbled to a halt. The people who were closest to the window inside were staring at us in growing surprise. I put my finger to my lips in urgent plea that they not point us out to everyone.

The car jerked as the train started moving again. I counted three more cars and then it was gone. "Let's get out of here, Mystify, before another one comes."

"It's not far," he assured me.

We reached a door I recognized—Mystify had brought us out this way last time. Now I knew how to find it again. I lightly ran down six flights of metal stairs until we reached the power room. Down the catwalk and through the archway was the catchments room. A long metal ladder was bolted down the side of the wall. The enormous tank nearly filled the round space.

Mystify went first, pointing at the dark rectangle about halfway up. "That's where it is. I have to lean out and stretch to grab hold of the rope. But I'll be able to pull you in once I'm inside."

It looked perilous the way he swung out to the side, holding on with one hand and one foot. His arm stretched, making my stomach turn from the *wrongness* of it. As if he were made of rubber.

Mystify swung from the lip of the opening, holding out one hand to me. I reached out and took hold of it. "Jump," he ordered.

I shifted so I could get a good launch off the ladder, and warned him, "Okay, here I come!"

I leaped for the opening in the wall. It helped that the wall was curved to fit around the water tank. Mystify lifted me with his supporting hand, pulling me in so I landed neatly beside him.

We were in a recessed compartment, a small square room no more than eight feet wide. It smelled of bleach and was bare except for a card table and folding chair.

Mystify pulled the laptop from where it was concealed on the underside of the table. "Just in case someone gets in and steals everything. But nobody can reach the rope now that I cut off the handle in the wall. I planted a broadband wireless relay at the top. The Grand Central network is really good."

I quietly sat on another folding chair that Mystify unhooked from the pipe running across the ceiling. There were a couple of plastic shopping bags from the Gap and Old Navy hanging there. An extra pair of sneakers dangled from their laces. "Where did you get all this stuff?"

He busied himself with booting up the computer. "Do you really want to know?"

It took me a second. "That means you stole it."

"Yeah, isn't that how demons get what they need?"

I thought about my patrons and how I took energy from them, stealing it away without them knowing. Shock did the same with her patients. What was more important than sustenance? Still . . . "I think it's bad enough we're parasites. Why do we have to be criminals as well?"

Mystify shrugged. "You had Vex. I don't have a benefactor."

That shut me up good. It finally dawned on me that this was Mystify's home. A hole in the wall. He might look like Ram's younger brother, but he didn't have any of the wealth or power of Ram. He had nothing but what he scratched up day to day, living on the edge.

It also occurred to me that other demons probably looked at my ratty little bar and thought the same disparaging thoughts about me.

As Mystify clicked through NYC government Web

sites and library files, he kept up a running commentary about the proximity of the Prophet's Center to the water, which apparently wasn't good. It was also far away from subway lines. So he focused in on the Williamsburg Bridge, accessing engineering plans that he got by hacking into the city DOT Web site.

So now I was an accomplice to cyberhacking on top of everything else. Apparently I had started at murder and was working my way back down the criminal scale.

I knew the Williamsburg Bridge well because it was the closest one to my bar. It was a lot like the Lower East Side, utilitarian to the extreme. Artists didn't paint it. I'd never seen a photograph of it. It was the ugly stepsister among the city bridges, and I loved it for that. Who needed fancy doodads and design thrills? The lattice of truss-work exposed raw mathematical formulas in all their glory.

It was also built in an era when security was not a concern. Mystify finally started exclaiming over a number of possible ways to get underground.

Once he had downloaded what he needed, he slid his laptop into a messenger's bag. He was so eager to get started that I said, "Why do you want to help? This could be really dangerous."

"Anything that mucks things up for the big boys is all right by me." The way he slung the bag over his shoulder and held on to the strap made him look much younger. He had nothing but this.

Now that he was focused on something other than trying to confuse me, I was starting to really like him.

Getting into Brooklyn wasn't easy. Too many people were flooding into Williamsburg to get to the Prophet's Arena and the Prophet's Center, where Cherie was said to be ensconced. The police had barricaded the bridge going into Brooklyn, and all of the streets on the Manhattan side were jammed up.

Though it was dark when we started out, by the time we walked across the Manhattan Bridge, south of the Williamsburg Bridge, the sun was rising. We couldn't find a cab for love or money, and there were no subway tracks in that direction, so we had to circle several miles around the Brooklyn Navy Yard on foot. It was cut off by manned security gates and tall wrought-iron fences with large shepherd's hooks at the top. The streets were littered with cars that had been abandoned in the chaos, snarling the early morning traffic.

Mystify was wearing Bliss's signature. It was almost as mild as mine, and most demons hadn't sensed it yet so they might think it was their own adrenaline pumping from the turmoil. Even though her signature was so light, I was hoping it would still cancel out mine, which was far more recognizable among Vex demons.

We didn't sense any demons on our approach, but things got really hairy when we entered the Hasidic neighborhood of south Williamsburg, marked by wrought-iron cages over the windows used to separate the dishes during holy days. Usually the streets were filled with men in old-fashioned black suits and women with their heads in colorful *schmattes* watching over dozens of children playing on every block, their bicycles and toys scattered across the sidewalks. But all of that had disappeared in the midst of the gridlocked cars with honking vans and trucks desperate to deliver their wares. Everyone ignored the lights, trying to fight their way through, so we had to wind across the street between stalled cars, avoiding the shouts around us.

The people who were out hurried by with their heads hunched, concerned only with their own destination. But Mystify stared around with a broad grin on his face.

"Exciting, isn't it?" he said with a wink, when he caught me looking at him.

At the same time, he brushed his hand across the arm of a woman shoving past us. His aura sparked rusty orange as he soaked off her panic. He shuddered slightly, briefly closing his eyes in delight.

He was feeding off her.

Disgusted, I snapped, "Can't you leave them alone? They're already being traumatized enough."

"I'm not hurting anyone," he protested.

"It's the principle of the thing." Disappointed for reasons I couldn't even articulate, I added, "I almost forgot you were a demon for a second there."

He nodded patiently as if he understood.

I got mad real fast. "Now you look like Ram."

"Ram knows you liked him better when you thought he was human. That's when he was pretending to let you be in control. I bet he's doing exactly what you tell him right now. At least until he gets his hooks good and deep in you."

Vividly I remember ordering him to be honest, with Ram meekly answering my questions with almost sickening honesty. Was that more manipulation? Of course, how could he resist turning me this way and that? As if he was playing with a fantasy doll made in the image of his one great love.

It made my stomach drop to think of Hope. The goddess. The perfect dead wife. She had shared lifetimes with Ram, fought and loved him. She was the original while I was a pale, insipid copy. So *nice*. And malleable.

Mystify laughed. "I'm right, aren't I? Pretty soon he'll have you thinking it's your idea you two should be together." He laughed again. "I bet he would *hate* you being here with me."

I remembered how Ram had flared up at the mention

of Mystify, right before I threw him out and ordered him to leave his offspring alone. "Oh, yeah. He would."

"Is that why you're with me?"

"No." I thought about it some more. "I knew you were the only one who would agree to help."

"What about the ever-adored Shock?" Mystify asked. "I thought she supported you in everything."

"She's working," I hedged. Then I had to admit, "We've been arguing a lot. About Bliss. And Ram. Even you . . . She thought I was crazy to go off with you without calling her."

Mystify got a faraway look, as if he was seeing a memory. "That's the way it is during chaotic times. You never know who's going to turn on you. It could be the person you trusted the most."

"You're thinking about Hope." I had seen that look in Ram's eyes. "She must be pretty amazing to be able to mesmerize you secondhand."

He shook himself out of it. "It's the stuff of legend."

Ouch. I managed to not say it out loud.

He was watching me closely. "Are you sure you want to do this? It could get really bad if we make a mistake. Dread's got that cage ready and waiting. Though I suppose Ram wouldn't let you stay cooped up for long." He paused. "Unless he's trying to prove a point, like you need him—"

I flung up my hands. "Stop it! I don't want to hear any more about Ram. I can deal only with my own responsibilities. I could have stopped all this if I hadn't been so afraid for my own soul, my own precious human soul. I should have killed Dread when I had the chance."

"Yeah, I've been meaning to ask. Why in heaven's name did you kill Pique instead of Dread?"

"I was in complete shock when Ram revealed himself. I shut down. I couldn't kill Dread. I just watched as

Ram killed Vex." I gritted my teeth. "And now everyone is paying the price because I was *weak*."

Mystify stayed silent. He agreed, but was too polite to say so.

That just hardened my resolve. "Don't worry. I'm going to fix it."

Mystify showed me an access door set in the base of the roadway leading up to the Williamsburg Bridge. It was several blocks away from the Prophet's Center, but I could feel the fringes of demon signatures in the distance.

It was definitely Goad, and maybe Stun. I figured their range was longer than my own, so Mystify hurried to break inside the door. I should have known he would be good at picking locks, any locks. Ram probably could have gotten us out of that cage any time he wanted to. But he had intended to give Dread to me, drained and tied up with a bow.

We entered a square passageway made of poured concrete. It was much cleaner than the tunnels. This was a worksite with exposed bulbs strung along conduit fastened to the wall just above our heads, providing a constant light.

Far down the corridor, we reached an abrupt end. The cables from the suspension bridge, each fatter around than my head, slanted down through the room. They were looped around an enormous drum lying in front of us, filling the corridor from wall to wall. Each cable fanned out to each fit into a groove in the drum.

I could feel the hum of tension on the cables, the motion creating vibrations in the air. It was the nearest thing to a mechanical aura I had ever encountered, as if the bridge was alive.

A heavy iron ladder was bolted into the wall. Mystify climbed up and worked at a panel in the wall where the electrical conduits joined a junction box.

"That looks awfully small," I whispered.

"You're going to hate it. But it's the best I can do."

Crawling through reminded me unpleasantly of the pipe leading out of the Grand Central condos. I felt squished in on all sides. But it was short and opened into a crawl space for the electrical grid.

"I knew we'd be in filth again," I muttered.

"We're about six feet under the street."

"Is that enough? Will it hide our signatures?" The thought of Goad roaming the streets above me made me want to run back to the bar.

Mystify pulled out a green glow stick. "I guess we'll find out."

It was reckless, it was barely thought out, this scheme of mine. I was flinging my life out there on a whim, just because I couldn't stand feeling responsible for all this pain.

I couldn't stop now.

I crawled after Mystify, sticking myself on cable-ties and worse. It smelled of mold and dog urine, a nasty combination. When we passed under a manhole cover, pencil beams of light showed through, blocked by constant movement. The racket on the street was shockingly loud. It sounded like a riot was under way at the Prophet's Center.

We crawled under it all until the noise disappeared. I figured we were below the sidewalk when Mystify whispered, "Hang on while I try to get this open."

I should have been forewarned by that "try." Despite everything Mystify did, he couldn't get through. A lock had been placed on the interior to keep people out of the basement of the Prophet's Center.

He sat down and pulled out his laptop to search through the plans he had downloaded. I didn't say a word. This was no time to jostle his elbow.

Finally he looked up. "You're not going to like it."

"What is it?" I craned my neck to see the glowing screen.

"An old sewage pipe."

I groaned. "How old?"

"It was replaced in the early seventies when the garage ramp was rebuilt. The new sewage lines are laid on top, so there will be some . . . leakage." He reached into his pouch and unfurled a plastic bag. "We'll have to take our clothes off."

I couldn't take my eyes off the plastic bag. "I don't think I can do it."

"You don't have to. We can go up and have a nice feed on the crowd, and forget we ever thought of bringing Dread down."

"I know you're loving it, but I won't profit off the chaos he's created."

Mystify shrugged, his eyes wandering upward as if he was thinking of all those juicy bamboozled people milling around up there. How many times would he ever be so close to a mob brimming over with his preferred emotion?

"Let's see this sewage pipe," I made myself say.

I kept telling myself I could back out at any time. I could go up to the street with Mystify and be all pious and disapproving while he wallowed in the mob. I could go on pretending to be human while I was really a demon.

Or I could act, and do something to stop Dread.

The pipe didn't look like much from the access tunnel. It crossed the floor at right angles. The top had caved in, opening up a large section. When we cleaned out the old chunks of brick and rubble fallen from the tunnels above, the floor of the pipe looked like it was partially filled in with dirt. There was just enough space to cr~
into it on your hands and knees. Above it was the
concrete bottom of the new sewage pipe, ha~
the old one.

"Looks fine to me," I tossed off.

Dubious, Mystify leaned down to put his face into the ragged opening. "It stinks."

"How far do we have to go?"

"About thirty feet."

I scoffed. "That's nothing. Where will we end up?"

"Subbasement. The plumbing in a lot of these old factories emptied into a well with a clean-out trap. From there, this old pipe goes down to the river. It used to be a tannery so there's no telling what awful chemicals they were dumping in the water."

"At least it can't hurt us. Do you want me to go first?"

As much as Mystify didn't want to crawl in there, he wasn't going to let me go first. He knew Ram would go charging in, and he took a deep breath as if girding himself to do the same.

When he saw me watching him, he made a show of popping open the button of his jeans. "I think the person in the rear will get more of a view."

I blushed, but it had to be done. I couldn't walk around the Prophet's Center smelling like that pipe.

After he bagged our clothes and tied it around him, Mystify dived right in. I crawled after him, noticing that he was wearing a particularly fine ass. The first few feet were not bad, but we quickly hit a "wet" patch. The crust broke under my hands and I was slimed up to my elbows. The upper curve of the pipe left a streak of mold down my head and back. The stench was unbelievable, and I finally stopped breathing, preferring the dizzying rush to actually being inside that pipe at that moment.

Mystify had to drag me through the opening at the end. I shifted rapidly, trying to shed my skin and the muck along with it. Mystify was wiping himself off as ʼl shaking his head and going instantly bald to rid ᵊᶠ the dripping mess.

I turned to hide myself from him, and quickly did the same. It was awful and wonderful at the same time.

The subbasement was chill and dark. The echo of the furnace sounded a long way off.

I gripped Mystify's arm. "We did it. We're inside."

I opened my pupils as wide as possible to see his proud delight. "I bet there's a way into every building in the city," he said.

"If anyone can find it, you can."

He leaned toward me, his intent clear, but I grabbed the plastic bag and gave it a tug. "Clothes time." I didn't want him to get any ideas. I liked Mystify, but he didn't make me fire up inside the way Ram did.

If Mystify was disappointed, he didn't let it show. We worked as if we had always been a team, making our way up through several basement levels without arousing any alarms. Just below the ground floor, I stopped him. "There's Cherie's signature. *Elude*."

"Like the tide is rushing out," Mystify agreed. "But where's Dread?"

"And Lash. And Zeal. We should have felt them before Cherie. Her signature is milder than theirs." Mystify was still wearing Bliss's signature, but it was easy to ignore. "Why would they all leave Cherie here alone? Without any demons to guard her?"

"We're inside their perimeter. They aren't expecting us to get past Goad's horde on the streets."

"It's just like Dread to be so sure of himself," I muttered. To Mystify, I added, "Go ahead, change into Missy van Dam."

Instantly it felt like Zeal was standing next to me, her pressing, squeezing signature consuming my own. He looked exactly like Missy van Dam, with her rugged complexion and messy updo, her expression shining with joy. His baggy pants and T-shirt suited her.

"What am I going to do again?" he ask

"Just talk to her. We'll figure it out from there."

Doubtfully, he asked, "Are you sure you don't want to kill her? It would solve the problem in one whack."

I glared at him until he held up his hands in defense. "Fine, it was only a suggestion."

I headed straight to Dread's private elevator, the one that didn't have any cameras in it. But with the Prophet's Center wired to the gills, I would run into surveillance at some point. So I changed my face into June, the perky Amerasian girl complete with pink braces and eager smile. It was very possible that June was somewhere up above doing the prophet's work, but I'd have to risk security seeing double rather than putting my own face out there. I bet there was an automatic alert that would sound if I ever wandered into view of a Fellowship camera.

I hated wearing someone else's face. It made me feel like a demon.

I had to step right over the patch of ground where I had lain in a straitjacket, with Goad leering down at me. When he had touched me and promised to violate me at a later time.

When I punched the call button, the elevator opened with a faint *ping*. The last time I had been in it, Ram had been about to explode and give birth to Mystify. He glanced around as if remembering that.

When we reached the top, we stepped into the private foyer between Dread's and Vex's sprawling apartments. The door that led to Dread's torture chamber didn't have a handle, only an electronic lock. I would have bet the bar that Dread hadn't dismantled his iron cage. A nice cell phone pic of it would make for handy bargaining material.

But we didn't have time, and I still didn't have a phone. I turned toward Vex's old apartment. Mystify was around as if he had seen it all in an old movie.

When we stepped into the hallway where the security cameras were watching, both of us kept quiet and tried to act nonchalant.

Mystify rang the bell to Vex's loft. I could feel Cherie inside. There was still no sign of other demons within range.

Cherie answered the door. "I thought it was you, Missy. I don't know why, a feeling, I guess. Weren't you going to help the prophet?"

"I didn't want to leave you alone," Mystify said in a fair imitation of Missy van Dam's gravelly warmth.

"But you said he needed you because of Mrs. Anderson." Cherie's eyes narrowed. With her perfect features, everything she did looked like a staged editorial. Even the bad lighting couldn't make her look unattractive. "After all that drama, she isn't going to be staying here, is she?"

So that was why Dread and Zeal were gone. They were taking Lash somewhere for safekeeping.

"I'll catch up to the prophet later," Mystify said blandly. "Can we come in, Cherie?"

"I hear sirens. It sounds like there are even more of them." Her gaze drifted back inside the loft. She seemed closed-in, and I was already doubting our success. Even her aura had the burnished hue of trepidation.

But she turned her back on us as if we meant nothing to her. Her fear was coming from someplace else. Did her demon memories tell her what she really was, and she was afraid of being exposed?

Fear . . . Dread was probably all over Cherie right now. He must be loving her confused suspicions; maybe he was even stoking her fears. But he also needed her to be stable in order to maintain the charade. What a conflict that must be for him right now.

As we went inside, I saw the loft was very much as Vex had left it, monochromatic with black leather and chrome, and the old wooden floor of the factory exposed. The windows had been covered over with swaths of muslin to block out inquiring cameras. It made the room bright but somehow stifling.

I stayed firmly in my June persona. I wouldn't put it past Dread to have surveillance cameras on Cherie. "I bet you're really confused right now what with everything that's happened."

Cherie tossed her head, a compulsive denial. She wasn't looking at me, as if she couldn't care less who I was. Just another flunky. "I'm fine. Everything's fine, or it was until *she* came back."

"The prophet took her away," Mystify said soothingly, much like Missy would.

"He shouldn't have let her come back," Cherie snapped. "She betrayed him. How could he stand being in the same room with her? She distracts him, and that distracts me because she's so needy. She's always been that way, interfering. . . ."

I shot Mystify a look. Maybe Glory had managed to do *something* by sending back Lash. With Dread caught between Cherie and Lash, no wonder he had decided to separate them. "I'm sure you have the prophet's undivided attention, Elude."

Her true demon name slipped out in spite of myself. I held my breath, but Cherie seemed to see me for the first time. "Yes, yes, I believe I do. After all, I have achieved perfection." She drew herself up to her full six-foot height, unblemished by time. "Mrs. Anderson hasn't achieved perfection. She's even older than me, and she looks every day of it."

"You were touched by God," I agreed. "Why do you think that happened? What did you do differently from the rest of us?"

"I accepted myself," she said promptly. She rapidly repeated the same cant she had been spouting since her resurrection, going on about herself and her perfection. She drifted over to the mirror, examining her face, pointing out the renewal of each delicate curve and stroking her skin to feel the softness.

"This could take forever," Mystify mumbled. He sat down on the back of a couch and crossed his arms, clearly waiting for me to make progress with her.

Dread was probably going to drop Lash at some fancy hotel with Zeal, and he could be on his way back home to Cherie right now. But breaking through the Teflon shield of self-absorption that surrounded Cherie was not going to be easy.

I had crawled through a sewage pipe to make this happen. I wasn't going to let a spoiled socialite stop me.

One step at a time. I went up behind her. "What is it you really want, Elude?"

I'd done it again, said her real name. This time she mouthed it after me. "*Elude.* That feels right, somehow."

She turned and took hold of my wrist, her long fingers easily circling my arm. Before I knew it, she was feeding off me. I kept my shields up so she got only drops from me. Her eyes glazed as if she had no idea what she was doing, as she greedily lapped up my desire to flee.

I wanted to run as far away from here as possible, before Dread and Zeal returned. I felt as if I were standing on an exposed mountain peak, vulnerable from all directions, and all I wanted to do was hide.

Hide . . .

Cherie closed her eyes in bliss. She had found what she was made for. Poor Fervor must have wanted to run away even more than I did now. Cherie latched on to me like she would never let go.

"Listen to all those people," she whispered. On the other side of the muslin, far down below, was the mob chanting and crying out for help. It was getting louder. "Why don't they go away and leave me alone?"

"Good idea, Cherie." I urged her toward the door. "Let's get out of here. Let's go hide. There are too many people here. We have to get away."

"The prophet said I couldn't. He said I was safer here."

She protested, but she wasn't going to let go of me while I was radiating what she wanted. I quickly led her into her closet and picked out some practical clothes for her, including sneakers instead of her stilettos. "We're going somewhere more casual, relaxing. You need to relax, to get away for just a little bit. The prophet will join us there."

"Why are the people so angry? Why do they yell at me? They want to get me. I can feel it. I'm immortal, and they want it for themselves. They'll try to kill me to get it. I'm perfect, so they can't let me survive. It's too much for them to take. A slap in the face. Don't they realize they can be perfect, too, in their own way? Why won't they listen and go home and be who they are? Why are they here?"

Mystify couldn't help himself; he took Cherie's arm, feeding off her confusion.

"I'm not a bottomless pit, here," I warned him quietly, as Cherie kept babbling.

I drew her down the hallway, leading her with my flight response, expecting to feel the return of demons any second. I didn't even bother listening to what she had to say. I had found a much easier way to manipulate her.

I punched the down button on the elevator.

Even as we passed the street level, I didn't feel any demons. I drew a deep breath.

As we stepped into the basement, I asked Mystify, "Can you find that access door with the inside lock?" I doubted we could get the princess to crawl through a sewage pipe.

He grinned. "I figured you'd want that."

He led us down another flight of stairs and over to the far corner. Behind a rack of old paint cans was a rusted panel. A padlock held the eyehook closed, but Mystify made quick work of it with a small crowbar he had brought along in his bag.

I expected Cherie to balk at slipping into the underground access tunnel, but she didn't say a word about it. Our flight fit perfectly with her need to hide, to secret herself away someplace dark and quiet. She finally fell silent when we crawled under the manhole cover where we could hear the pounding feet of the crowd and their shouting for her. I shuddered at how close we were to destruction. Those people would tear her apart in their frenzy if they could get their hands on her.

Cherie held on to my ankle even tighter, sucking up my all-consuming desire to stay hidden. I never thought it would be this easy. To think a little sewage pipe had almost stopped me.

"Good job," Mystify whispered back so only I could hear. "Considering it's your first kidnapping."

14

We paused inside the base of the Williamsburg Bridge, crouched next to the anchor drum that held the strands of cable. I gently pushed Cherie away from me. I needed my strength, and Cherie was plenty charged up. But she moved in close again, practically leaning against me, letting her aura overlap mine as if the taste of my desire to stay under cover was enough to satisfy her.

I was curious how much she understood what had happened to her, but I didn't want to frighten her back into the Prophet's Center. That was why I hesitated to ask her to change her appearance so we could walk out onto the streets.

"Can you find a way for us to stay underground?" I asked Mystify. It would also help conceal our signatures from the demon guards that Dread must have posted.

He nodded, popping open his laptop to access the Internet. "Let's go back this way. Whatever we do, we'll have to go inland." He keyed the pad as we walked. "The L train isn't too far. We could walk there in ten minutes."

Cherie was looking concerned, so I touched her, giving her a jolt of my desire to flee as I said, "I want to stay underground, even if it takes longer to get back to Manhattan. It's too risky up above."

Mystify found a way. From underneath the on-ramp for the bridge, he led us straight to another utility access tunnel under the street. "This should take us down Bedford to the station at North Seventh Street. But we'll be close to the surface the whole way. Our signatures will leak through."

"Then we'll have to move fast."

I distracted Cherie by feeding her as Mystify jimmied open the panel that let us into the access tunnel.

Then we started crawling. I had to prod Cherie more than the first time, giving her bursts of my adrenaline-fueled fear. She didn't know I was afraid that Dread was going to find us. I counted off eleven blocks by the tunnels that met at right angles to ours.

By the time we emerged in a small work area adjacent to the subway tunnel at the west end of the platform, I was shocked that Cherie hadn't complained once. I was ready to complain plenty—in pain and covered with that sooty, clinging dirt that was the city's own. We all wore shadowy charcoal masks of it, kicked up by our hands and knees. Their eyes peered at me whitely.

My knees were killing me in spite of expending energy to heal them. But I drew in my breath in shock when I saw Cherie's knees. Blood was flowing freely with dirt ground into the open wounds.

Then she healed herself right in front of me, lifting her face and hands as if to the heavens. "I am perfection. I am one with God now and forever."

The black stuff fell from her skin like rain as she shifted out from under it. There was no understanding in her expression, only ecstatic faith similar to what I had felt holding her hand during the Fellowship circle.

I exchanged a look with Mystify, whose round-eyed, openmouthed expression was clearly his despite the Missy van Dam guise he wore. He wasn't even bothering to act like Zeal's persona anymore. "Just what the world needs, another savoir."

Cherie didn't notice. She was too busy paying attention to herself, smoothing the skin on her cheeks, feeling how firm her neck was, rubbing her hands together sensually.

I leaned out over the subway tracks. The platform was back to my right while the tracks sloped sharply down to my left, heading through a tunnel under the East River to Manhattan. Our nook was lit by only one orange lightbulb, casting a lurid light over the blackened I-beams and piles of railroad ties.

Then I saw movement behind the farthest stack. Heads peeked over. People were here with us.

Cherie was practically glowing, her skin was so translucent, her eyes burning with fanaticism. Before I could stop her, she went over to them, circling the railroad ties to get to them.

I was afraid they were going to recognize her. I expected to hear them say her name. They were rapt, staring up at her, and one of them murmured, "Bless me, for I have sinned. . . ."

"I bring God's message," she told them. "Love yourself and you will become whole."

She reached out and placed her palm against the man's forehead, as the Fellows did during a healing. "I give you my blessing."

Her aura flared as she drew in a healthy dollop of his cringing fear that we would roust him and his friend out of their safe nest and back onto the streets. Cherie drew in her breath deeply, letting the sensation fill her entire body. Then she reached out and placed her palm on the other guy's forehead, sending off another flare of panicked energy, which she absorbed greedily.

I stepped forward, concerned that she would latch on to them and drain them.

But Cherie turned away beaming, as if she had given those two men the greatest gift they could receive. She rejoined Mystify and me, saying modestly, "They needed me."

"Yeah, right." I didn't want to burst her bubble, but she needed them. Or at least their energy. To Mystify, I whispered, "This is a really long tunnel. How do we get through?"

He also kept his voice down so the people huddled at the back couldn't hear. "There are alarms on the pedestrian walkways and the utility access along the top. They don't want terrorists getting in there and planting explosives. So we've got two choices. Either we get on a subway like normal people. Or we run."

"Run? You mean down the tracks?"

"I'd recommend running rather than walking because the trains are off schedule. Delays on all the lines, especially those connecting to Brooklyn." He pointed at something on his screen. "But there are nooks for workers to stand in if they're caught when a train comes by. We'd have to be very careful to get to one in time if we feel a train coming."

"I'd love to ride," I said longingly. But our clothes were a mess, and Cherie's famous face was practically a beacon. She would be recognized in an instant. "Run, it is."

Mystify slid his laptop into his pouch as I took hold of Cherie's arm. I gave her a blast of my feelings, knowing it would soothe her like a baby at her mama's breast. "Come on, Cherie. We have to move fast."

"Are there more people who need me?" she asked brightly.

"Sure, lots more." I thought of all the people I had seen in the deeper tunnels. "We just have to get back to Manhattan."

Cherie pulled out some cash from the pocket of her khaki safari pants. "We can take a cab."

"Not in this traffic," Mystify reminded her. "It'll take all day."

I nodded. "Yes, and the people waiting for you *re-*

ally need you. Now. Running through the tunnel is the quickest way to reach them."

Cherie didn't hesitate. She picked her way over to the tracks with Mystify and me stumbling after her. She reached the tracks and jogged off into the darkness alone.

"Should we tell her to wait until a train passes by?" I asked Mystify.

"You think you could stop her?" he retorted.

It wasn't easy catching up to Cherie, who was dashing along like she had a life to save. Mystify was huffing in the rear. I tripped and fell once despite my enhanced sight, we were moving so fast.

I found myself thinking that if a train came, I doubted we could turn Cherie aside into one of the safety nooks. It would smash into her, maybe causing enough damage and scattering her parts to keep her from regenerating. I hated the thought of it, but it would solve the problem of Cherie. Even if a jury of my peers would convict me of manslaughter.

We made a six-minute mile, or near enough not to matter, and got through the tunnel without being rammed by a subway train.

Not far from the first station, Mystify took us through a hatch with rounded corners set into the wall. A spiral staircase led down to a power room with emergency generators behind a locked door. We headed down a long tunnel that ran under the track and platform level.

I breathed a sigh of relief for the first time. We had escaped from Brooklyn without being detected, and now we were deep enough that demons couldn't feel our signatures.

As I relaxed, Cherie drifted away from me. I realized I was losing my one hold on her now that I wasn't fleeing for my life.

"Now what?" Mystify asked, lowering his voice.

"This isn't her fault. She's clueless. She doesn't know what she's doing."

"She's Dread's puppet. She's even more dangerous in her ignorance than if she understood her role in all this."

"I know, Mystify." I followed idly after her as she wandered into the gloom of the tunnel. "But there's got to be a better way."

Cherie suddenly knelt down near the wall of the tunnel. I hurried up to find her pressing her palm against some poor guy's forehead. He was dazed, either drunk or drugged or maybe so soundly asleep that he couldn't even wake up properly.

Cherie gave him her blessing and murmured her ritual words, "I bring God's message: Love yourself and you will be saved."

The flare of energy passing out of the man lit the tunnel brighter; there were huddled blankets dotting the floor along the walls. Cherie saw them and made her way to the next one.

I was afraid I had loosed a cannibal on them, but Cherie didn't show any signs of lingering and taking more than a hit of energy from each one under the guise of giving them her blessing. I was surprised that none of them protested more, though one guy flailed his arms at her until she easily held him still, giving him the blessing in spite of himself. The others seemed bewildered that a beautiful woman would so freely approach them, even touch them! Nobody ever touched them. They took her blessing in the spirit it was offered in, and only stirred themselves to sit up or stand to watch after her.

I kept an eye on those behind us. I had Plea's memories and the more recent sight of the religious mob to warn me. But these people truly did want to get away from everyone. And Cherie was eating it up.

"I think I know what to do," I told Mystify.

*   *   *

There were plenty of underground dwellers to keep Cherie occupied as Mystify and I laid our plans. I had to return to the bar as soon as possible so that it would appear I had nothing to do with Cherie's disappearance. That was crucial. I couldn't let anyone link me to her.

Mystify would take Cherie to the Grand Central condos. He was doing so much for them, hopefully they would take in a poor, befuddled girl. It wasn't a long-term plan, but it was something. At least it would keep Cherie off the streets for a while so Dread's "miracle" could be discredited.

First we had to stage a religious epiphany of our own. Mystify showed us an abandoned water main that we could crawl through for eight blocks to reach Sixth Street. There, it broke off inside a broad utility tunnel half filled with running water. It was so deep that the surface didn't ripple, and was flowing fast enough to be frightening.

"It's an underground stream. The water used to be on the surface snaking through the Village, but people built over it," Mystify explained.

"It's huge!"

"People do go across." Mystify gestured to the rope. "But you'll drown if you let go of the rope."

"I don't have to go any further. I can get out and walk home from here," I assured him.

Mystify gestured to the ledge that ran along the side of the tunnel. "I'll be right back."

He didn't go far, but I distracted Cherie by taking my time getting out of the narrow water main, blocking her view. By the time she emerged, Prophet Anderson was standing inches away from the black flowing water. His silver hair was immaculate, his tan recently refreshed by a visit to the golf course. He seemed bigger than Dread usually made him, and his hands were particularly ham-fisted—Mystify was exaggerating the prophet's characteristics. I gave him a hard look.

At least he definitely felt like Dread. Cherie ignored everything else, including the distinctly shabby clothing he was wearing. "Tommy!" she cried, running to hug him.

Mystify was caught off guard. But he responded lustily enough as Cherie molded herself to his body and planted a kiss on his mouth.

So that put Dread's relationship with Cherie in perspective. He always did mix his power games with sex, so I shouldn't have been surprised. I just wondered if he had sealed the deal before Cherie became a demon or afterward. Mystify was clearly uncomfortable with her all over him. He kept looking at me. He felt so much like Dread that I couldn't have cared less who he kissed.

"I told you I was bringing you to the prophet," I said to Cherie, firmly in my June persona. "He has something very important to tell you."

Cherie held on to Mystify's arm, hanging on him adoringly. Apparently she didn't hide their relationship from June, which told me a lot about Dread's relationship with his secretary.

"You've found your true calling, Cherie," Mystify said, imitating Dread's booming voice. "You carry God's message to all who need you, all those who hide away in fear of what life has to offer."

They were the words I had coached him with.

"Yes," she said firmly. "I feel it. This is the first time I've felt truly fulfilled since my transformation into the spirit. There was something missing up above. The voices told me so."

"The images you've seen confirm it," Mystify assured her. She was thinking of Fervor's memories. "People need you to be their spiritual guide, delving deep in order to reach truth."

"Yes! Like the whole world is reaching out to me, all at once, like they need something from me." Her eyes were burning again as she looked upward.

Mystify seemed to like that better than her passion. "You are made to bring light to the darkness."

Cherie nodded, her eyes once again fixed on his. Paying attention like she never had before. "Yes, it's too bright up there. All those eyes, those flashing lights . . ."

"You're needed here. Every person you touch is saved. A bit of their soul enters you, and you save them."

She nodded, too eager, too manic. "Hallelujah! We are saved."

Mystify leaned closer. "There are people who would take you away from your true purpose. The mob wants you. They want to crowd in close. All those eyes watching you . . ."

"I don't want to go back."

This was the tricky part. Mystify suggested, "If you could change the way you look, so people didn't recognize you . . . then nobody would try to take you back."

Cherie looked down at her palms, smeared with dirt. She had streaks on her face, and her clothes were in bad shape.

She rubbed her palms against her cheeks, turning her face into a macabre mask. "Now they can't see me."

It wasn't what I had been hoping for. I wanted Cherie to change her features. But in spite of healing herself over and over, she couldn't grasp the concept that she could look like someone else. The idea that she had achieved perfection *as herself* was too ingrained to shake.

"I don't know," I said doubtfully to Mystify. "Hopefully that will be good enough."

He shrugged. "It's better than I expected."

Cherie pulled on his arm. "Let's go, Dread. The people need me."

She didn't even realize she had called the prophet by his true demon name. She could feel Dread's signature in Mystify, and she was relying more on her demon instincts than her human ones. I could hardly think of her as Cherie anymore, and frankly, this creature was more appealing than the woman who had ritually starved herself for fame.

Mystify gestured to the makeshift ladders roped to the wall. "That will take you up top," he told me.

I nodded, and because we had been through so much, I reached out my hand. He took it without hesitation. It was strange for a demon to be so willingly vulnerable, almost human in fact. His eyes, his open expression, the pressure on my fingers . . . he bent his head and softly kissed the back of my fingers, a feather touch.

I felt a spark of attraction. Mystify was so genuine that even inside Dread's guise, he shone right through the facade.

In the darkness underground, time seemed to stop. Then he smiled and turned away.

I let out my breath. Okay, that was definitely something.

I watched as Mystify and Cherie headed back in the direction we came. Cherie wasn't talking nonstop anymore. She was losing that along with her Cherie-self. Soon the crunch of their footsteps faded away in the darkness.

It wasn't a final solution, but maybe it would keep Cherie off the radar long enough to shake Dread's resurrection story. Without Cherie, there was no miracle in Brooklyn.

I hoped.

15

As I emerged into the light of day, blinking like some nocturnal beast, I was thinking more about Mystify than the fact that I had just kidnapped a woman. Mystify and I worked well together. Like we fit together. Like we were on the same level. But I didn't feel that magic zing right to my core when he looked at me.

Maybe that "magic" feeling was dangerous. Maybe chemistry was nothing more than revved-up lust, and when it came to living with someone, partnering with a man, it was more important that he was good for you. And you were good for him.

Plus, there was that a spark between us. Maybe Mystify had all of the best parts of Ram with none of the baggage.

Now I'm really confused.

I hadn't asked Mystify anything about Ram this time. Funny, I hadn't even thought about it until I'd left him. The real question I wanted an answer to was, Why did Ram kill Hope? I needed to ask even though I was afraid to find out the answer.

The mood on the street was weird. There were a lot of people out walking, but it wasn't the frantic rushing of the night before, more like a massive street fair that had settled over the Lower East Side. A surprise holiday with work in the city shut down, giving everyone a three-day weekend.

Making my way through the crowds, I could tell the people were generally moving south and toward the river where they could stare and point across at the white sugar cube of the Prophet's Center. Radios blared out from cars and open windows, announcing a state of emergency in the city with all three bridges to Brooklyn closed to incoming traffic.

As I came down Avenue C, I didn't sense any demons at the bar. Maybe I was the first one back. Wouldn't that be lucky? Mystify had refused to cooperate in my plan to hide Cherie away underground until I pledged not to tell anyone, not ever. Not Shock, not Ram, not anyone. Dread would kill us both if it got out. Now we held each other's life in our hands.

I was opening the front door, warily keeping an eye out around me, when Ram emerged from the pedestrians passing by. He was looking at me steadily, as he always did. He was cloaked, but that couldn't hide the roiling in his aura—his golden joy to see me flooded over his purple frustration and pain at not being able find me.

My first thought was—where was he last night? Knowing about his other girlfriends made me more jealous than I liked to admit.

"I'm glad you're back, Allay." He joined me and took my hand, the same hand that Mystify had held, which finally shook me out of my reverie. I couldn't stand here on the street staring into his eyes like a lovesick girl.

"Come on in." I used the excuse of opening the door to pull my hand away from him.

He felt my confusion. "Are you sure? You're not mad at me anymore?"

"I'll always be mad when you lie and manipulate me," I assured him. "But we don't need to stand on the street talking about it."

I took him inside the bar instead of going straight up to my apartment. I needed to use the phone, even

though I didn't like being reminded of the last time
we were together alone in the bar. I avoided looking
at the bench under the back windows. The memory of
how he had reclined on the bench so manly and satiated made my knees week.

"So you got what you wanted," I said. "Dread got his
resurrection."

"I tried to stop him, Allay." His tone was quiet, reasonable, regretful. "I gave you Dread on a platter, but
you refused to end this. With him alive, this was always
a possibility."

"You want demons to be outed."

"I would have preferred it if superstition and religion
played no part in it. In this day and age, I thought it was
possible that a secular explanation of who we are could
have emerged. But the unknown is always the unknown.
Even science can only penetrate the true mysteries so
far: Who are we? Why are we here? What makes demons alive? I don't know the answers to those questions.
Maybe it's inevitable that religion and our existence are
entangled."

He was drifting closer, so I hastily went around to the
back of the bar. It felt more comfortable that way, with
some distance between us. Last time he had stampeded
me into sex without telling me about Cherie. "Now
what?"

"It's only just begun. The ERI machines are being
manufactured now. They'll start to be installed next
month, and then Cherie won't be the only one exposed.
It will take some time. First they'll see the unusual scans;
then they'll get orders to detain people who scan that
way. Eventually they'll get a demon into custody. There
are more than two hundred of us now, so it's bound to
happen at some point."

I sighed. "Imagine if it's Goad. Or someone like
Pique."

"It's out of our hands now."

The way he said it made me stop and think. "Is it? Isn't there something we can do to make this better?"

He raised one brow. "Only by killing Cherie. Do you want her dead, Allay?"

I swallowed. "No. This isn't her fault. Dread's to blame. Him and Zeal."

To deflect him from the subject, so he wouldn't realize I was trying to hide something, I turned to the phone. "I have to call Shock and let her know I'm back."

"So you weren't with Shock?"

His question was casual, but I didn't want to go down that road. I smiled and dialed her number. This time the circuits weren't busy, but her phone went straight to message. That usually meant she was inside a hospital. I told her to call the bar when she got a chance.

"Now what?" he asked, echoing me.

That was a good question. My first task was to hide the fact that I had just kidnapped Cherie with Mystify, so that meant I had to act normally.

"I'm going to open up." I gestured to the shutter. The sound of people was getting louder. "Plenty of customers to be had."

I didn't mention I needed to replenish myself. That was obvious from my feeble aura. Cherie had taken so much from me that I was in serious need.

"Let me help."

At first I started to shake my head, thinking he meant that he wanted to feed me himself, but then he added, "I'm not bad at pushing a broom."

"Are you kidding?" When he didn't back down, I said, "Sure, why not? The mop's in the closet over there."

It was a little strange opening up the bar with Ram. He was legendary, practically a god, and had experienced nearly the entire sweep of civilization. In fact, he'd been instrumental in the development of humans

toward enlightenment and progress. But he restocked
the toilet paper rolls as nonchalantly as Pepe.

To cover our lack of conversation, I turned on the
news on the television. The twenty-four-hour cable channels were each covering Dread's staged resurrection in
their own way: Fox's conservatives were denouncing it
flatly as a hoax; their traditional Christian views were af-
fronted by the very idea of a new messiah in their midst.
MSNBC and CNN waffled around, trying to be "ob-
jective" while focusing on Cherie's transformed looks
more than anything else, comparing endless photos
taken throughout the years. Bloomberg covered it from
a financial angle: the city was groaning under the influx
of too many people, including indigents looking for a
miracle of their own. Now they were sleeping on the
streets and jamming up traffic. NY1 featured eyewitness
reports of trucks blocked miles away from where they
needed to go, attempting to deliver supplies to stores
and restaurants. The entire city was under siege.

Unlike Shock, Ram didn't question my decision to
open the bar. He had probably sat through a hundred
sieges. What was one more?

As I watched the rush of ambulances at local hospitals, I wondered how Pepe was doing. He would probably be released soon. Even major abdominal surgery
was practically a walk-in procedure with all the city
budget cuts. I tried to call the hospital, but couldn't get
through. I couldn't even reach my trusty management
agent, Michael, to find out if he had heard anything.

So who shot me and Pepe in the bar? After Dread's
lies about the resurrection, I didn't believe that it was
Vex who had ordered it. Dread was protecting someone in his organization—who did he control who would
have a reason to try to scare me?

It came to me so fast I almost reeled—Revel. My
former lover had been ordered to protect me, and he

was angry that I was running away from him rather than running to him for help. When things had reached their pitch, maybe he was the one who staged that shooting in order to drive me back into his fold along with Shock.

Dread had said it was a pro who dismantled the surveillance camera. Who better than the PI who originally set up the camera for Revel?

Now I had two things to accuse Revel of—turning me into a demon and shooting my bar. Suddenly his little trip to Uzbekistan was looking more suspicious. Why wouldn't one of the richest demons in the world simply pay the asking price for the priceless manuscript and have it flown here pronto? Unless Revel wanted to get away from me for a while.

Maybe my allies were really my enemies.

Unnerved, I tried to call Glory. Instead of the emergency announcement, I got a recording that said the line was no longer in use. I figured it was a mix-up, what with the heavy traffic.

The only hint of Cherie's kidnapping came from channel NY1 announcing a closure of First Avenue because of a series of medical tests scheduled at NYU Medical Center for the "miracle supermodel." The traffic girl mentioned that the closures had gone on much longer into the afternoon than anticipated as officials waited for Cherie to show up. Ram didn't appear to notice it.

When I went outside to unlock the metal shutter over the front of the bar, Ram silently followed me. He stood nearby scanning everyone going by and examining the windows across the street, watching over me. It made me more nervous than before, but I wasn't going to let that stop me. Business as usual was the way to keep everyone from suspecting I'd had a hand in Cherie's disappearance.

The low whoop of an alarm warned me. Up the avenue, the lights on a red-and-white FDNY EMT truck were flashing as it slowly forced its way through the backed-up traffic. It had to stop up the block, unable to get any farther. From the passenger's side, a slight blond figure jumped down.

"There's Shock." Her signature was a welcome relief. I figured the other demons had bigger fish to fry than Shock, but it was good to see her safe. As Ram had said, there was no telling who would turn on each other during a time of chaos.

Then Shock saw Ram helping me push the shutter into place overhead. Her eyes narrowed and she slowed down her rush as she approached. I felt a pang of guilt, then lifted my head higher. I wasn't going to avoid Ram just because Shock didn't like him.

I have plenty of better reasons to avoid him, and those aren't working, either.

Shock crossed her arms, confronting me. "I've been calling you since two this morning, Allay, every time I could get through the lines. Where have you been?"

I glanced over at Ram, who was looking interested in the answer, as well. But Shock misinterpreted my look.

"Oh, I get it," she said flatly. "You've been with him. Why couldn't you call and let me know so I don't worry all night? Or have you stopped thinking entirely?"

I bit off my instinctive denial. "Don't be that way, Shock. Please."

"You've made it clear that you don't care what I think." She glared at Ram. "Or you'd keep better company. First him, then Glory, then Dread . . . and look at what it's gotten you." She gestured to the people bumping past us, some staring at us curiously while others were clearly intent on some internal need that drove them forward.

"I can't deny I'm responsible for letting this happen," I admitted. "I should have killed Dread. Then none of this would have happened. I've lived for so long treading water that I didn't act when I should have. I wish I could change that more than anything in my life, but there's nothing I can do about it now." Except for act when action was necessary.

But I couldn't stay that out loud. I had to let them both think I was a bump on a log, carried along by whatever current caught me. I didn't want them to think I could engineer Cherie's disappearance.

Shock wasn't paying attention to me, sadly enough. She was locked into a staring match with Ram. Then he smiled. "I've already apologized for nearly killing you, Shock—"

"Twice," she interrupted.

"I'm sure I've apologized enough for both times. I remember it was a long twelve hours while Allay was sleeping off Bliss's birth."

"I don't need apologies," Shock insisted. "You're a killer, Ram. And you're not even up front about it. You hide and sneak around and ambush us—you don't give anyone a fighting chance, do you? You've set yourself apart for thousands of years, thinking you're better than all of us. And I'm supposed to trust you? I'm supposed to think you're interested in Allay because she's such a sweet person? She's an infant compared to you. The only thing you want to do is mold her into a handy little tool that *you* can use."

Taken aback, I shook my head. "Wow, Shock. Is that what you really think of me?"

She waved me off. "This isn't about you, Allay. Don't you get it? He's the worst of everything that demons are—preying on gullible people, destroying them on a whim."

"He preys on demons, not humans," I pointed out.

"Allay, you're a demon! So am I, in case you haven't noticed."

Our voices had risen and more people were watching us. Two guys overheard us and stared back over their shoulders as they were carried past by the flowing stream of pedestrians.

I had to calm her down. "Shock, I want all of us to get along, humans and demons. Can you come inside for a while?"

"You're opening up the bar—you and Ram? I should have known. It's a state of emergency, and you're going to sell liquor. That should be a big help." Without meeting my eyes, she turned away. "I'm taking another shift. I have to get back to work."

I stared after her. Shock had never spoken to me that way. She had always been quiet and supportive, unemotional if anything. We had never fought like this.

I watched after her, knowing how much it revealed of my inner turmoil to Ram, but not caring. Shock climbed back into the truck, which had turned onto Second Street to avoid the backup on Houston. Just before it rolled out of view, Shock looked back at me, her eyes dark with hurt.

"Oh, no. . . ." I felt awful, but I didn't know what I could do to fix it. I couldn't betray Mystify's trust. And if I told her I hadn't stayed out all night with Ram and admitted the truth about what I had really done, she would be even more appalled.

"Why did you let her think we'd been together all night?" Ram asked.

I sighed. "Because that's really not the issue."

"She doesn't like how you're changing," he agreed.

"If I hadn't changed, I would have died. I wouldn't have killed Pique. She wanted me to do it even though I told her I'd be different. She didn't believe me."

"Shock has been the same from the moment she was born. Oh, she's changed personas, but even those have been similar. She's lived in that brownstone since 1905, going through the same routine, the same life over and over again. Isolating herself from everyone, including the people she works with. I'm not surprised she's not good at dealing with change."

I raised my hand. "I don't want to hear you talk bad about her."

Ram nodded, wisely keeping his mouth shut.

But inside I wondered—Shock and I had been living in an odd stasis. Was that why we meshed so well together? I hated to think that might be the foundation of our beautiful friendship.

I stepped inside the bar, looking around to make sure it was ready to open. Only the blackboard was empty. I didn't feel like making up a funny-awful name of a special for today, though a Resurrection Rum Cocktail did leap to mind.

Ram went back to the pool table and paid for a game. As the balls cascaded into the shoot, I wondered how long he planned to stay.

Patrons wandered in, some as nonchalantly as if nothing unusual were happening, while others were full of stories about the disruption. It felt as if a lifetime had passed while I was underground, but I tried to act the same as usual.

But I kept one eye on the news that played instead of the usual music. Nobody complained. Most patrons dropped in, drank fast, and bolted again. The afternoon crowd was like a staccato fugue, and I learned quickly I had to snatch and grab energy wherever I could get it. Slowly but surely I began to replenish myself.

In every emotion I drank, all were tainted with some kind of confusion. I started to think about Mystify and how anxious he would be to sample the mood on the streets. The more I considered it, the more I was certain that he would probably leave Cherie alone at the condos while he went upside to feed. How could he resist the feeling that was most savory to him?

I only hoped he made sure to convince Cherie to stay below the surface.

The news cut to a live shot outside the Prophet's Arena on the waterfront. First they showed a rather industrial view from the Williamsburg Bridge across the river to the arena with Brooklyn behind it, then a lovely reverse shot of the arena with the golden sunshine reflecting off the river between it and the Manhattan towers downtown. The rooftop park on the arena was lush with full-grown trees, and vines were hanging thickly down the sides.

I hurried to turn up the sound. " ... the site of last night's miracle, according to the Fellowship of Truth's leader. A few minutes ago, we saw Prophet Anderson's limo arrive here for tonight's circle. The top leadership of the church have gathered to commune with their new religious icon and the most famous member of the Fellowship of Truth, former supermodel Cherie."

Images of Cherie were flashed on the screen, as they had been all day. They loved showing those last paparazzi photos taken just before she was turned, looking like a cadaverous mummy, and comparing them to her pristine face as it appeared now. Yet they kept repeating that genetic and medical testing proved that Cherie was who she claimed to be.

Cut to the interior of the arena, where the camera panned the packed interior. People stood or knelt in front of their seats praying, while whole rows sang together, swaying back and forth with their arms locked together. It sounded like the crowd was spontaneously trying to get a huge chant going round the audience, but it kept breaking down because of the sheer size. Confetti drifted in the air along with streamers; it looked like a big tent revival smashed together with a Super Bowl pregame party.

Dread entered the stage to thunderous applause.

He lifted his hands saluting the thousands who had gathered at his command. He was probably going for "angelic" with his white suit, but reduced to a tiny size on-screen, he looked to me like a chef in search of his kitchen.

"How cheesy," I muttered as all of the church luminaries took their place on the stage in the center of the arena. Lash was prominent among them, her smile plastered firmly into place. The forgiven wife, the fallen woman among the saints. The camera kept returning to her, which made me snicker when I thought of Dread watching this afterward. He wouldn't like it that she had stolen some of his limelight, but clearly he couldn't let her go.

Then Cherie was announced. The applause was even louder this time, drowning out the commentators. Cherie's face was lovingly magnified on the JumboTron screens inside the arena, and on the television.

I drew in my breath. How did he get her back?

But as Cherie joined hands with Dread and closed the circle, beginning the chant, I realized something was off. Usually she barely bowed her head, as if she had an iron rod shoved down her spine. Even when we had walked through the tunnels, she bent stiffly like she had been drilled from childhood not to slump despite her height. But now she was hunched over like the most humble petitioner.

Everything was slightly off—her voice, the cadence of her words, even the perfect curve of her cheek. As the camera panned the people chanting in the circle, it was glaringly obvious to me that Zeal was not present.

At least, she wasn't there in her Missy van Dam guise. She was posing as Cherie.

I glanced back at the pool table to see if Ram was watching. His eyes were narrowed as if he was seeing the same signs. But it wasn't something that I would supposedly notice, so I continued watching along with my patrons. But inside I was gleeful—Dread's plan was falling apart!

"Do you think they'll cut off her head again?" one guy asked.

"Nah, that's already old. Did you see how she got shot in the chest?" the other retorted. "Blam! Left a hole through her that big." He gestured with his hands.

"What if they flatten her with one of those steamrollers?" somebody else suggested. "Would she inflate like an inner tube and spring back to life?"

"You guys are sick," a voice said over my shoulder. "Have you no respect?"

I turned at the same time I realized my mouth was watering. It was Savor, in a guise I had seen only once before—a young woman with pale silvery blond hair and waiflike features. She could be a coed from the art schools, pampered by an elite existence, yet somehow more vulnerable because she was untouched by the rigors of life.

The first time I'd seen Savor in such a disingenuous guise was a few nights ago, when she told me she was a double agent for Glory and Vex.

With one look at her, the guys tried to excuse their crude speculations, but Savor wasn't having any of it. She sniffed in disdain, moving down to the back end of the bar.

Ram was watching her closely, though she didn't know it. He still looked a bit like Theo Ram, with changes that reflected his true nature. He no longer wore the gear of a tradesman, but was dressed in thoroughly forgettable dark clothes with his face more weathered and taxed by time and experience. If Savor knew he was here, she was doing a good job of hiding it. I tried not to look at him over her shoulder as he graciously lost his pool game and gave up the table.

"Another beer," he said, coming up to the bar. I poured it for him and smiled politely when he over-tipped. He retreated to the wall around the storeroom, far enough away that Savor didn't notice him, but close enough to listen in.

I poured a glass of wine for Savor, at her request, and took her money. I wasn't going to be comping her any time soon. I still hadn't found out if she was telling the truth about Revel, but Plea's memory of her last en-counter with him was damning enough. Maybe my in-stinct not to trust Revel all these years had been based on that, as well as the fact that he had seduced me on Vex's order and made me fall in love with him.

He could have changed since then. But I wouldn't know that until I knew if he had shot my bar and nearly killed Pepe.

Savor was looking at me as warily as I was watching her. I poured a couple more drinks, then drifted back down in her direction. I needed information.

"What does Glory think of Lash's defection?" I asked her quietly.

"You don't know?" Savor's fragile voice matched her demeanor. "Glory left. She closed down all of her prop-erty and flew out with everyone this evening. When I went by, servants were packing up their belongings for shipping. One of them told me the house would be on the market by next week."

I couldn't believe it. "Glory left New York? Where did she go?"

"Dubai." Savor was glum. "She thinks the real estate opportunities there are prime, with the city only bound to grow as Middle Eastern influence broadens. Until another cheap source of energy is developed, they hold the balls of the world. Dubai has a foot in the modern day and another in the Islamic past, so they're perfectly positioned to take advantage of both."

I wanted to sit down. "Glory's given New York to Dread. There'll be no one to hold him back."

"Not unless your boyfriend takes a stand against him." Her voice was the barest whisper. "He did kill Vex, after all."

"He's not my boyfriend." I tried not to look at Ram, but I was sure he could hear us. "What are you doing here, Savor? Why aren't you going to Dubai with Glory?"

"She abandoned me. She found out that I told Dread about your deal with her."

My mouth fell open. "You said you didn't tell him! You liar."

"I had to tell him something juicy or he wouldn't have trusted me. That's part of being a double agent." Savor huffed as if misunderstood. "Glory never cared about the little things before."

"She's probably afraid you'll keep working for Dread. He'll have you as his eyes right in the middle of her camp. I wouldn't let you come if I was her. Why risk it?"

"Lot you know. You can't burn bridges with these high-powered demons, Allay. They never forget a grudge. I would have gladly gone with Glory and been loyal. I don't want to get mixed up in this nonsense that Dread has cooked up."

"You're saying that because you know *I* think it's awful what he's done."

"You should consider yourself lucky that I'd like to form an alliance with you, Allay. I'm now unencumbered by other associations."

"You're Dread's spy, Savor. Why would I want to get close to you?"

She waved one hand, reminiscent of her Sebastian-guise. "Because you know that's only my day job. I'm not really on his side."

I had to laugh. "Minions at work . . ."

"I'll prove to you how valuable my friendship can be. I have information you'll want to hear."

I leaned forward, encouraging her to lower her voice.

"There's something strange going on with 'Elude,'" Savor murmured. "Dread moved her from the Prophet's Center at the same time he installed Lash in a suite at the Beaumont Hotel. I talked to Goad, but he can't figure out where they've taken her. Zeal keeps popping back in from God knows where, but whenever I try to follow her, she manages to lose me."

I nodded thoughtfully, hoping I looked suitably intrigued. "Dread's probably afraid of Ram getting to her, so he's hidden her."

"Dread is holding her prisoner." Savor's voice lowered again. "That wasn't Cherie at the big Fellowship circle tonight. Goad was there. He said Zeal was impersonating Cherie. What if Cherie has already gone off the deep end? She could be raving about demons, and Dread can't let her out in public anymore. I tell you, this thing is bound to come to a messy end. He can't keep it up."

"That's the best news I've heard all day." This time I met Ram's eye. His expression was carefully blank, as if he was refusing to reveal what he was thinking. If I didn't know any better, I might think he had something to do with this.

Savor slid off the stool, ready to leave. "You might want to think twice about working with me, Allay. I could be very valuable to you."

Yeah, right. The most informative thing Savor had told me was that she was talking a lot to Goad. The last thing I wanted to do was align with someone who was friends with Goad.

16

I was saved from answering Savor by the approach of a familiar, if now rather irritating, signature—a vortex sucking me down.

"There's Crave now," Savor said, lifting her head. "So I guess Glory didn't forgive and forget."

I ignored her, going to the door of the bar. I couldn't tell if Bliss was with him, because his signature was so strong. And I couldn't see very far because of the busy streets. Savor came up beside me, but Ram stayed unobtrusively in the back of the bar.

I didn't have long to wait—Bliss blew in like a movie star, radiant and inhumanly gorgeous. She was wearing a tight sequined cocktail dress and extremely high heels. "Hi-dy, hi," she said breezily. "Why is it like a morgue in here?"

I broke off my initial pleased greeting. "We're watching the news."

She wrinkled her pert nose. "Whatever for? Let's get some music on, get the party going. Woo-hoo!"

Like an answering echo, guys all over the bar called back, "Woo-*hoo*!" A long wolf whistle and a few not-so-sotto-voce comments about the hot chick who had wandered in also came back.

Crave grinned like he was the proud owner of the red Jaguar parked in the driveway. He had long since dropped his "Mark Cravet" guise, but he was still in that general mold—a smooth Latino with fierce passions boiling beneath the surface. He was the seducer in pure form, strolling in and meeting every woman's eyes in the room, including mine.

Bliss slinked through the bar greeting the regulars she'd met yesterday, and saying hi to everyone else. She practically draped herself over a couple of young NYU guys, making their day as she ruthlessly sucked energy from them.

I corralled her and brought her to the back end of the bar. It was the only empty spot where she wouldn't harass my patrons, but it did put us within hearing range of Ram. He was sitting with his back to us, apparently watching the pool game and nursing a beer.

Savor clung to us like a barnacle, fascinated. She took a stool right next to Bliss. She had found Bliss to be distinctly unimpressive when she met her the day before yesterday, but Bliss had been a newly minted copy of me and was busy working the bar rush like a good employee.

"You're all grown-up," Savor told her. "What's your secret, darling?"

"Living *la vida loca*," Bliss said.

Suddenly Savor was looking older and less vulnerable. She wasn't trying to win me over at the moment; instead she was focused on getting a handle on Bliss. It showed me exactly why I couldn't trust Savor. She was in it solely for herself, all the time.

"What have you been doing?" I asked, trying to regain Bliss's attention. I didn't want her to get caught up with Savor. That would be almost as bad as Savor dating my bartender Lolita.

Bliss rolled her eyes to the ceiling as if overwhelmed by the question. "Too much to tell—that's for sure. We started out by going to this club—you don't know it, Allay—called La Trapeze. Did you know people go there to get naked and have sex? It's the most a-maz-ing thing I've ever seen."

"You're only three days old, Bliss."

"That includes everything *you've* ever seen," she added.

I cringed under the weight of the memories she had. She was probably the only demon in history to retain a full annotated set of her progenitor's life.

Well, I had changed, or so Shock kept telling me. So it wasn't like Bliss still had a spy cam looking directly into my soul.

Bliss was prattling on about their night. "Then we met these two couples from Germany who were ex-quis-ite. We went back to their hotel room and had sex until dawn. Insatiable. I didn't think anything could beat a demon's thirst, but this one woman, she wanted to or-gasm over and over again, endlessly." She sighed as if it had been heavenly.

Savor was veering into his Sebastian mannerisms. "Honey, you ain't seen nothing yet. I could take you to some parties that would knock your boobs off. I mean literally. The best ones are for men only."

Bliss's eyes lit up as if Savor had waved catnip in front of her nose. She was ready to pounce and bite. "Yes! Can we go?"

"It's too early," Savor said blandly, avoiding my glare. "I'll come by later to get you." She hesitated, looking at Crave. "You're invited, of course, Crave. Maybe you'd like to celebrate your liberation from Glory?"

Crave was leaning against the bar, the amused, so-phisticated boyfriend. "Glory ran away. My shop was emptied out today, but I managed to grab a few gems posing as one of the real estate agents." He patted his pocket as if there were jewels in it. "She tried, but she hasn't robbed me of anything. I'll be bigger and better than ever."

"Glory's merciless," Savor agreed. "Like a volcano. It's abominable what she's done to you. If you need a place to stay, my apartment is open to you night or day." She pulled out a card and handed it over. "You can call me anytime." She handed another one to Bliss. "You, too, scrumptious."

Crave wasn't buying Savor's flattery. Clearly he didn't know Savor had worked for Glory as a double agent; his sneer said he only knew her as Dread's messenger.

"I thought you were leaving, Savor," I said pointedly.

"Sure, sure." She turned to Bliss. "I'll drop by around midnight to see if you want to go out. There's one party that's only on Friday nights—you won't want to miss it, love."

Bliss agreed with a laugh. "Come on, let's go upstairs, Crave. I have something to show you."

They left before Savor did, but they were so intent on each other that they didn't say good-bye to anyone. They also didn't notice Ram sitting six feet away.

Savor watched after them, thoughtful. "So Crave doesn't know about my work with Glory. You won't tell them, will you, Allay? Dread would kill me if he knew."

"So that's why you came here."

"Believe what you want, Allay. I'd like to have an alliance with you. But if you're not interested, it's no skin off my nose. As long as you don't tell anyone my secret, then I owe you a big one."

I shrugged, trying not to look in Ram's direction. "I don't want to cause any problems for you. But what about Lash? Doesn't she know?"

Savor stared out the back windows of the bar. "I don't know. . . ."

"I'd be more worried about her than me, if I was you. That woman would do whatever it takes to save her own hide. She went over to Dread's side faster than it took to drive to Brooklyn."

Savor raised her brows. "I guess I won't know until my flame is snuffed."

"That's the spirit."

I went back to my work, wishing I could tell Savor to not come back for Bliss. But who was I to tell Bliss what to do? She was doing better for herself in a few days than I'd done in a decade. It was a little embarrassing.

The faint rhythmic bumping of the daybed moving upstairs echoed down. I looked up at the ceiling, rolling my eyes. Ram was smiling slightly, watching me, but I ignored him and tended to my neglected customers.

Happy hour swung into full gear, but the place never really got hopping. There was a tension in the air—in the subdued, worried voices and in the sudden arguments that kept breaking out between friends and strangers over Cherie's miracle. It upended everything—it was the fountain of youth suddenly made possible. Joining a church and chanting together every Sunday seemed like a small price to pay to live forever. Even the loudest skeptics were awed by the very idea, almost as if they longed in secret to be proven wrong.

I served drinks as I kept one eye on the news reports. The twenty-four-hour love affair with the story was now souring, as usual. Reporters and analysts were busy picking apart every bit of evidence amid a snowballing chorus of voices declaring Cherie's resurrection was a hoax. She had canceled all interviews today and missed her scheduled appointments for additional medical testing.

I was delighted to see a frame-by-frame dissection of the evening's Fellowship circle led by Cherie/Zeal. Facial recognition software detected a number of deviations from Cherie's features; nobody had been more documented from the time she was sixteen years old, and all of those images were consistent. They also found deviations in the footage of the beheading. Cherie's idealized face, thanks to her malleable demon physiology, was different in fundamental ways from her former image.

I touched my own cheek, wondering what I would really look like if I had remained human. Even though I had tried to be faithful to my original appearance, this face was a version of myself that I wanted to be.

Along with pseudo-scientific explanations that proved the beheading had been faked, the big sticking point was the fact that Cherie had idealized her features before she was beheaded. There was no evidence of her transformation from crone to beauty. I wondered if Dread had tried to make her resume her old appearance, as she really was at the time she was possessed. That would have made a much bigger impact. But having met her, I couldn't imagine her doing it. Her perfection was everything to her.

But I couldn't think about Cherie, not with Ram watching me.

As if reading my mind, he came down to the front end of the bar, where the hinged flap was leaning up against the wall. I was standing there watching the TV during the lulls.

"What do you think of this?" I asked him, heading him off.

"I think Zeal did a poor job of impersonating Cherie at the Fellowship circle. It was a bad decision on Dread's part because it's proof that his scheme is falling apart quicker than he had hoped."

Playing along, I asked, "Why would Zeal risk it?"

"Dread must have felt he had no choice. Cherie couldn't perform her role, for some reason. Maybe she's grown unstable very quickly. That happens with older humans when they're possessed."

I shook my head doubtfully. "I saw her up at the hospital, and she looked like she was holding it together just fine. She was talking to the doctors as reasonable as you could want. Albeit in an insanely fanatical way."

"Maybe she ran away from Dread. He could have Goad's horde out looking for her now."

I didn't like that thought. I hoped Mystify wasn't in danger. "But why would she leave him?"

"What did you do when you were possessed?"

"I ran," I admitted. "Like I was on a three-day acid binge. I ended up raving and tied to a gurney at the psych ward."

He didn't take it as lightly as I'd said it. His gray eyes seemed to draw me into him, and he lightly stroked the back of my hand, as if to reassure me that he was there for me.

It threw me. It was just what a lover would do. Someone kind and giving.

I pulled back, clasping my hands in front of me. I barely managed to keep myself from nervously wiping down the bar. I was already revealing too much to him. Why did he remain a mystery while I was clear as glass? Fear the unknown man in the shadows.

"Why did you hide from Bliss and Crave?" I asked.

"Savor was still here, and you didn't introduce me to her, so I remained concealed."

"You expected me to introduce you?"

"It's your bar, your call. I can protect you better if you don't, but you said you wanted me to come here openly. So I'll wait for you to decide which demons know who I am."

"I don't want Savor to tell Dread you're here." I grimaced. "But I didn't expect her to spill her secret."

"Too many people know about her and Glory by now. It's bound to come out. And Savor knows it. If anyone can walk across coals, it's that one."

"You won't tell anyone?" I asked.

"For you, anything." His sad smile blunted the cliché.

"Though I don't know why you're protecting Savor, of all people."

"I don't know, either. But it feels wrong for someone to spread information that I let them overhear. I don't trust Savor, but I don't wish her harm."

"Who else is on your list—" Ram started to ask.

The door flung open with a bang, interrupting him. Lolita stood in the doorway, with a huge silly grin. "I'm baaack, bitches!"

Her ringing laugh took all the sting out of her words. It was Lolita! My bestest friend, my rock, my shield against the world.

I laughed just to see her, and ran over to give her a big hug. I didn't mind it when she squeezed me extra hard. "You look great, Allay. A few days off suits you."

Regulars were calling out greetings, with some of her favorites coming over to say hi. She flirted and gave little put-downs for the guys who liked that, swaggering her way slowly to the bar. She was quite tall and imposing, with a coy sexuality that oozed out of her, all curves and special smiles for everyone.

When she saw Ram, she stopped in her tracks. "I remember you! Aren't you our hero?"

It caught me off guard—how could she recognize him when he looked so different? But Ram grinned right back. "You got it."

She gave me a special look of pride, like I had won a prize. "Good for you."

Now I was completely confused.

Lolita confided, "You know, I didn't like you at first. I even told Allay, here, to bounce you right back outside. But she wouldn't listen to me. I guess I'm not right all the time."

Ram looked surprised while Lo let out a loud laugh at her own expense. I didn't—I wanted to tell her that she had been absolutely right about Ram. I should have kicked him out when she warned me, because then he wouldn't have had the chance to try to kill Shock.

And none of this would have happened.

"I guess I'm lucky she's the boss instead of the other way around," Ram told Lolita.

"She usually does what I say." Lo looked up at the television. "Happy hour's over, so that goes off! We need to get some music going, liven things up."

Somehow it sounded different when Lolita said it instead of Bliss. Lolita never judged me.

I let Lo sort everything out. She plugged in her iPod and was pouring drinks before I knew it. Together we caught up on the restocking and washing, getting ready for the night rush. The mood in the bar picked right up, along with my own.

When we had a moment, Lolita chastised me. "Why didn't you tell me you were opening up, Allay? I had to hear it from a friend who lives nearby. He says the Den was open day before yesterday, too. What happened? I thought the owners were shutting us down."

I patted her arm. "I wanted to be sure it wasn't temporary. There are still things to sort out, but it looks like the bar is mine."

"Yours? You own it? Allay, that's fabulous! Mazel tov!" Lolita exclaimed in true New York fashion. "We have to celebrate—"

"No, not right now," I urged, keeping my voice down. "Things are too weird with the emergency and what with that circus over in Brooklyn. The Fellowship was involved in the ownership of the bar, so I don't want to make a big deal about it."

She nodded, understanding instantly. So when one of the customers asked if I really owned the bar, she told him to mind his own business. "You just relax," she ordered me. "I can handle this crowd myself."

"Are you sure, Lo?"

Lolita gave a quick glance at Ram. "You have *much* better things to do." Making sure he couldn't hear, she added, "He's more handsome than I remember."

"I'm not taking him upstairs for a little nooky." That reminded me of Bliss. I would have to explain her, but I hated to lie to Lo. "An old friend from California came to help me out. You can't miss her—she's a bombshell."

"Where is she?" Lolita looked around with interest.

"Upstairs, with a guy she just met. They should be down soon."

"A friend . . . that's really good, Allay. You should have more old friends come stay with you."

"Wait until you meet her before you say that." At this point I wasn't even sure I knew Bliss, much less could call her a friend. I finally understood what everyone had been trying to tell me: newbies need time to settle into themselves and shake off the vestiges of their progenitor. But the only thing that mattered was how trustworthy Bliss was—I didn't care how many orgies she threw or which demons she hung out with. As long as she didn't hurt people, I would support her.

"I can't wait," Lo assured me. Then she winked at Ram. "There's a pretty moon you should be able to see from the courtyard."

"Lo!" She was so obvious, it was embarrassing.

"I'd love to see the moon," Ram said seriously.

"Of course you'd say that." I made a face at Lolita. I didn't need anyone encouraging me to have a relationship with Ram. Why wasn't she warning me off him like she did the first time, like everyone else did?

Maybe because her instincts are right, and Ram no longer means me any harm.

It was tempting to believe it. I went outside with Ram, letting the door lock behind me, so we were alone in the courtyard. The bar wasn't licensed to allow customers in the back, so it was just a bare concrete pad.

I'd put a bench along the back fence, and Ram headed over to sit down.

I looked up at the second-floor windows of my back room, blazing with light. No shadows moved to indicate Crave and Bliss were inside. The overarching branches of the acacia tree blocked the moon from sight, but the glow lit up the sky. The city vibrated around us, filled with sirens, engines, and the thumping music from the bar, a perpetual mechanical racket. But in this little pocket of darkness, a dog barked a few houses down and then was quiet, emphasizing the calm of the interior of the block.

I wanted to say something ironic, like "How romantic." But it was romantic, too much so for me to point it out.

Ram took my hand lightly in his as we sat down. He could feel my hesitation, despite the fact that I could hardly stop staring at him. I knew it was all fake, that he didn't really look this way, but I was so attracted to him that my brain couldn't convince my body of that. It wasn't just his face and well-muscled body—it was the way he moved, how he looked at me, the timbre of his voice.

I wanted him to drop his shields so I could really feel his signature, that driving aggression that he rode so effortlessly. But that would sweep me off my feet and shut off my mind for good. And I wasn't sure I wanted that mindless oblivion. I wasn't sure I could risk opening up to him when I had to guard my secret about Cherie.

He leaned in to kiss me, his warm lips luring me in. I told myself it was only one kiss, only one long clench under the acacia tree. I wouldn't let myself go this time, I would show a little bit of restraint until I could get him into a proper bed. We had never made love on a bed, not once.

As our kiss went on and on, I wanted to go upstairs and kick Bliss and Crave out of my apartment so we could give the old-fashioned way a whirl.

"I love how you catch fire in my arms," Ram murmured.

"Yes, in spite of myself." I ducked away, feeling self-conscious. "You're like heroin. Not that I've ever tried heroin. You know what I mean."

He had me completely ruffled. I wanted to go back to kissing him, but I felt like I was floundering on shifting ground. Why did he always have the upper hand?

Putting both my hands to his shoulders, I looked him firmly in the eye. "I need to know something, Ram."

He settled back, unperturbed. "You've been dying to ask me, so go ahead."

"Did you really kill Hope because she betrayed you to Bedlam?"

His brow lifted slightly. "*That's* what you want to know? Ancient history?"

"Excuse me, but I think it's important to know why you killed your wife. Especially before I get more intimate with you, if you know what I mean."

He looked blacker than I had ever seen him. He could hardly speak. "I could never hurt you, Allay."

"Why, Ram? I want to understand. You said you did something that made her angry, and that I would sympathize with her. You can't tell me there's a mystery and then refuse to speak to me about it. What happened between you two?"

"I'm sure Mystify told you everything."

"I haven't asked Mystify. I want you to tell me." I didn't add that Revel was out of the country right now tracking down information on Hope.

"You've been spending a lot of time with Mystify. Did he touch you? Did he take your hand and kiss it?" Ram lifted my hand, his lips brushing the back of my fingers just as Mystify had kissed me.

I snatched my hand back so quickly that he knew he was right.

"You were with him since last night, weren't you?" he pressed. "He helped you, didn't he?"

"What are you talking about?" I had to keep our secret.

Ram saw the truth. "He helped you deal with Cherie. You did something, didn't you? If it was anyone else, I'd say you killed her. But knowing you, I'd say you've stolen her away and have her stashed somewhere. You do know how dangerous that is, Allay? When Dread finds out, he'll kill you. Unless I can get to him first."

I gaped at him. How did he know? Was it written on my forehead?

I might as well have spoken, because he said, "You weren't with Shock, Bliss, Crave, Glory, Savor, or me last night. Revel's out of town. The last time you disappeared, it was with Mystify, so that's who you were with this time."

Valiantly trying to recover, I insisted, "I went up to see Cherie at the hospital last night. Shock left for work, and Bliss and Crave went out to party. I was there when she was shot. Zeal did it."

"You and that misbegotten offspring of mine did something to Cherie. Let me help you, Allay. I can make sure that Dread won't find her. That way she won't tell any tales."

"I don't know what you're talking about." I stood up. "If you can't handle my friendship with Mystify, just say so. Don't make up wild stories about us."

Ram stopped me. "I know it's true, Allay. Because you didn't ask me if I did something to Cherie. That's bound to be everyone's assumption when it's clear she's disappeared."

I turned away so he wouldn't see my face. *I'm such a bad liar!* I never should have let him hang around and spy on me. I should have known he'd put it all together. Then he brought me out here and got me all softened up with his kisses so he could get an honest reaction out of me.

Mystify was going to be so mad.

I needed a few minutes to wrap my mind around this. "I have to go see if Lolita needs anything."

I made my way blindly back into the bar. He had peeled me like an onion. I never stood a chance. No wonder he could manipulate me so easily. Mystify was right—I *was* putty in Ram's hands. I had been trying to pin him down about Hope, and he had turned the tables on me but good.

Deny, deny, deny was my mantra as I marched through the bar. I didn't look to see if he was following. I figured on keeping busy and far away from him.

But as I neared the front of the bar, ready to slip behind the counter, a guy came in with his hood pulled up. It was warm out tonight, so that was odd, and even more so was the fact that the cord was tied tight over the top of his nose, hiding the lower half of his face.

His eyes met mine, fiercely bloodshot and filled with hatred. Then he pulled a gun out from his waistband and pointed it at me. It was sleek and black and looked heavy in his hand.

"It's your own fault!" the guy shouted. "You made me do it, Allay."

17

"Phil?" I blurted out. "Have you gone crazy?"

It was Phil Anchor, my first client as a bagman, one-time Pulitzer Prize contender, and lifelong coke addict. I had flirted with him, argued with him, kicked him out of my bar, and welcomed him in again. I'd recognize him anywhere, even with half his face covered.

His expression grew panicked as he realized I knew who he was. At that moment everything slowed down, as my brain caught up. Phil Anchor was pointing a gun at me. Phil Anchor was tightening his finger, intending to shoot me.

Like he had shot through the windows of my bar, killing me and nearly killing Pepe.

In one big rush, it all made sense. I'd been shot after I'd told Phil that I could reveal his petty dealings with the prophet. It hadn't been Mackleby and it hadn't been Vex. It hadn't been Revel, either.

It had been Phil Anchor.

I could see it in his eyes, the desperation, the paranoia, the greed that drove him to do whatever he had to in order to feed the beast. This man could fire six rounds through my plate-glass windows.

I held up my hands in a futile attempt to stop him. "Phil, stop—"

His finger flexed, and I heard the explosion as the gun fired. Behind him were the shocked faces of my patrons, some already lunging to get out of the bar. In the ringing echo, their screams seemed very far away.

I was jolted backward. I saw nothing but exploding light; then everything went black, abruptly, finally.

". . . but I just hung up the phone," someone was saying. "How did you get here so fast?"

"The lieutenant told us to keep an eye on the place. What happened?"

I listened to a jumble of voices trying to sort them out. Lolita was telling them Phil shot me, and she was crying, huge sobs. I wanted to reassure her, but my sight was only mistily coming back and I couldn't move my lips.

I was looking up at the ceiling of my bar. I'd been doing a lot of that lately, and in my gradual return to life I decided I was going to paint it some cheery color like blue or red. Peeling blackness with exposed ductwork wasn't my idea of inspiring.

Coming back to life was no easier the second time around. In fact, this time was much worse because I seemed to be aware and present before I could fully speak. Pain radiated from my nose and cheekbones, my sinuses were pounding, and my eyes felt like they were about to burst from the pressure.

"Oh, my God!" someone screamed.

I could vaguely see backward movement, away from me. Oh, shit. I was regenerating in front of my patrons. And the police, for good measure.

And Lolita. She dropped down to her knees next to me. "Allay!" The dawning hope in her voice made my throat close. I realized then that I wasn't breathing. Not yet. But I could see her leaning over me, begging for me to be all right.

The cops were standing at my feet, their hands on their guns, their eyes fastened on my face. Patrons fled, leaving overturned chairs and tables, but a good dozen people were ringed around me where I lay.

I reached up and touched my cheeks, feeling solid for the first time. "I think I'm okay."

"Your face was blown off!" a cop exclaimed.

Lolita took my hand, squeezing it. She couldn't speak for her tears, but she was laughing and crying at the same time.

Ram was kneeling on my other side. He took my other hand, letting me feel his comforting reassurance. He was the only one in the room who wasn't panicked.

That helped.

"What kind of stupid stunt is this?" another cop demanded.

I put my hands to the sticky floor, and lifted them to find it was my own coagulating blood lying in a vast pool around me.

Lolita was kneeling in it, her knees stained red. But she ignored it, helping me sit up. "Are you really okay, Allay?"

"Yeah, I'm fine."

"It's like the miracle in Brooklyn," one of my patrons said. "Cherie's head came back that same way, transparentlike until it was solid again."

I pressed my fingers against my cheeks. They were still sore with residual pain, my heart beating fast from the adrenaline rush. I wanted to throw up, but I did everything I could to control myself. Too many eyes were watching me in lurid fascination.

The female cop was leaning over me; I recognized the powerful fireplug of a woman. She had responded to Ram's 911 call when Dread came over to con me. "Explain this," Suarez demanded, holding up an exploded bullet, the metal peeled back like a banana. It was coated in blood. It must have fallen out the back of my head as I healed. "A round like this doesn't punch a neat hole. It blows your face apart, like your face was blown apart when I got here."

"It was," Lolita agreed. "Allay, what happened to you?"

Sirens were wailing in the distance, probably converging on the Den. Clearly the cops weren't doubting their own eyes. Maybe Cherie's resurrection had done that much to make people accept that such a thing could happen—people could rise from the dead.

But I didn't want everyone thinking this had anything to do with religion, especially not the Fellowship of Truth.

"I'm sorry I didn't tell you sooner," I said to Lolita. "I'm a demon. I'm immortal. I live off human emotions, but I don't hurt people, I promise."

I wasn't actually sure I'd said it in the ringing silence that followed. But Ram's expression and the shock wave of absolute surprise that tingled through his fingers were convincing enough. I'd managed to amaze a man who had seen everything in two and a half thousand years.

"That's . . ." Lolita lowered her voice slightly. "Allay, come on . . . a demon?"

"I was born human, like you. But I was possessed by a demon right before I graduated. See, this is what I looked like then." I transformed my face and body back to the fresh and innocent flesh of youth.

Gasps went up, even from the female cop. She looked left and right, as if searching for projectors. Or maybe for a camera crew to jump out and shout that they'd been punked.

I reverted to my usual facade. "Sorry about that. I'm just trying to prove a point. I am who I am, and I hate lying about it."

More cops spilled into the bar on high alert. Lolita helped me stand up and move out of the slippery puddle of my blood. I let go of Ram and lost sight of him in the surrounding blue shirts, puffed out with bulletproof vests.

Suarez snapped to and ordered, "Get her to the car. Button down this place. I want IDs on everyone here."

A general groan of protest rose, but I thought it best to do as they wanted. Cops liked order, and this clearly was a mess. So I went along with the cops, glancing back to catch Ram's rueful shake of his head. Then he turned away, transforming his features into an ordinary guy with neat hair and forgettable features.

Lolita argued with the cops to come with me, but they were curt in their demands that she stay and be questioned along with everyone else. "Don't worry," I told her. "I didn't do anything wrong."

"I'll close down and come after you as quick as I can," Lo assured me. There was no doubt in her eyes, none in her words. She didn't care what I was; she was my friend.

In a sudden rush, I knew I'd never regret telling her the truth. Never. Not when she could look at me like that.

I couldn't get the cops to tell me if I was being arrested or not. Suarez was closemouthed with her partner as much as me. I could see the hairs on the back of her neck standing up, and she sat slightly canted to keep an eye on me.

I realized that I could end this right now. I could run as soon as the car door opened. I could run faster than a human. I could disappear, change my persona, start over somewhere else.

I could even go back to the bar in a new persona. I could . . .

The only thing I'd lose was myself. I'd never be Emma Meyers again.

Having rejected my real name for so long, I suddenly didn't want to let it go. I didn't want to lose my own history.

I didn't want to lie anymore. So I went peacefully into the mint green cinder block cube that housed the police station.

They let me wash up in the bathroom and gave me a white NYPD T-shirt. I threw the blood-soaked one in the trash. Then they stuck me in a tiny one-person cell in an alcove off a dead-end hallway. I couldn't have lain down if I wanted to. I had to sit on the bench and wait.

"What am I being charged with?" I asked them.

"We have to figure that out," one of the cops told me. "Just cooperate, will you?"

"Hey, don't I get a phone call?" I wanted to tell Michael the truth myself, so he wouldn't have to hear it from Lolita first. But they were already gone.

Nobody came for hours.

I had plenty of time to think about what I'd done. And wonder if there was still a way out of this. As much as I wanted to tell the truth, I didn't want to out myself to the world. I didn't want the attention—my bar would become a carnival sideshow, my refuge would be ruined.

I also didn't want the responsibility. How could I represent demons to the world when I really didn't like them? They were a motley bunch of evil incarnate, except for a few of them, so why should I put a pretty face on it?

Because I could explain what we were, once and for all. I had one foot in each world; who better to bridge the gap?

I could take the religion out of it, defuse Cherie's resurrection with my own revelation, a demon revelation, not one of Dread's twisted truth. I could explain it based on science instead of mysticism, as Ram had suggested. After all, demons were going to be outed soon by the ERI machines.

But if I was the first, it would affect my family back home in California. They would be appalled, and besieged by people. That alone almost made me squeeze through the bars to escape. What right did I have to bring the media down on them?

Then again, it would only be fifteen minutes of fame, and they could shut the door in reporters' faces or sell my story to the *Enquirer* for a million dollars. Whatever they wanted, it wasn't mine to judge. Heck, if it made them feel better about me, I'd give an interview myself and give them the money.

I would finally be able to explain why I ran away from them all, why I had detached myself from their lives. It was because I didn't want to draw demons to their home when I visited, and I hated lying about not eating and sleeping and why I was still alone with no ambitions for myself after all these years. I could apologize and tell them how hard I'd struggled, and maybe my mom would put her arms around me like she used to do, and tell me it was okay.

I wanted to see the acceptance in her eyes like I'd seen in Lolita's. Suddenly, that was the most important reason to come out.

I could see now why I had wanted to turn Bliss into my daughter, so I could re-create the family I had left behind when I became a demon. But it was no substitute. I couldn't force Bliss to be something she wasn't.

But I could reach out to my own mom, my dad and sister, and her husband and kids. Because they were my blood. They were my family.

I settled in to get this over with. Then I could deal with the important stuff.

I didn't like sitting in a jail cell like a criminal. The fact that I deserved it for murdering Pique and kidnapping Cherie made it even worse. By the time Lieutenant Markman opened the cell door, letting me out to join

Detective Paulo and another plainclothes officer, I was ready to cooperate.

Paulo was watching me even more intently than before. Arrogance tinted his aura, that blood-orange mixture of fear and anger that usually came when someone was about to stomp on another person.

I sat up straighter, my feet hitting the floor, ready for anything.

Markman was tired of playing games with me, I could tell. He might have looked past his prime, but I knew better. He had uncanny intuition, nearly demon in his insight. Without Bliss to run interference the other morning, he would have peeled me apart as easily as Ram did.

"If we show you a lineup, can you identify who shot you tonight, Ms. Meyers?"

"Yes. Why? Did you catch Phil already?"

"Come this way."

It was weird. They didn't say a word about me being a demon. But Paulo never took his eyes off me, pumped up like he wanted to slam a wall or shout in some kind of twisted victory.

They took me to a room with a two-way mirror, a scratched and industrial version, not those sleek windows you see on TV. Phil was standing second from the left. He looked crazed, twitching and flushed, his eyes and nose weeping continuously.

"Pathetic," I muttered. How could someone do that to themselves? He could have gotten hold of himself somewhere along the way. During those years when he seemed to think he was doing so well, but he was really just clinging to crumbs of what he could steal as it slipped away. He had been successful, once.

Now he was going to be charged with attempted murder. I figured it couldn't be murder even though technically I had died.

I identified Phil, and a murmur went around the room.

Markman asked me, "What is your relationship with Phil Anchor, Ms. Meyers?"

I looked from him to the other men. "You don't want to know how I came back from the dead?"

Markman smiled. "We'll get to that, in due time. Right now, we're concerned with the crime that has been committed. We have witnesses who say Phil Anchor shot you in the face, but there's nothing like having the victim ID the perp. It helps us build a strong case for the DA."

I looked around again, seeing the clenched fists, the fierce nods. There was more going on here than the conviction of one sick junkie. "Why have you got such a hard-on over this?"

Paulo pushed forward. "We know about the church, buying the politicians in the city."

A corruption case. A big corruption case involving lots of publicity and kudos for the NYPD.

I met Markman's gaze. "Oh. I get it."

Phil was destroyed, a shriveled mess of a man. He must have told them I was the prophet's bagman, to try to save himself.

That was why they were all looking at me like I could deliver the crooked politicos and civil servants who had eluded them directly into their hands.

Problem was, I really didn't have much to give them even after ten years of passing off envelopes. I mostly dealt with messengers and used passwords instead of names. I could count on one hand the people I knew who were getting bribes, and a couple of those came from Savor's gossip instead of anything I had seen firsthand.

None of it involved murder, or at least I didn't think it did. Come to think of it, I didn't know much at all about what I'd been doing for the past ten years.

I cleared my throat. "I need to speak to my lawyer."

Markman's expression shut down, and they all nodded on cue. They were professionals. I fully intended to cooperate, but I was going to have a professional on my side to protect me. They wanted me to talk, right now, but Markman was willing to give me one last chance to come clean. Instead of spinning another story, I was finally doing it the right way.

I was shown into a conference room where I could call Michael and wait for a lawyer to arrive.

I stopped Lieutenant Markman on the way out. "Did you do a blood analysis on the bullets you picked up in my bar the first time?"

"Yes. I was going to ask why your blood is on two of them when you weren't injured."

"I was shot. Phil killed me then, too. He's the one who nearly killed Pepe."

Markman nodded thoughtfully. For the first time, I think he believed me.

It wasn't what I expected; it wasn't my choice. But I should have known it would come to this.

18

I liked my lawyer, despite how tight-assed he was. Michael brought in John Kosciusko; then with a worried look and a long hug for me, he left us alone. That was Michael through and through; all he cared about was making sure that I was all right. He wasn't just my management agent, he was my friend. He would ask his questions later, when I was out of trouble.

I was so grateful for Michael's support that I would have worked with any lawyer he had brought me. Kosciusko didn't look any different from any other suit on the street, with wiry reddish brown hair that was neatly groomed. He was in his late thirties with the brisk, no-nonsense air of a working attorney.

But I trusted Michael knew what he was doing, and I was completely honest with Kosciusko. I explained that after I was possessed, I had moved to the city from California at Vex's request so he could watch over me. He put me into the bar and ordered me to make the exchanges for Dread, who was posing as Prophet Thomas Anderson. I didn't go into Vex's recent demise or demon politics; Kosciusko had a way of keeping me on track and cutting through all the clutter in my story.

He also got out of me the lie I'd told to Lieutenant Markman, that the prophet and I had been lovers, and that was why he gave me the bar. Kosciusko asked a number of probing questions about the fact that the prophet had confirmed my story with the police. He asked about the first time I had met with the prophet, and his instructions to me on how I was to conduct the payoffs.

Everything else I had to tell him left him dissatisfied, according to his muddy aura. He didn't like it that all of my dealings had been with Vex, who had been in the guise of the prophet's nephew. The rest of my information was based on hearsay from Savor, who I identified simply as "another demon who worked for Dread." She's the one who told me about zoning commissioner Mackleby and pointed out the guy who was his driver. I rattled off the various people she said were involved in Dread's schemes, but Kosciusko didn't have any questions about them.

"Did you meet with anyone who directly received a bribe?" he asked.

"Other than Phil? I don't really know . . . there were some in the beginning who could have been picking it up themselves." I was feeling a little desperate. If I didn't have anything to give the DA, there would be no reason for him to cut a deal with me.

The lawyer tapped his pen against the desk calendar. That was when I noticed the ring on his right hand—on a crimson field was a tiny gold cross.

"Are you religious?" I blurted out.

For the first time, he hesitated. "Yes. I'm Catholic."

Uh-oh. "Do you have a problem with me being a demon?"

He shifted slightly. "That's unconfirmed. Regardless, I don't care if you're a two-headed cow—you're my client and I'll do everything I can to help you. But I can't do my job unless you're honest with me. Frankly, Ms. Meyers, you need to be honest."

"I am!" I racked my brain for anything I'd equivocated about. After lying for so many years, I found it weird to finally be telling someone the absolute truth. At which, he barely blinked. "You think I'm pulling some kind of scam, saying I'm a demon. But it's the truth. It's how I got coerced into doing this."

"Your motivations are unimportant. I need facts." Kosciusko looked down at his notepad. "Tell me about Phil Anchor. Why did he want to kill you?"

I wilted. Back to Phil again. "This won't get us anywhere. Phil's a no-account coke addict. He had a chance to be a good writer, maybe even a great one. Who knows? But he squandered it."

"He came to the bar himself to pick up his pay?"

"Yeah, he was my first customer. I saw him every month those first few years." That was when I thought he was cute, but I didn't want to tell Kosciusko that. Then at a slight narrowing of his eyes, I hastily added, "We flirted with each other, but we never took it any further. He was working a lot for Dre—the prophet, and he was being careful not to ruin a good thing."

"What did he do for Anderson?"

"Phil took tips for his articles, and he definitely slanted his coverage to favor the church. More recently, since he hasn't been getting the assignments, he's done research for them, smear jobs on certain people. He gave me a USB last weekend that he said had his life's blood on it for the prophet."

"What did he mean by that?"

"Who knows? Like he sold his soul to get the information. But Phil cares only about getting his next fix."

Kosciusko sat there looking at me, clearly thinking about something. I didn't want to interrupt, so I stayed quiet.

"I can offer them your testimony against Anderson," Kosciusko finally said, "and your corroboration on the payoffs to Anchor, along with any details or dates you can remember about those meetings. I can also offer them your hearsay evidence against these other individuals, which may be enough to get warrants in some cases, especially Mackleby, whom you called from your bar."

"That doesn't sound like much."

"Well, your other option is to argue that you didn't do anything illegal. You didn't confirm that there was money in the packets or that it was being paid for illegal purposes. Churches are exempt from taxes, so there's no IRS infraction in dealing in cash. You would have to take the Fifth because you couldn't confirm you had met with the prophet to set up a payment exchange system, and whether you had handed packets off to Anchor."

"You mean I'd be arrested and tried?"

"Probably not, but there's a chance if they're feeling vindictive over the collapse of their big case. You won't go to jail, not on my watch."

"But if I help the DA and I testify against the prophet, then it will be a much bigger case, won't it? A lot of publicity."

"It would be more sensational, yes. But I think you're in deep regardless. The DA will pursue this, and it will come out that Anderson gave you the bar since Anchor has admitted he was working for Anderson."

I stood up and paced over to the window, but it was so cloudy behind the wire mesh that it was hard to see the street. Kosciusko was offering me the easy way out. I could deny, deny, deny until I was blue in the face, and the police couldn't do much to me. I was small fry in all of this.

Or I could tell the truth. This was my chance to redeem myself. What if Dread had passed blood money to an assassin through my bar? I knew he had done bad things with that money, bilking the taxpayers at the very least when he built the Prophet's Arena on their dime on the unstable bank of the East River. The truth could be far worse.

Didn't I owe it to myself and everyone else to blow the whistle on Dread's dirty little scam? Wouldn't that help destroy any credibility the Fellowship had, and throw doubt on their "miracle" religion?

In fact, I didn't have the right to think of myself, my own needs in this. I had done wrong, and I should repay my debt to society. Whatever the consequences.

I turned to face my lawyer. "I'm telling the truth. That's why I came out. I'm not going to start lying again. Tell the DA I'll do whatever it takes to help them."

For the first time, Kosciusko smiled. "I was hoping you'd say that."

He stood up and reached out to shake my hand. I hesitated, but he didn't pull back. I gave it a firm shake. "Let's get to work."

After Kosciusko left to negotiate with the DA, the police let Michael come to see me in the office. He gave me another big hug, and was looking much less worried than before. But he was older now and heavier than when I first met him, and I felt really bad that he had been waiting for hours with Lolita, who had closed down the bar and come to the station house to stand by me. I told them both to go home, I was fine with staying at the station "for my own protection" until an agreement could be reached and I signed a statement for the DA.

They were both so worn out that they didn't need much convincing to go home. I gestured vaguely to the cameras in the ceiling when Lolita asked me about being a demon. They understood the station house wasn't the place to talk about it and with reassuring hugs left me there for the night.

Anticipating a long wait, I kicked off my sneakers and leaned back in the comfy desk chair. With only the old table and locked metal file cabinets, the place was completely boring. I sat and stared at the reflection of the traffic lights in the cloudy window. The red, yellow, and green got all runny and prismatic when it began to lightly rain.

Drifting off in that meditative state that most closely resembled sleep for demons, I felt strangely fine. If the overhead lights could have been lowered, I would have been perfectly content. You'd think I would be worried and trying to figure out what to do next, but now that I had told the truth, I didn't need to keep the balls in the air like a dancing monkey.

I could relax.

The door suddenly opened and slammed shut again. I leaped to my feet, my body faster than thought, immediately on the defensive.

It was a cop, middle-aged but trim, staring intently at me. At first I thought he was one of the policemen who had come to the bar after I had been shot.

Then I really looked into his eyes. "Ram!"

"I have a uniform for you in my bag," he said urgently, lifting the duffel slightly. "I can get you out of here now, Allay."

I sat back down. "You scared the living daylights out of me. Why do you come busting in here dressed like that? Impersonating an officer is a crime."

"I came to help you."

I leaned back to make a point. "Thanks, but I don't need any help."

He watched me for a few moments, taking in the fact that I had been lounging when he popped in. "Do you know what's going on out there?"

My eyes went back to the window. "No, I've been stuck in here for hours."

"Some of your customers at the bar are talking to the news. It's demon this and demon that. They're compar-

ing you to Cherie, and they found out the church gave
the bar to you, so they think this proves the resurrection
was some kind of hoax. They're running wild with it."

"That's better than people believing it was a miracle."

"Allay, why did you say you're a demon? Of all the
words you could have used!"

"But . . . isn't that what we are?"

"We're angels, we're fairies, we're shape-shifters, we're
vampires . . . you could have said almost any mythical
creature, and it was inspired by one of us."

"What do you call us?"

He said a word, a slurring sound that clipped at the
end.

"What does that mean?" I asked.

"Demon."

"Well, then!" I stared at him. "If it walks like a duck,
Ram . . ."

"You didn't have to call us anything, Allay. People
don't want to believe their eyes. If you had kept quiet,
they would have started convincing themselves that it
hadn't really happened. Or they couldn't think about it
because it was too awful—your face was blown off. Most
people block out things like that. The trauma of it is too
great."

I could have defended myself by saying I didn't want
to lie anymore, especially not to Lolita. But he didn't
care why I'd done it, he was too busy telling me that I
shouldn't have come out. "You're the one who said demons are going to be exposed by the ERI. You said it
was *inevitable*," I intoned, mimicking his dire word.

"I didn't mean it would happen to *us*. I can make sure
you're never exposed. And I can protect your friends,
too, since that's so important to you. All you have to do
is deny what you said, tell them you were delusional,
that the bullet must have been fake and it bloodied your
nose. Tell them you don't remember."

"So you want me to sit around and wait for someone like Goad to be discovered by the ERI. You want him to be the demon poster child?"

"We have to leave the city, change personas—"

"No, thanks. I'm not done with the city. I like my bar."

"Allay! You've never seen a pogrom before. They're going to burn you alive on a stake!" He was serious, his aura flushed deep red in anger. He wasn't trying to hide it.

I took a deep breath. "I don't intend to be a martyr, Ram."

"They've already got you in custody."

"That door isn't locked. I'm going to work with them. The NYPD doesn't care if I'm a demon or not. Bless their hearts. They've seen it all. The only thing they care about is their corruption case."

Ram groaned, rubbing his hand through his hair. "Why are you cooperating with the authorities? Who convinced you to do that, Allay? You're making an enemy of Dread."

"Dread is already my enemy. Look what he did with Cherie. I'm not going to let him get away with this."

"Let me punish him, Allay. It will be a lot cleaner my way. Did you know they had a warrant ready for Commissioner Mackleby because of that call you made to him? They rousted a judge out of bed and got him to sign it. That moron taped his own phone calls—they have the one you made to him, threatening to expose him. They also have his calls to 'the prophet,' demanding his help to shut you up."

"Wow . . . that's better than I hoped for."

"Allay, this is turning into a political scandal, with you at the center of it." His voice nearly broke. "I didn't know you threatened Mackleby so he would make Dread let me go. You didn't tell me that."

"That was when I thought you were Theo Ram. The first half of our relationship," I reminded him. "While you were manipulating me into doing what you wanted. Oh, wait a second—that's a lot like the second half of our relationship. I seem to remember you were prying into my secret about Cherie right before I was killed."

"I'm trying to help you," Ram insisted.

"I keep telling you, I don't need your help. I can handle this myself."

He sat down abruptly in the chair across from me. I doubted he was giving up, but he was smart enough to change tactics. At least I was catching on to him now. Sure enough, his aura paled as he got control of himself.

"I know this isn't your fault, Allay," he said more reasonably. "Who could expect Anchor to go off the deep end? I'm surprised Dread didn't kill him earlier, but up until last weekend, he was a functioning addict and still somewhat useful."

I shuddered lightly, thinking of the manic blankness in Phil's eyes as he shot me. Functioning addict, my ass.

"Unfortunately," Ram continued, "Anchor kept meticulous notes over the years, going back before you came on the scene. He was Savor's human counterpart—she gives demons their marching orders, while Anchor was Dread's deal maker with city, state, and federal officials. As a journalist, he could openly meet with anyone without it being linked back to the church. The cops are in the evidence room now, drooling over his spreadsheet. Dread was a fool—he controlled Anchor completely, but the vessel cracked."

Phil had killed me, but that was too cold even for me.

"It will be his word against the prophet's, if you drop this now, Allay. He's so far gone no jury would believe him, even with his spreadsheet. But if you back him up, if you confirm everything, this is going to blow up in everyone's face. Including yours."

My smile deepened, and then I laughed. "I have to hand it to Phil. To think that the weak link in all this turns out to be guy who'll bring down the Fellowship of Truth. I just hope Dread doesn't have him killed before he can testify."

"The hit has already gone out on him. But it appears Goad is no longer taking orders from Dread."

"That's even better."

"Allay, that means there's nothing holding him back from *you*. I got in here, no problem. I'm sure Goad could manage it with an offspring or two."

I held up my hands, showing him how charged up I was from feeding off my patrons all night. "I'm ready for him. I'm tired of being frightened into a tight, little ball. I've made my decision, and that's it. I'm coming out my own way."

"You said you didn't want to be part of Vex's plans for resurrection, but now you're doing it! You're putting yourself out there to be the new messiah."

"No, I'm not. Never that. There's nothing religious about this. I don't promise to save people's souls. I'm just telling them the truth."

Ram stood looking at me for a few moments, his aura flushed decidedly purple now. That dark bruised pain that came with only one name—Hope.

"I thought you were different from other hybrids," he murmured. "But every one of you suffers from delusions of grandeur. Because you're special, you think that it has to be about you. Who are you to give people the truth?"

That hurt. I didn't think he was right. But it was a great description of Cherie. "You said I wasn't like Hope."

"Maybe I was wrong."

I realized I was standing up, and so was he. Now there was only hurt instead of adoration in his eyes. Why would he be hurt? Because I wouldn't run off with him the first week I met him and say *fuck you!* to the rest of the world? This had to be about Hope again, always Hope. Like our entire relationship was an endless replay of a bad trip.

I almost said something I'd regret, but the door opened again. Kosciusko stopped abruptly when he saw Ram. My lawyer's freckled face flushed and he seemed to grow taller. I knew this was what he would look like defending me in court, like a warrior in a business suit come to my rescue.

"What are you doing in here?" Kosciusko demanded. "You're not questioning my client, are you, Officer? Because that would be a serious breach of trust."

"I was asking Ms. Meyers if she needed anything," Ram said easily enough, instantly back in cop mode. Always the consummate liar.

"I can take care of that. You go now."

Ram nodded shortly, giving me a sharp look before he left.

The tension was so thick that Kosciusko looked from the door closing behind Ram's back to me. "Was he harassing you?"

Yeah, sort of. "Not really. Nothing that needs to be dealt with."

"Are you sure? Because they've promised to treat you with respect."

I assured him that the NYPD had been nothing but nice to me, which was true. I hadn't run into the ones on Dread's payroll—yet.

Kosciusko sat down, gesturing for me to do the same. He opened up his fat briefcase. "The DA's office has agreed to drop all charges against you in this case and any future prosecutions that arise out of it, in exchange for the testimony you agreed to give. I've got the statement ready for you to sign. Once you do that, you can walk out of here."

"Did you work all night on this?" I asked.

"Oh, no. I went home and slept for a few hours. They were gathering the evidence to see how valuable your testimony would be, and apparently it is very valuable indeed. They would be most grateful for your help." He looked at me closer. "You look well rested. Did you manage to sleep in that chair?"

"Demons don't sleep." It was so nice to be able to say that. "I mostly sat here bored. What time is it?"

"Six in the morning. I can get you some coffee, and a donut. I saw a box out there."

"Demons don't eat or drink. We live off the emotions of other people."

His eyes narrowed. "So I heard on the news." He reached down into his briefcase. "You might want to see this."

It was the *New York Post*. The headline read PROPHET CONSORTS WITH DEMONS! A photo of me that looked like it was taken last night inside my bar by someone with a cell phone was splashed on the front page. The blood down my neck and white T-shirt was a stark black splash, and my eyes were wells of shadow in the dim overhead light. The other, smaller photo showed me flat on my back, my face a gaping wet pit.

"I look positively ghoulish! That's awful."

"The text isn't much better," Kosciusko agreed.

The story recounted how I had been shot and killed in my bar, and then it quickly veered off into a tale of a supposed love triangle between me, Phil Anchor, and the prophet. Somebody at the police department must have tipped them off, because it included details of my made-up affair with the prophet a decade ago, after which he gave me the bar in eternal appreciation for my charms.

Seriously? I wanted to gag. If they only knew Dread and what he was capable of.

The reporter managed to squeeze in the salacious

details that Mrs. Prophet had returned penitent to her hubby just in time for Cherie's staged resurrection, and that her former lover, Mark Cravet, remained mysteriously missing with his business summarily shuttered and emptied. It was all of the most lurid bits of the past few days, which the reporter had found and pasted together.

"Oh, my God. . . . Should I deny it? I mean, it isn't true that Dread and I had an affair."

"In my humble opinion, it's best not to respond to anything the *Post* prints. Maybe you should get a publicist? I could suggest one or two for you."

"I don't have the money to pay for a publicist." I gave him a sideways look. "How much do I owe you, by the way? You did a great job for me."

"You made it easy by making the right choice. When that spreadsheet came in from Mr. Anchor, I was ready to applaud. You fell on the side of angels, Ms. Meyers."

"I didn't fall, Mr. Kosciusko. I jumped."

19

"I wish you'd let me check you into a hotel," Kosciusko said for the fifth time as we were leaving the station house. "Or I could drop you off at the bar. You can't go back alone after all that publicity."

"Don't worry about me." I turned and walked away, gradually transforming myself until I was a dirty blond with a rabbity face. I waved back at Kosciusko, who was staring at me openmouthed. But to give the guy credit, he raised his hand in return despite his shock.

As I turned the corner, my smile faded. I came out so I wouldn't have to lie anymore. And here I was lying again by wearing someone else's face. It felt so wrong.

I wondered if Ram was somewhere nearby, watching me. Watching over me.

Or was he through with me? Maybe he didn't want me if he couldn't control me.

That was fine by me. But it did hurt.

Over on Avenue A, the early morning traffic looked more like rush hour during the week rather than a Saturday morning. There were more backed-up lines at the lights and more horns sounding distantly. I should have asked Kosciusko if the bridges were still shut down to Brooklyn. Hopefully now that Cherie's story was being openly questioned, that hysteria would soon fade.

But as I neared Avenue C, the sidewalk was so clogged with people that I could barely reach Third Street. I asked a guy standing on the stanchion of a streetlight, trying to see south, "What's going on down there?"

"It's packed right in front of the bar," he said, not bothering to glance down.

His girlfriend tugged on his pants leg. "Let's go, Ricky. There are too many people. We'll come see the demon later."

Me? I almost blurted out. These people were here to see me.

"I bet it gets worse," the boyfriend retorted irritably. "Like with Brooklyn. By the time we tried, we couldn't get across the bridge."

I eased away, feeling very self-conscious about hiding.

I was tempted to turn on my heel and leave, but I could sense Bliss and Crave ahead. They must be inside my bar.

I wiggled my way through the slowly shifting crowd that spilled off the sidewalk. There was only one lane of traffic getting through, and white vans with satellite antennas were double-parked. Everyone was looking in the direction of the Den, their attention focused sharply on it. Most people held up cell phones and cameras, taking pictures of my bar and the crowd in front of it, lifting them up toward the windows on the second floor, searching for movement and craning to see the apartment inside. I was glad the curtains were drawn. Bliss had taken over up there for the past couple of days.

Then the people separated enough to give me a glimpse of the closed metal shutter over the front of the bar. Something had been spray-painted on it in black, red, and white. When I got closer, it turned out to be a man-sized pentagram splattering the shutter.

Nice. Now I was branded a witch, a devil worshiper.

I let the crowd squeeze me back away from the bar. I was a coward, I admit it. I couldn't imagine going up to the door and brazenly opening it. I wasn't sure if I could get inside before they stopped me, nor could I keep them from storming through behind me.

I fought my way back out, hating myself, hating what I'd done. That girl was right—it probably would get worse.

I turned down Second Street, passing by the row of apartment buildings on the south side of my block. People were looking down from their windows at the circus that had erupted on their street, some were still wearing pajamas and rubbing their bed-heads.

I drifted down the inside of the sidewalk, keeping a sharp eye out for someone leaving. When a couple of teenaged Latina girls emerged onto their stoop, I quickly darted up and grabbed the door before it shut, telling them, "Watch out, girls. It's rough out there."

They skedaddled to get away from the lecturing grown-up. I made sure the door was closed behind me, then went through the inner door into the stairwell. It had a very high ceiling, with a staircase up the left. I went down the narrow hallway on the right to the back. Two apartment doors faced me, but on the underside of the stairs was a wood-panel door that led to the basement below.

I broke the old padlock easily. I left the door open so the tenants would see it needed a new lock. I didn't need light; I maneuvered around the pile of lumber and the old stove to find the rusted metal hatch that opened into the backyard. A pin held it shut from the inside. I was out and in the backyard with hardly a sound.

It wasn't much of a yard, only a dirt patch with weeds growing along the fences. I went over several fences, blessing my ability to heal when I jammed a big splinter into my palm and landed badly on the uneven ground jumping down. But I made it to my own backyard without any problems other than the dogs barking a few yards over.

I used my bench to climb down. Ram and I had been sitting there last night as he seduced my secrets out of me.

But brooding was out of the question as Bliss appeared in the window upstairs. She waved to let me know she was coming down.

I huddled against the back door—I was mostly blocked by the acacia tree, but there were some rear windows of the buildings along Second Street that I could see. I couldn't tell if anyone was staring down at the demon sneaking into her own home.

"Hi, Allay," Bliss said as she let me in.

I made sure the back door was locked, and the bars over the windows were secure. I had gotten in the back way easy enough, I was sure others would follow.

The bar was dark and in complete disarray. My own blood was on the floor in front. Crave's signature was coming from upstairs.

"The news said you were in jail," Bliss said.

"Not really. Just hanging out with the cops."

"Was it fun?"

I raised my brows at her. "More fun than getting home. How long have those people been out there?"

"Since you were shot."

I had almost forgotten that Bliss and Crave were here when it happened, having sex upstairs. "Have you been here ever since?"

"I thought you'd want someone to watch over the bar. There were people gathering out front and a news crew arrived before everyone was let go by the police. Lolita ran out of here so fast she was still wearing her apron."

I wondered at her calm, but then again, there had been nothing but chaos since she was born. Everything turning topsy-turvy was just another day for her.

A boom made us both jump. I realized someone had

slammed against the metal shutter outside. The rise in noise, loud voices and shouts, made me shudder. "Let's get upstairs."

The television showed the front of my bar being mobbed by people. The reporter was being jostled by everyone around her. It was surreal, as if I'd been dislocated in time. But I could hear them outside, growing louder and bolder as more people converged on the Lower East Side.

"Nice riot you've got going." Crave waved languidly at the window. "What are you planning for an encore?"

"Are you going to start in on me, too?" I snapped.

"Do I need to tell you that I've never seen anything so stupid in my entire life?" He started laughing. "If it wasn't so completely self-destructive, I'd think you were insane. But even insane demons have some sense of self-preservation."

"Coming from the guy sleeping on my couch, that doesn't count for much. It's not like you haven't fucked up your life, Crave. Last I heard, your mommy ran away without you."

"Good riddance," Crave snorted. "I don't need her."

"That's right, you have Bliss now. You can live off her for the next century."

His feet hit the floor. "I'm taking care of Bliss. If it wasn't for me, she would have rushed downstairs right into the arms of the police. She would have ended up in that cell along with you."

"He's stronger than me." Bliss was looking at Crave with a new wariness in her eyes. "He wouldn't let me go down when we heard the gunshots. Your signature went out, did you know that? I felt you die."

"She came back to life," Crave said impatiently.

"She died. And you wouldn't let me go down." Bliss rubbed her arm.

I pictured Crave grabbing on to her, locking his

arms around her, maybe even putting his hand over her mouth, urging her to be quiet. Forcing her to do what he wanted.

"That's not right," I told him. "People have to make their own choices. Their own mistakes."

Bliss nodded. "You can't manhandle me into doing what you want."

Crave lifted his hands in exasperation. "You're making it sound like some kind of domestic abuse. I kept you from running into a burning building, Bliss. If I saw you were about to throw yourself off a cliff, I'd sit on you to make you stop, if I had to."

"My life wasn't in danger," Bliss retorted.

"Yes, it is, as long as you're connected to *her*. You could have been outed as a demon, too. Don't you think the men in white coats will be here soon to escort Ms. Meyers to the closest hospital for a round of tests, just like that dried-up old stick Cherie? This time they won't let their miracle-worker disappear. Face it, Allay, you're going to be staring at the inside of a box before the weekend is over."

"I have a good lawyer." My throat was tight.

Crave laughed again, meanly. "You're going to need all the luck you can get, Allay. Forget about the humans; demons will make short work of you. They know how bad it can get when we're hunted and rooted out. You've launched Armageddon against us. You're a traitor and you won't have a demon on your side after this."

I looked from him to Bliss. "I take it that includes you."

A ghost of her usual smile lifted her lips. "No. I'll stick by you, Allay."

"Bliss!" Crave took a few steps toward her, and she backed up one, then held firm. "You can't stay here. This place is going to be firebombed. I keep telling you, we have to go now, before we're cut off completely. She's back now. There's no reason for you to stay."

Bliss kept smiling. "I'm not going anywhere. This is my home, remember?"

I felt such a flooding of relief, knowing that I'd been right to support her, to care about her. Shock had warned me that Bliss would try to kill me, and here she was, standing up for me against her lover.

Crave was undone by her refusal. He stepped closer, and this time she didn't flinch. He started speaking to her quietly, so I eased back, suddenly feeling as if I was intruding.

As they argued, I went into the back room and shut the door. I couldn't urge Bliss to stay when Crave was probably right—it was dangerous for her to be here. But I couldn't ask her to leave, either.

I didn't want to be alone. I was frightened.

I stared sightlessly out the windows, wondering what Bliss would decide. Then I heard the front door to the apartment close and their tread on the stairs going down together. They were in the bar for a long time; then the back door opened and shut. Crave emerged in the courtyard.

I hesitated, but Bliss didn't appear with him. Crave turned to glare up at me, and anger and frustration roiled his aura. He blamed me.

After a while, Bliss opened the door. "He's gone."

"He's still out there," I corrected. "Looking up at the window."

Bliss went close to the window and looked through the bars. She lifted her hand in a wave, then turned away. "Come on, let's go to the front."

I glanced out back as I followed to see Crave still standing there looking up at the empty windows. I kept expecting to hear him knock down below, but as the minutes passed in silence, his signature slowly faded as he left.

Bliss didn't say a word about it, so I didn't.

It wouldn't help to keep worrying over whether I'd done the right thing. I watched the television coverage of my own death and rebirth. It was an appalling repeat of Cherie's consumption by the media. Bliss flipped around the channels, idly showing me the highlights. There were a number of clips of patrons from my bar: people I barely remembered and others who had been coming here for years, all telling the same horrifying story of my murder and revivification. Except for Lolita. The sight of Lo's pout as she refused to comment warmed my heart. "You made the *Early Show*, *Today*, and even *Good Morning America*," Bliss pointed out. She had Tivo'd them all.

Currently playing was the midmorning inanity. Kelly was exclaiming to Regis in complete astonishment, as she did with every story. "Did you *hear* what happened last night? A bartender on the Lower East Side was shot in the *face* by her drug-addled lover." She waved away Regis's expression of dismay. "Don't worry. She's fine. Not a scratch on her. Customers who were there at the time say that she *died* and came back to life. Yes! Just like supermodel Cherie! Only this girl—Emma Meyers is her name—she doesn't claim she's a messenger from God. No, this girl says she's a *demon*." Kelly nodded solemnly, her eyes round. "You know what makes it even better? The *New York Post* has a huge headline this morning claiming that Emma is sleeping with Prophet Anderson himself!"

I put my head in my hands. If that wasn't proof that you should never lie, then I don't know what was. It was my own stupid story coming back to bite me. Someone could die and come back to life, and the salacious sex scandal would still dominate the news coverage.

"... Emma was born in Orange County, California, where she lived with her family in this humble home. She dropped out of high school, according to neighbors' reports, and moved into a fancy beach house in Malibu with an ... um, *older man* before moving to Manhattan ..."

The shot changed to one of the front of my besieged bar. "Go back!" I ordered Bliss. She reversed to the last clip. "There! That's my parents' house."

It looked so peaceful sitting there in the dawning light. The hydrangea was just blooming in heavy purple clusters, and my mom's SUV was in the driveway.

"Oh, my God! My parents." I put my hands to my mouth. "I have to call them."

I hurried downstairs, not even seeing the blood on the floor or hearing my name being chanted by the mob outside. The sight of news crews outside my bar had thrown me, but seeing them outside my parents' house was worse.

The line was dead. "I had to unplug it," Bliss explained, picking up the end of the phone line. "It was ringing incessantly."

As soon as she plugged it back in, it began to ring. I picked it up and hung up again. It took a few times before I was able to get a dial tone. My parents' phone was busy, and my sister Kathy's cell went straight to voice mail. People must be swamping them as well.

I stuck with it, determined to get through. I kept on having to hang up on people every time. It was a constant battle. I'm not sure how long it took, but my finger had a groove worn in it from the redial button.

The only time I paused was when I noticed Bliss mopping up the floor. "You don't have to do that," I told her, feeling bad.

"Got nothing else to do," she pointed out.

Finally one of my calls went through and the phone

began to ring. And ring. I hung on, refusing to hang up
and try again. I would let it ring until they *had* to pick up.
But what if they had unplugged it like Bliss? Or what if
they weren't there? What if they had been run off to my
sister's house or to a hotel?

I had almost hung up to dial my sister when she
snatched up the phone, breathless. "Hello? Is that you,
Em?"

She must have seen the caller ID. "Yes! Yes, Kathy, I
just saw the news—"

I hadn't returned home in six years, not since the last
time they'd tried to hold an intervention for me, complete with addiction specialists with their sympathetic
smiles. I'd last spoken to my sister at Christmas as the
holidays demanded, but it was always perfunctory at
best. I had to lie constantly to them, so how could we
have any kind of real relationship?

Now Kathy drew in a deep breath to better scream
at me. "What is *wrong* with you, Emma? What kind of
stunt are you pulling now? We've been calling you all
night. Don't you ever return messages?" Another con-
sequence of losing my cell phone. "Do you know what
you're doing to Mom and Dad? Do you want them both
to keel over from heart attacks right now? Haven't you
done enough damage—"

I was holding the phone away from my ear, so I had
to move quick to hear my mom's voice replace my sister's. "Emma? Is that really you?"

She had taken the phone away from Kathy, and
sounded as if she were holding a snake that would bite
her.

"I'm sorry about this, Mom. I really am. I should have
called you sooner to warn you."

Her voice quavered with real fear. "What's happening, Emma? What have you been saying to everyone?"

I tried to explain that I wasn't a drug addict, I was possessed by a demon, and it had happened that night at the beach, instead of a bad acid trip. I tried to explain everything, but she didn't understand. I kept having to repeat myself as Kath was shouting and crying in the background that it was another lie to get attention, that I was a born drama queen always trying to get more attention.

"Demons," my mom said. "You can't keep talking about being a demon, Emma. It goes against the Bible. I can't have you saying that, not to the TV people, not to the newspapers. I don't know what I'm going to tell my friends."

Kath called out, "Tell them she's nuts! I told you so. Didn't I say she should be locked up somewhere safe?"

I tried to stay calm. "I'm not crazy, Mom. I'm no longer corporeal. That's how I died and came back to life."

"That's wrong, Emma. You can't say things like that. Our savior died and came back to life, to take the burden of our sin from us. I know this is some kind of play or stunt with your city friends, that horrible cult you've gotten involved in. But it's wrong. You have to stop saying such awful things."

I was a little taken aback. She'd always been half-heartedly religious, taking us to the big church events and occasionally to Sunday school. But now she sounded serious, as if blasphemy were still a killing offense.

"Where's Dad?" I asked. "Can I talk to him?"

"She wants Dean." There was silence, then shuffling, and I realized my mom had simply handed the phone away without saying good-bye. If nothing else, I would have thought her devotion to politeness would have demanded a sign-off. But she was gone without a word.

Instead of my dad's voice, it was Kathy again. She was hoarse from yelling so much and was breathing heavily. "Do you really think he wants to talk to you? After all the times you've shamed him? Richard had to take the girls to a hotel so they could get away from the reporters. We only hope they can go to school next week. I don't know what you're trying to prove, Emma, but keep us out of it!"

"I will! Just don't talk to them. They'll go away—"

"*You* stop talking, Emma. Really. Just stop."

My sister hung up before I could say anything else. I couldn't explain it in one phone call, and it was foolish to try.

What hurt was my dad. It was my own fault. I used to be a daddy's girl, with a special bond with him. But he had given up on me a long time ago, when I refused to return for the holidays. I'd felt I had no choice, eaten up inside from the guilt of lying and frightened every second that some demon was going to attack my family to get to me.

The phone started to ring again. I unplugged it.

Bliss was watching me. "That didn't go over too well, did it?"

"No. It didn't."

Bliss flapped her hand. "Give them time. It's a lot to absorb."

"Meanwhile I'm ruining their lives."

"Allay, you can't live your life to suit other people. That won't make anyone happy."

Naturally, that would be her main concern. "I don't expect to make anyone happy. I just wish they would understand."

"Then explain it to them. Saying 'BTW, I'm a demon' isn't giving them much to go on."

"I'm trying, but it's hard—" I broke off at the distracted expression on her face. She was sensing an approaching demon. For a newbie, she had a very long range. "Uh-oh. Who's coming to visit us now?"

Bliss lifted her face, concentrating. "That's Shock. Definitely Shock."

I had deliberately put Shock out of my mind because I was afraid of what she would say about all of this. Now I had no choice; I had failed with my family, but I couldn't fail with her. I had to make her understand.

20

I could feel Shock coming from the west, but it took her a long time to get to the bar. She was coming in the back way, like I had done, so when I saw the flicker of a face in the back window, I let out a welcoming cry.

But the blur of hair was dark, and there were voices and laughter as a guy cupped his hands against the glass and tried to peer into the darkened interior of the bar.

I ducked down behind the counter, motioning for Bliss to do the same. The voices outside grew louder; then they called my name. The rattle of pebbles against my windows accompanied their calls.

It felt even worse having my backyard invaded, as if I were surrounded. Going down on a sinking ship, with the waves lapping around my nose.

Bliss lifted her head. "She's on the roof. Coming closer."

I reached out, but the buzz-tingle of Shock's signature was like a blanket, with no directional indicators. "Are you sure?"

"She's probably coming for the skylight."

Together we went upstairs, and Bliss was proven right when a thump came from Shock jumping down on my roof from the three-story apartment building next door.

"You have good radar," I told Bliss. "That could save your life someday."

"If I learn how to run in stilettos, it might."

I snagged the rope ladder and pulled it down. Bliss stepped on the end to hold it while I climbed to the top and slid out the pin that held it closed. As I opened the pyramid top, Shock was leaning over. Her aura was on fire, as if her body were going up in red flames.

Demon.

My own aura flared as orange as a caution sign, lurid with fear. I tried to tell myself this was Shock, I could feel it, but her cold, dead eyes staring through that crackling aura was almost too much for me.

I hurried back down the ladder and stood close to Bliss as Shock descended. She wasn't wearing her usual petite persona with the platinum blond hair—this guise was darker, more solid, like a wrestler.

"Who's idea was this?" Shock demanded before she even stepped off the ladder. "Was it Ram? Did Glory put you up to exposing yourself? Who was it, Allay?"

"I didn't plan it, Shock. Phil killed me in front of everyone—"

"Somebody put this into your head." Shock stood with her hands on her hips. "I know you, Allay. You don't make a spectacle of yourself. You're not into power or intrigue. So what made you announce to the world that you're a demon?"

"The ERI machines are going to expose us all—"

"That's nonsense! We always get around technology. We always will. You can't take something that Dread told you and blow it up into *this*."

"Shock, it's based on Kirlian technology, and it's real. It will unmask us. Ram has known about it for decades—"

"Ram! I knew he was behind this. He's manipulated you into doing this, Allay. He's trying to destroy Dread, and he's using you to do it."

I took a deep breath. "That's the third time you've interrupted me, Shock. How can I explain when you won't let me speak? First of all, Ram hates this as much as you do."

"He's letting you think that. He could make you cut off your own nose, and you'd think it was your idea."

I raised one brow. "Come on, Shock."

"I hate seeing him make a puppet out of you. And you don't even see it. Ram is the ultimate demon killer. Don't you think he likes the idea of a modern-day witch hunt? You're doing his dirty work for him."

"I don't want anybody to get hurt." But visions of the ragged eighteenth-century mob rushing at Plea were haunting. Bones being pushed in to close up the walls around me ... and suddenly I remembered emerging from the catacombs, into a cool clear day with a sky so intensely blue that Plea simply stood there laughing, her head back as she stared into the sky. Free.

She had almost died down there; I could feel it like my own recent bout with mortality.

I had condemned Ram for killing his offspring's offspring, but wasn't I just as culpable by putting other demons at risk?

It was too late now.

Like my doubts sprung to life, Shock said, "You've ruined everything." She stared at me like she hardly knew me. "Everyone knows I'm not your real sister. They're asking questions at work. There were two reporters outside my house. I'm going to have to sneak in the back way to get back in."

"Shock! I'll say whatever you want. I didn't mean for you to get caught up in this."

"What did you think would happen? Last night my partner kept joking with me about my 'demon sister.' I told him you've got multiple personality disorder, but he's started looking at *me* weird." For the first time, Shock shifted uncomfortably. "I'm not good at the warm-and-fuzzy feelings. Sometimes they call me the Ice Lady. They know I'm different, deep down, but they could push it away and ignore it until you dragged everything out in the open."

"I'm sorry. I feel awful, Shock."

"I don't see how that does me any good. I'm putting my house on the market. I've already quit my job. I'll stay somewhere else until I figure out what I'm going to do."

"Stay here," I said faintly. "I want to make it up to you."

"I'm not coming anywhere near you until you fix this mess, Allay. Tell everyone it was a publicity stunt to get customers for your bar. Tell them you set it up with a special effects studio. Tell them DreamWorks did a con job on them. I don't care what you tell them! Just fix it. Now."

"You want me to lie to everyone?"

"They don't believe you anyway! They think you're a nut job. If you don't retract it, it's going to get worse. Much worse, mark my words."

She was already stepping onto the ladder. Her aura wasn't flaming as brightly now that, having told me off, she figured I would fall in line and do as she said, as usual. Bliss and I watched her climb all the way to the top and through the opening. She never looked back as she left.

For the first time, I felt like I had made a huge mistake. I had considered what outing myself would do to me, but clearly I had underestimated what it would do to my family and everyone else around me.

"Shall I go lock up?" Bliss was apparently not bothered by the fact that Shock hadn't acknowledged her in any way.

"Thanks. Could you? My knees are a little shaky." I

sat down on one of the green linoleum chairs and leaned back in the generous curve, as Bliss neatly climbed the ladder and pulled down the skylight.

"I remember this pin," she said from up above, carefully sliding it into the holes. "Ram took it out so he could make a quick escape after he killed Shock. But you interrupted him. Then he got back in this way, and tried to kill her again. That's what made you go to Vex to get help."

"I was trying to save Shock," I agreed. I had been ready to do anything, even give my own life if I had to.

Bliss jumped lightly back down. "Maybe Shock forgot about that."

"She blames me for bringing Ram inside in the first place." I watched her use the broom to stuff the ladder back into the slot under the skylight. "Bliss, tell me something. Do you think I should denounce what I said? Take it all back? Disappear without a trace and become someone new?"

"Why would you do that?"

"Because everyone is telling me I'm being an idiot, that I should slink away with my tail between my legs."

Bliss wrinkled her nose. "That doesn't sound like fun."

I shook my head. She certainly looked at the world through a narrow lens. Maybe it was easier that way.

I was saved from answering by the sound of a cell phone ringing downstairs. "That's mine," Bliss said, darting away.

I shook my head after her. Bliss had taken the time to get a cell phone. Surely I should do the same. I needed a way for the important people to reach me.

Bliss called me downstairs. The noise from the crowd outside was louder now, with more raucous laughter, more shouting going on. The shadows moving in the back had multiplied. I could almost hear the drums beating in the distance, driving on the hunters. And I was the prey.

Bliss showed me she had her finger over the speaker hole. "It's for you. It's Dread."

I stopped in my tracks. Then forced myself to meet her and take the phone. "What do you want?"

"You've been a busy girl, Allay." For a second, I thought he had found out that I had kidnapped Cherie. But that was old news now. "The pictures don't do you justice."

"You like resurrections, so I thought you'd appreciate it." Not. But I figured I might as well be flippant. I didn't need to explain anything to Dread of all people.

"I could tell you had a death wish the first time I met you. You told Vex to fuck off when he ordered you to serve as my drop-off. You really thought you could say no. Vex made you, he owned you, and now that he's dead, I own you."

"I know Vex ordered Revel to kill Plea to make a hybrid." There was silence on the other end, as if Dread was surprised I knew that but he didn't want to admit it. "I think I've proven that nobody owns me."

After a moment, Dread said, "You do realize this is the end for you."

I was chilled by his tone, and very glad we weren't having this conversation face-to-face. "You do realize this phone is bugged, don't you, Prophet Anderson?"

There was a tinge of admiration in his voice. "I'm going to enjoy this. See you soon, Allay."

The line went dead. He actually thought I got the police to put a tracer on Bliss's phone!

"Uh-oh," I told Bliss. "I think I turned him on."

"He does love that fear." She took her phone back. "I wonder how he got my number."

"Savor probably gave it to him." She nodded, so I knew that Savor was one of the first people to get her number. "At least I don't have to worry about Dread sending an assassin. He'll want to kill me himself so he can get off on it." I grimaced at the ugly thought. Dread's cage had been bad enough once. I'd felt such helpless rage when his henchwoman had burned Theo. . . .

Dread could do the same thing to Lolita. Or Pepe, or one of my patrons. It could turn out to be the same horror show all over again.

With a crash, glass exploded into the back of the bar. Someone had thrown a rock through the window. The yelling was much louder now.

Bliss had ducked her head, but her eyes were shining. She grinned when I looked up. "Exciting, huh?"

"You could call it that." We both flinched as someone hit the metal shutter out front. Then Bliss laughed.

"Aren't you afraid?" I asked.

"What are they going to do, kill me? I'd just come back to life. It's not like they're going to nuke the bar."

"But what about other demons? They could kill you."

"Oh, that's inevitable." She waved it off. "It's just a matter of when. So why worry about it? Make hay, and all that."

"You're right," I said slowly.

"Of course, I'm right. You're just afraid. You're afraid you'll lose Shock. You're afraid it will hurt your family. You're afraid the other demons will hate you and hunt you. Which they're doing anyway, by the way. And you're afraid Ram won't like you anymore."

"I never said that."

"You said he hated it more than Shock," she reminded me. "And since you're obsessed with him, that must really gut you."

"Obsessed is a strong word. I don't think all that much about him. I've spent far more time with Mystify the past few days."

She gave me an eloquent look. "I know how you feel about him."

"That's more than I can say. Bliss, things have changed since you were born. And I was confused about him back then."

Bliss smiled as she shook her head. "You want him. More than that, you have to have him. Don't you think it's unfair that I have *that* to compare all of my liaisons to?"

I blushed, a human response too quick for me to stop. It felt as if Bliss were looking over my shoulder every time I'd had sex with Ram. To deflect her, I said, "I don't think Ram wants to be with me anymore. He called me a megalomaniac. Like other hybrids."

Bliss laughed out loud. "He's mad because you won't do what he wants. He'll be back, trying to wheedle you some other way. You'll see. Nothing will drive him away from you."

"How do you know that?"

She put her hand on her belly, over her core, serious for once. "I'm not sure you did me a favor, Allay. It's hard to find bliss. People feel good, they laugh, they have sex, and they orgasm. Fleeting, scarce moments. Actually, I haven't felt any true bliss since you were lying on the riverbank kissing Ram. Don't you think he could feel it, too? How could he ever let that feeling go? How could he ever turn his back on you?"

I had to ask, "You don't feel that way with Crave?"

"It's nice with Crave, very easy because we understand each other. We have the same needs. We're both up for anything, so it's fun. Most of the time. But you had something else with Ram. Something powerful."

Maybe she was right. But that kind of love was overwhelming, and I wasn't sure I wanted to throw myself into it. If I trashed everything and ran off with him, what would be left of me? "I felt like I finally have a chance to be who I really am. Now I have to run and hide again, instead of being myself and living openly."

"It's like choosing to live in the tunnels or on the streets," Bliss agreed. "The streets are more dangerous, but there's a lot more to do up here."

I nodded. "You're right. Even if it does mess things up for people I care about, I can't live for them. I'm out. I have to stay that way."

"Fly your freak flag proudly. That's what I say."

I laughed, feeling lighter with relief. Doubt was a killer, but I couldn't doubt my decision anymore. It wasn't going to be easy, but I had to do it. I had to be myself. Every step of the way. "Are you sure you don't want to leave? Crave is right. This could get rough and I'd hate for you to be caught in the crosshairs when demons come calling for me."

"Are you kidding? I wouldn't miss this for the world. I can't wait to see what happens next."

I looked around my little world, listening to the echoing crowd out front. "First things first—this isn't the eighteenth century. I don't have to let myself be mobbed. I'm calling my lawyer."

Kosciusko was divine. He agreed to pressure the cops and the DA into providing better protection for one of their key witnesses. Then I was on the phone with Michael, who suggested that we arrange for a private security firm to send several men over to serve as guards for the bar. That was when Lieutenant Markman arrived. A squad of uniformed cops moved the people back from my dented metal shutter, and a truck with blue police barricades pulled up behind the news vans.

I let Markman into the bar. The lines in his face seemed deeper. "Get any sleep, Lieutenant?"

"Not yet," he said grimly. "I heard the situation was escalating over here."

"Just around the edges. Are you going to cut off the

whole block with those barricades? My neighbors must be furious."

"That's to control the foot traffic, to keep it flowing. We'll have those news vans off the street soon. Somebody in the mayor's office gave them permits to park there. We're trying to track down who gave that order."

One of Dread's men, no doubt. "People are getting in the backyard, too." I showed him the broken window. "I'm told I can hire private security."

"I can suggest a firm, if you'd like. Trustworthy people, if you get my meaning."

"Sure, thanks." I was glad to have his help.

In fact, he was so accommodating that I reached out to touch his arm in gratitude. But he started back, avoiding the swoop of my fingers.

My blush betrayed me, as usual, though I quickly got hold of myself, quieting my pulse. *He knows I want to feed from him.*

He knew it before I did, with the quick instincts of a predator himself, of a man who watched others and pounced on their little weaknesses and lies.

"I'm sorry," I manned up, not without some difficulty. "I promise I'll never feed from you, Lieutenant Markman. Not that I hurt the people I do feed from, you understand. I take only drops of energy when people have bucketfuls overflowing."

"So you claim." He looked at me as if words didn't matter much in situations such as this, only deeds. He didn't believe I was a demon, in spite of his own instincts.

"There's no way to prove it to you. Unless you want to shoot me in the face yourself. Go ahead. I don't have anything else to do."

Bliss groaned on the other side of the bar. "Allay! I

just got finished cleaning up from the last time. I'm not doing it again. You'll have to mop up your own blood this time."

Lieutenant Markman shook his head to himself. "I'll be out front, if you need me."

I followed him into the vestibule and shut the door securely on his order. I watched through the tiny window in the door as the cops ordered people to move away as the barricades were unloaded.

As the blue barriers were placed in front of my bar, walling me more securely inside, I grew even hungrier. I needed to feed, and clearly I was going to have to ask Bliss. She was charged up enough for both of us.

Or I could change my facade and go out among those people, soaking up energy through another lie. Why, when I had caused such pain for everyone around me, did I still have to lie? I exposed myself so I could be honest, but in order to eat I would have to pretend to be someone else.

It wasn't right.

I watched as the police cleared the street and got the people moving in an orderly line past the front of my bar, going north to south. Presumably they were circling around the block and walking by again because the stream was endless. It was done so smoothly that it made me suspicious.

When Lieutenant Markman returned to the bar, Bliss was nowhere to be seen. But I could feel her signature coming from the storeroom. So I felt free enough to say, "You could have done this before, Lieutenant. Why'd you wait so long?"

"Flushing out the perps. Put the pressure on, and it usually works."

I perked up. "You got someone?"

"Mr. Anderson shouldn't have called and threatened you, Ms. Meyers. Juries don't take kindly to that."

"You heard that?" I was astonished.

"You said the line was tapped."

"I was just trying to poke at him. You really bugged Bl-Belissa's phone?"

Markman tilted his head. "You referred to someone else ordering you to serve him. Vex. Who is he? Is he with the Fellowship, too?"

It was innocently asked, but I was instantly on alert. To hear Vex's name from his lips! I wanted to tell him, to be honest in everything, but my tongue froze.

"Let me guess," Markman said dryly. "You want to talk to your lawyer first."

I managed to nod. "The important thing is you heard the prophet threatening me."

"The DA sent some of our guys over to bring him in for questioning."

It boggled my mind to think the system was this efficient against one of the most powerful demons in the modern world.

I had to ask, "You don't believe me, do you? That I'm a demon?"

"That's immaterial. I don't care what you are, only that you're protected like any other taxpaying citizen. Will there be anything else, Ms. Meyers?"

He was going to leave me here boarded in as if a hurricane were coming, fearing for my life. He didn't understand; no one did. They thought I was lying or pulling a scam. They would use me for what they needed, all of them, and then leave me lying in the gutter where they found me.

Nothing had changed, I was still isolated in my bubble, only now the walls had hardened around me, driving away everyone else. I remembered Bliss's bored expression and wondered how long she'd be content to hang out in the dark, empty bar with me. This time tomorrow, I was going to be completely alone.

"Ms. Meyers?" the lieutenant repeated. "Anything else?"

"Yes." I roused myself. "Yes, could you please have the security company send those guards as soon as possible? I want to open up the bar."

"Open up? You're going to let people in?" Markman asked in surprise, his politeness gone. "We just got them under control out there. Do you want to start another riot?"

"No, I don't think it will be a problem. You can keep the barriers up but leave a space for people to come in. I'll tell the guard who can come through, and the rest can pass by like they're doing right now. At least then they'd see something instead of the shutter pulled down."

"You *want* people to come here?"

"I need customers. I have to pay my lawyer. And the guards, come to think of it." I also needed to feed, but I didn't have to tell him that.

"You want to open the bar," Markman repeated, as if he still couldn't believe his ears.

"Open the bar?" Bliss popped out from the storage room, grinning. "Are we opening up, Allay?"

"Sure, why not?"

"I'll tell you why not," Markman snapped. "Some guy tried to murder you! Then another guy threatened to kill you. Don't you take that seriously? You could be shot."

"What else is new?" I retorted. "Maybe you should stick around and get that proof you're looking for."

"Someone else could get shot, like your janitor."

My expression fell. "I'd hate for anyone to get caught in the line of fire again...."

Bliss marched up. "Full disclosure—tell everyone it might be dangerous. If they decide to stay, like I did, then it's not your responsibility."

"I don't know," I said. "It would still be my fault."

"No, it's not!" Bliss was getting worked up. "Are you going to stay stuck inside forever? Grow up, Allay! You're not the center of the universe. You're not responsible for everything. Let people make their own choices. You concentrate on deciding what's best for you."

"That hasn't worked out very well so far."

Bliss held out her hands. "What's not to like? I know you—you're glad you can atone for working for the prophet all those years. He deserves what he's got coming. Plus you're out and proud, and you've got great friends like *me*. Not to mention you have a rocking little bar, with lots of eager customers outside."

I was nodding, feeling lighter by the moment. "When you put it that way . . ."

"Do it," Bliss said softly, coming closer.

I was done with doubts. I had made my choice; now I had to live with it. I wanted nothing more than to run my bar and talk to my patrons, to be honest and not have to do dirty deeds to pay for protection. I had to be exactly who I was, out in the open.

"Okay, I will."

Bliss stroked my arm, stealing away some of that golden stream of happiness that flooded me for so brief a moment. "I knew that's what you wanted."

"You vampire," I said fondly. Then I took hold of her arm in return, drawing on her energy, soaking up enough to blunt the immediate edge of hunger.

"Same back at you." She smiled.

Lieutenant Markman cleared his throat. "I hate to interrupt you, ladies, but I have to advise you against this."

"You said you wanted to draw out the perps. This will do it." I realized Bliss and I were still holding each other from the way he was trying hard not to look at us. She was content to snuggle and continue feeding right in front of him, but I gently disentangled myself. At the very least, he was getting the wrong idea that Bliss and I were a couple.

What we had was even more intimate and deep; she was my offspring. Shock had been wrong about that, as she had been wrong about a lot of things. I was very lucky to have Bliss in my life.

I squeezed her arm as I pulled away. "If you could call the guard company, Lieutenant Markman, I'd appreciate it."

21

Markman gave way, and worked with me. He had to. My lawyer sent over a notice to be posted on the door stating that the owners of the property took no responsibility for any violence that was out of their direct control. The guards showed up and I carefully searched their auras—there was no sign of deception when I mentioned the prophet and the Fellowship of Truth. They were solid men, and they immediately took control of the flow of patrons into my bar.

I picked out my regulars—the few I saw—and made sure to greet everyone who entered. One girl cried; she had been here the night before, and had seen me die. I spoke to her for a while, leaving the bartending to Bliss.

I barred the press in any form, but I couldn't stop people from taking pictures with their cell phones. The press of eyes boring inward was unnerving until the bar fairly filled up, and I had to serve drinks along with Bliss to keep up with the demand. We were well into the first hour before I realized, "Where did you get the ice?"

"I fixed the machine. I opened it up and saw that a wire had worked loose." Bliss hardly glanced at me, pouring the beers. Bartending was hard work when it was busy, and she was doing it with the skill I'd gained over a decade.

But I would never have thought of opening up the ice machine to see what was wrong. "More power to you. Maybe you're destined to be an engineer when you grow up."

Bliss laughed, a perfect peal of delight. "I am all grown-up, Allay." Then she was gone.

When the rush eased off and everyone was seated, nursing their drinks and watching me, I went to talk to my patrons again. They were listening to me; even the ones passing by outside were straining to hear. It kept giving me flashbacks of Plea, preaching to one group or another, saying stirring, inspirational things about the glory of God. But I tried to answer honestly about everything—I did it because I wanted the truth to be known, not a religious lie, not superstition.

They thought it was a big joke, with nervous laughter erupting from every part of the bar at nearly everything I said. They didn't believe I was a demon. But they wanted to believe. They wanted proof that there was more out there than their eyes could see.

Then a woman held out her arm and said, "Feed from me, then. Let me see how it feels."

It was unexpected, especially in front of so many people watching and recording the moment for posterity. I hesitated, but it was exactly what I wanted, to be able to feed honestly, freely taking what was offered.

"You won't feel anything," I warned her. "I'm only skimming off the excess that your aura sheds."

I lightly touched her arm, feeling her instant thrill along with a slight shiver of her skin. "Your hand is cold," she said.

"I'm always that way." I let go of her.

She grinned, rubbing her arm where I had touched it. "How do I taste?"

"Very good, brave and daring, with a pleasant thrill of fear to top it off. You were really scared, weren't you?"

"A touch, I think. It's so strange to think you're a demon." But her voice was filled with doubt.

"I'm human, too. I grew up like you did, only I was waylaid before I could finish." That led to questions about my past and how I was turned. A few of the young men called out snarky comments, trying to make everyone laugh. But mostly they were so fascinated that people began to call from the street asking to be let in.

The guards warned me that some turnover would be helpful, so I asked everyone but my regulars to go. They could stay as long as they liked; this was their bar as much as mine. But a new crop of tourists joined us, and Bliss and I were busy serving drinks once more.

Old Jose showed up at his regular hour, and had not one word to say about the crush that he had to fight his way through. He sat at the bar downing his beer as usual. He had been sitting in that very spot last night when I was shot, but he didn't ask a single question or act like anything was different tonight.

I was laughing about it with Bliss when there was a commotion by the front door. "I work here!" Lolita drawled, holding out her hand to introduce herself. "I'm Lolita. What's your name?"

Bemused, the guard was trying to usher her back into the stream and was having no luck, when I arrived to welcome her in with a hug. "Lolita! I told you everything was fine." I had called this morning while we were prepping the bar. "What are you doing here?"

"You didn't say you were opening up, you little brat! You need my help. Saturday is always our big night." She gestured to the pedestrians shuffling slowly by, all holding out their cell phones to take photos. As if I hadn't noticed them. "I'm thinking it'll be a *really* big night tonight."

"I'm so glad to see you, Lolita. But . . . I have to warn you." I felt obligated to gesture to the legal warning posted on the door. "Someone could try to kill me again.

Just to prove a point. I'd hate for you to get hurt like Pepe."

"Yeah, yeah!" She breezed past the guard and me into the bar. "I'd like to see someone try. This time we'll be ready for 'em. Nice security, by the way," she added, lowering her voice. "What do you know about him?"

I laughed. "Nothing, yet. I'll leave that to you, Lo."

I thought she would be stilted or feel awkward around me. Of all of them, Lolita knew in her bones that I was different, that I was demon. But she was far too polite to ask me personal questions. She knew how much I valued my privacy.

"You don't know how much I appreciate you," I told Lo. "You've backed me up every step of the way. I'll never forget it."

Lo pooh-poohed that. "You're part of my family, Allay. What else does family do?"

I thought of my mom's wary voice, Kathy's shrill resentment, Shock's anger, and couldn't answer. Lo was my foundation, solid and immovable.

Together, we went back to work, rotating the looky-loos every hour or so. We sold a lot more drinks than usual, so it took all three of us to keep up. There had been no deliveries this week, but since we'd been closed for several days, we had plenty of stock. Still, at the pace we were going, I was wondering how we'd finish out the night. I was going to have to double my orders for next week. Being a demon was good for business.

So I made sure to entertain the crowd by answering questions, glad to see some nod thoughtfully as I spoke about the huge number of myths based on demons. We had always been a part of history, coexisting with humans and working together. A few caught the mystery of it despite their sightseeing spirit. They had come just because they wanted to be a part of something new and different, to see for themselves as YouTube videos hit the Internet and were picked up by the broadcast media. I ended up turning off the television much earlier than usual because it was too surreal to see myself up on the screen talking to people in my bar.

I fed from those who offered, and by the evening, they were lining up to let me touch them. The girls giggled and the guys strained as if trying to feel me drawing their energy out. It was a freak show, yes, in many ways, but it was honest. I was getting what I needed, and they were getting what they needed from me.

Bliss was not so honest. She stroked my customers, stealing away more than I took consensually. But they knew the risk; I warned them that the only way a demon could take their energy was by touch. And it took a demon only ten, maybe fifteen minutes to drain a human of vital energy. So I told them to only let someone touch them that long if they trusted them with their lives.

It made them smile knowingly, even the ones that Bliss was draped over at the time. She nodded right along with them, laughing at my expression. She didn't touch anyone for very long, so I didn't protest. Clearly she wasn't interested in outing herself, so I was very careful to make no sign that she was also a demon. Not even to Lolita, who was again tolerant enough not to ask about my frisky blond friend from California.

But as gratifying as it was to be able to explain to my customers, and to see some of them trying to understand instead of making a joke out of it, I kept waiting for the other shoe to drop. I kept waiting for demons to come.

I wasn't quite sure how my rule against no-outing would apply if demons tried to hurt me or my patrons. I still didn't know when Bliss finally gave me the nod, abruptly serious, telling me that she sensed a demon approaching.

I joined her at the front of the bar, feeling only the

first tingles of warning, when she sighed in relief. "It's Mystify," she murmured, then returned to fill an order.

I waited at the open windows, smiling back at everyone who was pointing at me, when Mystify drifted into view. He was wearing his elfin urchin persona, and was looking good, relaxed and enjoying himself. He gave me a slight wave as he passed by, bumping and jostling with everyone being funneled past.

I rolled my eyes. He was feeding off them. He trolled along time and again like a grinning shark, making the most of the confusion I had created. I laughed and pointed him out to the guard, giving him a pass if he wanted to come in. For a long time he cruised the sidewalk, charging himself to a nice, bright glow before he finally entered.

He gave me a big hug, ignoring the eyes and cell phones focused on us. He was euphoric from soaking up his favorite emotion. "Allay, how sweet of you. Throwing a party in my honor!"

"Hush," I warned, wondering if he was drunk on their confusion. He was going to out himself with another word. If that was his choice, fine, but I didn't want him to stumble into something he'd regret.

Firmly taking his arm, I led him to the storeroom. Through the half-open door, I could see the end of the bar where the nearest patron was a guy deep in a flirtation with a Chinese girl with caramel-streaked hair.

I kept my voice low to ask, "Where is she?"

"Ch—" He stopped as I gestured quickly with my hands to keep him from saying her name.

"She's"—he pointed downward with his finger, and then he frowned and pointed uptown and down—"to be exact."

So Cherie was still underground at the condos. "She didn't follow you up?"

"Nope. She's happy to be there."

"Really?" I shuddered to think of her white eyes peering out of her blackened face. "Did we do the right thing?"

"She loves it, Allay. Don't argue with madness."

He shifted, putting his arm up on the shelf behind me. We were already close, whispering over our secrets, our faces together.

"Don't argue," he murmured. He closed the distance to kiss me.

It startled me, and I drew back. But he held on to my hand, trying to keep me from retreating. "Do I only get a kiss good-bye, not hello?"

His touch sent a spark through my arm, igniting me inside. I couldn't deny it; he saw the verdant blush of my aura. He could feel it in my trembling hand.

He leaned closer again, to kiss me. I wanted to, but I couldn't let him. As much as I was attracted to him, I couldn't pursue this now. Ram loomed between us, an impassable divide. The things Mystify did were a constant reminder that he was Ram's offspring. It was too weird, too incestuous.

"No, Mystify. I have to sort out things with Ram."

"Allay, in case nobody told you, demons aren't monogamous. Ram certainly isn't. He never has been."

I remembered Ram promising he would drop his girlfriends. I wondered if he was with one of them now. He could be anywhere, even in my bar, hiding among the patrons I hadn't touched.

But it was different now; now that I had come out. He was disgusted with me. "Do you think I'm a megalomaniac?"

"You? No, definitely not. Who said that?"

"Ram. He said I had delusions of grandeur, like Hope."

He looked puzzled.

"Mystify, you, of all people, should know what he's talking about. You have Ram's memories. Why does he think I'm like Hope?"

Mystify pulled back. "I wish I could tell you, Allay."

"Why can't you?"

"It's my memories, or rather Ram's memories. Everything's fairly clear for the past week—the rest is fuzzy. The things I know about Hope are from memories he recalled when he met you. But it's vague, little glimpses. Memories are tricky. The things that happen closest to the time of fissioning are the strongest."

"But you must know something," I pressed. "Ram said I would sympathize with Hope. It had something to do with why she betrayed him to Bedlam."

He gave me a sideways look. "You don't know? Ram killed her offspring. Hope was close to her, sort of like you and Bliss. So she stole the map he made of all the human civilizations in the world and gave it to Bedlam in revenge. Bedlam used it to destroy them."

"Ram killed her offspring?" I gulped. "That's awful! Why?"

Mystify shrugged. "Ram always has his reasons when he kills a demon."

"Then why did he kill Hope?"

"Ram doesn't think about it—it's like a big black hole that swallows him up from time to time." Mystify narrowed his eyes. "Why don't you ask him?"

"I did, but he turned the subject back on *you*. He thinks you're manipulating me, trying to confuse me."

"Right back at him." Mystify smiled. "He's hiding something, from me as well as you, and that's no small trick."

I knew I had to confess. "He knows about . . ." I gestured downward, imitating him. It took him only a moment to realized who I meant—Cherie. "He hung around watching me all day and figured it out. I'm sorry—"

Mystify titled his head back, letting out a groan. "Allay! You promised."

"I didn't mean to. He sees through me like I'm glass."

He paced back and forth in the narrow storeroom, shaking his head. Ram had something on him now, something that could be used against him. But Mystify didn't fling that in my face. He took the blow and considered it from all angles.

Finally he said, "Ah, well. What can I do? Ram could tell Dread, but that's the least of Dread's worries right now. Is it true you're cooperating with the DA?"

"Yes, Dread's about to be indicted for a number of felonies."

Mystify shook himself, as if he were loosening up after a fight. "I'll just have to remember you can't keep secrets from Ram."

"I'm a very bad liar," I agreed.

He was preoccupied and distant. As soon as we left the storeroom, he returned to the sidewalk, where he started making his rounds again, giving me little waves the few times our eyes met, concentrating on enjoying himself.

I was getting comfortable again when I felt another demon signature approaching. Maybe I was more attuned to this one, because I met Bliss's eyes as we both recognized it—Revel. Returning from Uzbekistan.

When he came to the door, I didn't recognize him. Instead of exposing his Giles Fortunay persona, he was wearing a Euro-trash ensemble complete with bleached blond hair, mirrored sunglasses, and white cargo pants.

"You look like an asshole," I told him. "Could you be a little more obvious?"

"I figured it would read well on TV, love. I tried calling, but your phone was busy."

"I had to unplug it." I would have spent more time on the bar phone than with my patrons if I had tried to keep up.

He glanced around. "Is Ram here?"

I blew out my breath. "Damned if I know. Come into my office."

I took Revel to the storeroom, feeling a little self-conscious at the eyes following me. Revel was right; he'd be featured as a "mystery man" who spoke in private with the "alleged demon." Somehow with Mystify it had been more casual, maybe because Revel lived for attention.

"You need a better office, Allay." He looked at the stacks of napkins and boxes of sugar packets with raised brows. "Shock says you've lost it, that you're Ram's puppet now."

I shook my head. "Ram hates it that I came out. He thinks I'm as delusional as she does."

"Allay, I was gone for only three days. What happened?"

I wanted to tell him that I had found out the truth about him, but I had to hear what he had discovered first. "Shock and I have been fighting since I woke up from having Bliss. She hates Bliss, hates Ram, hates Mystify—"

"Mystify is here now. Why is that?"

"He's a friend. He's been . . . helpful."

I could see a slice of the bar through the half-open door. Mystify had followed Revel back inside. He came all the way nearly to the door to lean against the wall at the back curve of the bar, where I could see him. He was there to help me if I needed it. "What did you find out about Hope?"

With his back to the door, Revel couldn't see Mystify, but he knew he was close. "The scroll is authentic. A real find. There's some damage that has to be X-rayed in order to get a complete translation, but I got a preliminary reading from a local scholar. It tells the story of a god who kills his wife's daughter—the wife's name is Hope. She revenges herself by selling his soul to a fellow god. Thus enslaved, she flays her husband alive for forty days and forty nights, killing him over and over again."

"Seriously? Did that happen to Ram?" The thought of Ram tied spread-eagle to a tree, flayed alive every day for six weeks ... "It can't be true."

"That's what the story says."

A demon could be killed over and over again, deliberately, slowly. *I'd go insane if someone did that to me.*

"The scroll says that the god finally broke free and ripped his lover into a thousand pieces and buried them at the ends of the earth, traveling around the world for a hundred years to complete the task."

I wanted to cry. Vengeance, hatred, cruelty ... it was the stuff of nightmares. No wonder Ram didn't tell me. He didn't want to see me recoil in horror. To think he'd gone through that ...

"Allay?" Revel's tone lost that cynical edge. "Are you all right? It's just a story, a myth."

Mystify had said there was a big black hole in Ram's past, where he fell into despair. I met Mystify's eyes. Revel's words had called up memories in him, just as I suffered flashbacks of Plea's tragic moments. He looked like he was stricken dumb.

"It's true," I whispered.

"Maybe you don't want to hear about this?" Revel said.

"I do." I added, not so sure, "I did."

He shrugged, a little miffed that I wasn't exclaiming over his find with him. "You've got bigger problems, Allay. You need to lie low for a while, let this all disappear."

"Let Emma Meyers disappear, you mean."

"Exactly. It's time to move on. We all do, Allay. It's

how it works for us." His eyes lit up. "You could go any-where you want. The pyramids, the Left Bank, the Great Wall of China. It's time for you to travel and get a feel for the world, not just this little corner of the city."

I crossed my arms. "You think you can tell me what to do."

He heard the warning in my voice though not the exact words. "I'm making a suggestion. I'm offering to be *helpful*. I think you should get out of New York for a while, make yourself scarce. So I'm offering to travel around the world with you, to see that you're not harmed. You should be warned—Dread has put the word out that he would be very appreciative of anyone who arranged a 'meeting' between you and him."

"If he wants to see me, he can come here. Let him do his worst in front of twenty cell phones recording his every move."

"You're being naive, Allay. Dread's vendetta against you will last centuries beyond this bar. You need my help."

My arms were still crossed. "I'm not going anywhere with you, Revel. You were working for Vex when you killed your own offspring to make me. He ordered you to ambush Plea."

Revel was a very old demon, but even they could be caught by surprise. There was only an instant when he wanted to deny it; then he immediately went into ap-peasement mode. "I was forced to do it, Allay. Do you think I wanted to kill Plea? I liked her, though we ran in different circles. But Vex insisted. I did my best to get out of it, and I saved Shock from being his intended vic-tim, but I couldn't save Plea, as much as I tried."

"So you killed her. Or rather, I killed Plea. You tied her up and laid her on the tracks so I could run over her." I was angrier than I had a right to be, since I al-ready knew he was a liar. Every single thing in our relationship was based on a lie, by Vex's order. "Why didn't you tell me?"

"It was the only hold I had over Vex. I used our secret to stay involved in your life, to help protect you, though you wouldn't let Shock or me do it properly. He knew I could tell you at any time; I could turn you against him for masterminding the whole thing. Now I know why it was so important for him to retain your goodwill—he intended for you to be in Cherie's place. But Vex is gone now, and we can start fresh, without him between us."

I was already shaking my head. "Get out, Revel. I can't even look at you."

"Allay! I just went all the way to Uzbekistan for you—"

"You did it for yourself. I bet there are things you're hiding from me about that scroll." He didn't look guilty, but he also didn't leap to deny it. "You always do what's best for yourself, Revel. I'm so sick of how selfish you are. Go away."

His aura flushed a surprisingly deep shade of red, a sudden, blinding anger. For a second I was frightened.

Mystify straightened up, seeing my fear. He took a step toward the door, but Revel was already turning to leave. He ran into Mystify. "Quick work," Revel muttered at him. He didn't glance back at me as he left.

Mystify and I exchanged relieved looks as Revel stalked through the bar like a rejected diva. For a second back there, I was afraid Revel was going to explode. But I should have known he was too civilized for that.

Mystify opened his mouth to say something, but the guy who had been flirting with the pretty Chinese girl got down off his barstool and stepped between us. "Now it's my turn to have a moment with you in the closet."

I looked into his eyes and knew—it was Ram. There was a spark, a connection between us, and like a transparent overlay, I saw *him* instead of the ordinary guy.

I had wondered if I would be as attracted to him in a different guise; I had grown to love the rugged, darker version of his Theo Ram face, but it made no difference that now he was blond and smooth. It was Ram; even shielded I could see him like a blaze of light within. Why hadn't I noticed it before? Why hadn't I felt the magnetism that drew me toward him even now?

"You should have told me you were here." I tried to keep my voice low. He had been flirting with that girl! It was the perfect disguise for deceiving me, because I hadn't imagined him doing something like that right in front of me.

Bliss noticed and knew instantly that it was Ram. Mystify realized it almost as quickly. He was trapped by Ram against the wall at the back of the bar.

To relieve Mystify, I stepped into the storeroom. Ram followed, and was careful to shut the door. "Something about the acoustics—you can hear everything that's said in here when you're sitting at the end of the bar."

I wondered how many private conversations I'd had with Lolita had been overheard by the patrons who loved those stools. "You should have told me you were here. Instead of sneaking around and eavesdropping on me."

"Even if you were mostly talking about me," he agreed. "Allay, you've heard everything, there is nothing more to tell. Except for this: you're not like Hope. She never helped people, she sought out those who were in agony and she gave them hope, only to deliberately leave them hoping and never rescued. She did the same for me, telling me she would release me as she tortured me, feeding from me all the while. When I finally broke free of her, in my madness, I killed her. But it was better for the world that she was dead."

It hurt to hear him admit it, but I also felt bad for him. "I wish you had told me yourself, Ram. I asked you, but wouldn't tell me."

"Yes, then you wouldn't have to hear it from my rivals. But they are always there trying to control you." His hands clenched. "Allay, come away with me. Close down the bar, stop making a show of yourself. It can come to no good."

We were already standing apart, but I drew back even more. "Now you sound like Revel. At least he lets me know when he's coming."

"I have to conceal myself because of the fuss you're making. This is too dangerous, Allay. You're going to get killed, really killed. Come away with me, and we'll be together."

"Give up this megalomaniacal nonsense, right?"

"You can't change the world, Allay. You'll only get hurt trying."

"*You* try. Isn't that why you kill so many demons?"

He almost smiled. "That's how I know I'm right. It's futile, Allay. Let's go away together and forget about this. Let everything run its course without us. Let's take some time for us, to be together, to see what kind of a future we have together."

It felt as if I were tied to him by a thousand strings, and those strings were tightening between us, drawing me back to him. I felt like I had to give in; I wanted to say yes, to throw myself in his arms and let him take care of everything. I could love him as fiercely as I had always longed to, give him everything, live for him, with him.

I wavered forward, and he reached out for me, his face alight with eagerness, ready to crush me to his chest. I wanted to bury myself in him.

I stopped myself. "I can't."

"Allay . . ." His arms were out to take me. "Why not?"

"I can't leave. I belong here. I want to be here. I don't want to run away and hide anymore." I gestured out to the bar. "I want to talk to them, to explain what I am, to make them understand. It's working, Ram. I think some of them believe me."

"This is the lull before the storm, Allay. You're about to be engulfed."

"I'm not a natural disaster."

"It's going to be a disaster if you don't stop."

I was breathing faster at his condescending tone. I had kicked Revel out so easily; I should have done the same with Ram. But some traitorous part of me wanted to throw my arms around him and kiss him, to demand he love me for who I was.

A hesitant knock on the door interrupted. I opened it to find Bliss. "Um, Allay, your customers are getting antsy. They came here to see a demon, you know. And there's a woman here to speak to you. She said Michael sent her. She's a publicist."

I glanced back at Ram, who was shaking his head. "No, Allay, don't do this."

"You're very tempting . . . but I can't run away with you, Ram. This is my home."

I joined Bliss, whose eyes were round, as she pointed out the publicist. Ram stood in the doorway of the storeroom as I headed over to the stylish woman who was wearing too much makeup for my taste. I expected him to leave, or make a scene, but he just stood there openly watching me along with everyone else. Except for the pretty girl he had been flirting with. She was smiling at him in question, wondering why he didn't return to her side.

Rather than disappoint my patrons by retreating to the storeroom, I met the publicist in the front of the bar. She shook my hand with a tighter grip than was necessary, with tiny, hard fingers.

"I'm Marissa Perone with the Perone Publicity ~~G~~ up. Michael Horowitz contacted me. He tried to call ~~but~~ your phone doesn't seem to be working. I've been watching you on the news. Not bad, not bad at all. He says you don't want any coaching, you just want a booking agent who knows her way around the industry. That's me. I won't tell you to do anything—well, I'll tell you but you don't have to listen. Like that dark shirt, it really doesn't work on the small screen, and with the low-rez clips that are coming out, it's not working."

I laughed. She was so überpolished herself, there was no way she could understand my style. "No offense, but that's exactly the sort of advice I don't need."

She lowered her voice so the others couldn't hear. "What about advice on your sound bites? First of all, must you call yourself a 'demon'? Why not 'vampire'? People really like vampires right now. They're very hot. And that's really what you are—an emotion vampire, *right*?"

I looked over at Ram, and laughed again. He had said the exact same thing, yet they couldn't be coming from opposite poles. That didn't make me doubt myself, though. "I call things what they are, Ms. Perone. I don't think this is going to work."

I started to turn away, but she stepped aside to block me. "Look, Ms. Meyers, I'll stick to setting up the bookings and your fees. I'll brief you on each interviewer, tell you their quirks and what they're going to ask you about. All of this barroom chat is wonderful stuff, but you could reach millions on *Good Morning America*. Why not spread the word to as many people as possible?"

I considered her. "Can you give me final approval on everything? No little deals behind my back."

For a second, I saw through her Botoxed mask to her shrewd eyes. "Yes, I can do that."

Over her shoulder, I saw Ram watching me. I shook her hand. "Then it's a deal."

22

Ram left right after that. Watching him go out the door hit me deep in my core, as though my eternal flame had been snuffed. I didn't want him to go, I wanted to hold him, but he didn't want me. He wanted some other kind of girl.

It felt very empty without him, even with all the people who were eager to be here.

Mystify cruised the sidewalk, never saying a word to me about what he had overheard. He was wrestling with the knowledge, too. Our ancestors had such bleak terror in their lives, monstrous deeds. How could Ram live with it?

Bliss asked me about Ram, but there was nothing to say but "He wants me to run away with him. And I can't do that."

"Fuck 'em," Bliss said, imitating Lo's pet phrase. "You do what you want."

I kept the bar open as long as the beer held out. What was supposed to last until Monday ran out by eleven o'clock Saturday. I called and left a message with the distributor, but I wasn't sure if they could deliver on a Sunday, and through all this traffic. My neighborhood was still snarled, along with the streets around the Prophet's Center and Arena.

I called a car and made the security guards go out to Lolita so she wouldn't have to deal with any of the passersby. Even after we closed down the bar and pulled the shutter, there were too many of them strolling past.

Bliss said she was going out on the town, so I offered to join her to be safe. She laughed at the idea of me at a swing club, and I had to agree it wasn't something I was interested in exploring at the moment. She had no fear, while I had more than my fair share. She left at the same time as Lolita.

My first task after pulling down the shutter was to get rid of the spray-painted pentagram. Earlier I'd asked one of my regulars, Anthony, to paint over it, and he returned with all of his supplies to work on it as soon as we closed. We agreed on an undersea motif. I hoped it would be pretty enough to keep people from defacing it.

Then I settled down inside with my new publicist, Ms. Marissa Perone, to get to work. I could feel Mystify circling outside along with the curious stragglers, who were doubtless much more curious and less satisfied than when the bar had been open. It felt good knowing he was there. It also felt good having security guards stationed in the front and back.

But I knew there was nothing that could stop a gang of demons if they really wanted to break in and get me.

So I decided to tell all and tell it fast. I might have only a few days to get my message across before someone decided to stop me.

Marissa laid out a list of interviews I could do right away on the Internet—it was early morning in Europe, and there were plenty of people who wanted to speak to the American demon. I also did text interviews with bloggers and made Webcam appearances in several on-line conference rooms. Then she left to get some sleep before my big morning show appearances, which started bright and early at five thirty a.m.

I was waiting for her, wearing a dark shirt that had a nice collar and cuffs along with black jeans and ankle boots. I had only a couple of silver chains around my neck, tucked discreetly inside my shirt. She screwed up her lips, dying to tell me everything that was wrong, but I cut her off, trying to explain in her terms, "I can't be polished, Marissa. I have to look awkward and natural, I have to look *real*."

At the studio, she fussed with my hair a bit, and she tried to get me to sit down in the makeup artist's chair, but I refused. I could make my own skin matte, and darken my lashes and lips just enough so they were still natural but would "read" on camera, as Marissa kept insisting.

As she was watching me adjust the tint in my cheeks, Marissa got a strange expression, a flash of revulsion. It was the instinctive xenophobia that humans had for bipeds who are like them, but different.

It made me uncomfortable. It was a bad way to begin my television debut.

I felt awkward and unreal sitting in a tiny three-sided set floating in a big sound stage filled with people and equipment with cables snaking along the floor and grids of lights overhead shining hotly into my eyes. I barely had time to meet my interviewers, Jamie something, and who was the guy? I should have known, but couldn't remember despite Marissa's last-minute briefing. Both were literally caked with foundation with their features carefully drawn on. I had seen their faces on the television screen, but now suddenly they looked older and uglier. Their warm personas were swallowed up by an ironclad professionalism that had gotten them to the top of their game.

Jamie didn't like me, not one bit. Her scorn was palatable. She thought I was a two-bit hustler who was too naive to make it in Peoria much less New York City. She was barely civil, joking with her cohost about "this bullshit" right before someone called out of the darkness offstage, "Rolling!"

I knew millions of eyes were watching me right *now*, and if I made a mistake, I could ruin everything. Adrenaline spiked, and I tried to control it as Jamie switched on her perky All-American persona, and was off and running. I couldn't keep up. Looking in her eyes, I saw her contempt. Surely everyone else did, too. She kept mentioning that this must be good publicity for my bar.

"How much did you make last night with your Q-and-A sessions?" she asked brightly. "Was it twice the usual Saturday night take? Maybe three times as good? These little stunts make for good television, don't they? We've seen it all here, haven't we, Bob?"

I was so self-conscious that I froze, groping for words that had flowed off my tongue so easily at the bar. The only time Jamie mentioned "demon" was to put air quotes around the word, with a smirk in her voice and a knowing look at her cohost. Mostly she wanted to make snide comments about my seamy love affair with the prophet, including the fact that I must have some kind of daddy complex.

Having had hours of practice overnight, with Marissa's handy advice, I didn't suck as badly as I would have. But that wasn't saying much.

As soon as the segment was over and the lights were killed, Jamie unclipped her mic and clicked away without even a good-bye. A techie wearing a headset waited impatiently as the wire of my microphone got caught in my necklaces. I stilled my shaking fingers and dragged it out from under my shirt. A girl with a clipboard was waiting to show us through the long industrial corridors to a black car waiting outside.

I felt as though I were being put out with the garbage.

After that, I was whisked from one studio to another tucked into various cavernous buildings throughout the city. I had no idea there were so many. I didn't watch morning shows myself, but had always considered them to be fluff. If this was bad, what would the news interviews be like? I'd be going to CNN and MSNBC later. Even Fox wanted a piece of me.

I had to keep my panic under control. I didn't have much time between each show, waiting in tiny rooms with television screens displaying the guest before me. Sometimes another guest was waiting there too, watching me as if I were a pregnant panda about to pop. I felt like there should be bars around me keeping the visitors back.

Everyone was much more interested in my relationship with Prophet Anderson and the fact that he bought me the bar. I kept having to repeat that I couldn't comment on that because of pending litigation, just as Kosciusko had insisted. I was glad because I didn't want to speculate about what Dread would do now that he was considered a "person of interest" in my shooting. My lawyer also told me to not speak about Phil Anchor, which was a relief. I didn't mind doing as Kosciusko said, whereas if Ms. Perone had asked me, I would have refused. Marissa was concerned with appearances, whereas my lawyer was trying to protect me.

But I did talk about Cherie. In fact, I told people I had come out, in part, because of the things Cherie had said about herself. She was the only one I pointed to and said, "That's a demon." She had set this in motion, using her demon nature to misrepresent herself as a religious miracle, whether intentionally or because of Dread's con game. So I said it: Cherie hadn't become immortal through faith. She was possessed like me.

I denied any knowledge about her motives, or that anyone else in the Fellowship knew that Cherie was a demon. But I explained the mechanics of how we both became possessed, the only two alive. They asked where she was, but I took them at their most literal meaning and replied, "I don't know."

Then one interviewer asked, "So, if you're a demon, how many of you are there?"

"Over two hundred."

That was the first time that I got a real reaction. Not just the interviewers, but there was a slight intake of collective breath from the crew behind the equipment. They didn't believe I was a demon. But just the notion that a couple hundred parasitic creatures were out there, living among them, feeding off them . . . it sparked a deep-seated evolutionary fear. Demons had always preyed on people. And they knew it, though they didn't want to admit it.

"Not all demons are bad," I hastened to explain. "We have strong desires, usually based in our emotional signature. For me that's relief; for others it's sadness or pain. But that doesn't mean a demon will cause pain—a demon doctor could soak up pain from people, lessening their suffering and helping them. We all have our flaws, but we aren't all bad."

"What are your flaws?" the interviewer asked.

It wasn't the usual question, so I had to think about it a bit. "I doubt myself. I avoid problems. I've done things I regret for selfish reasons. I . . . think I have a hero complex. I'm not sure how else to explain why I want to ruin my own life in order to tell everyone the truth."

They always wanted more, but Marissa kept me moving. As the day wore on, the shows picked up on what I'd said in previous interviews, and clarified things or asked me to expand on my own comments. By then I'd found out that my distributor couldn't deliver until Monday morning, so I had to keep the bar closed. I let everyone know, and the guards reported that Bliss had returned and gone out again.

With nothing else to do that evening, I agreed to a round of tests at NYU Medical Center, the same hospital where Cherie had gone. I had an eerie sensation of déjà vu, even though I had a different perspective lying on the table where Cherie had lain, looking up at the mirrored slanting windows. I knew there were dozens of people watching me from up there.

The surgeon cut me with a knife again and again, his fascination oozing from his aura. He didn't seem to care how much he touched me, holding my skin taut, so I shamelessly fed from him, and any of the other hospital staff that touched me. I was nearing my peak capacity.

It felt good.

Along with Marissa Perone, Kosciusko came with me to the hospital, along with a couple of his lawyers. I liked the show of strength. I knew that one false step could land me in a "secured facility." I wasn't going to let myself disappear.

I got a much more thorough grilling from the doctors than the media. They were taping me, and I wondered if these clips were also going to end up in the blogosphere. I almost hoped so. At least some of the truth would be out there.

One of the questions the doctors asked that I couldn't answer was: How did demons come to exist? The fact that I had a distinct DNA and blood type was understandable because I had started out human. But every demon was different, with a unique physiology. Where did that imprint come from? Was there a human out there with the exact same biology that a demon's body mimicked? Or were demons as truly unique as humans, who relied on the joining of two strands to make a whole gene? What made demons the way we are?

I wished I could refer them to Revel. He could probably have a serious discussion with them and get somewhere. "I am only an egg!" I wanted to cry.

I didn't get home until nearly midnight. There were just as many people passing by as last night, but this time I had a chauffeur, my publicist, and security staff to clear my way to the door. The first thing I saw was my shutter, transformed. It looked like a giant aquarium with underwater plants and colorful fish swimming in the midst of a light-filled, Mediterranean blue.

I could sense that Bliss wasn't home, and Mystify wasn't among the stream of people filing by my beautiful shuttered bar. Marissa was still by my side. She had worked out a deal with Michael for a five-thousand-dollar retainer and a one-month commitment. I wasn't sure how I was going to pay it, but she had certainly earned it. She left me with a list of more interviews I was supposed to do overnight, and planned to join me again at five a.m. so I could go to some different morning shows. There was a whole new lineup on Monday mornings.

All I cared about was making sure I was home by ten a.m. for the beer delivery. I needed to open up the bar and get some cash to pay for all of this.

Marissa had asked the car to wait, and I headed outside with her to tell the security guard to make sure nobody bothered her. She stopped me at the door. "Allay, I've been with you since five this morning. You didn't sleep last night because I checked all of your online interviews. You haven't eaten a bite, while I've been pigging out on the greenroom buffets. You haven't had to so much as blot your face or blow your nose or go to the bathroom. You look exactly the same as you did this morning. You're inhuman!"

"I know you're making a joke, but I can tell it bothers you. That I'm different."

"I admit I'm a bit squicked about the whole thing. But as long as you don't touch me, we'll be able to work together. I make it a point not to discriminate against anyone." She sniffed, a honed skepticism still warring with what she had seen with her own eyes. "Demon, huh? Who would have figured it?"

She had been listening to me all day, and was possibly the foremost expert on demons other than demons. But most of the time she had appeared to be paying no attention, concentrating on her BlackBerry during my interviews. I wasn't sure how much she had heard.

Apparently it wasn't my words but my deeds that were convincing. That was the problem—how could I convince millions of people one at a time that I was telling the truth?

A few hours later, I got a call on the cell that Marissa had given me to do my interviews. It was an AP reporter. "Ms. Meyers, would you like to comment on the fire burning in the Fellowship complex?"

"It's burning?" I blurted out.

"Yes, it appears to have been started by rioters on the street."

I turned on the television so I could see for myself. The Prophet's Center was on fire, and it wasn't just one corner of the building. The windows were broken and spewing flames. The whole middle was going up in smoke. The fire trucks were jammed in at odd angles to get close enough with their ladders, and people were hanging out of the upper windows. Hoses were run out and spewing water.

"No comment," I said, hanging up on the reporter.

Sickened, I hoped that nobody had been killed. I felt like I had to take some responsibility for this. I'd been denouncing Cherie as a demon all day.

According to the news, Prophet Anderson had been asked to a meeting at the DA's office and had been unavailable for comment ever since.

I knew Dread was busy determining what to do to counter my multipronged attack. Even if he killed me now, the power base he had built for half a century was falling apart around him.

* * *

Not long after that, I felt Shock approaching. I jumped to my feet. I had never been so glad to feel her buzzing sensation. I knew Shock, and she wouldn't be coming unless she had something to say. Maybe she had heard me.

Maybe she understood what I was trying to do.

I strained to tell the direction of her approach. I should have guessed it would be from the rear, and when it became clear she was making her way through the backyards, I went downstairs. After waiting a few minutes, I realized she had stopped moving. She must have seen the security guard and didn't want to approach.

I hurried outside and told him to step into the bar for a few minutes. He didn't ask questions. He was being paid too well for that.

"Shock!" I called softly. "You can come out now."

Rustling in the weeds next door alerted me, and then Shock appeared at the top of the fence. "Where did that guy go?"

"Inside," I whispered.

"Watching us," she murmured, hesitating on her perch. This time she wasn't blazing red with anger. She glowed almost a pure white, as controlled as a demon could get. Revealing nothing.

"He can't hear us," I said barely above my breath. "Come down, Shock. I don't want the neighbors to see you." It was three in the morning, but someone could be watching.

She dropped down and we stood close together in the shadow of the fence. Her eyes were dead. A shiver of fear ran over my skin, rusting my aura.

Scared of Shock. It blew my mind.

"I almost didn't come," Shock said quietly. "But Revel insisted that I try one last time. He said I'm the only one who can stop you from going off the rails. But

I told him you wouldn't listen to me. You stopped listening to me a while ago."

My heart sank. Cold and mechanical was almost worse than blazing with fury. She couldn't be further away, even standing right next to me. "I'm sorry I hurt you, Shock. I didn't mean for that to happen."

She shrugged as if that meant nothing.

"I'm trying to change things, so we don't have to hide anymore," I said. "We won't be able to much longer, and if we don't deal with this now, in the right way, people like Dread will use it to their advantage."

"Like you're doing."

"You think this is helping me?" It was the same accusation I'd been hearing all day, but I couldn't believe Shock was saying it. I was so taken aback that I couldn't speak for a moment. "Shock, you have no idea what I've been going through."

"Yes, I do. I've seen it before, Allay. I tried to tell you. Everyone's tried to tell you. Whenever demons are discovered, it causes a panic until half of us are killed and everyone else goes so deep underground that we don't dare make a peep for another century. Do I have to actually say 'Salem witch trials' for you to get it?"

"That was a different time, more superstitious. People believe in science now. I can prove what I am."

"Maybe a few will believe you, but that just fuels the hysteria against us."

I was frustrated, not just with her but with everyone who wouldn't listen. "If you think it's so dangerous, I guess you better keep away from me."

"I'm going to Africa." She stared at me blankly. "You're a demon now. I can't trust you."

"Shock . . . you're the one who keeps telling me I'm a demon."

"I was wrong. You were human, and that was why I trusted you. Now that you're a demon, I can't. You'll hurt every one of us if it suits your purpose. You've already destroyed my life."

It seemed useless to protest that that hadn't been my intention. "I told you I would change if I killed Pique. I told you, but you wouldn't believe me."

"I won't make that mistake again."

She was so far away already. I could easily imagine her joining Doctors Without Borders and helping victims of famine and civil war. But the fact that she was going now, because of me, made it hard to accept.

"But I need you, Shock. Now more than ever."

"Someday—maybe not soon—but someday you might try to kill me." She shrugged as if it didn't matter. "I can't guard my back for that long."

I felt like I was tearing off my own arm. Last week I would have died for her. This week she looked at me like I was a stranger.

I waited in vain for some kind word, some hint of concern, some consolation I could use. Some sign of interest in me. But she had been ordered to come say good-bye by her progenitor, and that was what she did.

Without another word, she jumped up on the fence and swung her legs over. She gave me one last look, indecipherable, then disappeared on the other side.

It was my own doing. I had destroyed our friendship with my own hands. But then again, if Shock couldn't remain my friend as I grew and changed, then what could I do? She was the one person who had known me the best for the past decade, yet she had just walked away as if I was nothing.

I had been convinced that in the end, Shock would come back to me. I couldn't believe how wrong I was.

23

I had to admit I went about my interviews over the next few days in a stunned state. It felt like I was repeating myself, facing the same disbelief, the same mocking tones, the same dismissive attitude as if I was just another pawn in the big media game of one-upmanship. The more I talked, it seemed, the less headway I made.

Losing Shock had been a real blow. As the days passed, I was also becoming certain that Ram would not return. Now that I knew his past, I could see that my coming out couldn't have been timed worse for the start of our relationship together. I was grasping for power because I had to protect myself, and if that meant he couldn't love me, then I had to accept it. I had no other choice. It was either take care of myself or become somebody's chattel again.

I settled uneasily into a new routine. I opened the bar from two to ten p.m., and then out of respect for the neighbors, closed down for the night. I sold twice as much liquor in nearly half the time, and the tips were incredible. Who wants to stiff a demon?

Every day Bliss showed up in time to help open the bar and work a full shift, raking in the cash. I think it financed her after-hours activities. She mentioned seeing Savor once—they went to a sex party together and Bliss could hardly stop giggling as she described some of what she had seen. I asked her if she ever saw Crave, but she said no. According to Savor, he had disappeared. Perhaps he had gone to Dubai after Glory. It didn't seem to bother Bliss.

Mystify came by every day to join the curious crowds around the bar. He fed for hours but it never seemed like he came close to being fully charged up. Maybe because he was Ram's offspring. He cruised along letting the curiosity and amazement wash over him, getting high on his favorite emotion. Whenever he came inside to talk to me, he was giddy and babbled nonsense. I was grateful; I didn't want to fight off his advances. Or be tempted into giving in.

The only time he got serious was when he reported on Cherie's activities—always without saying her name. She roamed the caverns under Grand Central Terminal, staying with various groups. Rumors were spreading among the homeless that an angel had come down from heaven to live underground. Mystify said she sometimes referred to herself by her demon name—Elude. But I had a sinking feeling that Cherie would emerge soon, and then I would have to deal with her. Would she align with Dread? If that tender scene with Mystify was an indication, then yes, absolutely she would.

When the bar was closed, I moved on to print interviews, talking with magazine reporters and journalists and having my picture taken at the bar. Lolita brought back my cats, so I posed with the Snow-monster and his minion whenever I could. Who could fear a crazy cat lady? The print interviews went more in-depth with the questions, but such large chunks of my life involving Dread, Phil, Ram, and the other demons couldn't be spoken of, so I doubted people really understood me personally. But I kept my fingers crossed that they were getting the general picture of what it meant to be a demon.

All sorts of bizarre comments were made on the Web

site Marissa put up for me. I wrote the introduction and I spent several hours a day replying to questions on the chat boards. I got at least a hundred offers a day of marriage, from both men and women. I was single-handedly creating a new sexual preference—demon-amore.

It was still odd to look at the TV and see my face, or glimpse my picture in the papers. Marissa pleaded with me to go to some of the swanky parties I'd been invited to, arguing that people with money had power, and I needed to suck up to them along with everyone else. I finally agreed to go to an art opening, and it turned out to be a pleasant change. The people in attendance weren't dying to meet me like the tourists who came to the bar. I could relax and ease out of the spotlight. I actually had a nice conversation about American Chardonnay with an older woman in a Chanel suit who didn't indicate by word or deed that she was speaking to the latest media sensation. Maybe it was polite breeding. Maybe it was narcissism—they were all much more into their own image and reputation than other people's. After that I started showing up at social events around the city, shunning the paparazzi, but happy to watch the celebrities for a while instead of being the one in the fishbowl.

Everyone surrounding me served as my protection. No demon came close, though several times a day, if not more, I felt Goad at the fringes of my range. I'd have to deal with him soon. But he was camera-shy, like the other demons, and doubtless he was trying to figure out how he could cut me out of the herd.

After another futile call with my mom, I was starting to think I needed to go to California to see my family. They weren't being besieged anymore—the media had no need of photos of them with me deliberately overexposing myself. But when I suggested that once I got my finances under control, I'd close down the bar and come out for a week or two, they weren't enthusiastic. It was a moot point, anyway, since I was barely treading water at the moment, what with my suddenly extensive and expensive staff.

Mostly I thought about Ram. A lot. It didn't help that he never really loved me. It was the same with Shock—if she had really loved me, she would have stood by me like Lolita and Michael. Even careless Bliss had been more faithful. How could I miss Shock and Ram when they had abandoned me?

Yet how could I not?

Then one night just before closing, I felt the faint signs of Savor's approach. Swallowing, I turned to Bliss, who pumped her fist, jumping up and down a bit. "Yeah, baby! It'll be a hot time on the old town tonight. . . ."

"You really like her."

"Why wouldn't I?"

"Bliss, you can't trust Savor. You know that, don't you?"

Bliss waved one hand, dismissing me and my concerns. "What has Savor ever done to you, Allay?"

I had to think about it, and that proved her point. It was true that I couldn't say there was any time in the past ten years that Savor had hurt me. Sure, she had given me my marching orders, and I had to put up with her coming to my bar, but that was it. "I haven't gotten in her way. Yet. Savor's all about what's good for her, so it's bound to happen sometime."

"Don't be such a downer, Allay." With that, she breezed off to greet Savor, who was wearing her favorite Sebastian persona. The guards glanced at me when Bliss ordered them to let Savor in, and I nodded. They knew who was the boss here.

I was busy saying good-bye to the patrons who were lingering as long as possible, but I could hear Bliss say, "I've got the cutest little outfit. Do you want to go up while I dress?"

I abruptly straightened, startled at the idea of Savor going inside my apartment. Savor shot me a look; that sly grin was so Sebastian, yet completely Savor. He knew exactly how uncomfortable it made me.

"I'll wait down here," he drawled.

Savor plunked himself down at the bar and winked at Lo. She laughed and said, "I thought I was your favorite bartender."

"Would you like to come with us?" he asked, taking her hand and stroking it. He was feeding off Lo, but she was loving it. "It's a private party, just a few dozen beautiful people in a loft in Midtown. Clothing optional."

I briefly closed my eyes at the thought of Lolita attending an orgy with Bliss and Savor. But Lo declined, having worked hard all day, asking for a rain check.

When Lolita went to the back, I asked Savor, "Are you planning to fuck everyone who's close to me?"

"I can't help it if I love the company you keep."

I had to be plain. "Are you working for Goad now?"

"Allay—what makes you say that? You know I offered to be your ally."

"I think you're too used to being a double agent to start aligning with only one side. I think you're in it with everyone. And you're passing around information as it suits your purposes."

He leaned his chin on his hand. "You don't say."

"How's Glory settling into her new digs?" I asked. "I hope she likes the heat. The desert can be brutal if you're not used to it."

Savor didn't reply, so I knew he had been in touch with Glory. And with Goad tickling at the edges of my territory, Savor had to know he'd be identified inside my bar.

"That's why I can't trust you as an ally," I told him.

"Allay, in my heart, you're my only real ally."

I raised my brows. "What about Dread?"

"Dread's gone AWOL. Goad says he's not going to fight the Manhattan DA. It seems Prophet Anderson is kaput."

Kosciusko had told me that Dread's lawyers were delaying the DA shamelessly, but a hard deadline had been sent for him to appear on Monday. Apparently Dread wasn't planning to make that meeting.

Savor was watching me closely.

"Where is Dread?" I asked.

"Who knows? I didn't get the memo. As far as I can tell, only Dread and Lash have gone. Zeal is firmly in control of the Fellowship and its assets."

"What about Goad?" I hated his stinging signature, dancing around the edges of perception as annoying as a mosquito.

"Goad's demons have spread throughout Manhattan, taking over Glory's Harlem territory. Stun pulled out of the Lower East Side and took over the Village."

"Sounds like I'm surrounded." I wondered how long it would take before Goad attacked. Surely with Dread no longer holding his leash, he would try sooner rather than later. "I can't believe Dread would give up his power base so easily."

"It was never his. Vex controlled everything, and everyone. And after the Prophet's Center was professionally firebombed, on top of everything else you did to Dread, what could he do?"

"What are you talking about?"

"That's why Goad is staying away from you. Ram made his point, dear. He struck at the very heart of Dread's empire, and burned him out like a rat."

"That was Ram?"

He gave me a funny look. "You didn't know?"

My gut clenched at the thought of those frantic, helpless people waving their arms from the upper floors as firemen raced to save them. Ram did that? He had endangered dozens of people to kill one demon? Perhaps that was business as usual for him.

It made me sick. How could I love a man who did that? "How do you know it was Ram?"

"Goad told me. So far they seem to have split up and there hasn't been any horde activity like there was under Dread. Goad seems happy with his conquest—he personally took all of downtown. Now that he doesn't have Vex and Dread to check his appetite, he'll be churning out demons like clockwork, just you wait and see."

Now I was really nauseated. "Well, I'm not Glory. I'm not running away and leaving this city in his hands."

"You go, girl!" Savor beamed at me, as doting as if he had made me himself. "I'll bet on you, hands down. You and Ram will be the new power couple—with Vex gone, and Glory at the other end of the world."

That was it—that was why Savor was so interested in aligning with me.

Ram.

Savor just wanted to get on the good side of our mean demon-daddy. When it was clear Ram wasn't coming back to me, a whole lot was going to change. I'd better be prepared for that.

"What's wrong, Allay?" Savor asked.

To distract him, I asked, "Why don't you come out, too? We could do it together."

He froze, and his Sebastian persona seemed to disappear for a moment. "Don't be silly."

"Might as well make it on your own terms. Live free! That's my motto."

"Allay, that motto is 'Live free or die.' You can't leave out the 'die' part."

"Fine, don't come out. Bliss hasn't. Neither will Mystify, he says it's too time-consuming."

Savor was saved from answering by Bliss's arrival. She was tricked out in a skintight champagne dress that showed off her bust, and the highest heels I'd ever seen strapped onto her toes and ankles.

Bliss came over and gave Savor a twirl on request. They were giggling like kids, much more poke-and-tickle than sexy, not at all like she had been with Crave.

They ran off together, waving good-bye as I pushed the last of my reluctant patrons out the door. Some of the regulars had stopped coming. They didn't like my early closing hours, and they hated dealing with the crowds. But old Jose was always on his usual stool, and I had acquired scores of new loyal customers who came back night after night, offering to feed me. It seemed to mean something to them.

At least the lines of people passing by the bar were much more thinned out. Now they were mostly out-of-town tourists visiting the city. I had become another attraction, a must-see along with the Brooklyn Bridge and the Statue of Liberty. I had to ban flash photography inside the bar.

There weren't many left at closing time. I was getting ready to go outside to pull down the shutter when I felt Revel approaching. Fear was my first response, my gut reacting faster than my head. I was alone and Revel had killed on command before. Would he have any compunction in killing me, just like he had killed Plea to make me?

I had only a few minutes before he arrived, so I turned to the one tool I had denied for so long. I closed my eyes and tried to ease past that barrier in my mind, to see what Plea's memories could tell me about Revel. It was hard; I had shored up my defenses for years, but cracks had appeared over the past week, and I was finally able to merge my mind into the random stream of what Plea saw and thought.

Revel, I murmured, trying to direct myself in the confusion.

I caught a glimpse of Revel laughing and helpless with mirth, at Plea. She shrugged, turning away.

Then I remembered a tiny dab-and-wattle hut with a dirt floor. There was no door, only a window with a drape over it. An arm thrust through, palm up, questing, as a voice outside murmured tearfully, "Blessed Mary, help me." Plea grasped her hand, soaking up her outpouring of grief and despair, begging for mercy. Plea shuddered in ecstasy.

The hand withdrew, and instead of another hand the curtain opened, and Revel's face appeared in the too-bright square of light. He was laughing again, openmouthed, holding himself up by the windowsill to see Plea robed in a hair shirt and living like a hermit crab while people by the hundreds offered themselves up to her to feed. He was just checking in on her as he passed through the Pyrenees, to be sure she was doing okay.

I opened my eyes to see Revel, rocking his moneyed EU look, and smoothly chatting with my security guard.

It took a second for me to come back from the eighteenth century. I nodded to the guard to let him in, and said to him, "Shut the door behind you."

There were a lot of people outside looking in, so I felt safe and exposed at the same time. The guard was also keeping an eye on me as per my coded gesture to be on alert.

Revel was unusually somber. "I came to apologize, Allay. I'm sorry I didn't tell you before about Plea. I thought at first when I told you I was a demon, you would realize it from your memories. Plea knew it was me who had drained her. I couldn't understand why you didn't remember it, and I kept waiting day after day."

"Why you? Why did Vex choose you?"

"He'd made dozens of hybrids over the decades, but they always knew from the memories that he was the one who destroyed the demon progenitor, draining them to be taken by a human. The hybrids never trusted Vex."

"Even without the memory, instinctively I knew you couldn't be trusted," I agreed.

"Vex knew that would happen, and now we know he wanted you to cleave to him so he could use you in his resurrection. Instead, you've done it on your own, without him."

"That's not true," I protested.

"I know you aren't religious, but that doesn't matter, Allay. The Fellowship was just a medium for Vex. He was so seeped in the demon instinct to hide, he never would have thought of doing what you did—tell the truth. If he was alive, I bet he'd be backing you a hundred percent. He survived this long by periodically shaking things up. He was a genius at making the most of the transformations that civilization passed through. He thought it was time for a new paradigm."

I didn't know what to think of that. "Maybe he should have tried to work with me instead of twisting my arm."

"Seeing as he's dead now, you're right."

There was a touch of admiration in his voice. Always before he had talked down to me, as if I were still the naive teenager he had introduced to demon life. Now he was watching me closely, like Savor, as if waiting for me to surprise him again. Since I didn't trust either of them, I suppose that was a good thing. A moving target was harder to hit.

"Why Plea?" I asked. "What did you have against her?"

"Nothing. I tried to get Stun while he was in Barcelona, but he wouldn't cooperate. I knew Shock didn't care about her offspring, so I wouldn't have to deal with any other demons if I killed him."

I shuddered to think what it would have been like to have Stun's memories. Awfully ugly. Some teenager in Barcelona dodged a bullet on that one, for sure. I seriously doubted Stun's last emotion would have been relief to see a girl come to the rescue. More likely he would have wanted to hurt her.

Revel admitted, "I didn't think it would bother me like it did, betraying Plea. I didn't have much of a relationship with her. We had nothing in common, of course. She was a leader of religious fanatics, while I ran brothels. But she was the only demon other than Shock who would come to me if I called. So I was able to set up the ambush where a teenager would be able to 'accidentally' find her."

I shook my head. "You should have refused. You should have told Vex no."

"I couldn't."

"Why not?"

His expression closed. "I would have lost my standing with Vex. It could have cost me everything."

"I don't see how."

"You didn't refuse when he told you to pass money to bad politicians, did you?"

"You're trying to wiggle out of your own guilt by pointing the finger back at me."

He frowned. "Allay, you know that when you're subjugated to someone, you end up doing things that you normally wouldn't choose to do. By your own experience, you know that's true."

I noticed the guard had moved closer to the door and was frankly staring through the window at Revel's defensive body language. I approved.

"I don't trust you, Revel. I think you helped Vex because it suited your own purposes. Then you hid it from me ever since because you knew I wouldn't forgive you."

He heaved a big sigh. "You're right. But I'm not going to stop trying to prove myself to you."

Ever since he had let me do unspeakable things as a

new demon, he had been trying to make it up to me. But I had trusted my gut feeling, courtesy of Plea's buried memories, and avoided him.

"Maybe this will help," he said. "I know that you want to tell people the truth about what really happened with Dread and Vex, and how you got caught up in their illegal doings—"

"I'm not going to out you, if that's what you're asking."

"Thank you, my dear, but that doesn't really matter. I have several other personas I could transition to, and Giles would simply die a peaceful death." He smiled, as if to show me that he didn't feel threatened. "In fact, I encourage you to speak about your personal life. It's the only thing that will convince people you're telling the truth."

"I can't say anything because of the legal proceedings."

"For now, but that mess will be over quicker than you think now that the prophet has disappeared. And you don't have to go into the specifics of any crimes. But you can tell your story. Dread will never be able to come back as Prophet Anderson and deny what you say."

"Why not?"

"You've destroyed his persona, my dear. You got him to lie about being your sugar daddy, and then you came out, irrevocably tying the two of you together in the public eye. You blew him up, in every sense of the word. Dread will have to find a new shtick."

"You could always come out, too," I told him.

He laughed as if the idea was absurd. "I'll sit back for a while and leave this one to you, my dear. What a bizarre idea you had . . . to live openly as a demon."

I wasn't going to tell him about the bad parts, like the most recent *New York Post* headline over a photo of my bar that screamed FREAK SHOW ON C.

"I'm told you're here alone every night," Revel said. "Do you think that's safe? You could come stay with me when the bar is closed."

Alarm bells went off. Darn, and we'd been having such a nice conversation. The better to manipulate me into giving up control to him.

"Oh, I'm never alone," I assured him. It was true. I was referring to the Snow-monster and his minion, but I wanted him to think I was talking about Ram.

I knew Revel would broadcast the news far and wide that Ram was a regular at my bar after hours. They would assume he was cloaked, and that was why they couldn't sense him here.

Another lie. I still couldn't get away from deceit, to protect myself. It almost made me sick. I had to find another way.

But Revel swallowed it whole, smiling and nodding as if he was in the know. He didn't seem to mind that I barely uttered another word as I ushered him out the door. I did give him my new cell number in case he needed to get hold of me.

I might have to count on him again someday. He hadn't let me down this time. Even though he had destroyed my life, someday I might need his help again.

24

A few days later, in the dead of the night, I was cozied up in my armchair working on my laptop when I felt Bliss outside. It was really early for her to return, so I went to the front windows to look down at the nearly deserted streets.

Mystify waved up at me, standing next to the guard who was on duty. He was wearing Bliss's signature, along with his Theo Jr. persona. Mystify always wore another demon's signature because it was safer than being himself. Goad's demons would take him down just because he could infiltrate their ranks. And it didn't help that Ram was his progenitor. Nobody trusted him, apparently, except for me.

I let Mystify in and showed him up to my apartment. As I crossed the threshold, I realized it was the first time he'd been in my inner sanctum. From the way he looked around, he was remembering it from Ram's memories. The almost reverent way he touched the back of one of the linoleum chairs made my heart skip a beat. He kept saying I'd made a huge impact on Ram, but seeing his reaction made it all the more real.

"Do you want to sit down?" I asked.

His gaze lingered on the door to the back room, where I'd made love to Ram that first night on the chaise. He sat down in the same chair Ram had sat in as a battered Theo. "I came to tell you about . . . you know who."

I nodded at his discretion. There was no telling how many directional mics were aimed at us. "Yes?"

"Somehow . . . I can't be sure how because everyone was keeping watch . . . we lost the package."

"Lost it? As in . . ." I drew my hand across my throat.

"Oh, no, not that. Just gone. Vanished. I think it's gone deeper. Much deeper."

Here I'd been expecting Cherie to surface at any moment. I kept having nasty premonitions of Cherie facing off with me in front of the cameras. That would be a show nobody would want to miss—the demon vs. the saint.

I gulped. "You don't know where?"

"We've got ears all over. People are looking. But there's a whole other world below that one, Allay. I had no idea the extent of it."

I sat back, considering it. Cherie was a time bomb that could go off in my life at any moment. Leaving aside my public attacks on her, Cherie also knew my signature, even though I had been wearing June's guise. What if she realized I was the one who kidnapped her from the Prophet's Center?

My uneasiness rose as Goad's stinging signature flickered over me, making my skin crawl. I rubbed my arms. "I hate that guy! Why can't he leave me alone?"

"You're too tasty," Mystify said quickly. I looked at him, and he had the grace to look away.

"I know it will always be like this, a struggle to survive every day. But I get so tired of it."

Mystify smiled slightly. "I have an idea . . . I could blast a little 'Ram' at him. That might keep him away for a while."

It was tempting. It would reinforce the rumors I'd set in motion that Ram was here with me after hours. It could deter demons from testing me further, especially

Goad. I could ask Mystify to do it every few days; I could carry on the charade for a good long while.

"I don't want to live another lie," I forced myself to say.

"The only person you're lying to is Goad. And he wouldn't know it if he wasn't here bothering you. He should go back to his own territory and leave you alone. If it takes a bazooka lie to send him there, then I'm all for it."

"You're right. I guess using a lie as a weapon of defense is a lot like aikido—deflect the attacker." Maybe rationalizations like that were what Shock meant when she said I was a demon now instead of human. But Goad's stinging was getting stronger. "Do it."

It was like flipping a switch. One moment there was barely anything, a vague sense of well-being that typified Bliss, and the next second a Harley motorcycle was thrumming in the room with me.

It was exhilarating—I started breathing faster, my body responding just like it did with Ram.

I had to look at Mystify, telling myself it wasn't Ram that I felt. His signature wasn't nearly as strong, and there weren't those chasms of emotion like with Ram, the weight of the millennia he evoked. I wasn't carried away like I was with Ram.

I just needed a second to get hold of myself. It was similar enough to spark a full-on lust-fest inside me.

Mystify saw it. He grinned as he stepped closer, teasing in his eyes.

"Mystify," I said, reminding myself who he was. Even his persona looked like Ram.

He touched my arm, just brushed it without trying to feed from me. He'd always fed from me before when he touched me. This was much better.

"Goad's gone," Mystify told me.

"Is he? I hadn't noticed," I said breathlessly.

"You feel it, too," he murmured. "There's something special between us."

I swayed, unsure of myself. I did want to touch him, to kiss him. To feel loved again. I trusted him more than most of the people in my life. He had just chased off a persistent menace from my door by hardly lifting his finger. What more did I want from a man?

Mystify stroked my face, leaning down to kiss me.

Then he felt it. He stiffened and strained upward, in a way I'd come to associate with the effort to sense other demons. It wasn't until he abruptly dropped Ram's signature, returning to his own, that I realized what was happening.

Ram was coming.

The pounding, driving signature continued to grow stronger, coming up the block. He was letting me and everyone else know he was there.

Mystify was now wearing his own signature, the floating void. I hadn't felt it in a while.

I went to the front window in time to see Ram arrive. He paused to shake hands with Glenn, my favorite security guard because he didn't try to be all chummy with me. The two men sized each other up, and my cell phone rang in the kitchen as Glenn called up to get permission for Ram to enter.

I ducked back before Ram could see me. "He must be mad because you're wearing his signature. Do you want time to get out the rear? I can deal with this."

"He won't do anything to me. Not in front of you." Mystify sat down and leaned back against the chair as if he didn't have a care in the world.

"I'll talk to him downstairs." I didn't think it was a good idea to throw them together. I was the only one who knew Ram had lost interest in me. His only reason for being here must be to squash Mystify for imitating him. I had to fix things now or he would kill Mystify.

I took a good look at Ram as I let him in downstairs. His expression was perfectly pleasant, as if he hadn't a care in the world. The guard was smiling and laughing at something Ram had said, completely comfortable with him. It was a little scary that Ram had won Glenn over so easily. It was usually hard to get a word out of him, but Ram had managed to find a way.

But I knew that under Ram's genial mask lay a killer. I had discovered that four people had died in the fire that had destroyed the Prophet's Center. Apparently the police also believed the fire had been deliberately set on the inside, not by the rioters as had been reported. Ram had cold-bloodedly killed them all. He was not the man I thought he was.

I let him into the bar. With the shutter down, Glenn couldn't see inside and sound the alarm if I needed help. But I didn't have any defenses against Ram. If he wanted me dead, then I was dead. Nobody could stop him.

As Ram followed me inside, there was a tightening in his eyes as he glanced back upstairs where Mystify was.

"Is he too scared to come down?" Ram asked.

His voice echoed in the stairwell. I'm sure Mystify heard it inside my apartment.

I walked into the bar and waited until the door closed behind us. "You're here to see Mystify?"

"He is the one wearing my signature."

To all appearances, Ram was not angry at all. He was still letting his signature roar, and it nearly knocked me off my feet. It was also doing funny things to my nether regions, making me want to run my fingers through his hair and wrap my legs around him. . . .

"I asked him to do it," I said. "Goad has been hanging around lately, and I thought if *he* thought you were here . . . he would keep away. So if you're mad about it, you can be mad at me."

It was embarrassing to admit it. But it was my fault after all. Ram walked deeper into the bar, standing in the middle of the darkened room. He was so guarded I had no idea what he was thinking. Here was a man who had been flayed alive repeatedly by his first great love. Only a fool would have believed he wasn't a monster.

The click of the bolt behind me was my only warning. Mystify opened the door, grinning just enough to show Ram that he didn't care. He was still wearing his Theo Jr. persona.

"The whole package," Ram said thoughtfully.

I gave Mystify a hard look. What was he trying to do, provoke Ram? "I was just explaining to Ram that I asked you to wear his signature. That you were helping me."

Mystify shrugged one shoulder. "That's right."

He being nonchalant, with an undercurrent of cockiness. He was glad to have the chance to finally push back at Ram. After all, he couldn't avoid his progenitor forever—

Ram burst into motion, slamming into Mystify. With hardly a sound, Ram drove Mystify back against the wall. Mystify's breath went out in an agonized whoosh, like his chest was crushed. Ram wheeled and dropped Mystify to the floor like a bag of cement.

"Stop it, Ram!" I cried.

Sprawled on the floor, Ram had Mystify in a choke hold, arching him backward. Mystify's face was turning blue. But Ram wasn't trying to drain him.

"You kissed her, didn't you?" Ram growled. "While you were wearing my signature. You made a move, didn't you?"

"Let go of him!" I ordered. "It's none of your business."

Ram ignored me. This was between him and his off-spring. Mystify grabbed at his arm, trying to dislodge him, but Ram had beaten him in his surprise attack. Clearly Ram didn't care what I thought of his brutality.

"Answer me!" Ram demanded.

"Yes ..." Mystify managed to get out.

"Allay didn't want you while you were wearing your own signature. She only wants you when you're wearing *mine*. Isn't that right?" His arm tightened.

"But I love her...."

"You don't love her. You're feeling the echo of my love." His anger flowed out now in a violent red gush. "In another month or two, you'll hardly remember these feelings. Then who will be around to protect her? I will. So stop playing games with my woman, boy."

My mouth fell open. "Your woman? Since when? You disappeared when I refused to go away with you."

Ram was still focused on Mystify. "Do you understand me?" It looked like he was barely holding himself back from ripping Mystify's head off. At any second, I expected him to start draining Mystify. I'd seen how quick it had happened with Vex; it would take no time to overcome a newbie like Mystify.

It was frightening, overwhelming, because I knew Ram would do it if he thought it was necessary. Right in front of me.

I picked up a chair, holding it over my head. "Let him go, Ram. Or I'll make you stop, I swear."

Slowly he seemed to back away from his killing rage. The crimson cleared from his aura, as he warned Mystify, "What you know about me will get you killed. Remember that."

He let go of Mystify, pushing him away.

Mystify rolled over, gasping for breath. I dropped the chair, kneeling down next to him. "Are you okay?"

Mystify nodded, but he was rolling in agony. He had

sadly misjudged Ram. He almost died because of it. We both knew it.

My phone was ringing and it was the guard outside. I started to assure Glenn that everything was fine, even though I didn't believe it. But he interrupted me. "There's a guy here who wants to see you." His voice lowered. "I'm not liking this, Ms. Meyers."

"Someone's outside?" I repeated, looking instinctively to Ram.

Ram moved quicker than I could think, ready to defend me. I had to leave Mystify gasping on the floor, and barely caught the door as it swung shut behind Ram. He was out the front before I could catch up to him.

The guard was holding out both arms, warding off a skinny guy in a trench coat. He was staggering with his head down, barely able to stand. "Some car drove by and rolled him out," Glenn said. "Then he started calling for you, Ms. Meyers."

"Allay?" Phil Anchor raised his head. "Is that you?"

"Phil!" I exclaimed. In his bloodred eyes, I could see it—he was bingeing on drugs again. He was so high he hardly knew where he was. "What are you doing here? I thought you were in police custody."

"You ruined my life, Allay," Phil slurred.

Everything happened at once—Phil pulled back his coat to reveal a bulky pack strapped to his stomach. The guard, to his credit, leaped toward Phil to try to catch his arm as he reached for the device.

Ram got there first. He caught Phil around the middle, slinging him around like a discus. Phil let out a loud *ooff* and nearly doubled over, his feet swung off the ground by Ram's force. The guard and I fell back as Ram spun and then flung Phil as hard as he could.

Phil flew through the air, much farther than humanly possible. As he arced back down into the middle of the intersection, Ram turned and leaped on me, his eyes blackly determined.

I didn't know what was going on until the explosion hit us. The boom made my ears ring, and chunks of asphalt rained down on us. Ram shielded me with his body, his warmth pressing against my cold skin.

Car alarms went off, filling the ringing in my ears with horns and sirens. Cries rose above the din as people began calling out from open windows.

I tried to push Ram aside so I could see, but he took a good look around first. When he finally let me go, he warned, "Watch out for the glass."

The ground glittered with shards of glass everywhere. It looked like every window on both blocks had broken. The middle of the intersection was now a concave hole, revealing broken pipes and a gusher of water that shot higher than the two-story building on the corner. The streetlights were fallen over like matchsticks, and people were coughing and carefully picking over the debris as they emerged from the surrounding buildings. One woman was screaming and crying, but I couldn't see her.

"Suicide bomber!" Glenn exclaimed. "That guy blew himself up."

My stomach heaved. What was that whitish thing over there?

I'm not going to think about it.

Ram tapped on the shutter down over my bar. There were a few scars in the new undersea mural. "The windows didn't break. Bulletproof, just as I ordered."

"*You* ordered?" I repeated.

"I couldn't let you risk getting shot again." He grimaced. "I didn't know the idiot would shoot you in the face the second time."

Stunned, I asked, "Did you know Phil was going to do this?"

"No! Of course not. He was in police custody the last I heard." He lowered his voice as Glenn stumbled over the chunks of asphalt, closer to the crater in morbid fascination. "I knew Dread was going to try something against you. That's why I've been watching over you. But I never expected him to use Phil again."

It took me a second to catch up. "So Dread sent Phil to shoot me and Pepe the first time. I should have known Phil couldn't pull it off alone. Dread is the one who disabled the surveillance system."

Ram nodded. "But it backfired on him. The last thing Dread wanted was for Phil to murder you the second time in front of everyone. Dread should have known he couldn't control a drug addict." Ram kicked a chunk of asphalt. "There goes the DA's corruption case."

"And he almost killed us." That would have taken care of all of Dread's problems in one blow.

"I wouldn't let that happen." The look he gave me was full of tenderness. After his killing rage with Mystify, it was too much.

Fire engines pulled up with sirens blazing. An ambulance came slowly down the avenue on the far side of the crater. Only my habit of locking myself inside at night had prevented a large crowd of tourists from being outside my bar. There were only a few people sitting here and there who had gotten caught in the blast.

But for the first time, I didn't feel like it was my fault. Despite what Phil had said—I didn't ruin his life. He did. He let Dread fill him up with coke and strap dynamite to his waist. He was trying to push the button when Ram stopped him. I felt more sorry for the NYPD, who no longer had a witness or a defendant for their big corruption case.

This was the last time Phil Anchor would try to kill me.

"Come on." Ram ushered me inside. "The cops will be here soon enough to question us."

Mystify was still sitting on the floor, still healing his injuries. He scooted back warily away from Ram, holding up a hand to ward him off.

"You can't come in here and beat up my friends," I told Ram. But my protest didn't have much heat in it— not after Ram had just saved my life again.

"I'll do whatever it takes to protect you, Allay."

"Including setting fire to a building full of people? You killed four people in the Prophet's Center, Ram. Just to hurt Dread. How could you?"

"I didn't do it. Dread set that fire."

A disbelieving noise escaped Mystify's lips. I felt the same way. "No way," I protested. "Dread wouldn't destroy his own home. The church is his power base."

"Not after you got through with him. There was evidence he needed to destroy, and what better way than an incendiary fire? He didn't care if his employees were inside." His voice tightened. "You really thought I did it?"

Suddenly I remembered how Ram had spoken about helping humanity, guiding their civilization to enlightenment and balance so demons and humans could live together in harmony. He cared about people. He killed rogue demons, not people. "Not really. But the others think you did it."

Ram shot Mystify a look that pierced the darkness. "You better not tell them otherwise. I want them to be scared of me. I want them to think nothing will stop me from protecting Allay."

"Dread knows the truth," I said.

"I'll make sure Dread doesn't hurt you," Ram said.

A warm feeling began to spread through me at his tone. "Do you mean that? I'm out, you know. You won't be able to hide."

"I know."

"So you want to be here, standing by my side, helping me like a partner? You want to be the boyfriend of a famous demon?"

"Just try to get rid of me." His smile was just for me. "Maybe I'll come out myself."

He had beaten me to my own line. There was no mushy stuff; he wasn't saying he couldn't live without me. He didn't apologize for nearly killing Mystify, or trying to strong-arm me into going away with him.

"Allay, you know he's a killer, a thug," Mystify protested, giving voice to my own doubts. "He's saying what you want to hear."

"You can feel the truth, Allay. Do you feel the same way about him as you do for me?"

I stared at Ram, who drew me in like a magnet, making my mouth water and my hands yearn to touch him to hang on for the ride of my life. When I glanced at Mystify, his signature was a void, nothingness.

Mystify shook his head. "Don't believe it, Allay. He seduces women, carries them away in spite of themselves. Like he's doing with you now."

Like Revel used his titillating signature to convince me I was in love with him. But once I knew what that feeling was, I'd been able to resist it. Actually it had hardened me against his advances.

Was it the same with Ram? I lost my head when was around him. Who knew if it was real or a response he was evoking in me? Like Crave manipulating women into an obsessive passion for him.

With both of them staring at me, waiting for me to make a choice, I realized I didn't know for sure.

But I didn't have to. Not right at this moment. I had long, long time to figure it out. I was a demon—I could live for a thousand years, two thousand years, maybe even more if I played my cards right. My first steps were crucial—where I ended on this long journey would be very different depending on how I began.

My choice was Ram. He was the oldest of us, the strongest, the most deadly. Being with him wasn't without its risks, but if I wanted to be the kind of demon who lived through the ages, there was no better way to learn to sink or swim.

I didn't accept some of his behavior, but he wasn't capable of something truly reprehensible. Like Dread.

I'd be lying if I said the danger humming through Ram wasn't an aphrodisiac. Just being close to him, I could hardly keep my hands off him. Watching him expertly choke out Mystify seemed to have stoked my cavewoman instincts, as sick as that was.

I have to be honest with myself, if nothing else.

I helped Mystify stand up, then patted him on the shoulder. "You should go, Mystify. The police will be here soon."

He glared at Ram, who instantly flushed verdant, he was so ready to grab hold of me. He was only restraining himself because of Mystify.

The poor boy crumpled like a dead leaf. I had the uneasy feeling I'd sparked another filthy little Oedipus tale by choosing his father over him.

Distantly I heard the door close behind Mystify as he let himself out. I might have ruined any chance at a friendship with him, but we definitely weren't ready for anything more.

Ram's signature seemed to intensify when Mystify left, as if the void had managed to dampen even his tremendous power.

I could no longer help myself—I reached out for Ram. His arms were strong around me. In them I felt safe, happy, and full of hope for the future.

His lips met mine softly, as if savoring every second. He poured into me with a touch, letting me soak up his power, giving everything he had to me. It was more than I had dreamed of, his devotion, his passion. His mouth drew me in further, making me drown in him.

I wish I could say we made it upstairs before my jeans came off, but I can't. But I did make sure that after our interview with the cops, the second round finally took place on my bed, the old-fashioned way.

ABOUT THE AUTHOR

S. L. Wright has lived in New York City for more than twenty years, exploring every part of the city, from rooftops to underground tunnels. She moved to Manhattan to get her master's degree in fine arts, and not long afterward met her husband, Kelly Beaton. Together they have spent the past decade restoring a big brick house on the edge of Bushwick, Brooklyn. Wright is an activist at heart, saving wild cats in the city as well as helping people who are persecuted for their personal choices.